ONLY CHARLOTTE

ONLY CHARLOTTE

By

ROSEMARY POOLE-CARTER

A tale of Dr. Gilbert Crew's entanglements in the city
of New Orleans as told by his sister, Lenore James.

Top Publications, Ltd.

Top Publications, Ltd.
Plano, Texas

ONLY CHARLOTTE

© COPYRIGHT
Rosemary Poole-Carter
2018

Top Publications, Ltd.
Plano, Texas

Library Edition
ISBN 978-1-935722-99-1
Library of Congress Control No. 2018963474

With love to Gilbert Rome

and in loving memory of John Crew

Acknowledgments

Only Charlotte and I owe much to many. For wisdom, wit, and immeasurable patience, I offer my affection and gratitude to the Three Graces of my writing life: Katherine Parr, Sarah Harris, and Marly Rusoff. Thank you, Shannon Jamieson Vazquez, for urging Lenore into the limelight and William Manchee for letting her shine. Thank you again, Sarah and Katherine, for giving Lenore three husbands and a song to sing. Thank you, Vaughan Siviglia, for the gift of a pivotal research book and Jeri Fahrenbach for being my personal reference librarian. Thank you, Gilbert Rome, Cynthia Rome, Janis Terry, Lisa Qualls, Chris Humphreys, Stephanie Cowell, Anna Louise Bruner, Dolores Rieger, Mary Pat Trenkle, Luisa Amaral-Smith, Debra Osterman, Kitty Jordan, Mikha Mitchell, Jean Seidl, Peggy Ann Lyle, Cecilia Eichenberger, and John O'Malley for the myriad ways you have assisted and inspired me, whether you knew it or not at the time. Thank you to my husband, children, and grandchildren, the darlings of my heart, who sustain me. To one and all, I am much obliged.

A Noiseless Patient Spider

A noiseless patient spider,
I mark'd where on a little promontory it stood isolated,
Mark'd how to explore the vacant vast surrounding,
It launch'd forth filament, filament, filament, out of itself,
Ever unreeling them, ever tirelessly speeding them.

And you O my soul where you stand,
Surrounded, detached, in measureless oceans of space,
Ceaselessly musing, venturing, throwing, seeking the
            spheres to connect them,
Till the bridge you will need be form'd, till the ductile
            anchor hold,
Till the gossamer thread you fling catch somewhere, O my soul.

Walt Whitman
1819 - 1892

Perdita: . . . bold oxlips and
            The crown imperial; lilies of all kinds,
            The flow'r-de-luce being one! O, these I lack,
            To make you garlands of, and my sweet friend,
            To strew him o'er and o'er!
Florizel: What, like a corse?
Perdita: No, like a bank for love to lie and play on;
            Not like a corse; or if, not to be buried,
            But quick and in mine arms.

The Winter's Tale, ACT IV, Scene IV
William Shakespeare

Act I
Interment

Chapter One

Draw the shadows, and the shapes will appear. Charlotte taught us that—my brother Gilbert and me. Before my witnessing her profound effect on Gilbert, I might have argued against the idea, whether as art lesson or metaphor. I had once been a fanciful girl but had matured into a sensible woman. I had taught myself to avoid lingering long on the romantic and the ephemeral, for I knew the tangible was as tenuous as anything for those of us who had come of age in the midst of the War Between the States. I had encouraged Gilbert, ten years younger than I, to do the same, to cultivate some commonsense—not that he, as a boy, would listen to me. Nor when he, as a man, first laid eyes on Charlotte. Oh, then how I watched my brother shade truth and circumstance, as if they were no more than charcoal shadows in one of Charlotte's sketches, and he could conjure out of the darkness the shape he most desired.

While I have never learned all the details of what happened to my brother on the night he first met Charlotte, I saw the alteration in him the morning after that particular evening in October of 1879. Gilbert and I sat as usual in the parlor, engaged in quiet pursuits, he reviewing his medical case notes and I writing a letter of tender advice to my married daughter in North Carolina. But our domestic tranquility did not hold. A sudden frantic rapping at the front door gave me a start, causing the pen to jump in my hand and ink to blotch my final words of wisdom. I should have taken that as a sign. Gilbert dropped his notebook and answered the summons.

But I get ahead of myself. Months before that particular evening, I had urged Gilbert to leave Baltimore and join me here in New Orleans to share my home in Faubourg Marigny. I had discussed the idea with Ella, my long-time housekeeper and friend, and we agreed Gilbert needed looking after. He had only been married a year in 1878 when he lost both wife and infant son to a difficult lying-in. His father-in-law and mentor, Dr. O'Brien, blamed Gilbert for their shared loss—despite the fact that Dr. O'Brien had shut Gilbert out of the bedroom in which Estelle labored on grounds that the young husband could not maintain proper professional detachment. Meanwhile, O'Brien, himself, wasted precious minutes arguing a course of action with the attending physician. My poor brother was now detached, indeed, from wife and child and mired in melancholia. He needed to get away and begin again elsewhere.

On his arrival here, Gilbert expressed little confidence that the change of scene would change him. I remember he said to me: "Lenore, you know I've just traded one turbulent port city for another." I saw his point. Although the war had ended more than a decade ago, the indignities of defeat, Union occupation, and purported Reconstruction still rankled with the population of New Orleans. Every household was in some way haunted by its losses, whether from the collective grief of the war years, or from a summer's devastating outbreak of yellow fever, or from other sorrows, intimate and unnamed. Would it be any wonder if Gilbert's own sorrows grew more importunate traveling south with him? But even if they had and even if Gilbert were what he appeared to be—a haunted soul—he had come to us, and Ella and I welcomed him. And until October, he seemed to be settling well enough.

Ella was fond of saying, "Mr. Gil scatters himself and sometimes he needs gathering up." Indeed, for as far back as my memory of him went, fragmentation of thoughts had plagued him—as it had me on a few occasions. Our mother with her sharp voice, our father with his leather strap, and a schoolmaster with a hickory switch had all tried and failed to keep the boy in the moment. But later, Gilbert had found his own way: work was his salvation, as it had been mine. I felt sure his mood would lift after that dark time in Baltimore and his confidence return when he built a new practice in New Orleans.

My brother kindly gave me credit for inspiring his choice of profession, both pleasing and surprising me. I had thought Gilbert would follow in our father's footsteps and become a pharmacist, especially given Gil's early curiosity about and experimentation with *materia medica*. Besides, I was gone so much of his boyhood, we rarely saw each other. A slip of girl considering herself a woman, I had run off from our strict household to marry a soldier in wartime. Oh, the romance and the squalor! And then the horror of it all—losing my gallant young husband at First Manassas. Galvanized by grief, I turned my energies to nursing the wounded sweethearts of other girls. Then, on my few trips home, I shared tales of some of my adventures with Gilbert, hoping to turn him away from any notion of enlisting as our brothers had—I had seen a twelve-year-old courier lose his right arm to a Minié ball. Gil had hung on my words and, sure enough, he concentrated himself, not on soldiering, but on the healing arts.

Soon after Gilbert came to New Orleans, I introduced him to Dr. Rufus Baldwin, whom I knew slightly through mutual acquaintances. The old gentleman, as I'd heard, had lost interest in treating all but the wealthiest of his patients and was willing—for a fee—to refer less desirable patients, mostly laborers and tenant farmers and children of all sorts to Dr. Gilbert Crew. This arrangement suited my brother well, for his sympathies, whether moral or political, had always rested with the downtrodden and the vulnerable.

Which brings me to October and the rapping at the door.

Gilbert left the parlor for a moment or two, and on his return from the front hall, even before he spoke, I surmised he had been called to a sick bed. He was holding a note, transferring it from hand to hand as he stuffed one arm and then the other into the sleeves of his frock coat.

"A boy is ill—a baby," he said.

I heard the catch in his voice, knowing the memory he carried of his child, and rose from my desk. He would be fine when he got to work. Gilbert would focus entirely on treating the child, whether the babe were one of a dozen in a boisterous family in a crowded house or alone but for an anxious mother in a single room.

"The messenger came by way of Dr. Baldwin's house," said Gilbert. "Who knows how long the old man dithered before sending the boy here?"

My brother was already on his way back to the hall, gathering his hat and medical bag from the stand, when I caught up with him. "Do you know where you're going?" I asked. His six months in the city were hardly time enough to learn all its streets and byways.

"Yes," he said, glancing once more at the note before stuffing it in his pocket. "Just off Frenchman Street. I can walk it in minutes." Gilbert opened the door. "The house of Victor Eden," he called to me over his shoulder before he was gone.

Victor Eden—I knew the name, knew the man mostly by his reputation as an ambitious architect with influential patrons. Some of them had been associates of my third late husband. Yes, after my love-match with Grady, my doomed private, and before the war was half-over, I married again—and years later, yet again. My

4

second husband, Samuel, was a major, then a college professor in peacetime. Our companionable union was blessed with twins, and somehow we made ends meet in those lean years of the war's aftermath. But before the children were grown, their father's heart failed him. Thus, I accepted a third suitor, the wealthy, aged Bartholomew James, and entered a marriage of expedience—by which I acquired the funds to raise my children, send my son to a university in Virginia, and provide a dowry for my daughter, who married as young as I had my first time around. Add to all that a lovely Greek side-hall cottage in Faubourg Marigny and the wherewithal to travel, enjoy art and theater, and support my charitable concerns, and I had profited well from the hardest work of my life—that last marriage.

And so my thoughts turned back to Victor Eden—whose name sparked my recollection of his wife, Charlotte, not yet Mrs. Eden when I first met her.

Mr. James had passed just before Christmas 1875. His prominence in life dictated the lavishness of his funeral and of my mourning couture. Of course, I went to Madame Joubert's Hat Shop for my bonnet, where her most talented young assistant, Charlotte Varcy, created exactly what I requested: a dream of midnight with an impossibly long, weightless veil. I told the girl I envisioned myself wafting my way through the cemetery with that endless veil trailing after me in the breeze, like a ribbon of smoke.

"Or like a dark ghost following you," Charlotte had whispered.

"Who will never catch up with me," I whispered back, and we shared a fleeting smile.

She had charmed me—soft-spoken, pretty, and artistic. Or had she really been artful, then and later? I may never quite make up my mind.

I barely had time to order another hat of her design in Nile green, a shade that particularly complements my auburn hair, planning to wear it as soon as my period of mourning was over, before Charlotte abruptly left the hat shop to wed Mr. Eden. Ensnared him and married above herself, said the gossips, who predicted a baby's arrival within six months of the wedding day. The ladies preferred to believe that society had lost a dashing and chivalrous bachelor to his sense of obligation, not to love. They were disappointed when the first child, a daughter, appeared a decorous eight and half months later. By then, I was resigned to the loss of Charlotte's millinery magic and thought no more about her as she disappeared into the duties of wife and mother.

It never crossed my mind that one day—in fact, late one night—Gilbert would discover that Charlotte had not disappeared at all.

As a thrice widowed lady, who had sworn off ever marrying again, I had, on occasion, considered writing my memoirs. I had even begun and abandoned several versions of my experience. But I have always been too caught up in living to finish the undertaking. Besides, at shy of forty, I may yet have time for reflection. Or perhaps I am not compelled to write my own past because I do not mystify myself. It is my brother's story—what I know of it, what I was told, what I suspect but may never know for sure—that I wish now to unravel.

Chapter Two

Gilbert had no sooner climbed the three steps to the front porch of the Eden house than Charlotte had flung open the door. She stood before him, her dainty form silhouetted in the frame, apprehension surrounding her like air wavering in the heat of lamplight, the lamp burning behind her within the room.

Gilbert introduced himself to her, for he was not the doctor she had summoned, only the one who had come in his place.

"Dr. Gilbert Crew," Charlotte repeated the name and, quick as her next intake of breath, drew him forward through the doorway of that long, narrow single shotgun house, all its rooms arranged in a line, all connected, like a chambered nautilus unwound. In that instant of his crossing Charlotte's threshold, had an image crossed his mind, as well, of his traveling ahead of himself, beyond past grief and lingering regret, on down the hallway to the last room and into the garden? Perhaps so, but they had stopped that night in the front room.

The three of them—Charlotte, the baby, and Gilbert—huddled in the little sitting room at the front of the house, so the baby's coughing and crying would not wake his sister. Nor disturb his father? It was unclear to Gilbert whether or not Mr. Eden was at home.

The room was close and warm. Before setting to work, Gilbert asked Charlotte's permission to remove his frock coat. "Of course," she said, taking it from him, saying, "here, let me," as simply as if she were welcoming him home at the end of the day, laying his coat over the back of a chair. Then, while he removed his

7

cufflinks, dropped them in a trouser pocket, and turned back his shirtsleeves, Charlotte hurriedly recounted her baby's symptoms.

"He's been feverish all day but so much worse tonight, and his coughing comes in terrible fits. My little girl is well, sleeping in the next room. But my baby—" Charlotte lifted her son from his cot and turned him, so Gilbert could see his round, flushed face in the lamplight. "His name is Wilfred," she said.

"Wilfred," Gilbert repeated, taking the baby from Charlotte.

He asked her to sit and arrange a folded towel across her lap. Then, he laid Wilfred on the towel, removed the baby's nightshirt, which was damp with spittle and regurgitated milk, and set about bathing the feverish little body with a solution of water and witch hazel taken from his black leather medical bag. Charlotte cradled Wilfred's head in one of her hands and assisted in bathing him with the other. As they worked, doctor and mother, their hands momentarily touched over the heat of the baby's skin, her hand brushing past his. She looked up at him, her dark eyes seeming to search his face for an answer to the fate of her child.

"They're all gone," she said, "all my family, before I met Mr. Eden and began again—this family—my children who must survive me. You understand, Doctor?"

Yes, Gilbert understood—if we could choose and have our way. As Wilfred spluttered and coughed, Gilbert lifted him from her lap, held him and waited for a break in his coughing before placing the baby in the cot. Then Gilbert continued examining his patient, following the order in which he had learned the process: observation, palpation, percussion, auscultation. *The quartet*, his mentor had called them, and he had thought of music, still did when tapping an abdomen to discover tenderness or listening to a chest to hear the beat and breath of life.

Even as Gilbert worked, he remained aware of Charlotte moving back and forth, into and out of the circle of light cast by

8

the single lamp burning on the table near the child's cot: the mother of his young patient, someone to reassure, someone to circumvent if she interfered with his treatment methods, as anxious mothers sometimes did. Yet she did not interfere, not in any usual sense, although in other ways she might have scattered his thoughts.

She moved too quietly, gliding away, startling him with her sudden reappearances—removing soiled cloths and bringing fresh ones, filling the basin with cool water, offering a sponge. Anything Gilbert asked for she had already anticipated, and she brought him coffee unasked. She showed him too much deference, and that became a distraction he struggled against. While he fixed his attention on the sick child, the mother shimmered at the edge of his vision. The charcoal gray expanse of her skirt faded away into the darker circle of the rug, while the starched, stark whiteness of her blouse, cinched to nothingness at her waist, and the pale hands and face floated in and out of the lamplight. The perfume of sweet olive moved with her, close to her as her shadow.

Gilbert took a deep breath and concentrated on his work. Although the baby fussed and cried, Gilbert would not administer opiates, not if he could help it, in such a case, with a patient so young. Laudanum could bring a permanent silence. Instead, he chose a mild syrup of elm bark, one of his own concoctions, hoping to loosen the phlegm and clear the chest, reassuring Charlotte of its safety and efficacy. Again, she held her child on her lap, and he knelt in front of her. A few strands of her hair, dark as umber, clung to her brow, where a glistening had gradually appeared, as if she were drawing the fever away, into herself, to spare her son. Gilbert eased a few drops of medicine past Wilfred's pursed lips, while Charlotte hummed and cooed to him and stroked his little feet. Her palms looked as pink and soft as the soles of her baby's feet.

A quiet moment passed, which Gilbert would have prolonged if Wilfred's reaction to the medicine had not come with such violence. Convulsive coughing doubled him over, impelled him forward, breaking his mother's grasp of him. Charlotte cried out as her son left her arms, and Gilbert caught him, falling back on his heels, clutching Wilfred to his chest, feeling the tiny ribcage near to splitting with the force of the baby's coughing.

Charlotte slipped from the chair to her knees, reaching out to regain hold of her son. But Gilbert did not hand him over. Rising to his feet, Gilbert lifted the child above her and looked down on her where she knelt. Suppose he gave her back her child to die in her arms, would that be her comfort in times to come? Was that the best he could do? Waver, hesitate, lose precious seconds and so lose all? Such things happened, he knew too well.

The pale oval of Charlotte's upturned face floated above the dark circle of her skirt, a drowning pool of darkness. She stared at him with the wide-eyed look of panic. Giving way so soon to accusation? His failure and his guilt foregone. Charlotte had opened the door to him, let him in and trusted him, and now she would see her mistake. Gilbert heard a different sound then, but not the baby's coughing—there was no longer any sound from the baby, not a choking, not a strangling, not the eerie crepitation of the lungs. The only sound in the room came from Charlotte, drawing her own breath in a long gasp. Gilbert turned away from her. That was how he would help her, not think of her, think only of the child. Cradling the baby in one arm, the little head fallen back against his shoulder, with his free hand Gilbert yanked a syringe out of his black bag and set to siphoning the mucus that obstructed the airway. Clearing the passage, such a simple thing. If it were not too late—difficult to tell, moment from moment.

The baby's eyes rolled beneath fluttering lids as if spinning towards consciousness. His pink tongue arched and thrust itself forward from his mouth as he spat phlegm and curdled milk over his nightshirt and over Gilbert's hands. The slick feel, the sour smell coated his hands. Within the moment, Charlotte was beside them, a wet cloth in her trembling fingers, wiping her son's face and the backs of Gilbert's hands. She must keep busy tending to her child; his needs were proof of his living. Gilbert must disengage, not look at her, only at the tasks they performed together, the repetition of bathing and dressing her child. Charlotte changed Wilfred's cotton diaper, too, then swaddled her son in a small flannel blanket before handing him back to Gilbert.

All the while, the air rasped in and out of Wilfred's open mouth in shallow, ragged breaths that did not fill his lungs. Yet he breathed. Gilbert held the child out in front of him, one arm around the legs, the other supporting the back, the head resting in his cupped hand. His fingers spread out through the downy, nut-brown hair and curved to the rounded shape of the baby's skull. Gilbert breathed more deeply, himself, exaggerating each of his inhalations and exhalations, demonstrating to Wilfred what was expected of him. And when, at last, Wilfred complied and drew several full breaths, Gilbert brought the baby to his shoulder and patted his back. The baby nestled into him. Just above his collar, Gilbert felt a soft, plump cheek against the side of his neck, felt its warmth, no more the blaze of fever. The fever broken, Wilfred gradually drifted into sleep.

Gilbert held Wilfred against his chest and supported his drowsing patient with one arm. Exhausted, himself, Gilbert dropped the other arm to his side and, in the next moment, felt his limp fingers caught in Charlotte's hands. With the baby's round head tucked beneath Gilbert's chin, he could not look down into her face but was aware that she knelt at his feet. He heard her repeated, whispered thanks, felt her pressing her cheek against the back of his hand. Over and over, "thank you, thank you, Doctor, thank you," embarrassing him with her gratitude for a simple mechanical action. He felt the smoothness of her cheek turning, then the pressure of her lips, three kisses hard on the back of his hand. It was a spontaneous gesture expressing a mother's profound relief, yes, moving him with its intimacy. But there was something else—disquieting, unseemly—something that came too easily to her and should not have done. What in her nature would lead her to such a display of subservience, to kneel and kiss his hand? He was a physician called in to treat her child. He was a stranger to her—and he was no one's master.

Gently, Gilbert drew his hand away from hers and upward to hold Wilfred more firmly, before lowering himself to sit on the footstool. The child whimpered, and again Gilbert patted his back. A weary smile flickered on Charlotte's face.

"You have saved him," she said.

Gilbert shook his head and mumbled something about merely doing his job, perhaps about the randomness of Nature, but she stopped him.

"Call me superstitious, if you will, Dr. Crew, but now you have worked a part in my fortunes—the ones that were told to me in Jackson Square." This time her smile more than flickered as she gazed at her child in his arms, and Gilbert at her, seeing everything she said. He watched her in the square, as if he had been with her that day beneath an oak in dappled light and shade, when she drew from a deck of tarot cards, their thick paper softened and creased with use, with daily readings sold to passers-by. She had laid out the cards on a green velvet cloth, dark as the rug now surrounding her in the sitting room, and turned over each card to the reader's view: "Contentment, struggle, love," she said. "In that order. The card reader promised me." Then, Gilbert saw her standing on the flagstones, pigeons circling and cooing around the hem of her skirt, as she offered her hand to the palm reader, who cooed her future. "It's all there, love lines and life lines—and three healthy children. I was promised." Charlotte held the very hand out to him, palm up, as if in proof.

"One more to come, then," Gilbert said, and she dropped her gaze.

Charlotte rose and moved to the upholstered chair. In a little while, she leaned back her head, the wavy mass of her dark hair falling loose from its pins. Her eyelids drooped and closed. Then her breathing, like her son's, slowed to a whisper of breath, the stillness of sleep descending upon her. One of her hands dangled limply over the armrest, the other lay across her lap. The white fingers twitched and stilled in the dark gathers of her skirt. Her white blouse, starched and crisp hours ago, now damp after the bathing of the child and with the heat of her own body, lay pressed against the lace of the garment beneath it. Gilbert's gaze ran up and down the line of tiny shell buttons on her blouse and over and over the edging of her camisole, where the cotton blouse had melted into the lace. He could not look away.

All through the night, Gilbert held her child and watched her sleep. At dawn, Wilfred started to whimper, rooting against Gilbert's shoulder, gumming the cotton cloth of his shirt. As the whimper rose to a cry, Charlotte opened her eyes, confusion darting in them before she focused on her son. She touched the shell buttons at her throat, in an instant releasing the top one from its buttonhole, the movement quick as a reflex. Then her eyes met Gilbert's, hers a light hazel, not as dark as they had appeared in the shadowy room at night, and she, no longer frightened for the boy, or not yet recalling her fear. Charlotte took her hand away from the neck of her blouse and with both arms reached for her baby.

"He's hungry," she said.

Gilbert handed him over. "I'll leave you then."

"No. Stay, please"—a hint of alarm, then softly—"His coughing might return. What if he should choke?"

"As you wish." Gilbert turned his back to her to respect her privacy, perhaps to guard his own.

The baby fussed. Charlotte must have hurried to unbutton her blouse, lay it open on one side, lift her nipple above the lace edging of her undergarment, for the fussing had risen towards a crescendo never reached, replaced by the sound of the baby's suckling and humming into his mother's breast.

Gilbert stared at the wall, at a picture hanging there, a small engraving behind glass, surrounded by wide crimson matting and framed in black. He willed himself to focus his bleary eyes on the image fixed before him, but it would not be still. The mass of dark corrugated lines undulated across the cream paper, running upward to the jagged edges of cliffs, and on the highest cliff a castle stood, cut out of rock and into the rock, all turrets with rippling flags and towers piercing the clouds—foreign and impossible. But then, or so it might have been, his vision took him deeper, and he could see through the castle's stone walls and hanging tapestries and into a solitary chamber that slowly resolved itself into the little sitting room, where a young mother nursed her child. As Gilbert's eyes grew accustomed to the visions behind him, captured in the sheen of glass before him, other shapes within the room melted away into the shadows, and Charlotte lifted her face to his full view. Had she felt the concentration of his gaze and, in reflection, chosen to meet it with her own?

Chapter Three

Naturally, there were things my brother did not choose to share with me. Although, he shared more than he might have realized, for I could decipher expressions, construe gestures, and interpret silences, as well as words, with skill to rival a reader of cards or palms.

After Gilbert had departed that evening to attend the Eden baby, I grew uneasy, worrying for the baby and for my brother, who suffered in sympathy with his patients. Still, I kept occupied, finishing and sealing my somewhat ink-stained letter to Arabella and writing another to her twin, Allan, for my son, although a college man, was not past needing my encouragement in his studies. My correspondence complete, I still couldn't quite settle on going to bed, so I dozed in my wing-back chair, stocking feet on the footstool and calico cat in my lap. There I was in the morning when the sound of the front door clicking open and shut woke me. The next moment, I saw Gilbert looking in at me from the archway between the front hall and the parlor, his hat still on his head and medical bag in his hand.

"You've just come home." I stated the obvious.

"You never went up to bed," he returned the obvious to me with a whimsical smile, then turned away to set his things on the hall stand.

"Well, you know when Dulcie gets comfortable, there's no shifting her," I said, moving the cat from my lap to the rug while Gilbert's back was turned. Then I stood and called to him: "Is the baby—"

15

"Fine," Gilbert finished my question with his answer as he entered the parlor. "Wilfred Eden will be just fine."

"Still, you stayed the night."

"Yes. I did." He sounded as if the thought had taken him by surprise. "Mrs. Eden seemed so in need of . . ."

I took a closer look at my brother as he let that sentence trail away and began another.

"The baby has a respiratory illness," he said, his own voice sounding a trifle hoarse to me. "While he's much improved this morning, his condition was very worrisome last night. Mrs. Eden is concerned, too, that her little girl, Amy, keeps well. I tried to be a comfort to mother and children."

Gilbert's gray eyes had a glassy appearance, and his lids were heavy. Exhaustion from lack of sleep was one explanation. But I had sensed, even then—hadn't I?—that Gilbert looked not so much fatigued as halfway to beguiled. Or is that hindsight toying with memory?

"And Mr. Eden?" I asked. "You comforted him, too?"

"I never saw him. No sign nor sound of his presence—and it's a small house." Gilbert sank into the sofa, leaned his head back against the cushions, and massaged his temples with the heels of his hands. "Strange," he said, "I might well have spent the night there alone with Mrs. Eden and her children. Then, this morning, with the baby in her arms and the little girl tugging at her skirt, she saw me off at her front door—almost as if I were the husband leaving for work."

I reminded myself that this was what Gilbert had hoped for and lost—a family of his own—and thus he mused.

Even so, after the midday meal of Ella's sublime shellfish étouffée, when Gilbert announced that he was off to call on his new patient, little Wilfred, I announced that I would accompany him to renew my acquaintance with the child's mother, Charlotte Eden, née Varcy.

16

"You know her?" Gilbert stopped at the front door.

Pausing before the hall mirror, I skewered the crown of my hat and my chignon beneath it with a long amber-jeweled hatpin, before replying: "Yes, slightly—not socially. I haven't seen her in forever."

"Yet you absolutely must see her today." Gilbert's tone might have been teasing.

"Before she married," I replied, "Charlotte worked in Madame Joubert's Hat Shop, where she trimmed my most unforgettable mourning bonnet. So, now that she's a young matron, I'm interested to see how she's getting on."

"Curious," he said.

Curiosity was a trait we shared, I considered, as we began our walk of a few blocks and my brother turned the conversation from Charlotte to her husband, inquiring if I knew Mr. Eden's profession and if his work took him much from home.

"Victor Eden is an architect," I told Gilbert, though whether or not the man traveled in his work, I really couldn't say. He might. "In the newspapers," I continued, "I've noticed Mr. Eden's name linked with those of certain powerful men—his clients and patrons. A plague of hypocrites, if you ask me, making a fuss and bluster about states' rights, while assiduously guarding their own personal privilege." My voice carries well, and I didn't much care who heard me as we passed a couple of puffed-up looking gentlemen on the banquette.

Yes, I was venting a little spleen with my last remark, thinking of my last late husband, who had belonged to the self-serving inner circle—one of my unpleasant post-nuptial discoveries. Bartholomew James had courted and wed me abroad, on a Mediterranean cruise, I traveling as companion to my great-aunt, while the twins summered with their grandparents. Only after the return voyage, when Bartholomew moved me and my children into his house in Faubourg Marigny, he lost the luster afforded him by a foreign setting. And I was confronted daily with examples of how entitled he believed himself and how uncharitable he was to others. Well, he has gone to his reward. My equanimity returned.

As Gilbert and I approached a tidy shotgun house that shone in the slant of the west sun, there was Charlotte on the front porch, sweeping away dead oak leaves. Seeing us, she set the broom aside and met us at the top of the steps, where we exchanged greetings. Charlotte was surprised to see me, had no idea that Dr. Crew was my brother, and so forth. I, in turn, exclaimed over her lovely home—with all sincerity, for the white louvered shutters, closed against the autumn chill, and the white wooden quoins edging the mint-green slats of the drop-siding truly appeared like the fluting of cream on a frosted layer-cake.

"A wedding-cake cottage," I pronounced it.

"Oh, Mrs. James, that's what I thought, too, when Mr. Eden first brought me here after we married. He added those especially for me," Charlotte said, lifting her eyes to the white-painted brackets supporting the overhanging roof of the front porch. They were cut like lace along the eaves and curved like a lady's open fan where they attached from roof to wall.

Then, I glanced towards my brother. What was he thinking when that scowl passed over his features? My guess was that he envied the bridegroom, who had carried this peach of a girl up the porch steps, under those lacey eaves, across the threshold, and down the hall to the bedchamber, kicking the door shut behind him.

Charlotte had been no more than fifteen years old when I first saw her in the hat shop, hardly more than that when she married, maybe twenty now. She looked just as I remembered: a wistful beauty with a cupid's bow mouth. Gilbert couldn't take his eyes off her.

"Please come in," said Charlotte.

She led us into the little front room, which I took in at a

glance: a settee, an armchair with footstool, and an oaken pedestal table matched with a pair of ladder-back chairs, all arranged on a worn green rug; a desk and chair and a glass-fronted book case against one wall; a low pine chest under the window and a basket of mending beside it. Serviceable furnishings, I thought, for a room that must serve a number of purposes in a small house; perhaps the couple even dined here. On the walls hung a few framed drawings, some of grand houses. I had just moved in for a closer look at an engraving of a castle on a cliff when I noticed in my peripheral vision that Charlotte was leaving the room for the narrow hallway, with Gilbert following.

"The children were napping," I heard her say, "but they should be waking up now."

I called after her: "I'm so looking forward to seeing your children, Mrs. Eden." And Charlotte called back that she would bring them to the sitting room—she and Gilbert together, apparently, since he went with her to the next room in line of the shotgun house, the nursery, I supposed.

They returned shortly, Charlotte with the baby on her hip and Gilbert with the little girl by one hand, the child's other hand, a tiny balled fist, rubbing sleep from her eyes. What a picture they made! Rosy-cheeked baby Wilfred, looking about him and blinking those large, curious hazel eyes, like his mother's. His cupid's bow mouth was like hers, too, the downward curve of the wide upper lip gave both faces a pensive expression, a hint of melancholia that was dispelled when they smiled. Little Amy had inherited her mother's abundant dark hair, the child's tousled with sleep and falling in tangled ringlets. But her eyes, unlike Charlotte's, were a smoky gray, like Gilbert's—although, of course, she must have her father's eyes.

Charlotte sat in the armchair with Wilfred across her lap and Amy standing close beside her. Gilbert dropped to one knee to examine first the baby, then the little girl, meeting Amy eye-to-

19

eye—much less intimidating to a child, Gilbert believed, than looming over her. He was all professional decorum, inspecting the children's throats and listening to their lungs—hardly glancing at Charlotte until he had pronounced Wilfred on the mend and Amy quite well.

"Mrs. Eden, your children are darlings," I said feelingly, warmed by an early memory of my twins on one of those rare occasions when they were well-behaved in the parlor.

Gilbert gave me a sideways look and a smile, as if to say he remembered what a time I had with Allan and Arabella. Then, he returned his attention to Charlotte, encouraging her to get some rest—she did look a little weary—and take care of herself, for her health was important to her children's wellbeing, a typical comment for a family physician to make. But he followed it with a more personal question: "Was Mr. Eden much disturbed last night by the baby's coughing?"

Charlotte did not reply right away. Wilfred had begun to snuffle and fuss, and she brought him to her shoulder and patted his back before she spoke in a low, level voice: "He was not at home. On his way out, Mr. Eden told me that he would send for Dr. Baldwin. But Dr. Baldwin sent you in his stead."

It was customary for a married lady to refer to her husband as Mr. Such-and-Such when speaking of him to others, while in private she might call him whatever he permitted her to call him. I had no reason, nor had Gilbert, to interpret Charlotte's speaking of *Mr. Eden* as anything other than custom, yet her avoidance of the intimate *my husband* combined with her lack of inflection to create an impression of distance between them.

"I make a study of children's health," Gilbert said. "It's my specialty, Mrs. Eden—not only treating children when they are ill but finding ways to keep them well."

I gathered that my brother was winding his way towards requesting that Charlotte always call him in place of Dr. Baldwin, when she made it simple for him, agreeing without his asking.

"Please, Dr. Crew, will you continue to treat my children?"

"I am at your service, Mrs. Eden."

There was something—nothing inappropriate, mind—more an undercurrent in my brother's tone that stayed with me all the way home.

Since Gilbert had come to New Orleans, I had introduced him to several young ladies of my acquaintance, encouraging him to think of his future. When he showed no interest in any of them, I worried for him. Had his tragic loss so affected him that he no longer believed himself worthy of love or capable of it—or even dared to acknowledge his masculine proclivities? And now this change in him, as sudden as a flash of lightning. I saw it in his eyes and heard it in his voice—this fancy he had taken to Charlotte Eden. His energies must be channeled in another direction before he made a fool of himself—or worse. I was never prudish, but I have learned to be practical. The relations between a man and a woman are difficult enough without the added complication of one or both being married to someone else. And in gaining that insight, I am a sadder but wiser woman.

Chapter Four

In the months that followed, if Gilbert sometimes appeared abstracted—well, I reminded myself that it was not unusual for him to spend a little of his time building castles in the clouds. He always had, and, whether bemused or not, he applied himself to his work.

His clinic for children was set up at the end of our small yard in what had once been slave quarters—the two-story structure connected by a covered walkway and narrow gallery along one side of the garden to the back of the main house. As Gilbert and I had overseen the renovations of the quarters, we had speculated between ourselves about the nature of lives claimed by a master and eked out within the box-like rooms, for our parents had not been slaveholders and our experience of the institution had been limited. The front room of the clinic was brighter now with freshly white-washed plastered walls but was still no more lavishly furnished than it had been in the old days, when property and persons belonged to the late Mr. James. The plank floor remained mostly bare, with a wooden bench against one wall and a few cane chairs hanging from hooks above to be brought down as needed—a room that was easy to sweep and mop, I had advised, as Gilbert prepared to open his practice. And so it was, except in one corner, where Gilbert wisely chose to construct a sort of pen with low sides, lined with a braided cotton rug and furnished with a changing array of playthings—building blocks, rag dolls, and gourd rattles, which sometimes disappeared with departing patients to be replaced by other novelties, for which Ella and I enjoyed shopping.

As she and I knew from personal experience and Gilbert understood from observation, harried mothers arriving at the clinic with a brood of small children appreciated a place to set down and safely confine their offspring.

When Gilbert was not seeing patients in his clinic, he sometimes attended residents at a shelter for women and children, a charitable concern begun by a committee of ladies to which I belonged. The committee chairwoman's husband served as primary medical consultant, but my brother stepped in as needed. And then, of course, Gilbert made house calls.

Over the winter and into the spring, I really couldn't say for certain how many times Gilbert was summoned to the Eden house or how often the children were poorly. As far as I knew, Charlotte never brought Amy and Wilfred to the clinic. But Gilbert saw them out and about, so he mentioned to me, at the market or the park—by chance. Or not by chance? One sultry afternoon in late spring, from a carriage window, I caught sight, myself, of Charlotte by a market stall, dickering with the vendor over heads of lettuce, while Wilfred wriggled on her hip and Amy pulled at her hand. Then, I saw Gilbert, too, just passing on foot, stopping in mid-stride to speak to Charlotte. He took Wilfred on his shoulders as Charlotte completed her bargaining, then proffered his arm to carry her basket of parcels, and together they walked off in the direction of the little shotgun house.

I rode away in the opposite direction in the carriage of my new acquaintance, actor-manager Ambrose Parr. His cousin, my friend Geraldine Ivy, had recently introduced us, knowing how I enjoy the performing arts, and Mr. Parr had invited me to witness the auditions for a musical revue at his theater. Stimulating as the afternoon proved to be, I was still home before dark and was relaxing on the front porch in one of a pair of wicker armchairs when Gilbert returned home.

I asked him to join me. Then, while he settled in the other chair and loosened his tie and collar, I filled the little bowl of my briar pipe and struck a match. In my wartime nursing days, I had taken up smoking to clear my head in the evening of all the putrid odors breathed during the day. The finely carved pipe and my special blend of vanilla-sweetened tobacco were post-war luxuries. As the tobacco kindled and I drew and exhaled its perfumed smoke, I heard Gilbert draw a deep breath, too, and release it with a sigh. Perhaps he was anatomizing the mixture of vanilla with nearby tea olive blossoms and a cool evening breeze. He had a discerning nose.

I opened the conversation: "Many house calls today?"

"Only the two this morning," he said. "I went to the shelter this afternoon to deliver my new tonic for the children with diarrhea."

Gilbert often concocted his own quite effective remedies, improving on our father's old formulas, compounding plants grown in our little garden with ingredients from the pharmacy and flavorings from Ella's kitchen. If medicines were palatable, my brother reasoned, his young patients were more likely to swallow them. And outbreaks of the common ailments that ran through the shelter would be more likely limited.

He talked on a few minutes about matters at the shelter, the comings and goings—one woman who had found a better situation, another who had returned to her misery. Missing the devil she knew, I thought. Still, Gilbert made no mention of Charlotte, so I brought her up: "But didn't I see you in the early afternoon at the market, talking with Mrs. Eden?"

"You may have," he replied. "For I'm sure I saw your plumed hat bobbing at the window of Mr. Parr's carriage."

As much as I'd hoped my brother would brighten up with his move to New Orleans, in this instance, his amused tone vexed me. "We were only passing the square . . ." I began.

"As was I, Lenore, when I chanced on Mrs. Eden and lent a hand with her children and her parcels." *As innocent as that*, said his inflection.

"Well, it's a pity her maid doesn't help her with her shopping," I said.

"I asked her where her maid had got off to," said Gilbert, "and she told me the girl only works a few hours in the morning—and not every day."

Then his reply to my remark led him on, not to any admission about his afternoon with Charlotte, but to his opinion about Victor Eden's failings as a husband. Through her marriage, Charlotte had altered her status from orphaned shopgirl to wife, mother, and maid-of-all-work for a seemingly successful architect-about-town, who was strictly parsimonious at home. Oh, dear, I had seen this pattern before now: an outsider, perceiving the strain between a husband and a wife, finds a means to play upon that strain, and then anything might happen. Would my brother do such a thing?—make himself ever more a contrast to Mr. Eden, parlay Charlotte's gentle manner towards him into affection—into an improper attachment? Or would Charlotte, dissatisfied with her husband's treatment of her, tempt my brother into a tangle?

"I've seen the evidence with my own eyes," Gilbert said, "and the difference from the way other professional men's households are run."

This was a sensitive topic for my brother, as I knew. A lady should have one or more servants to help with cooking, cleaning, mending, and washing, for housework was heavy work, his late wife had assured him—Estelle, who had wanted no part in domestic labors. Just after they married, when his income could not provide her with what she considered sufficient staff, Estelle had gone to her father for a second housemaid. And Dr. O'Brien had obliged his daughter, then lectured Gilbert on increasing his fees and decreasing time spent with each patient. Gilbert, so said his father-

26

in-law, was not a man of business.

"But what is Mr. Eden's excuse?" Gilbert continued on, sounding a trifle heated, and I realized my mind had wandered and I'd missed some of his remarks. "You've told me, yourself, he caters to a prosperous clientele, who surely pay him well. His fortunes are on the rise. So where is he spending his income? Does he gamble? Or philander? Little enough goes towards any help for the mother of his children."

"Does Mrs. Eden complain to you of her situation?" I asked gently.

Gilbert shook his head.

"Did she invite you in today?"

"No," he said. "Why would she?"

I assumed his question was rhetorical, and his musings that followed bore me out.

"I stopped on the porch steps," Gilbert said, "while she shepherded her children into the house. Wilfred's big enough to toddle now with Amy holding his hand. Then, Mrs. Eden turned back to take her basket from me. I was standing a step or two below her, close to the level of her eyes—"

Those wide hazel eyes, luminous as amber in the afternoon sun, enchanting him, I thought but didn't interrupt. Sure enough, a girl doesn't grow up as beautiful as Charlotte without discovering her effect on men.

"—when she glanced away from me, over her shoulder, sweeping her gaze across the façade of the house, saying to me: *I've been happy here, Dr. Crew. I wouldn't choose to leave.*" Gilbert took a breath, then added, "You see, Lenore, she doesn't seek my sympathy. She doesn't invite me in, except to treat her children."

Well. I had his word.

Chapter Five

Hardly more than a month later, Gilbert paid his last visit to the Edens' single shotgun house, calling to see if Amy, who had been poorly with a sore throat, had made any improvement. The maid, working her few morning hours, paused in mid-sweep of the porch to open the front door for him. But he found his own way from there, past the series of dim rooms, the chambers of the unwound nautilus, to the back of the house and to the garden.

At the top of the steps, still in the shadow of the doorway, he stopped. The patch of ground before him was cut into pieces of light and shade, slivers of green and ocher, flecks of gold and purple. His patient in a pink nightgown sat on a white wicker *chaise longue*, swirling a paintbrush across a sheet of paper held in place by clothespins clipped to the edges of a wooden tray. Charlotte, a spotless white apron covering the front of her indigo dress, moved between her daughter and a low table, where the painting supplies were laid out. As she mixed colors on a palette and rinsed brushes in jars of water, Wilfred toddled around her, unsteady but determined, tugging at her apron or stretching up on tiptoe, trying to catch hold of Charlotte's sleeve. Each time mother and children moved, the scene changed and reshaped itself in the way fragments of colored glass, turned within a kaleidoscope, shift from pattern to pattern.

As a small boy, Gilbert had enjoyed painting, regardless of the results, but now he confined himself to illustrating case notes in his journals, controlling the lines as if they were veins of a sort, transporting the essence of one thing to another. He would have enjoyed having a talent for watercolor, the freedom of it, especially, to capture and keep on paper an impression of this moment before it changed again. That had been his difficulty with brush in hand—no sooner outlining a shape than seeing it turn, unexpectedly, into something else.

Charlotte must have sensed she was being watched. A look of alarm crossed her face as she turned towards him, but disappeared when their eyes met. Then, in that moment of distraction, Wilfred succeeded in catching her sleeve, jolting the palette she held. A rainbow splattered across the boy's upturned face and over Charlotte's apron. Amy clapped a hand to her mouth and stared at her mother.

Involuntarily, Gilbert's right hand tightened in sympathetic response, as if it would be stung with Wilfred's in reprimand. But Charlotte struck no one. Instead, she took up a cloth and a jar of clear water and knelt by her son to wipe away the paint from his cheeks and forehead. Wilfred giggled and bounced and upset the jar, drenching the top of his mother's paint-spattered apron. She set aside the jar and caught him by his wrists, holding him at arm's length for a moment. Instantly, his face puckered in preparation for a burst of tears, but then, just as suddenly, his lips stretched into a grin. Charlotte let him go, let him tumble forward onto her lap, his fingers busily smearing muddied colors across her breast, over the canvas of her apron.

"What am I to do with you, Willie?" Her voice broke with a laugh, but even as it did, Charlotte brushed the back of one hand across her cheek, just below one eye, flicking something away. A drop of paint, a strand of hair, a tear?—Gilbert couldn't say for sure.

"Papa says no *Willie*," Amy corrected her mother.

Charlotte looked towards her daughter. "That's right, dear. We must call your brother Wilfred and hope he grows to the name." Then, as Gilbert approached, she turned her attention to him: "Dr. Crew."

30

"Mrs. Eden." He nodded, and then gripped her elbow, his forearm firm beneath hers, assisting her to rise, while her other arm still encircled Wilfred, his chubby legs now wrapped around her waist.

A sudden dryness in Gilbert's throat reminded him of the reason for his visit, and he turned his attention to Amy, whose own throat, he found on examination, was pink and moist with health. "All better," he told her. "But just in case, you and your brother should take one of these," and from his bag, he produced a couple of soft golden butter-mints to melt in their mouths.

"You're very good to my children," Charlotte said. "Thank you, Dr. Crew."

"It's a pleasure to see them well." Gilbert closed his bag, preparing to depart as he had come through the house, but Charlotte gestured him towards the side gate of the garden.

"May I send your fee along later?" she said as they moved away from the children.

"Don't trouble yourself, Mrs. Eden. I was hardly needed today. And I do apologize for startling you when I appeared at the backdoor. The maid said to go on through, but—"

"At first, I thought you were Mr. Eden home early." Charlotte unlatched the gate and stepped back, allowing it to swing open between them.

"I beg your pardon?" Gilbert said.

Charlotte glanced towards the children, who were still engaged with the watercolors. "My paint box was nearly empty," she said, "so I borrowed a little from my husband's supply—his paints are very fine, you know, an architect's watercolors for plans and designs. I shouldn't have. I wanted to cheer up Amy and Wilfred. And now—" her fingertips brushed across the paint smears on her apron. "I must clean up this mess before Mr. Eden returns."

✛ ✛ ✛

31

The next time Gilbert passed the shotgun house, he did not see Charlotte there. Strangers to him sat on the front porch, an old woman and an old man stiff in a pair of ladder-back rocking chairs, their determinedly asynchronous rocking suggesting deeper disharmony between them. In turn, on the forward rock, one glared at him and then the other glowered. Who were these elderly people with their suspicious, proprietary airs? Charlotte's parents were both dead, as was Eden's father, his mother the only remaining grandparent to Amy and Wilfred, who were nowhere in sight. A sensation of cold started suddenly at the back of Gilbert's neck, as if someone had dropped ice shavings down his stiff collar. A fantastical thought struck him. What if he had lost track of time, as he sometimes did? What if, somehow, he had lost track of years, gone away and come back—the years in between momentarily slipping his mind—and now he had found Mr. and Mrs. Eden grown old and alone in each other's company? Gilbert shook his head, dispelling the absurd notion. The ice melted away, leaving a trace of dampness within his collar. He went on his way without asking either the man or the woman what had really become of the Edens.

Instead, Gilbert asked me, knowing that, amid my usual activities—hosting ladies' study club meetings, attending lectures, supporting various philanthropic organizations—I managed to keep abreast of city news and gossip. He sometimes accused me of being more curious than my cat, unless he wanted to know what I knew. On those occasions, over the past months, he made bungling attempts at insouciance, slipping questions about the Eden family into our supper conversations—as if my answers would be of little consequence to him.

But one night he spoke openly, telling me details of his last call on the Eden children, they painting in their garden, then Charlotte dreading Eden's displeasure. "Is that what Charlotte expects from her husband—to be chastened?" Gilbert said. "What's wrong with the man that he cannot see how fate has favored him?"

We had just finished a supper of my making, for Ella was away visiting one of her granddaughters in St. Martinsville. My repertoire of dishes is limited, but I'd made a passable meal, drowning snapper and vegetables in an excellent French wine and accompanying our repast with another bottle of the same.

Over the last glass, Gilbert related his experience of that afternoon, seeing the dour old couple rocking on the porch of the shotgun house and feeling himself, however briefly, lost in a distortion of time. As he spoke, I felt a shiver travel my own spine—oh, what we can lose, time and love and all in the blink of an eye. My brother's imaginings were too vivid. But I knew the prosaic answer to his confusion.

"The Eden family has moved," I said.

"How long have you known?" His question sounded rather sharp to my ears.

"A few weeks," I replied. "It's no business of ours, Gilbert."

"But her children are my patients."

"They were when they were ill. If Mr. Eden chooses to change doctors as well as houses, that is his affair."

"Did they leave New Orleans?" Gilbert asked. "Is that what you're not telling me?"

Oh, Gilbert, I thought, *let her go. Such carrying on can only end in disaster.*

"Hardly," I replied aloud. "The Edens have moved up in the world, is what I heard, from that little confection of a shotgun house to something more substantial in the *Vieux Carre*. A townhouse that once belonged to old Judge Royce Placide. I suppose he kept a quadroon mistress there before the War." I touched my linen napkin to my lips, then returned it to my lap.

In the old days, a man of the planter class keeping two households was not an uncommon custom—the lily-white wife and legitimate children in the plantation mansion off the river road and the coffee-and-cream-colored mistress and illegitimate offspring in a townhouse in New Orleans. According to Ella, Bartholomew had indulged himself in the arrangement before the war—before his first wife gave up the ghost and his mistress understandably deserted him, taking her son and all her jewels and sailing for France.

I recalled myself to the dining room. "Gilbert, listen to me. If Charlotte—Mrs. Eden—does send for you, you must remember that she—"

"What?" Gilbert cut in. "Do you think I ever forget?"

I took a last sip of wine and let it linger in my mouth before swallowing, then sighed and said, "I think that you are as mortal as the rest of us."

Gilbert was my last brother, the only one not taken by the war, and so dear to me. For the time being, I would let go of whatever I suspected of Gilbert's feelings for Charlotte and believe he had not yet acted upon them.

Chapter Six

Weeks passed before Charlotte sent for Gilbert by way of the same young maidservant who had worked half-days at the shotgun house. Ella met her at the front door and directed her to Gilbert's clinic behind the house, the maid saying Amy Eden had fallen on the staircase, offering her opinion: "Can't be too bad. Child's strong enough to holler."

Grabbing up his medical bag, Gilbert departed with the maid. Keeping pace with the girl, or urging her to keep pace with him, the pair of them traversed the several blocks out of Marigny to the crossing at Esplanade into the Quarter. From there, she led him to a townhouse on Dauphine Street, tall and narrow, built of brick, plastered over and painted a dark, dusky plum color. Even darker gray shutters covered the casement windows, and a black scrolling cage-work of cast iron framed two tiers of galleries above the banquette. Something more substantial, his sister had told him. The arched glazed transom was barred in a radial pattern above the solid door, which the servant unlocked and held open for him, then shut behind them.

From the heat and full brightness of noon, Gilbert entered a cool, dim passage, momentarily blind to his new surroundings. "This way, doctor," said the maid, and he followed the click of her footsteps down the bricked entryway. Along his right side, the dense plastered wall dissolved itself into an archway, beyond which he made out a curve of polished banister lit from somewhere above and the suggestion of a stairwell. "Here?" he asked the maid. "No, sir," and she led on across the interior courtyard, its shade dappled and broken by what little daylight filtered through a screen of

35

potted lemon and banana trees and lines of laundry strung from the upper loggia across to the second floor gallery railing. Beneath the lower arch of the loggia, Gilbert glimpsed the first steps of a back stairway and, in the shadow of it, the ripples and corrugations of a woman's skirts spread over the pavestones. In the pool of fabric was Charlotte, herself, Amy's head resting in her lap. Charlotte stroked her daughter's hair, murmuring to her, while the child whimpered. Near them, Wilfred stood barefoot on his mother's hem, in a loose white shirt that hung past his knees and gave him the appearance of a tiny bewildered wraith. He flicked his tongue against the roof of his mouth in the approximation of a sympathetic "tsk."

Charlotte looked up at Gilbert. "Amy fell, Dr. Crew. She was trotting ahead of me down the stairs. I should have held her hand, but I was carrying a tray of dishes. Three, four steps from the bottom, something startled her. A mouse? I don't know. She squealed and tumbled and hurt her leg, crying so—I couldn't touch it. I don't know what I'd have done if Bette hadn't been here to fetch you."

While she rushed through her explanation, a quaver running through her voice, Gilbert set down his bag and moved aside a fold of Charlotte's skirt to kneel directly on the flagstones. "There now, Amy. Show me which leg hurts." The little girl pointed to her left leg and drew the right one up close to her body, lest he attempted to treat the wrong one. "May I have a look at it?" he asked, and Amy cast a glance at her mother before nodding consent to him. Carefully, Gilbert unlaced and removed her small brown shoe, rolled down and slipped off her white knitted stocking, examined the leg for injury from the thigh to the sole of the foot. "Are you sure this is the leg you hurt?" he asked.

Amy looked warily at him, then whispered: "Will you cut it off?"

"Oh, no. It's a good leg and you should keep it." Gilbert

caught Charlotte's eye in a moment of shared understanding: her daughter's question was hardly strange for a child growing up in a town where war veterans, many of them missing limbs, were commonplace. "Let's have a look at that other leg, too," he said, "just to make sure it matches this one."

While completing the examination, Gilbert was peripherally aware that the maid had finished gathering shards of broken china onto the wooden tray. "Rubbish now, ma'am," the girl said. Charlotte reminded her to sweep up the last slivers to prevent Wilfred from finding them and putting them in his mouth. "But I gots to go, ma'am"—her half-day done here, another household awaited her indifferent service. "A quick sweep," Charlotte said with a sharpness in her voice that was unfamiliar to Gilbert. Then, she turned back to her daughter with her customary gentleness of expression.

Amy was quite perfect, Gilbert assured Charlotte, every bone in place, not a scratch or a bruise or the swelling of a sprain in sight. Still, he carried Amy up to her bed in the nursery and prescribed lemonade and picture books, followed by a nap, for both his patient and her little brother, who had begun to fuss. Nearly an hour later, when the children were, at last, settled and sleeping, Gilbert stepped outside the nursery with Charlotte, who softly closed the door behind them, and stood with her on the inner gallery of the second-floor.

"I apologize, Dr. Crew," she said, "for summoning you when there was no need."

"You did the proper thing. Amy could have been seriously hurt in such a fall. And she was frightened," he said. "You both were."

Charlotte moistened her lips, as if preparing to reply, but said nothing. Gilbert watched the slight movement of her throat above her high collar as she swallowed and then the lowering and lifting of her hazel eyes.

"Is there anything more I can do for the children?" he asked. "For you? Some way I might help relieve your mind?—for as much as Amy and Wilfred are napping peacefully, you look as worried as when I arrived."

"I am," she said. Her gaze swept upward to the third-floor gallery overhead, then down, over the railing to the courtyard below them. "What mother wouldn't worry in such a house?" Charlotte had swayed slightly as she spoke and now gripped a post that connected the two narrow galleries.

Gilbert offered her the support of his arm, and her free hand hovered in the air above his coat sleeve, as if she were considering his offer before drawing away from him. "What is it?" he asked. "What about the house?"

"Oh, Dr. Crew," was all she said.

"Mrs. Eden, are you ill?"

"No, sir, not ill. Dizzy with work and worry, I suppose. I managed in the little house—you saw that for yourself, didn't you?" Gilbert nodded, saying, of course, she had, and then her words tumbled forth: "But here—with all the tasks to be done, with all Mr. Eden's requirements and expectations—how am I to keep my babies safe? Everywhere there are stairs and balconies and galleries from which the children might fall at any moment. All these rooms spiraling up, turning in on themselves around a hard stone courtyard. And the walls of the courtyard are covered with bougainvillea, beautiful in bloom, yes, but every leafy branch is lined with thorns." Charlotte caught her breath. "Dr. Crew, this house is a danger to us."

"My dear Mrs. Eden." This time she allowed him to take her arm, and Gilbert felt a tremor run through it as, side-by-side, they walked the few paces to the stairwell. "If I can be of service to you—"

"I'm sorry, sir. Forgive me, please. The house is new to me. I must learn to manage it better." She composed herself, resuming her wifely role, ending the intimacy of the moment of her venting her emotion.

"And if Mr. Eden moves you overnight to a mansion on Bayou Teche, will you manage there, too, with a maidservant who comes half a day and no help with the children?" The thought had run through his mind, and from the startled expression on Charlotte's face, Gilbert realized he had given voice to it—and to the bitterness with which he regarded her husband.

She drew her arm away from his. "If you will wait here, sir, I'll get your fee."

"No"—not out of her pittance of housekeeping money—"don't concern yourself, Mrs. Eden. I'll send the bill to your husband."

"I will learn to manage, Doctor." Whom was she trying to convince?

"Even so," he said, and his tone softened, "even so, may I bring you a cat?—to rid the house of mice that might startle someone on the stairs."

Briefly, Charlotte smiled at Gilbert, amused by his offer, perhaps, or in an effort to restore the polite distance between them, which her confession of domestic discord and his outspokenness had breached. Then her mouth curved down again into the cupid's bow, and he took leave of her on the gallery, minding his step on the descent.

Chapter Seven

Gilbert mentioned to me a notion he had of calling on Victor Eden at the gentleman's office to have a word with him about the strain on Charlotte's nerves as she made do with so little help. I wondered if my brother had completely forgotten his own reaction years ago to his father-in-law's meddling in Gilbert's domestic arrangements. But more than that, I worried over the prospect of Gilbert coming face-to-face with Charlotte's husband. However carefully and professionally Gilbert phrased his recommendations, Mr. Eden might well see through my brother. And what if Gilbert's tender regard for Charlotte were then exposed beyond denying?

I nipped that possibility in the bud.

"Far better," I said over morning coffee, "for me to call on Mr. Eden's mother."

"But what good would that do?"

"She could speak to her son—use her maternal influence."

Would Gilbert bring up my twins and wishful thinking? No, he had no time. The bell on the side gate leading to his clinic began to jangle, signaling the arrival of his patients. But just in case he decided to spare a moment to object to my plan, I rose from the table, adding: "I'll go now. I'll touch on your concern while I'm soliciting contributions for the orphans' fund. Widow Eden made a donation last year, I'm almost sure of it, and might well wish to do so again . . ." My voice trailed away from him as I moved down the hall towards the hat stand.

Widow Eden lived in small but elegant apartment not far from Jackson Square. I had attended an afternoon recital there some years ago on the arm of an architect with whom I briefly kept company, a gentleman associated with Mr. Eden and also the cousin of the performer, a young lady with aspirations above her talent for opera. Oh, I suppose everyone in New Orleans is entangled with everyone else in some way or another, at one time or another—if one follows a thread far enough.

I had left home far too early to make a polite social call, so I ambled, nodding to my neighbors along Rampart and lingering on the banquette along Royal to window shop. Then, at midmorning, I knocked at Widow Eden's door and was admitted by a bright young housemaid, who, it occurred to me, might be well suited to looking after her mistress's grandchildren on occasion.

Widow Eden looked surprised to see me, blinking at me like the bird she resembled, a crane, lifting and arching its thin neck. But I soon put her at ease, making a quick mention of being out on orphanage business, without making any direct plea to her for a donation, and deciding to look in on her. "I haven't seen you at a concert or the theater in ever so long, ma'am," I said. "Have you been keeping well?"

"My headaches, you know." With one long-fingered hand, she traced a vague circle in the air near her forehead.

"Oh, dear, Widow Eden, I am so sorry to hear that."

"I grow old," she said with a sigh. "And my Victor keeps so busy, I hardly see him."

This was my opening. If Widow Eden lacked for company, visits from her Victor's adorable children would brighten her hours—while, perhaps, giving her daughter-in-law a brief respite from the never-ending demands of hearth and home. I suggested as much to the lady, then remarked, "We women are tried at every stage of life's journey, are we not?"

"I certainly have been," Widow Eden said. "But Charlotte—that girl worked in a shop before she married." Born for servitude, the woman's tone implied. "Charlotte is now fortunate enough to keep my son's home. What more does she expect? What would she do with time to fritter away?"

Clearly, Widow Eden expected no answer from me. She made a modest donation to the orphanage, reminded me of her headaches, and bid me good morning and goodbye.

✛ ✛ ✛

In the few months that followed, I doubted Charlotte was ever far from Gilbert's thoughts. He called on her in the *Vieux Carre*, a couple of times that I was aware of, though there may have been others, to inquire after the children's health and once to deliver a gray-stripped mouser he had found roaming on the wharf. The same indolent maid worked her few half-days, so my brother told me, and Charlotte remained patient with her children and busy with housekeeping—for a man with exacting standards, according to Gilbert. Charlotte remained troubled, too—of that, Gilbert felt sure—troubled by something apart from her leaving behind the shotgun house, where she had been happy, apart from her moving into the townhouse, which she had called dangerous. Perhaps she met with it—with whatever disturbed her—where Gilbert next beheld her, in yet another house—indeed, a mansion.

October had come again.

A year to the month since Gilbert first met Charlotte, he drove Dr. Baldwin in the old man's carriage out along the river road west of town. By late afternoon, I imagined my brother had left Dr. Baldwin at Testament, a plantation belonging to the eminent Judge Royce Placide, for a social visit, shooting and feasting. Gilbert planned to return for his aging colleague in a couple of days after making rounds, staying overnight in the spare rooms of other great houses farther along the course of the Mississippi River.

Part of Gilbert's practice included his visiting planters' estates and tenant farmers' shanties in between, where he treated whole families of laborers, old and young, some so very young—children of four or five, who picked cotton and dug sweet potatoes and suffered with cuts and blisters, fevers and worms. They were my brother's calling. And, though circumspect about his ambitions, which I encouraged—both the ambitions and the circumspection—Gilbert had hopes of playing some little part in preserving the life and improving the health of the next generation of the struggling poor, who might someday challenge the ascendancy of the next generation of the powerful.

When Gilbert had set off, I'd no idea that Mr. Eden and his wife would, like Dr. Baldwin, be guests of Judge and Mrs. Placide. I wondered if Gilbert had known. Not until the third day that my brother was gone did I learn of the situation from Ella. She had some passing acquaintance with Widow Eden's housemaid, Narcisse, and had chatted with the girl at the market that afternoon. Our lives are all entwined, haven't I said? Apparently, my suggestion to Widow Eden that she might enjoy seeing more of her grandchildren had made some impression on the lady, after all. Amy and Wilfred were staying with her while Charlotte accompanied her husband for a couple of days at Testament.

On the evening that Gilbert was due to call back at Testament for Dr. Baldwin, to stay the night, himself, and return to the city tomorrow, I had a prickly feeling at the back of my neck. My late third husband, who had invested in various business schemes with the judge, had brought me with him, on occasion, as a guest at Placide's plantation. Something about the Placides in their great house had disquieted me then, and I had avoided them since Bartholomew's death. I'd never quite decided if that rambling mansion of theirs were haunted more by the past or the present—by the long-dead ancestors and their slaves or by the living boorish master and his haughty mistress. Then, as little scenes and stories were wont to intrude upon my thoughts, inventions of the mind, I suddenly envisioned my brother, bemused and wandering

Testament's maze of corridors without a thread to follow to find his way out.

"Perhaps," I said to Ella, who was arranging my hair before the dressing table mirror, "I shouldn't go out this evening. The weather is threatening. And I have a feeling about Gilbert—an apprehension. Mr. Parr will simply have to understand."

"You staying home fretting over him won't keep Mr. Gil out of trouble," Ella said. She went on coiling and pinning up locks of hair.

"You may be right, Ella—as usual." I wanted to be persuaded, even as I sighed and handed her my favorite silver comb, with which she secured my coiffure. "I have been longing for this opening night. *The Winter's Tale*—the title, alone, gives me an anticipatory shiver"—which, that moment, crossed my shoulders. "The play is under Mr. Parr's direction, did I tell you, Ella?"

"Yes, Miss Lenore—a time or two."

"Mr. Parr has acted the role of Leontes, himself, on tour," I rattled on, regardless of repeating myself to Ella, "but he told me he didn't wish to be bound to nightly performances this time in New Orleans."

"No, Miss Lenore—not when he got himself other plans for his evenings."

Oh, how I was distracted by anticipation of the drama on the stage. Then, as the curtain would rise, I would fall under a theatrical spell and, for hours to come, spare not a thought for Gilbert nor imagine his descent into anarchy.

Chapter Eight

On Gilbert's return journey to Testament, heavy clouds had brought an early twilight. He urged the carriage horse up the long drive towards the Placides' great house, hoping to arrive before it faded into utter darkness, shades and curtains drawn. He had been invited to spend the night, grudgingly, as a convenience for Dr. Baldwin. Still, if he were not too late, he might be asked into the parlor. Dr. Baldwin had mentioned to him that Mr. and Mrs. Eden were also guests at the plantation for the weekend, and Gilbert hoped to see Charlotte and ask after her little boy and girl. She might smile and thank him for his interest—gracious and careful, while her dour husband stood by, as if none of them could see past the role Gilbert played, the professional services he rendered. But such a scene was not to be, no gentle banter, no smile.

Instead, a gust of wind scattered dry leaves ahead of him, like shriveled thoughts. An oak branch cracked, broke, thudded and splintered on the drive. The horse shied. A stableboy dashed out and caught the traces. Then Judge Placide, the master himself, met Gilbert on the steps of the verandah and ushered and hushed him into the house.

Something had changed. When Gilbert had deposited the old doctor at Testament, Judge Royce Placide had barely nodded in his direction, yet on his return the judge leaned on him and squeezed his arm, as the two of them crossed the threshold. Gilbert supported him along the marble hallway and, by the light of the sconces, saw the judge's features in profile, quivering like aspic. On this chill night, beads of sweat glistened over Placide's puffy brow and balding head, on which were plastered a few remaining strands

47

of hair, some still reddish, more white. His lower lip flapped as he muttered: "The ladies are beside themselves . . . Mrs. Eden . . . just up and collapsed . . ."

Gilbert's heart quickened. What had happened? What was the judge rambling on about?

The pine-paneled pocket doors had been slid back halfway into slots in the walls on either side of the grand parlor's threshold. The open doorway framed a *tableau vivant* into which Judge Placide lumbered on gouty legs, while Gilbert, the spectator, stopped just outside. He scanned the scene for a glimpse of Charlotte. Had she fainted, resting now in a chair or lying on a settee? Collapsed, the judge had said. There was no sign of Charlotte. Instead, Gilbert saw the judge's wife, Helene Placide, half-reclining on a barge of a sofa, swathed in violet silk, the focal point of the composition before him.

Old Judge Placide took up his place behind his wife, who was young enough to be his daughter, and laid a thick-fingered, proprietary hand upon her shoulder. Then he mumbled something to her about Dr. Crew's arriving just in time to take care of the matter, although Gilbert did not yet know what the matter was. Dr. Baldwin, his back hunched forward, clutched at the small of it with one hand and with the other held a brandy snifter under Helene's nose. Kneeling on the rug beside her hostess, half-obscured by the expanse of a tufted ottoman, was Mrs. Duvall, whom his sister had once noted was inseparable from Mrs. Placide. The two women's fingers were laced together. Only Victor Eden was remote from the others, sitting apart in a wing-back chair.

Gilbert stepped through the doorway as if entering from the wings onto a proscenium set with over-large furnishings, the scene lacking proper proportion. Then, like an actor unsure of his lines, Gilbert ventured: "Judge Placide, you said Mrs. Eden—"

The instant he spoke the name, Helene Placide flung up one bejeweled hand, striking the snifter from Dr. Baldwin's grasp.

Amber beads flew in an arc, spattering the old man as he recoiled. Margaret Duvall flinched as near her the vessel splintered against a table edge. A pulse beat of silence passed as the shards flew outward, another as they fell, glass slivers scattering over the carpet.

A moment later, Helene lifted her chin towards her husband. "Royce," she sighed his given name, "you said you would take care of this—" She finished her statement with a wave of her fingers towards the hallway from which the judge and Gilbert had entered, then sank back against the cushions. Margaret Duvall fanned her. Dr. Baldwin dabbed at his jacket with a handkerchief, muttering to himself. The judge rounded the sofa and was once again at Gilbert's side. That was how it was. Or had Gilbert forgotten some detail in his later retelling to his sister? Yes. Victor Eden had not moved.

The judge gripped Gilbert's elbow and turned him away from the scene, speaking to him as if the two of them were alone in the judge's private chamber.

"You must understand, Dr. Crew, my wife is highly sensitive. We have to do something, don't you see? Under the circumstances, and to spare Mr. Eden, of course—"

"I beg your pardon, sir. What are you talking about?"

"Poor Mrs. Eden." The judge licked his lips, then dropped his voice: "Such a pretty thing. Pity." He glanced back at his wife, who gave a little sniff.

"What has happened?" Gilbert asked.

"What? Why—Charlotte Eden has passed away."

A moment elapsed. Somehow, between the judge's speaking and Gilbert's hearing, the words must have become jumbled and arrived out of order in Gilbert's head. But in what order would the words have made sense to him? None, whatsoever.

"No. No, sir, that's not possible," Gilbert said, refusing to be taken in by the judge's bizarre jest.

But Placide was without humor, breathing his words into Gilbert's face with the frowsty odor that escaped his mouth like foul air from a tomb: "All of a sudden, she up and died."

"No, sir," Gilbert repeated, "that cannot be true." She cannot be dead. In a moment, he would turn back into the room and see her sitting on the ottoman by her husband. Or if she were not there, she was upstairs reading or sketching in her notebook or preparing for bed—anything that she might do, Charlotte would go on doing because she could not be dead.

"You'll take her remains back to town *tonight*. Best for all concerned," Placide said close to Gilbert's ear. His voice firm, he was giving an order. His earlier unsteadiness, which Gilbert had first taken for a case of nerves, more likely had resulted from Placide's exertions to and fro, taking command of the situation.

Gilbert shook the judge's heavy hand from his coat sleeve and spun around to stare at Victor Eden. Surely, the man had heard Placide's ludicrous statements, issued in a stage-whisper, yet Eden said nothing to contradict the master of the house. He said and did nothing, and the nothing, itself, gave Gilbert pause. Others might have interpreted Eden's lack of expression as a lack of feeling, others who could not share the particular language of his particular grief. The man's face was set and blank, his back straight, feet close and parallel. His hands, placed on his knees, were still, only the fingers barely moved, curling and digging themselves into the fine wool of his trousers.

Two years ago, hadn't Gilbert looked just the same as Eden?—ashen and vacant, disbelieving death? Was Gilbert not, even now, looking into the mirror at that same self, the man bereft? For an instant, hardly more than that, a lightness came over Gilbert, as if he had left his own body, floated just beyond it. Quickly as he could, not quickly enough, he caught his image and folded it back into his flesh. Something in the room had changed; Gilbert had missed something and could not recall it.

Again, he felt the judge's hand, this time weighing on his shoulder. "Take care of this for me, young Crew, and I won't forget it," Placide said, then let his hand drop as he moved away, while Gilbert remained standing near the doorway, stunned. Next thing he knew that woman had materialized beside him, Helene's bosom-friend, Margaret, her profile cut as sharply as a paper silhouette. As she tilted her head to him, Gilbert noticed her alarmingly high cheekbones—a trick of the light, perhaps, or some intentional cosmetic illusion. For a moment, looking at a face another man might find alluring, he was only aware of the skull beneath the skin.

She urged him away, preceded him across the hall, and then stopped at the foot of the staircase. "Dr. Crew, will you lead us up?" What did she think?—that he would try to lag behind her for a glimpse of her ankles?

Gilbert's thoughts were all of Charlotte, only Charlotte, as she had looked the first time he had seen her, not as her body would become—not as all of us, all mutable flesh, would become. Somehow, he climbed the stairs, his legs taking his weight even as his knees seemed to loosen and come unhinged. At the summit of Testament's massive staircase, he halted, his hand tight on the banister railing. Gilbert shut his eyes and pressed his lips together, as if doing so would contain emotion, catch it and keep it, as a living spirit is kept within the body.

Then, Margaret Duvall reappeared at his side. "Her body must go out by the front door, the door she entered," the woman said. "Feet first. It's all superstition, of course, but my dear friend Helene is very particular."

All superstition, indeed—in the cards, in the palm of a hand. If Charlotte lay dead in a room down the corridor, what part could Gilbert work in her fortunes now?

Chapter Nine

"Come along, Dr. Crew," said Margaret Duvall. "We must hurry you off before the weather breaks—and before dear Helene faints away entirely."

Hurry—hurry the body out of the house. Why was that? Why was Helene Placide's reaction to a death so much more important than the death itself? Gilbert thought he understood Eden's reserve. If the husband could not register a discernible emotion, that might well prove the depth of his grief. But Helene's excess of feeling more likely arose from a desire to maintain her position as center of attention, not to be upstaged by a beautiful houseguest dying young.

The room seemed small—in such a vast house. Gilbert stepped in and stopped near the foot of the bed. Margaret brushed past him, and he caught a whiff of musty jasmine rising from among the ruffles encircling her shoulders. She crossed to the window and pulled down the blind, shutting out the cloudy evening sky—gold, rose, purple disappeared from the room. A single lamp burned on the table, lighting the scene that had been transformed from a watercolor to a sketch in pencil and chalk.

Charlotte's face appeared as a pale oval in a pool of darkness, which was her hair, loose, brushed back from her brow and spread across the ivory-colored pillow slip. The tatted-edged bed sheet was folded over and back, turned down to her waist and revealing the dressing gown she wore, which was overly large, excessively fancy. The line of the shoulder seams of the pleated sleeves fell past the curve of her shoulders beneath, and the silken ribbons tied at her throat and across her breast had length to spare.

The gathered tiers of lace at the cuffs scrolled over her folded hands and left only her fingers from the second row of knuckles exposed.

Gilbert said what came to mind: "That can't be her dressing gown."

"Why, no, it isn't. But how would you—"

"It doesn't fit her."

"How very observant you are," Margaret said. "The gown is one Helene no longer wears. Poor Charlotte's own was so frayed at the hem. Helene said it should be cut up to dress a doll for the children."

For Amy and Wilfred Eden. Was that to be their comfort, their keepsake, a doll clothed in scraps of their late mother's dressing gown?

While one of Gilbert's hands gripped the bedpost at the end of the bed, the other reached out and, for a moment, touched the coverlet, which was pulled taut and tucked over Charlotte's feet. Then, as quickly, he withdrew the hand and stuffed it in his pocket.

Margaret came to the bedside and drew a tiny, glinting pair of scissors from her pocket, which was seamed and hidden among the gathers of her shirt. She lifted a lock of Charlotte's hair and snipped it off at the scalp, close by Charlotte's left ear.

"No. Stop," Gilbert said, too late.

"Oh, it's only customary, you know. Victor may want a piece of mourning jewelry. Perhaps a fob for his watch." A trinket made of Charlotte's woven hair, a souvenir. Margaret coiled the lock around her forefinger, forming it into a tight circlet, before slipping lock and scissors into her pocket. What might she have collected next? Nail parings? A finger bone?

Gilbert heard a rustling coming from some dark recess of the room. His old sorrows moving along the wall, perhaps, reminding him that they had preceded him here, anticipated his arrival in a chamber for the dead—come to join him and meet his new sorrow. But no. Out of the background, a pair of dark-skinned women in darker dresses emerged into the lamplight and pulled back the bed sheet. One of them lifted Charlotte's head and shoulders, the other her legs swathed in the ivory gown, as the women moved her from the bed. For a moment, Charlotte's body was suspended between them, and the women disappeared again into the shadows while Charlotte's body floated as if levitated by a magician. Then, the women moved and materialized yet again and laid her body within a coffin, itself suspended between two wooden chairs. No, not a coffin. This was no more than a storage chest, a rectangular pine box with a hinged lid. Charlotte was not tall, but still the chest could not contain her full length. One servant bent Charlotte's knees and slightly turned her legs, moving her easily, no rigor yet to break. The other adjusted her shoulders, laying her more on the left side of her body, her head on a small square pillow, not laid out at all, but positioned as if Charlotte had turned and curled herself in sleep.

How these servants must have rushed at the master's command to empty a chest and carry it between them to the bedroom, leaving behind in another room or in a hallway, the former contents tossed out and scattered on the floor—linens, old clothes, odds-and-ends in confusion. Moving through the shadows of this room, Margaret cleared away the toiletries from the dressing table into a holdall. Combs and hairpins and little glass bottles disappeared, while Gilbert gazed at Charlotte, tucked in the pine box.

Her children were so small, two and four, and the palm reader had foretold a third child. Impossible now—as was Gilbert's hope of calling at the Eden's home for years to come, whenever Charlotte summoned him to listen to Wilfred's lungs or inspect Amy's throat. Gilbert could not back his way out of the great hall of Testament, unwind himself from the tiers of balconies and the curving staircase of the townhouse, and ever again open door after door after door of the single shotgun house until he found them in the back garden—as he had found them before, Charlotte and Amy on their knees, their bare hands pressing the loamy soil around the roots of violets and pansies, velvety purple and gold. Then, Wilfred, with tiny fists clenched, had toddled towards his mother, opened his hands and tossed clumps of soil over the pleats and furrows of her skirt.

Another image appeared unbidden from Gilbert's memory—of himself dropping a clump of earth onto the polished wooden lid of a coffin visible in an open grave. Within it lay the body of Estelle O'Brien Crew, in her arms the son she had never held in life. Gilbert should have left her alone, he had confessed to his sister, after Estelle was gone. At what had seemed the proper time in his career, he had wed the proper young lady, his mentor's daughter, vowing to care for her while she vowed to please her father. Estelle had shown little interest in the getting of a child, and the delicacy of her condition might have come as a relief to her, excusing her from further intimate duties, before ending her life. Conception and confinement were fraught with danger and should only be risked by a woman mad with love. Then the memory of her passion might be a salve for the widower's conscience. More salve to Gilbert than that God had ordained women must suffer and bring forth children in sorrow.

One of the servants started to shut the chest. "No," Gilbert said, "leave it." The pair of servants backed against the wall, while Margaret went on filling a carpetbag, tying up a hatbox.

Outside the bedroom, from down the hall, Dr. Baldwin's repeated dry coughs announced his approach. When Gilbert knew the man was behind him, without turning, he asked him, "How did this happen?"

"Heart," replied Dr. Baldwin, as if that one word explained everything.

"Did she faint? Fall?" As a woman with child sometimes fainted. Had she again been with child?

"No, nothing like that. Slipped away in her sleep—peaceful-like."

Margaret paused in her packing and looked towards Dr. Baldwin, one brow lifting, and Gilbert wondered if she were questioning—or doubting—the old man's pronouncement.

"She hadn't been ill," Gilbert said. "Her daughter had a cold a few weeks ago, but Mrs. Eden—"

"Oh, these delicate little women always look a trifle ill, wouldn't you say? Affect the look so often, hard to know when they are really on a decline." So Dr. Baldwin excused himself.

"Had you treated her recently?" Gilbert asked.

"Not recently, no. Pity I wasn't called in before—"

"Maybe she was taken by surprise."

"Mrs. Placide is my concern now," said Dr. Baldwin.

"Is *she* on a decline?"

Dr. Baldwin approximated another dry cough but did not answer. Instead, he edged around Gilbert, moved to the pine box, and looked down at Charlotte, then adjusted the placement of one of her hands. The next moment, Margaret ceased packing and joined the old doctor, each of them at one end of the box. Together, they began to lower the lid. Gilbert caught his breath so suddenly, audibly, that he must have startled Margaret, whose narrowed eyes darted in his direction. He hoped his place in the shadows hid his face from her, concealed the shock of finality and pain of loss twisting his features in an expression befitting a grieving husband.

With the creak of the hinges, the dull thud of the box lid settling into place, the closing up and hiding away of Charlotte's beauty, Gilbert still caught at a filament of hope. Suppose the whole lot of them were mad, suffering from some shared derangement of their senses. Couldn't that happen among such people as these in their rarified world?—the puffed-up judge and his histrionic wife, her fawning companion, the rich man's physician of easy accommodation and questionable skill, and the insensible husband, who allowed the others to carry on with their perversity. They had brought Gilbert in not to share their madness but to witness it, and by witnessing it, make the impossible true.

But Gilbert would thwart them. He would be Charlotte's witness, not theirs, and act for her upon his observations. Between the lying in and laying out that opened and closed a life, were not physicians called upon to attend and record the intervening disasters, whether caused by illness or injury? Whether owing to happenstance or malice?

Chapter Ten

By the bedroom doorway, Gilbert listened to Dr. Baldwin issuing instructions about where Gilbert should deliver the pine box containing Charlotte Eden's remains. The old doctor's head bobbed as he spoke, and his hunched back and rounded shoulders, loosely draped in a black frock coat, rose in shadow behind him on the wall like the folded wings of a raven. Then, he moved past Gilbert, into the corridor, with the pair of servants coming after—more shadows, carrying holdall, carpetbag, and hatbox. Gilbert waited for Margaret to follow the rest of them out, to give him a moment alone in the room, but still she busied herself.

She straightened the bed linens and brushed one hand across the pillow, smoothing out the indentation where Charlotte's head had lain, removing the last clue that Charlotte had ever occupied the bed. Then she turned down the lamplight. Was she preparing the room for Charlotte's husband, as if he would return to it for a sound night's sleep? Margaret seemed unaware that Gilbert had not left with the others, that he watched her lift a delicate bone china cup and saucer from the bedside table. An odd expression crossed her face: one moment her mouth formed a plump moue and the next a thin-lipped line, as if an idea had struck her in one instant, and in the next, she had tucked it away. At the same time, curiosity struck Gilbert, and he wanted to know what Charlotte had drunk from the cup before her sudden collapse.

As Margaret skirted the bed and started for the door, Gilbert stepped forward, nearly colliding with her, begging her pardon, catching the rattling cup and saucer before she could drop them. A brief flurry ensued, in which she reached for the cup, he assured her he had a good grip of it, and she brushed at her bodice and skirt in case the remaining contents of the cup had spilled, saying: "You gave me such a start, Dr. Crew. I didn't see you there."

"My apologies, Mrs. Duvall. I hope your gown has not been damaged."

"Not at all." Again, she reached for the cup and saucer. Lowering them from where he had held them up and away from her, Gilbert brought the cup past his nose, inhaling, catching a whiff of stewed mint and an intimation of something fruity and sickly sweet. As Margaret resumed possession of the china, Gilbert cast a glance at the dark leafy dregs within the cup.

"Some kind of tea?" he asked.

"Oh, this?" she said, almost lightly, as if she had not just snatched the cup from his hand. "A tisane from an old recipe." Her expression was bland, a contrast to the thoughtful one her face had worn earlier, when she had first picked up the cup. She rattled on: "Dear Helene ordered it mixed for little Charlotte, who had complained of feeling poorly. But then she didn't finish it."

"Did you bring her the tisane in the afternoon?" he asked.

"Not I," Margaret replied with a trace of amusement at his foolish question. "A servant."

"And the end came soon after," Gilbert said, his throat closing over the words.

"I suppose so." Margaret lifted and dropped one shoulder. "Charlotte had been drooping around most of the day. Dr. Baldwin didn't take any particular notice—but then he was out shooting. Still, he's right that her low spirits were nothing new. That's how she was whenever Victor brought her here. Oh, shame on me for saying so, but it was very tiresome for the rest of us." Was that it, then?—Charlotte's demise had rid the house party of a tiresome guest. "When she went off to her room," Margaret added, "I

60

thought she'd gone to have a little pout after the spat she'd had with Victor out in the garden."

"They had an argument?" Gilbert asked.

"Trivial, I'm sure—neither here, nor there." Margaret sighed impatiently. "Well, really, Dr. Crew, how were any of us to know she had a delicate condition?"

Because they only saw her when she was subdued in the presence of her husband's patrons and associates.

As if Margaret's impatience were suddenly contagious, Gilbert joined the hurry to remove Charlotte's body from the house. Within the vastness of Testament, he had sensed a paucity of air and was anxious to be gone, out of sight and sound of the Placides and their houseguests. Gilbert took up one end of the coffin as a manservant took the other and backed down the stairs and out the front door. Then, they lifted their burden into the bed of the wagon that a groom had brought from the stable, and Gilbert set off, on the open road.

There was no time for him to out-distance nightfall, which was nearly upon him, nor was he likely to out-run the brewing rainstorm, so Gilbert chose to meet them when they came. He welcomed the night and, behind its cover and away from Testament, let his features fall with the grief he had restrained and that now overcame him. Beyond that, he welcomed the storm that forced him from brooding and into the moment.

White lightning cracked the bowl of black sky, and thunder caused the bay mare drawing the wagon to shy and falter in her gait. Gilbert gripped the harness reins, calling out to her, "Easy, girl. Easy now." Briefly, they slowed, then gathered speed again as the rainfall increased, down the road barely visible in the wagon lantern's paltry light.

Approaching a curve in the road, Gilbert sensed the pine box shift in the bed of the wagon, and he glanced back. Was the improvised coffin water-tight, air-tight? Its boards were thin, but its

lid had fitted snuggly enough into place. Gilbert looked away from
the road ahead, glanced back only for an instant, the time it took
for a lightning bolt to flash above him and delineate the pine box
askew in the wagon bed. Surely, that was all the time it took.

In the moment of his hearing above the boom of distant
thunder the close crack of a whip, Gilbert again faced forward.
Wind-driven rain slapped his hunched shoulders as if that cracking
whip were laid across his back. Lightning broke the darkness, and
Gilbert saw a black carriage rip through the curtain of rain,
charging like a demon hearse in a nightmare. Its pair of slick black
horses sped directly towards the wagon. Instantly, Gilbert yanked
the reins and braced his boots against the foot board, throwing his
whole weight back and to one side, turning the head of the bay
mare. Or had the mare anticipated him?—already swerving as the
carriage horses hurtled towards her. At the instant, not of impact,
but of passing, the wet flanks of the bay and of one of the pair
struck, slapped against each other, then tore apart.

The carriage rocked and pitched—first veering away to the
far side on two wheels, then swinging back, striking the side plank
of the wagon. The wagon careened onto the rim of the
embankment, the left wheels rising from the ruts, the right ones
digging more deeply into the muddy incline. The carriage vanished.
The bay thrashed against the weight of the listing wagon that
dragged her to her knees. The reins slipped through Gilbert's
leather-gloved hands. He let go. He could not stop himself—not
from tumbling from the wagon, nor from falling down the bank,
nor from striking one shoulder, then the other against a rotten log,
rolling over and over, nor from feeling the spin of the earth for
moments after he lay sprawled on crushed weeds.

At last, gaining his footing, his precarious balance, Gilbert
stared from the river's edge up the embankment. Flashes of
lightning revealed the scene before him as if it were a series of
stereoscopic photographs: image, blankness, image, blankness. The

mare, her neighs like shrieks, as she struggled up on her forelegs—blankness—the mare raising her hindquarters, the wagon bed tilting behind her, back over the rim of the embankment—blankness—the pine box shot from the back of the wagon, plummeting down the slope—blankness. Through the darkness, Gilbert lunged towards the splintering sound of the box breaking in its fall. Jagged branches of lightning lit again the pine chest, its lid twisted away on the hinges, the side panel split open, and through the fissure, through a torn sleeve, dangled a white arm.

In darkness, Gilbert knelt beside the coffin, his knees sinking into the mire. He ran his gloved hands over the broken pieces of pine and the fragile bared arm, as if he might somehow gather the fragments together and reassemble the whole. A last flash of lightning revealed the body, twisted to one side, face hidden in the pillow. Darkness fell again. Time passed, the rain slackened to a drizzle, and the thunder faded to a distant reverberation. Gilbert peeled away his leather gloves, then reached into the coffin to turn Charlotte's head, to arrange her arms by touch, for he could not see her. How long ago had Dr. Baldwin said she had died? She was limp and soft. Her cheek was a little pillow of its own against the palm of his hand. His hand, trembling with the chill, with the shock of the fall, cradled her cheek.

Gilbert slid one arm beneath her shoulders and lifted her towards him. Her body yielded, and her head lolled back against his shoulder. Then, he held her to his chest and rocked her there. All Gilbert had felt at Testament and stifled he now released and wept like a fool in time, who could not carry Charlotte backward or forward from the moment in which they were trapped. *If this were all—this was the first and last time he would ever hold her.*

Chapter Eleven

On our carriage ride to the theater, Ambrose Parr devoted himself to broadening my knowledge of the performing arts, to which I found myself drawn, and to the works of William Shakespeare, in particular. "The tragedies, undoubtedly, end in death, and, of course the comedies in marriage. But the romances," Ambrose said, covering my gloved hand with his, "lie somewhere betwixt and between. There may be death for some and marriage for others, betrayal followed by forgiveness, vengeance by redemption—even resurrection is possible—in a romance, which, in short, contains the very chaos of human passions."

I would soon find out, when ensconced in Mr. Parr's private box at the theater, overlooking the proscenium—that little world within a larger world. Ambrose had just offered a quick word of encouragement to his cast of actors backstage before joining me. From our box, depending on the placement of the plush red velvet chairs and the arrangement of the box's draperies, we could also view as much or as little as we chose of the audience on the lower floor and in the boxes opposite us. Certainly, I was curious to see who was in attendance and how they were paired or clustered. But when the stage curtains parted, I was soon sitting on the edge of my seat, entirely focused on the tale unfolding below me—*The Winter's Tale*.

The play began with an immediate reversal—the cordial friendship between Leontes, King of Sicilia, and Polixenes, King of Bohemia, was corrupted in moments by Leontes's savage jealousy. As the play proceeded, I felt increasingly relieved that Ambrose was sitting beside me and not strutting the boards as he had on tour, portraying that green-eyed fool—who accused his wife of infidelities conjured from his own lascivious imagination. I quite shivered when Leontes called Hermione *slippery*, the very term Bartholomew James had once flung at me. Oh, if only I could have been as eloquent as Hermione in defending my character. Or if Bartholomew had only been more interesting with the rest of his accusations, for I held my breath as Leontes delivered these lines:

"There may be in the cup a spider steep'd, and one may drink, depart, and yet partake no venom, for his knowledge is not infected: but if one present th' abhorr'd ingredient to his eye, make known how he hath drunk, he cracks his gorge, his sides with violent hefts. I have drunk, and seen the spider."

My stars! Shakespeare's language quite lifted the story above the usual melodramatic fare I had too often seen in recent years. I was transported. Never mind that Mr. Parr had earlier explained to me some of the craft behind his scrim of illusions. Never mind a slight grinding sound of machinery when a ship sailed from the wings across ribbons of azure waves from Sicilia to Bohemia and back again. As the voices rose and fell and the figures appeared in the flare of gaslight and vanished into shadows, my heart pounded and my head spun.

That brute, Leontes, destroyed his family and then believed his wife dead, but her loyal friend Paulina hid her away from him—a nice touch, I thought, to make the man suffer remorse for his villainy. Especially, since he had already gone off half-cocked taking Hermione's newborn baby from her—claiming it was the offspring of adultery—and commanding his minion, Lord Antigonus to abandon little Perdita in the wilds of Bohemia. Antigonus was just fleeing the cruel scene, pursued by a bear—no more than he deserved—when the terror was further heightened by a boom of thunder.

A gasp escaped my lips. Ambrose squeezed my hand, then let his fingers slip round to the inside of my wrist to the row of pearl buttons on my long cream-colored gloves. His forefinger found the gap between a pair of buttons, where his fingertip touched my pulse. He must have felt the blood jump in my veins. In the moment of that charged contact between us, I recalled we were not lost in Bohemia but nestled in a box at the theater. And I realized, too, that the crackles and rumbles I continued hearing were no theatrical devices. Outside, a storm had broken. I blinked and remembered my brother was abroad that night, blinked again, and saw him in my mind's eye, not sheltering at Testament, but caught in a tempest.

Chapter Twelve

Whether Gilbert were maddened by loss or impossible desire, whether desperate or demented, he did not know and would be loath to confess. He had denied Charlotte's death, believed in it, denied, believed, denied. In that whirl of credulity and incredulity, where was he in the moment of his tasting the rain on her lips and drinking it from the locks of her drenched hair? No one may ever know the answer. His fingers caressed her damp cheek, stroked the length of her neck, traced the ridge of her clavicle, dipped into the hollow of her throat, and then slid upward again to the tip of her chin and along the line of her jaw, until his hand once more cupped her face. With two fingers, Gilbert smoothed strands of her hair behind the curve of her ear. Then, in the hidden place, just behind the soft lobe of her ear, his fingertips came to rest, and Gilbert found what he longed to find and felt the gossamer thread of a pulse.

The overwrought silken dressing gown swallowed Charlotte's body. Gilbert rifled through the convoluted gathers of the gown's lace as if plunging his fingers through the layered feathers and down of a swan. He grappled with the rain-soaked tangle of ribbons, tore at them, bit at them, until they loosened and lace and silk opened to the tissue of cotton shift beneath. In the space he had forced between the gown and the shift, Gilbert pressed his ear to Charlotte's breast, willing himself to hear her heartbeat above the pounding of blood in his temples. But he could not. Was that all it had been, then, all he had felt?—his own pulse imagined into hers, the gradual warming of his palm on her face imitating the heat of life that was gone from her flesh.

Gilbert caught his breath and held it and, in that moment, against his cheek, he detected the merest rise and fall of her chest, the faintest whisper of breath drawn in and exhaled. He touched the inside of her wrist and felt the pulse, feeble but quick. Here was her life, not gone, only for a time, suspended.

Gilbert lifted his head and stared around him and up the embankment, straining to see anything in the darkness that might be of use, or be a danger. The clouds had thinned across the half-moon and opened on patches of stars. By the wan moonlight, Gilbert gained a sense of his surroundings. Above him, shapes on the edge of the bank, darker than the night sky behind them, were the wagon and the mare, now standing quietly.

Kneeling still, Gilbert slowly began to lift Charlotte from the wreckage of the makeshift coffin. He encircled her shoulders with one arm, supporting her head in the crook of his elbow, and slipped the other arm beneath the back of her knees, gathering her legs and the heavy folds of the dressing gown—made heavier, he realized, by viscid blood soaking through her garments and into his coat sleeve. Then, she moaned and shuddered and convulsed in his arms. His heart seized before he was brought back to his senses by the odors of sickness and blood, sour and metallic. Charlotte was injured. In her falling, had she been cut, impaled by a sliver of wood, when the pine box splintered and broke apart? Gilbert threw open the skirt of the dressing gown and blindly skimmed her body with his hands, seeking the source of her injury. But he found no external wounds, only the blood soaking the lap of her shift and slick between her thighs. A woman's cyclical bleeding, yet to excess—the result of a miscarriage? If that were so, Charlotte could have fainted at Testament, as any expectant mother might, and then, somehow, slipped away into a deeper unconsciousness, which Dr. Baldwin had mistaken for death. Surely, he should have known the difference, should have suspected the possibility of pregnancy in a woman of child-bearing age, a young wife, already the mother of two children. What had been the rush to another judgment?

Again, Charlotte shuddered and convulsed, again fell limp, moaning. Gilbert carried her up the bank and to the wagon, where he laid her down. He bunched the skirt of the dressing gown between her legs to staunch her bleeding, then covered her with his jacket and folded his waistcoat as a pillow for her head. Still unconscious, she began to shiver, her teeth chattering. Gilbert scuttled down the bank again, retrieved the blanket that had lined the pine box, and brought it back to the wagon. Parts of the blanket were drier than his jacket, so he rearranged the covering, tucking the blanket around her first and adding his jacket on top.

All the remaining way to town, the wagon axle shuddered with every revolution of the wheels. The mare stumbled, and Gilbert limped and stumbled beside her. All of them damaged, but Charlotte was alive, might go on living if he could bring her to shelter. As Gilbert embraced that hope, his physical discomforts fell away. Elation drove him forward. And then, of a sudden, he halted, went again to Charlotte in the wagon and felt for the pulse behind her ear. Yes, it was there. They traveled farther, halted again. He touched the pulse at her wrist and then resumed the journey.

Chapter Thirteen

After *The Winter's Tale*, Ambrose Parr and I shared a late supper and champagne with friends—including his cousin Geraldine, who had introduced us and was pleased to see us getting on so well. Indeed, we were, as we chatted and smoked after supper, my vanilla-scented tobacco blending well with his bay rum. Ambrose was a silvery-maned gentleman, a widower for some years, but not past his prime. He was tall, trim, and still vigorous and creative in his career. On our carriage ride home, after we had been stirred by drama and mellowed by wine, I began to view him in an ever more favorable light.

The hour was late. The storm had passed, and only a fine mist lingered along the quiet lanes of Faubourg Marigny, droplets suspended in glistening auras around the streetlamps. The driver kept the carriage horse to a leisurely pace, then rolled our conveyance to a gentle stop outside my house, where Ambrose did not merely hand me from the carriage. He lifted me up bodily and carried me to my front steps, where he set me down after having gallantly saved my slippers and the hem of my gown from the mud puddles. I laughed with delight, then let the hood of my evening cape fall to my shoulders and angled my cheek to receive Ambrose's kiss.

"Oh, Lenore," he whispered against my ear.

Whatever his intonation implied, I simply thanked Mr. Parr for a memorable evening and bid him goodnight at my threshold. There would be time, I told myself, there would be other evenings—and anticipation was as delicious as anything.

Ella, with her customary kindness, had left a candle and matches for me on the hall stand before she retired for the night. I found them easily enough by touch, fumbling only a little in the darkness before the wick took the flame. Then I hung up my evening cape and peeled off my gloves, tossing them on the stand. I moved into the parlor, carrying the candle upraised in its holder. The single flickering light brought my shadow with me, following me along the wall, graver and more dignified than I—for I felt a trifle light-headed. Thinking a brandy might steady me, I poured one and breathed the heady fumes while tipping the snifter to my lips.

Oh, I had been a sensible woman for far too long. How else could I explain the effect that Mr. Shakespeare's play had played upon me? I had spent years of my life guiding the twins to their young adulthood, while managing Bartholomew's tempers and fits and final apoplexy, then devoted my resources and organizational talents to charitable and artistic causes . . . But tonight I had seen Paulina pull back the curtain on the *statue* of Hermione, in truth, a living, breathing woman, whose blood could still rise. I took another sip of brandy. Of course, Leontes did not deserve to have his wife restored to him, not after the way he had behaved. But this was Romance, and he was penitent and she forgiving to a fault.

With Ella asleep upstairs at the back of the house and Gilbert away for the night, no one would have been disturbed if I had allowed Ambrose to share a brandy with me in the parlor. His presence might have soothed me, as well, for I felt myself becoming agitated by an odd feeling—a suspicion coming over me that I was not, after all, alone downstairs. I sensed movement. I glanced about for Dulcie, who was a large cat and could make a floorboard creak, and found her curled on the wing-back chair, heedless of my existence or choosing to take no notice.

Then I heard a shuffling from somewhere down the hallway in the direction of the kitchen, so it seemed, the sound coming nearer. Ella, I reassured myself, wakeful, coming to see if I'd locked the front door on my return. But no, the approaching footfalls were not Ella's. The sound was too heavy and uneven, a limping gait, stopping just before it reached the archway to the parlor. I held my breath. A notion of spirits abroad darted through my mind before the sound in the hall resumed as a dull, terrestrial thud of boots mounting the stairs. I counted the steps the boots took—halfway up the narrow staircase that ran along one wall of the hallway. Silently, I came to the arch and peered around it into the hall. Then, with lighted candle in one hand and brandy snifter still in the other, I stepped forward, my gaze ascending the stairs, stopping halfway up like the figure, who seemed to be readjusting his shoulders—shifting his burden?—as he turned towards the candlelight: my brother, disheveled and in his shirtsleeves, with a woman limp in his arms.

"Gilbert." I spoke his name, not knowing with what meaning I should imbue the word.

"Lenore, there's been an accident," he called down to me, dispelling other interpretations I might have made of appearances. "I need your help," Gilbert said, at which statement, I shut my mouth—had it momentarily gaped?—and set aside my brandy on the hall table. The dark liquid rolled up one side of the snifter, sloshing almost to the rim before it settled. Raising my candle, I mounted the staircase, catching up with my brother as he continued his ascent, then passing him to open the spare room door near the top of the stairs. I turned down the counterpane, and Gilbert limped over the threshold and laid Charlotte Eden on the bed.

"My stars and planets," I barely heard myself utter. "What's happened to her?"

Gilbert rushed through the briefest outline of a story of his being run off the road while transporting Mrs. Eden to town, of her sudden illness and the possibility of a miscarriage, at which point he stopped to draw a full breath. I had been staring down at Charlotte's unconscious form in the mud-spattered, bloodstained dressing gown. Now I looked at my brother and addressed him in a harsh whisper: "Whatever possessed you, Gil?"

"I did what was asked of me." One of his maddening sort of replies, the words sounding reasonable enough, level in tone, but as vague as if someone outside himself had spoken them.

I pressed on: "But *who* asked you? Did Mrs. Eden choose to go? Or did her husband send her off like this?" My hand, palm up, swept through the air above where Charlotte lay.

Gilbert stared blankly at me, perhaps too exhausted to quite take in the meaning of my questions. Then he blinked with an apparent effort to focus on my face.

Narrowly, I eyed him back. "Gilbert, you have brought Mrs. Eden here in a *nightdress*." My voice sounded disputatious, even to my own ears. Still, I persisted in the same vein: "How do you explain that, brother of mine? Did you spirit her away from her bed? Is this some mad elopement? Obviously, followed by disaster. Oh, my shooting stars, say it isn't so."

"Would that it were." Gilbert actually muttered those words aloud.

I took hold of his shoulders and gave him a brisk shake. "Gil, you are not yourself."

Then I gathered what commonsense and compassion I still possessed at that hour and resolved to drop the subject of why we were in the current predicament, instead assuring Gilbert that I would take charge of dealing with it. I shooed him out of the way to dress his own injuries, whatever they were—a sprained ankle, cuts and scrapes. I woke Ella to assist me in caring for Charlotte.

Both Ella and I had some experience treating the ill and wounded, I in wartime and Ella as a plantation slave and a mother and a grandmother—her experience with midwifery far exceeding mine. Charlotte was in a bad way with pain and bleeding, and Ella sadly confirmed the miscarriage. For perhaps half an hour, she and I came and went from the little spare room, fetching water and fresh linens and carrying away soiled and bloodstained items.

Gilbert kept well clear of our activities, leaning himself against the wall at the opposite end of the hallway, outside his own room, apparently in a stupor. At some point, pausing in our ministrations and with Ella out of earshot, I placed a hand on my brother's arm, gave it a shake, and brought him around with a question: "What did you mean, Gil, when you told me that you did what was asked of you?"

He shook his head, perhaps to clear it. "You see—they told me to—" he began, stopped, then began again with a revision. "No, they *insisted* I take her body to town."

"Her *body?*"

He nodded. "They told me Charlotte Eden was dead."

"*What?*" I exhaled the word.

"At Testament. Dr. Baldwin, Judge Placide—all of them. They said she had passed away." Gilbert seemed to force the words from a dry throat. "They wanted her body out of the house. Judge Placide ordered me to bring her remains to town in a pine box." His voice echoed oddly in the hall, the sound distorted by the strangeness of what he was saying. "It was the wreck that saved her from suffocation—the box falling from the wagon, down the embankment, and breaking open."

I clasped my hands over my bosom.

"Has she miscarried?" Gilbert asked.

I nodded, whispering: "The poor creature."

"You're certain?"

"I am." I had seen the evidence in the bloody linens before Ella took them away to burn them in the stove.

"You will fetch me if her condition worsens," Gilbert said. "Promise me that."

"Of course, Gil." My tone to him had softened. How could it not? "Ella and I will manage for now," I said. "Go clean yourself up. You look—and smell—like something the resurrection man dug up and dragged in by the heels."

I put a firm hand on his shoulder and turned him away from me, so that he faced the oval gilt-framed mirror hanging above the credenza. By the low flame of the wall sconce, he might just discern the murky shape of himself, his mud-smeared visage, as I had described it, appearing newly unearthed—like the cadaverous subject of one of Dr. O'Brien's anatomy demonstrations, which Gilbert had once described to me in chilling detail.

I moved along the narrow hall, which paralleled the length of balustrade above the stairwell, then opened the door to the spare room, now our guest's room, just beyond my own. Before entering, I glanced back at Gilbert, who had turned from the mirror and was looking towards me—no, past me for a glimpse into the lamp-lit room, where Charlotte lay. From within I caught the gentle sound of water dropping on water—Ella with her strong hands wringing out a sponge over the washbasin. Then the fragrance of fine-milled gardenia-scented soap met me and traveled into the hall, perhaps reaching Gilbert, before I shut the door behind me, and Ella and I were closeted again, attending to Charlotte in the delicate process of returning her to life.

Chapter Fourteen

Gilbert did not immediately follow my admonition to take care of himself. From the window of the guest room, I looked down on the side garden and saw him carrying a lantern and limping down the path, leading the wagon horse, also limping, under the gallery for shelter from the drizzle. Yes, Gilbert would rub the shivering animal down with sacking and improvise a mash for it, perhaps oat cereal and cornmeal drizzled with molasses, before ever thinking of himself—before stripping away his mud-caked trousers and rain-soaked shirt to salve his own bruised body. That's how he was.

Some while later, leaving Ella watching over Charlotte, I stepped into the hall, thinking to finally go to my room and change out of my rumpled evening gown. But I abandoned the notion on seeing Gilbert again upstairs, now clean and in a fresh suit of clothes. He had brought a ladder-back chair from his bedroom and sat on it beside the credenza, as if he had taken up his post for the night. We needed to talk, and I approached him.

"Charlotte's sleeping now, peacefully enough," I began. "And the bleeding has slowed—a good sign. But she was sick to her stomach and in pain, moaning and tossing about while we bathed her—and bathed her again."

"I know," Gilbert said, shutting his eyes. The sounds had been muffled behind the door, but he must have heard them.

"What happened at Testament?" I asked. "More than you've so far told me."

"I don't know what happened before my arrival." Gilbert's eyes were still closed—he might have been conjuring a memory of the scene—and a shudder passed over his shoulders before he spoke again: "I can only tell you what I observed, Lenore—without understanding it. Call it what you will—there was something hanging in the atmosphere—obliqueness in the grand parlor, oppression in an upstairs bed chamber, something . . ." Gilbert gave up his attempt at explanation as he opened his eyes and stared beyond me, down the hall towards the door that concealed Charlotte from his view.

I found myself on the move, restless, my mind stirring with speculation. I passed in front of him, to and fro, took up my smoking things from the credenza, then paced away the length of the hall and back, filling the tiny bowl of my pipe and tamping down the tobacco, scattering bits of leaf the length of the hall rug. At last, I came to a stop in front of Gilbert, eyeing him where he sat, while I lit the pipe and drew on it. "When I saw you holding her on the stairs," I said through a veil of smoke, "I thought—"

"You were mistaken," my brother stopped me.

"I must have been." With two fingers of one hand, I pushed his tangled hair, his forelock I used to call it, off his brow. "There is something very wrong when sleep—or a faint, or whatever it was—can be mistaken for death," I said. "It worries me."

Gilbert nodded. "Me, too."

I resumed my pacing, but only across the little width of hall floor in front of Gilbert, not along the greater length that would have taken me down to Charlotte's door. "The fall may have brought on the miscarriage—hard to know for certain," I said. "You saw no cuts or bruises on her limbs before you took her away?"

"She was covered from her neck down, laid out for dead."

"Ah." I continued: "One of her arms is badly abraded and freshly bruised, and there's a lump rising on the side of her head. Ella and I pulled out splinters here and there and bandaged a few small cuts. All those injuries could have resulted from the accident. But what explains her collapse at Testament?"

80

"Dr. Baldwin claimed it was her heart," Gilbert said. "Sounded to me like he was making up an excuse."

"For what?"

"For not knowing what he was talking about."

"And he didn't," I agreed. "I think it was very high-handed of the judge to rush you away to town. Odd, as well. If Charlotte had been dead, why shouldn't her body have remained there overnight?"

"The judge said something about Mrs. Placide's sensitivity," Gilbert said. "I could hardly take it in."

"She is known in some circles for her interest in spiritualism. Surely, the dead can't upset her too much since she carries on conversation with them." A trace of scorn entered my voice.

"Mrs. Duvall mentioned that Mrs. Placide holds some peculiar superstitions."

"Peculiar, indeed. And she has the leisure to indulge them." I completed another circuit at the edge of the rug, then said: "When Charlotte can talk to us, we might learn something useful. For now, Ella and I have found no signs of acute infection—no fever. It was all we could do to bring some warmth to her flesh. And her eyes—when she finally opened them— had that odd look I remember seeing in some soldiers' eyes in the hospital, pupils no bigger than pinpoints."

"But sensitive to light?"

"Yes, she winced and turned away from the lamp. Gil, I'm wondering—" I tapped the bowl of the pipe against my palm. "I find it difficult to believe she fell ill of a natural cause—ill enough to be presumed dead—without some warning symptoms. I suspect she took something she shouldn't have."

"You mean she was given something," Gilbert interposed.

I tilted my head, looking sideways at him. "Do you have reason to think so?"

"If we're speculating, we can't rule it out. Dr. Baldwin is just the sort to push laudanum for the vapors and who knows what else."

"And I strongly suspect laudanum was part of the concoction," I said. "But only part. I'm not satisfied that's all there is to it."

Nor was Gilbert. He reminded me of our father, quoting Father's idol, Paracelsus: "*The difference between medicine and poison is the dose.*"

"Whatever she swallowed," I mused, "a home remedy, patent medicine, or something she was prescribed—did she take too much accidentally? Or intentionally? And to what purpose?"

"What purpose?" Gilbert repeated, more to himself than to me. "For an illness I knew nothing of?"

"If she took it with intent," I said, "might it have been an abortifacient?"

Gilbert stared at me. "What? Why would you say that?"

"Because of what happened to her, Gil—her sudden collapse, falling into a stupor, becoming violently ill, and then miscarrying. I've seen this sort of thing before."

"She'd have no reason," he said.

"We don't really know, do we?" I spoke through a puff of smoke, as if a little cloud could soften what I had to say. "Even married women can believe they have reasons—another mouth to feed in hard times, trouble in the marriage, a child not the husband's."

"A husband can believe a child is his, be persuaded," Gilbert said.

"Some differences can't be easily explained away. It's not so common, but men aren't the only ones who've ever consorted with servants," I said. "And then, there are those discrepancies between dates of conjugal visits and a conception."

"None of this has anything to do with Charlotte Eden." Gilbert sounded certain. As far as his knowledge went, his statement might be true.

"I never said it did."

"Mrs. Eden fell down an embankment," Gilbert reminded me. "That can cause a miscarriage, if anything can." While speaking, he had come to his feet, one hand gripping the top rung of the ladder-back chair.

"Oh, do calm down, Gil. I'm not gossiping about this particular woman. Just—we cannot always know what others endure, what drives them to take extraordinary, desperate, even dangerous actions."

If he thought I were alluding to something in my own experience, he could wonder. There was a gap between us in those few years when I had become a young woman and Gilbert was still a boy, which I had never chosen to fill, no matter how close we had become later, after the brothers born between us had gone to war and not returned, and only the two of us remained.

I ceased my pacing, puffing on and gesturing with my pipe, and the curls of smoke that had trailed after me like thin, white ghosts faded away. "Suppose," I said, "a woman finds herself in a situation that allows her no choice. And then she fears the consequences as much as if she had invited the man's attentions."

"Are you talking about seduction?" Gilbert asked. "Or rape?" Then, when I did not answer, he went on: "Mrs. Eden drank some sort of tisane. Apparently, not long before she—before Dr. Baldwin mistakenly announced her passing. A mixture of leaves and petals, some recipe belonging to her hostess."

"Well, then," I said. "What if the tisane were meant for a particular condition? Suppose Charlotte had turned to Mrs. Placide, or Mrs. Duvall, for advice—or for the concoction, itself. Both women are older than she, both married. Either one is likely to be more knowledgeable of certain matters than young Mrs. Eden. That could explain why this happened at Testament."

"You're still talking about an abortifacient," Gilbert said.

"Not necessarily." I tapped out my pipe in the enameled tray on the credenza, then added: "This was early days—Charlotte might not have known or been sure that she was with child."

"Then what?"

"I don't know, Gil. Some women get together and brew up this and that for any number of reasons—"

"Whether or not they know anything about the effects of pennyroyal and the like," he interjected.

"Yes, whether or not. Hoping to cure minor ailments or enhance their beauty—darkening their eyes with belladonna." Although, if I were any judge, my brother had already found Charlotte's eyes beguiling beyond artifice. "Why not these women?" I added.

"Their husbands associate with Victor Eden. That doesn't make the wives her confidantes."

"Do you know that for certain?"

Gilbert shook his head. "I don't know anything for certain, anything at all. Will she be all right? Will she recover?"

"Time will tell," I said.

"I must see her."

Even as Gilbert said the words, Ella had opened the door and beckoned me to come into the guest room. Gilbert followed. Then, as he limped past me to the head of the bed, I heard his hiss of breath, the only hint he had given of the pain in his ankle. Charlotte lay motionless on the narrow bed, a heavy quilt pulled up to her chin. With her closed eyes and pale face, her dark hair spread over the pillow, she must have looked as she had in the bedroom at Testament—laid out for dead. I saw Gilbert's fingers tremble as he lifted Charlotte's eyelids.

"She be sleeping, Mr. Gil," Ella said softly.

Yes, sleeping—and her pupils were no longer pinpoints, nor were they excessively dilated. For a moment, her eyes seemed to focus and fix on Gilbert, before he released the lids, and the eyes closed again. He waited, Charlotte did not stir, and then he touched her, felt the coolness of her forehead with the back of his hand and the subtle pulse in her throat with his fingertips.

"Thank you, Ella," he said.

Ella nodded to him, but she was whispering to me: "I's changing the cloths again—she's still bleeding some—and I seen something we missed before, when we was in such a hurry with the bathing."

"An injury?" I asked.

"Maybe." Ella moved to the foot of the bed and lifted the edge of the quilt and the hem of Charlotte's nightgown to just below the knee of one leg, then carefully turned the leg to reveal more of the curve of its calf. "There," she said, pointing. "That didn't happen tonight."

I brought the lamp closer, and then Gilbert and I saw for ourselves dark bands, not purple but yellow-brown, striping the soft white flesh—old bruises.

✛ ✛ ✛

Charlotte might have received the marks by accident some days ago, perhaps from a tumble on the stairs, falling against a bannister. But I could have challenged myself with the same objection that Gilbert raised: hadn't I seen similar, intentionally inflicted injuries on women at the shelter that I helped support? Yes, and I was of a mind with him and with Ella, whose early life had taught her a thing or two about canings, that Charlotte had been deliberately struck. Much as the thought sickened me for her sake, I worried for Gilbert that his dislike of Victor Eden, his envy of what the man possessed, was twisting into hatred. And where would that lead my brother?

"You don't know, for a fact, that Mr. Eden is to blame," I said. "Do nothing rash, Gilbert. Promise me. No rush to judgment. We don't know the circumstances. Wait and hear what Charlotte has to say when she wakes."

If she wakes. Gilbert and I were again in the upstairs hall, my thoughts whirling as he rushed through recommendations for Charlotte's care. A little castor oil, forced, if necessary. Bland food, when she was able to eat. Clear liquids. He ran over and over the delayed effects of certain herbs and plants—pennyroyal, tansy, ergot, and yew—raising my anxiety with his. We didn't know what we were dealing with. What if the worst were yet to come?

Trying to calm us both, I linked my arm with his, turning us away from the bedroom door and towards the French doors that opened to the gallery above the back garden. The sky, visible through the upper panes of glass, had begun to lighten. We talked of his leaving again for Testament, and I assured him that either Ella or I would remain with Charlotte until the danger was past.

"Mr. Eden may already be on the river road," I said. "You should meet him on his way, if you can, to give him the news—to prepare him."

"By all means," said Gilbert, "to spare Mr. Eden the embarrassment of calling at the funeral parlor and finding his wife absent."

"Oh, do mind your feelings, Gil. If you give them away to Victor Eden, you may do Charlotte a harm you never intended."

I understood that Gilbert might not bring himself to return to the Placides' estate with the same urgency with which he had been dispatched from it. His swollen ankle, tight within his boot, would pain him at every step—reason enough for him to move slowly in taking Judge Placide's lamed mare and battered wagon to the livery stable. At the same stable, I kept my rig and carriage horse, and Gilbert kept a dun gelding. How his shoulders must have ached as he slung pad and saddle over his horse's back, cinched the girth, pulled himself astride, and thus began another journey, without having eaten since I didn't know when, without having slept at all. He might have spared a moment to take a little better care of himself—I wouldn't have begrudged him. But he didn't. Perhaps Gilbert wanted to go on feeling all the reminders—the injuries, the hunger, the exhaustion—of the night that had, however briefly, brought Charlotte into his arms.

Chapter Fifteen

Gilbert wound his way through the noisy confines of city streets to the openness of the river road. There, the morning sky expanded like a vast unhinged oyster shell lined in washes of color—slate gray, lavender, and rose—one overlapping the other, lustrous as mother-of-pearl, while on the ground lay murky reminders of the night's storm. Dead leaves floated in dark pools of rainwater, banked by mud and broken branches. An aged, water-logged oak had fallen near the roadside, leaving a wound in the earth of tangled roots torn out of the ground, exposed and clotted with mud. He road slowly, dangling his injured foot outside the stirrup, letting the dun choose the way among the ruts and through the mire. Gilbert had a duty to perform and must be careful, deliberate, not risk laming the horse or further injuring himself. There was his excuse for dawdling like a boy on his way to school. A *dillar, a dollar, a ten o'clock scholar.*

His head throbbed, and thoughts of the past night swirled and hovered before him like a swarm of midges after the rain. Victor Eden could not blame him for his course of action, surely not. After the wreck, whether Gilbert had brought Charlotte back to the estate or forward to town, as he had done, the main thing was to bring her to shelter and safety. He could tell her husband that, and tell him, too, that Gilbert could not have left her in better hands than his sister's and Ella's, especially in light of her having miscarried. But had the man been aware of Charlotte's condition? Or would Gilbert be the first to inform him?

Gilbert did not encounter Eden on the road. But suppose he had, Eden demanding an explanation for Gilbert's tardiness, for his prolonging of Eden's distress. Gilbert could say that events had consumed more time than they actually had—the journey slowed and made hazardous by lashing rain, then the carriage charging out of the darkness, never stopping, running the wagon off the road. Gilbert had been injured, perhaps knocked unconscious, which could account for any number of lost moments. Certainly, he had been disoriented, which might explain any lapse of judgment at the riverside. *What lapse?* Eden would want to know, but Gilbert would remind him that the misadventure on the road had, in fact, served as Charlotte's deliverance. Would she not have suffocated in the pine chest in the time it took to reach the city and then have been dead, indeed?

Gilbert rode onto Testament land, acre after acre, past harvested fields. In one, where the dark wet earth was still flecked with white bits of cotton, young laborers knocked down brittle cotton stalks to prepare for the next planting. In another field, hogs roamed among broken cornstalks, fattening themselves on fallen ears missed by the harvesters. Approaching the drive, Gilbert saw Judge Placide, himself, alone on his broad verandah, standing between a pair of white columns, legs planted on either side of the cane in front of him, bracing himself, hand over hand pressed on the bulbous golden top of his cane. A guard of the old order. The judge lifted the glob of his chin from among the fleshy folds of his neck and scowled at the overcast sky. So Gilbert's first encounter this morning was to be with the head of the household, of the sprawling body of this house that could have sheltered a hundred in comfort and was occupied by two—and the servants they required and the guests they invited.

After tethering the dun at a post, Gilbert limped forward, gritting his teeth, and mounted the wide front steps.

"Back so soon?" Judge Placide's voice rumbled from above, no quivering lip this time.

"Yes, sir." Reaching the verandah, Gilbert leaned his weight against a column, allowing his injured ankle some ease. Although his limping had not aroused the judge's curiosity, his return apparently had.

"What brings you?"

"I have news, sir, for Mr. Eden." Gilbert had no desire to give the news first to Victor Eden's host, to hear the judge repeat the tale to his wife, who would turn and repeat it to her friend and the old doctor, all of them twisting the various details to suit themselves before they presented the story to Charlotte's husband.

"News? What further news can you have? We all know the man's just lost his wife."

"The news pertains to his wife, sir."

"Funeral arrangements?" The judge looked skeptical. "Time enough for that." Yet the judge had rushed him away last night with the makeshift coffin. Now there was time, when Judge Placide said there was time.

"Is Mr. Eden here?" Gilbert asked. "Or have I missed him on his way to town?"

"Eden's here. In the parlor, most likely. You know the way."

"Thank you, sir." Gilbert shuffled to the door and turned the latch.

"Mind your tongue around my wife, you hear?" the judge said. "No talking about the dead with her. I've had my fill of rappings and revenants and cold spots in the hall. Don't you set her off. You understand me?"

"Yes, sir."

Nearing the open parlor doorway, Gilbert glimpsed, not Victor Eden in solitary mourning, but Helene Placide and Rufus Baldwin together on the sofa. They took no notice of him. He stopped and leaned his back against the wall just outside the room to adjust the fit of his boot on his swollen foot before entering the room. Then he hesitated to move, to interrupt them, for he could hear their voices, casual in conversation about the forbidden subject.

"No, not in the least surprised, Dr. Baldwin, I really was not. That little woman was forever moping. But here, under my roof?"

"I worry for your nerves, dear lady," the old doctor said.

Helene responded to that remark with what sounded to Gilbert like a twitter of amusement. "Worry you may. Just don't offer me that bitter tonic you gave Charlotte. I won't take it, sir, you hear." Her tone was teasing—callous, rather—hardly that of a lady on the verge of a nervous collapse, as her husband would have had Gilbert believe.

"Oh, now, you don't think that I had anything to do with her—"

"Suicide. No, no, no."

They were talking madness, Gilbert later told his sister, after they had been so quick to give Charlotte up for dead.

"I'm putting *weak heart* on the death certificate," Dr. Baldwin said. "Easier for Victor."

Easier than admitting medical incompetence or negligence. If Dr. Baldwin had prescribed some noxious mixture for Charlotte, then panicked when it appeared to have proved fatal, was he now trying to cover up his mistake by latching onto a trumped-up tale of suicide?

Gilbert retreated from the doorway. Surely, neither of them had seen him. One of them would have said something, demanded like Judge Placide to know the reason for his return. Instead, they put their heads together and dropped their voices, intent on further private conversation of which he could hear no more. But the speculation he had heard was as unbelievable to him as his sister's suggestion of an abortifacient. Charlotte had been with child. Devoted to her children, to her husband, too, as dutiful wives were bound to be, Charlotte would not have harmed herself and so harmed a child—that was Gilbert's conviction. Then, to hear her disparaged by this pair of vanities. It was too much for him.

He limped away from the parlor door. Then, in the moment of turning the corner at the end of the hallway, he collided with the oncoming Colonel Frank Duvall. The colonel's booted wooden foot came down heavily on Gilbert's injured foot, exacerbating the pain already throbbing there. But with some effort, Gilbert suppressed the impulse to cry out, believing temporary injury hardly compared to amputation.

The men stumbled back from one another, muttering apologies.

"Pardon me, Colonel. I was looking for Mr. Eden."

"And I am looking for my wife." He tugged at the hem of his jacket, straightening the line of brass buttons. The army with which Colonel Duvall had fought no longer existed, but he had kept his title and a certain cut to his suit, a certain so-called bearing. Perhaps he also belonged to one of those covert organizations that defended lost causes.

"Shall we try the back garden?" the colonel said. "We might kill two birds." Then, as they set off, both limping, he added, "Did I break your foot just now?"

"No, I had a fall last night."

"Ah."

At the rear of the house, the verandah, which wrapped the entire lower floor and whose columns supported a broad gallery above, opened onto a lush and complicated garden. Sinuous paths followed the curve of the lawn, winding among terraced flower beds and trimmed hedges and past vine-covered trellises. Nearly as many gardeners as field hands slaved over Testament's verdant paradise. Two of them now chased about with rakes and baskets, whisking up withered red oak and pecan leaves scattered on the ground after the storm, which had left untouched the evergreen sweetbays and magnolias.

Like the colonel, Gilbert could not hurry his halting gait, descending into the garden and moving along the flagstones towards the octagonal gazebo. Their slow progress gave Gilbert time to observe Eden with Margaret Duvall in a pantomime of a conversation. The lady paced behind the white latticework, within the confines of the gazebo, while Eden sat on a low bench looking up at her, now and again shaking his head or flinging up one arm. Was he despairing, even as she urged him to rally? Did he want her gone, to be alone with his grief? The structure that contained them slanted away at an odd angle, and Margaret seemed to grow taller, then shorter, as she circled within it. Perhaps the ground had subsided unevenly beneath the platform, or had never been level. Off kilter, like the pairing of Dr. Baldwin with Mrs. Placide in the parlor, discussing Charlotte's death, and now of Mr. Eden with Mrs. Duvall outside—comforting the widower?—while the ladies' husbands lacked their company.

Although the colonel would not lack for long his wife's attention. He labored forward, shifting his weight from his sound leg to the artificial one, which he swung out from what remained of his thigh. As if forcing his limbs to keep pace with his will, he propelled himself forward, reaching the archway of the gazebo ahead of Gilbert, gripping the door frame to catch his balance. Colonel Duvall stopped just inside the entrance and drew a full breath before speaking his wife's name: "Margaret."

Lagging behind, Gilbert was still close enough to observe the shifting and reconfiguring of relationships among those in front of him. Margaret turned away from Eden and took a step towards her husband, her face lifted. Her fair skin stretched taut over the line of jaw and chin, the high cheekbones and the brow above her deep-set pale-blue eyes, over what lay beneath, the latticework of bone. But, despite the tightness in her face, she had puckered her mouth into a little pout with the corners slightly turned up. Perhaps it was a look she had practiced as a girl, and no one had advised her to give it up. The cultivated simper was a very different expression from the one Gilbert had seen slide away from her face in her turning from one man to the other, when the thin set of her lips had hinted at a thwarted will.

Behind her, Eden came to his feet, adjusting the set of his waistcoat and the line of his jacket, careful of the formal appearance he presented. Although, his having been seated while Margaret had not suggested a familiarity between them that his slow rising had done little to belie. "Colonel," Eden said, "Mrs. Duvall was offering her suggestions—"

"For funeral arrangements." Margaret finished the sentence, as her husband came forward and took her by the arm.

Gilbert reached the archway. "Mr. Eden, may I have a word?"

For an instant, Eden looked blank, as if not recognizing Gilbert, then nodded and passed by the Duvalls, now engaged in some low-voiced exchange of their own, to join Gilbert on the garden path. They walked together, slowly, the better for Gilbert to underplay his injury, which he could explain later. Eden, himself, seemed in no hurry to arrive at any particular destination.

"My mother is minding the children, Dr. Crew. You haven't been to my house?"

"No, sir."

"Good. I should be there when they . . . I should be the one to tell them."

"Mr. Eden—"

"Charlotte hadn't been herself for a long time, you understand, not since Wilfred was born." His voice sounded dull and distant. "But why should you have noticed? You're the children's doctor. She was a good mother," Eden said, "I'll give her that."

95

Now was the moment for Gilbert to plunge into his story. But he held back, for once the truth was out, Eden would say no more to him of what Charlotte had been to her husband. And Gilbert wanted to know what she had been, what she was to Eden, needed to know if there was any love between them on which Charlotte might rely on her return to him. Even if Eden had frightened his wife, even if he had hurt her, he might believe his authority over her was evidence of his affection. Some men did.

Eden stopped on the hedge-lined path and looked at Gilbert from his slightly greater height. "Where did you take her body? I wasn't thinking clearly last night. I want Pascal's Funerary Furnishers. You know the place?" Gilbert nodded, waiting while Charlotte's husband, her widower, seemed to measure his next words before speaking them. "I appreciate the service you rendered last night. The ladies were most distressed. But even I . . . the prospect of spending the night here in the same house with her remains but without her animate spirit."

Eden's tone might have been sincere. Right then, Gilbert could have told him that Charlotte lived and put an end to his mourning. But Gilbert had also heard the suggestion behind the words—that Eden knew his allowing Charlotte's body to be rushed away had left him open to a reproach, for which he had tried to excuse himself. Gilbert decided to provide that reproach: "Holding a wake is common custom"—then was unsure whether or not he had actually spoken the words aloud, for Eden made no response. He stared off, beyond Gilbert, who gazed past Eden, too, in the opposite direction. For a moment, Gilbert stood in a chamber of memory, staring down at his wife and newborn son, wakeful and exhausted, watching all through the night and far into the next day for the pair of them to move in their sleep, for the coffin to transform itself into a four-poster bed with canopy, or into a raft with billowing sail, floating them away into the distance, out of harm's reach.

Coming back to the present moment, Gilbert caught sight of Eden's return, as well, the refocusing of his eyes on Gilbert's face. The men had lost their opportunity to speak further in private. Over Eden's shoulder, Gilbert saw Colonel and Mrs. Duvall approach, coming from the gazebo, the wife a pace or two ahead of her husband. Then Gilbert looked over his own shoulder at the sound of rustling silk behind him, and saw Mrs. Placide, arm in arm with Dr. Baldwin, advancing from the back of the house. They were all closing in.

"Just look at that sky!" Helene called out. "Come along, everyone, before you are drenched. Inside, now, before you all catch your—"

Death. She did not say the word, but replaced it with a half-smile and a little shrug, as if she had, momentarily, exposed something naughty and was hiding it again.

Soon, with a wave of one hand, Helene had assembled them in the parlor, almost as they had been the night before: she angled along the grand parlor sofa, Rufus Baldwin at her side, Margaret Duvall nearby on the ottoman, then Judge Royce Placide taking up his post behind her. Only this time Victor Eden joined them, drawing up an armchair for himself and offering another to Colonel Frank Duvall, who had not previously been present. It seemed to Gilbert that Eden's inertness, which had separated him from the gathering last night, was supplanted now by an energy connecting him to those around him, though in a pattern Gilbert could not yet discern. He recalled the judge's odd comment, something about cold spots in the hall, and a chill passed through him where he stood. If Gilbert had been a spirit medium and shut his eyes and suggested the invisible forces in that chamber, he might have said he felt the presence of apprehension, arrogance, hostility—curiosity. He blinked and found they were all staring at him.

"Well, young man. What's this news you have for Mr. Eden?" the judge asked.

"He has news for Victor? This is the first I've heard of it," said Mrs. Placide.

"If you'll allow me, ma'am—" Gilbert began.

"Proceed." She inclined her head of henna-colored curls, and Gilbert obeyed.

"When I arrived here last night, you were all so sure that Mrs. Eden"—he caught Judge Placide's warning glare—"so sure she had passed away."

There was a murmuring in the room, someone clearing a throat, someone forcing a little cough, someone expelling a short blast of air through pursed lips. The lot of them seemed to be treating his statement as a social transgression.

"So sure? What are you getting at?" Dr. Baldwin muttered.

When the old doctor had touched Charlotte's wrist, what had he felt there before he and Margaret lowered the lid of the pine box? Might his sense of touch be all of a piece with dim eyesight and dull hearing? It was possible.

Gilbert cleared his throat, preparing to continue his barely begun narrative, when an image of Charlotte laid out in the shadowy bedroom overtook him, and he said what he saw in his mind's eye: "Mrs. Eden was laid out in a fancy dressing gown that swallowed her."

"I wanted her to have something nice," said Helene, the sly half-smile on her lips. Something nice or some castoff, either way she would never miss it.

Perhaps Gilbert had begun to feel light-headed with hunger, his stomach twisting in emptiness, for the judge's parlor had taken on aspects he'd heard described by a patient troubled with fainting spells. The edges of the room darkened, the spot where he stood deepened as if it had become a dry well. Then Margaret surprised him, rising and coming to his side.

"You look worn out, Dr. Crew. Do sit down." She indicated the settee. "You should have a drink. Shouldn't he have some brandy, Helene?" Her hostess nodded permission, and Margaret poured from a cut-glass decanter and brought Gilbert a snifter, chatting all the while, watched by her husband all the while. "What a night you must have had! The storm breaking just after you left. And yet you didn't turn back but went right on to town. Very brave of you. Have you had any sleep at all, sir?"

"Thank you." Gilbert took a quick swallow of brandy, following it with a slow one, which he let burn its way down his throat, before answering: "No, ma'am, I haven't slept."

"There, you see," she said to no one in particular. She joined Gilbert on the settee.

He scanned the expressions of those around him, trying to assess the receptivity of his listeners before telling them his story. The longer he hesitated, the greater his difficulty in beginning. The judge fidgeted with an unlit cigar, and the colonel wound his pocket watch, that little ratchet noise breaking the silence. Then, Dr. Baldwin sighed and frowned, apparently with mounting annoyance, as if he were anticipating a difference with Gilbert in their professional opinions, or perhaps Gilbert's revelation of some discovery made by the undertaker that would reflect poorly on the doctor's skill at diagnosis. Margaret cocked her head towards Gilbert and blinked several times, as if she were practicing the look of inquisitiveness she had learned as a girl in elocution class. Eden appeared grim, somewhat hostile. Or had Gilbert misread them. Helene Placide, arching one thin brow, leaned slightly forward, possibly indicating her interest, possibly challenging him to say anything that could be of significance to her.

Gilbert started off: "I was on the river road in the midst of the storm, when a carriage came out of nowhere, its pair of horses at full gallop. I did all I could to control your mare, Judge Placide, and narrowly avoided a crash. But the mare was terrified. At the top of the embankment, she reared, and I was thrown from the wagon."

"Hence your injury," Colonel Duvall said. Gilbert noticed then how shadowed the colonel's eyes were, how sallow his complexion. Was he ill or simply as weary as Gilbert?

"A turned ankle," Gilbert said, his explanation of no apparent interest to anyone else.

"And my bay mare?" the judged wanted to know. "Is she ruined?"

"No, sir. Lamed—temporarily, I think. I stabled her and left the wagon in town."

"What about the carriage?" Margaret asked. "Didn't the driver stop to assist you?"

"No, ma'am."

"He must not have seen you," the colonel said.

The instant after he had spoken, his wife released her breath in a short, derisive huff. Gilbert looked from one to the other, Margaret, then the colonel, and back. There was a pause in the room, enmity felt and noted and then dropped out of sight, as if into a pocket.

Gilbert sensed Eden's gaze and turned towards Eden as the man spoke: "A storm, an accident, an injury—yet you've wasted no time in coming back here. Why is that?"

"I would have come sooner, Mr. Eden." Gilbert plunged into a list of excuses, just as if Eden had demanded to hear them, as if the husband had expressed concern for the fate of his wife's remains. Only gradually, while rambling, Gilbert realized the difference between what Eden had asked him and what he was answering. "I must have lost track of time. Difficult for me to see anything with the darkness and rain. The pine box—the coffin—had fallen from the wagon, too, and slid down the embankment."

"Dr. Crew." The judge spoke the name as if it were a warning to a lawyer or a witness speaking out of turn.

"Let him finish," his wife said with her own authority.

"But your nerves—"

"My nerves, Royce, will stand the strain—for my curiosity must be satisfied." She fixed her gaze on Gilbert.

"The lightning flashed again and again," he said. "I could just discern the chest had broken open, the lid lying askew. I made my way towards it, and when I reached it—" Gilbert halted in mid-sentence. They were watching him, each one of them, all of them together, with what he could only describe later to his sister as morbid fascination. That was the moment when the story turned and started down a different path.

Somehow Charlotte had been caught up with this gathering, associated with its members by their association with her husband. But she did not belong among them. Perhaps Victor Eden had seen an opportunity to advance his career by catering to the likes of the Placides, the judge fattened and his wife plumped by a cancerous old system that war, occupation, and elections had damaged yet failed to excise. And who were the Placides' friends but those who were useful to them: Colonel Duvall, a sometimes-lawyer, who shared the judge's politics and lent his faded military glory to the assembly; Mrs. Duvall, the lady-in-waiting, who flirted and fawned; and, of course, Dr. Baldwin, for a corruptible physician might have no end of uses. The Placides' were well-situated. Privilege was rank, and its odor hung in their gilded parlor.

Looking past his audience, over them, Gilbert's eyes fixed on a small chink in the crown molding, the egg and arrow motif circling the room, signifying life and death. He began again: "When I reached the broken coffin, I found that the corpse was gone." The words had easily escaped him, and Gilbert would not take them back.

"Oh, good God," Colonel Duvall murmured. "Her remains fell out of the coffin?"

Here was the opportunity for Gilbert to retract his statement, but he did not.

"No, sir. Gone entirely."

"Impossible!" Dr. Baldwin declared. "Plain ludicrous. She couldn't get up and walk off. I pronounced her dead, myself."

"I didn't say she walked away, sir." That much was true.

Victor Eden gripped the arms of his chair, his face as ashen as it had been the previous night, his breathing quick and shallow. Margaret, sitting beside Gilbert, barely moved, yet a sort of tremor seemed to travel through her, through the cushions of the settee, itself, through the threads of its brocaded weave, and into and up his spine. It was just as he said, just as he told them. A dead body was not in the coffin. That was not a lie.

Then, Helene Placide made her pronouncement: "Alligators!"

The others turned to stare at her—Gilbert, too, but then turned swiftly back to Eden, in time to catch the flicker in his eyes, first of shock, then of something else, difficult to name.

"Well, it must have been gators," said the judge's sensitive lady. "They take a body down in the water—and keep it there."

Gilbert half expected her to expound further on the dining habits of alligators, although he could complete the image her words suggested of these creatures who preferred their repast well-tenderized in the river's depth. Well-rotted. Fleetingly, he thought of the sauerbraten his late grandmother had served and felt a wave of nausea.

Recovering himself, Gilbert looked again at Eden, whose arms hung over the sides of his chair while his fingers curled into his palms. Had Eden used a strap or a stick to leave the marks on his wife's bare legs? A calculated form of discipline, not like a sudden blow of knuckle against cheek leaving a bruise that could not be hidden. Eden shut his eyes, drew a deep breath and let it go.

102

Gilbert would not shift his gaze from Charlotte's husband, even as he felt Margaret's solicitous fingertips light on the back of his hand.

"You were fortunate, indeed, Dr. Crew," she said, "not to have been taken as well."

Chapter Sixteen

Bit by bit, I discovered the appalling truth of my brother's lie. I have recounted the lie, itself, before my learning of it because I desired to explore my vision of its unfolding—perhaps for an episode in a memoir or, better yet, a scene in a play of my own devising.

After imparting his news of the disappearance of Charlotte's remains, Gilbert left the Placides and their houseguests in the parlor, planning their search along the river road. Colonel Duvall would lead the expedition. The judge would provide the hounds. Such a man had always kept a pack of hounds on the plantation for hunting or tracking one thing or another. And what did the Placides and the Duvalls and Victor Eden hope to find? I shuddered to think. Fragments of the broken pine box, shreds of the dressing gown, claw prints in the mud leading down to the water? Some morsel of tender flesh that had not been consumed? Proof of the grisly end Helene Placide had imagined for Charlotte.

Entering the stableyard to retrieve his horse from one of the grooms, Gilbert had paused to exchange a few words with another groom, whom he found engaged in polishing the side of a black carriage. The groom confirmed for him that the carriage belonged to last night's late arrive, Colonel Duvall, who had not employed a coachman but had driven himself through the storm. "Ought not've done that," the groom added, slowly rotating a chamois over the carriage door, where a long gash ran through the glossy black-lacquered surface, revealing pale wood beneath. But Duvall had done it and, whatever his reason, had been in such a swivet to reach Testament that he had run a wagon off the road

105

and sped away. Indeed, he would be just the man to send the judge's hounds down the bank and put them on the scent at the river's edge.

All this and more I pieced together after Gilbert returned to Marigny towards evening.

The downpour, which had seemed imminent that morning, had not come to pass, the clouds dissipating, and Gilbert's ride back to town, this time, was uneventful. As he entered the house by the back door, I met him in the kitchen.

"Charlotte Eden?" were the first words out of his mouth.

"Is still with us," I replied. "Ella's sitting with her now. Didn't Mr. Eden come back with you?" I looked past him, in search of Charlotte's husband.

"No," Gilbert said, then added, "not yet."

I gave him a sideways look, already feeling something was amiss. "But he is coming?"

Gilbert said nothing, simply looked worn out. A moment passed.

"Hungry?" I asked.

Nodding, he sank into a cane chair, resting his elbows on the scarred, scrubbed surface of the oaken table and his head in his hands, pressing his fingertips to his closed eyelids.

I set to work, my preparations creating a series of familiarly comforting sounds: the sizzle of butter hitting the hot iron skillet, the sharp crack of eggshells against the skillet's edge, and the rasp of a dulling knife sawing through crusty bread. No matter the time of day, breakfast is the meal of restoration. Out of the corner of my eye, I glimpsed Gilbert dropping off while I cooked. Only when all was ready, did I gently jostle my brother's shoulder, and he raised his head from where it had come to rest on the tabletop. The heat rising up in a mist from the plate of fried eggs and toast set before him and the aroma of coffee filling the kitchen soon revived him, and Gilbert ate like the starving man he was.

I joined him at the table, maintaining my patience—and prolonging my ignorance of his mendacity and the madness he had set in motion—keeping quiet while he cleaned his plate and drained his coffee cup. I imagined Gilbert relaying his strange news of Charlotte's return to life, stunning Victor Eden and the other listeners. Then, Gilbert broke the silence between us by asking again after Charlotte, requesting details of her progress, further delaying his report of what had actually transpired at Testament.

"She finally stirred about an hour ago and fluttered her eyelids," I said.

"Then you've spoken with her?" he said, the weariness suddenly gone from his voice.

"No. I spoke to her—and she may have heard me—but she hardly murmured a reply."

"I'll go to her." Gilbert pushed back his chair, beginning to rise when I stopped him, laying my hand on his arm.

"Stay where you are. Charlotte's pulse and breathing are steady—I made sure, myself, right before you came home. Ella will call us if we're needed. For the time being, sleep is the very best thing for Charlotte." Gilbert slowly resumed his seat. "Now, tell me," I said, "what did Mr. Eden have to say to you?"

Gilbert exhaled a huff of scorn before he answered me, quoting Eden: "*She was a good mother. I'll give her that.*" Then my brother offered his opinion: "Stinting praise. Perhaps Mr. Eden was more impressed with Mrs. Duvall—considering herself fancy-free to attend a house party unencumbered by her husband. But Colonel Duvall apparently disagreed. Why else did he bluster through the night and the storm to reach her side? And on the way, he ran a wagon off the road—without a backward glance."

As from the wagon spilled a man and a woman together over the edge.

Abruptly, Gilbert changed the course of our conversation: "Lenore, I want you to go through Charlotte Eden's things—the luggage sent with her. I've brought it in, left it in the hall. Look through everything, and bring me any medicine bottles, pills, powders, anything you find."

"I did ask her if she took any medicines," I said, "and she may have murmured no. Although, I can't be sure she understood my question."

"Then, there's the tisane," Gilbert said. "And back at Testament, I overheard Mrs. Placide speaking to Dr. Baldwin of a tonic he had prescribed. I swear, the pair of them sounded—conspiratorial."

"Gilbert?"

"Something's not right," he said.

"Well, I can see that." Saw it in a single sideways glance at my brother.

"Lenore, you've known these people longer than I—"

"I've known of them longer," I said.

"Mr. Eden told me that Charlotte hadn't been herself since their son was born. Then, some of the others were talking as if she meant to—as if they believed she had harmed herself."

I took my time refilling his cup with coffee and pouring some for myself. "That is one possible explanation," I said, for it had occurred to me.

"No. Not for Charlotte."

"Some women have a low spell after giving birth, sometimes very low."

"Wilfred is already two years old," Gilbert countered.

"Even so. And here she was with child again. As she recovers, we may learn more about her state of mind. Until then, we can encourage her recovery," I said, "and hope her husband will be careful of her and—"

"Her husband won't touch her."

Then it all came out.

"He believes she's dead."

108

Soundlessly, I returned my cup to its saucer. "You mean he believed she *was* dead."

"No. He still believes it."

"Gil—" I clapped a hand to my breast. For a moment, I imagined myself in the theater, where I had been last night, but this time forced onto the stage—unrehearsed, racking my brain for a line to make sense of what Gilbert had said to me.

"If you had seen them, Lenore, the whole lot of them . . . "

My heart pounded. "You didn't tell Mr. Eden what happened? You didn't tell him his wife is alive?"

"No, I didn't tell him." I heard the obstinacy in Gilbert's tone that said *Yes, and I'm glad I didn't tell him.*

I gasped before I could speak. "Why, that's just plain cruel! What possessed you? Imagine how he feels. Oh, you *know* from your own losses how he feels. And those little children . . ." I reached across the table and shook his arm. "Gilbert, what *did* you tell him?"

"What he wanted to hear, what they all wanted to hear—that Charlotte Eden has disappeared." Gilbert's voice sounded even, almost reasonable, as if he believed himself.

With an effort, I slowed and deepened my breath. I was upset with my brother, but I did not rush at him. I must consider what he had done and how best he could undo it. Pushing my chair back from the table, I rose with deliberation and began circling the room, shaking my head as if that would clear my brain of Gilbert's rashness.

On coming back to face him, I replaced astonishment with sternness: "Gilbert, why? Don't you give me that stubborn expression of yours. Don't you let those eyes glaze over as if you live in some other world. Tell me why and how could you do such a thing."

"Naturally, what I did seems strange to you," Gilbert answered with maddening calm. "But you'd understand if you had been there, seen them as I did, heard them—the way they sneered and patronized. She never belonged with them, and they couldn't wait to be rid of her."

"*Who* couldn't wait?"

"Judge Placide and his grand lady-wife. Mrs. Duvall, Dr. Baldwin, all of them."

"Not Victor Eden?"

"Yes, Victor Eden. He is one of them. Oh, he looked shocked enough last night, or seemed to, but today he was relieved. The man actually sighed with relief."

"Relief is not the only cause of sighing," I said and heaved a sigh of exasperation before taking my seat again opposite Gilbert. Then I covered his hand, splayed on the tabletop, with my own. "What did you tell Mr. Eden?"

"That the wagon was run off the road, the pine box fell down the bank. All true. I said I was injured—I was. When I reached the box, Charlotte—her remains were gone."

"Gone? That's what you said? Simply gone."

Gilbert nodded. "Mrs. Placide, herself, supplied the explanation."

"Which was?"

"Alligators. Mrs. Placide said alligators must have taken the body into the water."

I removed my hand from his. My brother was out of his senses.

Gilbert rushed on, I imagined much as he had in the Placides' grand parlor, letting a story create itself while I listened in flabbergasted silence.

"I described the spot on the road where the wagon nearly collided with a carriage," he said as he wound towards the end of his tale. "Although I'm sure Colonel Duvall, leading the search party, will have no trouble finding the very site. Then, they'll all see the churned up mud, pocked with hoof prints and wheel ruts.

They'll all see the broken coffin, half in the water, half out. Their imaginations will take care of the rest."

"Stop it, Gil. This is grotesque. Oh, I could just slap you. You go back to her husband—at once—and tell him she's alive. I'll go with you. We'll think of something. Some excuse for this madness. You were without sleep, without food, battered in the fall—knocked out, we'll say. You suffered from confusion, a temporary loss of memory. Mr. Eden may forgive you once he has his wife back."

"I won't give her back to him."

"Oh, brother of mine, are you utterly insane?" I clutched at my head with both hands, endeavoring to contain an explosion beneath my skull.

"I don't believe so," Gilbert said. "A loving husband would not have remained unmoved while his friends swept away all evidence of his wife's existence. If he had held Charlotte in his arms that night— if he had embraced her and wept over her—"

Oh, what a naked tenderness exposed itself to me in my brother's words.

Gilbert swallowed, then continued: "Eden would have found out for himself how wrong Dr. Baldwin was—not left it for me to discover."

I pinched the inner corners of my eyes, forestalling a threat of tears.

"You and I saw the bruises on her," he said.

But neither Gilbert nor I knew how Charlotte had come by her bruises—or come by her collapse at Testament. We should not be as hasty as hot-tempered Leontes had been to draw conclusions, which could prove false. Since Gilbert's arrival with Charlotte last night, I'd not spared a moment for reflection on *The Winter's Tale*, but now aspects of the drama swept over me anew—strangely mingled with actual events and muddled with Gilbert's obfuscation of truth. Perhaps I was fatigued.

Gilbert's voice cut into my thoughts: "If her husband would beat her, he would do anything."

Anything? Leontes had done far worse than strike his wife.

"If you have any evidence, Gil, any proof of wrongdoing by Mr. Eden—or someone else—go to the authorities. Go with your suspicions if—"

"You're forgetting, Lenore, that Eden's patron, Judge Placide, is one of those authorities."

Gilbert knew I disliked the judge and his ilk. On occasion, I had been outspoken on the topic of those men, including Judge Placide, who ran the state's labyrinthine legal system—a system that had allowed them to buy and sell human beings before the war and that allowed them still to wield power in one way or another over entire classes of other people. The War of North Aggression and a few years of Union occupation had been interruptions of their business as usual, but business had resumed. At the whim of such men, who controlled courts and governments, and if such men chose, crimes—beatings, rapes, even murders—might go unpunished, including violent crimes against women and children perpetrated by the very men whose duty should have been to protect them.

"Something happened to Charlotte Eden at Testament," said Gilbert. "Something befell her, not of her choosing."

I wondered. What kind of man had Charlotte married? Had she given him offense? And was I so overwrought—or so worn down—by Gilbert's actions that his words were beginning to make a kind of sense to me? I did not yet know the answers to those questions. But I knew this: a man who believed he had *drunk and seen the spider* behaved as if he had, indeed, whether or not it were true. I thought of Hermione suffering the ill-treatment of Leontes, then of Leontes suffering remorse—before their love was reanimated when Paulina unveiled the statue of Hermione. Then, what had seemed lifeless drew breath.

"We must keep Charlotte here a little longer." My brother's voice had become a persuasive hum in my ears. "If only you and Ella will help me keep her a secret from Eden until we can discover what happened to her—until we're sure that she'll be safe to return to him."

I inclined my head, not quite a nod of agreement. "There's danger—" I began.

"We must, Lenore." Gilbert's hand covered mine. "Please, will you help me?"

Surely, he could not have asked that of me, his own sister, with such innocent eyes if he were responsible for strife between the Edens—if he were Charlotte's lover. Even so, right then, I might have said no to him, but I wavered. If Mr. Parr had not introduced me to *The Winter's Tale*—but that was hindsight. In the moment, as my brother entreated me, I felt myself slipping into the role of Paulina, directing another woman's fate.

Chapter Seventeen

I headed straight upstairs to sit with Charlotte and allow Ella a respite. Gilbert followed me, limping but refusing my offer to help him carry Charlotte's luggage. After he deposited the carpetbag, holdall, and hatbox in our guest's room, he lingered in the doorway, casting a searching gaze beyond me, towards the bed. But I sent him off, as I had Ella, to get some rest, then shut the door after him.

Turning towards the bed, myself, I barely discerned Charlotte's presence, for she seemed to have all but vanished under the heavy quilt and into the mattress. No wonder Gilbert had peered into the shadows to find her. As I approached the bedside, her three-dimensional form revealed itself only in the curve of one arm, the bandaged one, lying atop the patchwork. Then I saw the shaded contours of her cheeks and brow, her head deep in the feather pillow. A shadow appeared, too—no, a darkening purple bruise on her forehead, above her right temple. The cotton nightdress, one of mine, was high at her throat and indistinguishable from the cotton bed sheets, both white fabrics turned ashy gray in the half-light. Silent and still, heedless of my presence, Charlotte had yet to wake, sleeping on like the proverbial dead. Had she looked like this at Testament, so lifeless that those who had gazed upon her had been deceived into believing they beheld only her earthly remains? Someone had been hasty to believe it.

I felt for and found the gentle pulse in her wrist before beginning the task that Gilbert had asked me to perform: *Lenore, I want you to go through Charlotte Eden's things . . . look through everything, and bring me any medicine bottles, pills, powders, anything you find.*

I moved the lamp from the night stand to the dressing table and turned up the wick, the better to examine the contents of Charlotte's luggage. If she woke to find me rummaging through her belongings, I'd say I was unpacking for her. That was true enough. Certainly, the disorder within the holdall required some sorting. First, I removed the two largest items, a sketchbook and a pencil box, glancing at the pages of the sketchbook, which contained only a few drawings—charcoal shadings, really, one of curtains half-draping a windowpane, another of a pillow indented as if a head had rested there, another of a counterpane folded back from empty sheets. Charlotte must have been practicing a technique for drawing textiles. I extracted her few toiletries and other items, then arranged them on the marble surface of the dressing table in front of the mirror, glancing now and again at the reflection of Charlotte enfolded in the bed clothes behind me. Before me were things any lady might have taken with her for a night or two away from home: a hairbrush, shell combs, a handful of hairpins, a ribbon, a handkerchief, a pair of gloves, a pair of amber drop earrings, and so forth. From the bottom of the holdall, I withdrew a couple of small jars and a tiny white frosted-glass bottle. These, which I would bring to Gilbert for his inspection, appeared innocuous to me—one jar containing toothpowder scented with clove, the other a waxy lip salve, and the bottle holding a few drops of sweet olive perfume.

In the hatbox, I found a simple shade hat, finely woven straw with a speckled feather in the olive-brown band—far plainer than any bonnet Charlotte had trimmed for the customers of Madame Joubert's Hat Shop. I placed the hatbox on the upper shelf within the narrow armoire, then turned my attention to the contents of the carpetbag. The first articles visible to me and which I extracted were a pair of button boots, followed by a rumpled dark

116

gray skirt and white blouse, stockings and undergarments, including petticoat, corset, and corset cover trimmed with eyelet lace. Charlotte must have been wearing these things when she fell ill, and they were removed from her and later stuffed into the carpetbag—their untidy condition implying hurry or carelessness, or both. The skirt's hem appeared mud-stained and the blouse smelled slightly of sickness; neither had been sponged. I set them on the floor with the boots.

Other garments, which had lain beneath the jumble, were clean and neatly folded. I unpacked and arranged them in the armoire. The russet-colored cambric basque and matching skirt with apron drapery she must have intended to wear for dinner—her best dress, perhaps, although more modest than any gown Helene would have worn to the table. I remembered that woman's displays of rounded shoulders and swelling bosom, encircled by a froth of tulle, when Bartholomew and I were guests at Testament. Some of Charlotte's better items, such as her lisle hose and sateen wrapper, had been darned and mended. Evidence of Charlotte's economy? Or what Gilbert had called Eden's parsimony? Perhaps, in happier days, Eden had given his wife nice things, which she had made to last when he was no longer so generous to her.

As I closed the door of the armoire, its latch clicked sharply, and Charlotte whimpered, stirring at the sound. Then, just as she settled again, silent and still, a question snapped for attention in my mind: had Charlotte been aware, even for a moment, drifting in her death trance, that she had been shut up in a pine box? How must she have felt in such a moment, trapped, fearing the nightmare of premature burial? Mr. Poe had described such horrors in his works, and I pictured myself in Charlotte's place—in a makeshift coffin, unequipped with an interior spring latch to open it, devoid of a bell contraption to ring for aid. Then I shivered away the abhorrent image. Imagination may kindle empathy, but sometimes mine was too vivid for my own good.

Gathering the soiled clothes, intending to set them outside the door and later take them downstairs for a washing and the boots for a scrapping and polish, I felt something small and hard within the folds of the skirt. Along a seam, I found a pocket and, inside it, a brown glass vial—a little four-sided vessel with two ridged sides, the type indicative of dangerous contents within, so I remembered my father warning me as I watched him work in his pharmacy. I tucked the vial into my own skirt pocket.

Chapter Eighteen

In the wee hours of my vigil at Charlotte's bedside, I must have dozed in the rocking chair. As gray haze filled the room, the beginning of daylight filtering through the lace curtain at the window, I sensed there had been a gap in my thoughts and felt a sharp crick in the back of my neck. I blinked a time or two, then looked towards Charlotte, who was looking back at me.

"Mrs. James?" Charlotte whispered, giving my name the inflection of a question.

Perhaps she believed herself still at Testament, waking from a bizarre nightmare to the face of someone she had not expected to see. I hurried to explain that she was safe in my home, transported here by Gilbert after being taken ill at the Placides' house. While I spoke, Charlotte's brows knitted and the fingers of her left hand traced over the bandage on her right arm, then touched the purple swelling at her temple.

"During the thunderstorm," I said, "you had an accident on the road to town. You fell from the wagon." I did not mention the pine box. "My housekeeper, Ella, and I are looking after you until—" Well, I really didn't know until what.

Charlotte filled the moment of my hesitation with a question I could answer: "My children—where are they?"

"With their grandmother."

Her brow smoothed for a moment before her face tightened again as she suppressed a whimper of pain. Charlotte placed her hands, one over the other, on top of the quilt that covered her body, covering the ache and the emptiness inside her, which echoed in her voice: "I've lost my baby," she said. "Haven't I?"

"I'm so very sorry, my dear." I brought her a handkerchief, then murmured comfort and stroked her hair while she sobbed, until her sobbing eased.

Soon, Ella, with her sixth sense for others' needs, brought up cups of hot tea for Charlotte and me. Ella had left the bedroom door open as she entered, and I saw Gilbert behind her, standing out in hallway, one hand on the stairwell railing, craning his neck, the better to see into the room—to catch a glimpse of Charlotte.

"He's fit to be tied," Ella said under her breath as she set the teacups on the bedside table.

"Let's have him in," I said.

While I arranged pillows at Charlotte's back, then steadied her hand as she brought her cup to her lips, out of the corner of my eye, I kept my brother in view.

The moment Ella called to him from the doorway, Gilbert lurched forward, catching the toe of one boot on the rug or nearly tripping over his own feet. But Ella slowed him down, extending one broad hand towards him and undulating it against the air as if she were patting a large, soft, invisible beast. "There now, Mr. Gil," Ella said, her tone soothing. But, as he limped past her over the threshold, her eyes cut towards him with the sharpness of disapproval. Later, I would sound her out on what he had done to merit that look; for now, Ella left us.

His sprained foot evidently paining him, Gilbert shuffled to the end of the bed, where he took hold of the brass bedstead rail and shifted his weight to his uninjured foot, skewing his posture. I stood at the bedside, observing, as Charlotte, whose face had been turned towards mine, slowly shifted her gaze in Gilbert's direction. His gaze, of course, traveled over every detail of her—her trembling hand giving me the teacup, the fingers of her other hand closing over the crushed white handkerchief, her cheeks blotched and eyelids reddened, the glinting beads of tears trapped in her lashes.

Gilbert took in the distress in her countenance, mirroring it in his own. He cleared his throat, then spoke: "How are you feeling today, Mrs. Eden?" Perhaps not knowing what else to say, he had fallen back on the usual question that doctors pose.

Charlotte looked up at him, saying nothing.

"Has Mrs. James explained why you are here?" he asked.

Charlotte nodded.

"Do you understand?"

"No," she said.

I stepped closer to the bed, placing my right hand over Charlotte's left, idly running my thumb over the narrow gold band on her ring finger. "We've only spoken of her illness and the accident on the road—and its aftermath," I said to Gilbert.

For a moment, Charlotte shut her eyes, and the movement set a tear free from her lashes to slip from the outer corner of her eye and into the pillow. Then, she opened her eyes and looked again at my brother.

Gilbert pressed the heel of one hand against his forehead, the gesture that had become his habit when he had suffered bouts of neuralgia as a boy, and I wondered if his head were splitting now. Letting his hand fall to his side, he said, "I'm very sorry, Mrs. Eden. I did all I could to avoid the collision—in the dark, in the rain. If I could have prevented—"

"Gilbert." I spoke his name in an effort to bring him back to the room, even as I suspected he was veering away in his mind, down the river road and over the bank.

"Yes." He glanced my way, then looked back at Charlotte. "Well. My sister and Ella are excellent nurses, Mrs. Eden. They'll take good care of you. We want you to rest here and regain your strength." Gilbert finished with a half-smile, first at Charlotte, then at me, widening his eyes at me as if in hope of my approval of what he had said.

121

Charlotte lay still, only her eyes shifting from Gilbert's face to mine and back again. "Where is my husband?" she asked. Had I heard a waver in her voice?

"He'll be along," I answered, matter-of-factly.

"He didn't come back with you, Doctor?"

"No, ma'am, he didn't."

"He sent me away with you," Charlotte whispered, as if only to herself.

Still, Gilbert nodded in response.

"While he stayed at Testament without me," she said. "With them."

"Yes, he stayed," Gilbert echoed her words.

The shadow of a line between her brows faded, then deepened again. "My children," she said. "I want my children."

I bent towards Charlotte, again murmuring assurances that they were in the care of their grandmother. Charlotte looked confused, seemed not to comprehend, her eyes searching the space beyond me, as if she expected to find Amy and Wilfred somewhere across the room. I patted her shoulder and repeated: "Your children are safe with their Grandmother Eden." This time Charlotte took in the words, and her anxiousness appeared to lessen.

She murmured in return: "Yes, of course, ma'am. Forgive me. You're very kind. Please, forgive me." Her tone echoed the submissiveness Gilbert had heard in her voice on the night he had first met her, which he had described to me. *Thank you, Doctor, thank you*, she had said and kissed the back of his hand. Just then, I saw Gilbert's hand tighten, his fingers clinched around the bedstead rail.

A bell rang, the one on the gate to the side garden, signaling that patients had arrived. Ella would let them into the clinic behind the house. Gilbert must go to work soon and leave Charlotte to me, with nothing settled. I saw him hesitate, could

122

almost read his thoughts darting away to the various cases awaiting him across the yard and back to the dilemma in front of him. What was he to do for Charlotte? *What was he to do with her?*

For a start, he might discover what had precipitated her collapse. With that thought, I slipped a hand into my skirt pocket and withdrew the glass vial, two thirds empty of whatever liquid it contained. I held it up for both Gilbert and Charlotte to see, saying: "I was unpacking a few of your things, Mrs. Eden—setting them out on the dressing table—when I saw this. I don't wish to pry, but if it's something you take . . ." I arched one brow and let my sentence trail away.

Charlotte looked at the vial, then answered, "No, ma'am. It isn't mine."

"Are you sure?" I held it closer for her inspection. "Perhaps a tonic Dr. Baldwin prescribed?"

"That was in a blue bottle. I threw it away months ago."

"But this was among your belongings," I persisted.

"I don't remember packing my belongings." Charlotte's breath quickened, and the pitch of her voice rose with her words: "I don't remember leaving Testament, the journey, the wreck—what you've told me. I don't remember—" She pressed a hand to her forehead, her gesture so like Gilbert's minutes ago, and I read pain in her eyes.

A child's wail sounded from the garden below, insistent, rising over the gallery railing and crossing through the glass of the bedroom window.

"Wilfred!" Charlotte cried, struggling to raise herself from the bed.

Before Gilbert could reach her side, I had caught her by her shoulders and eased her back. "No, my dear, it isn't Wilfred," I said and, with a look, sent Gilbert back to the foot of the bed. "Dr. Crew's patients are coming to his clinic downstairs—that's what you heard, dear. Someone else's child."

"Someone else's child," Charlotte repeated, each word fainter than the last, as she turned her face away and spoke into the depths of a feather pillow. The child's wailing grew louder.

Gilbert had not anticipated Charlotte's distress, her fearfulness, her sadness. I saw as much in his stricken expression.

I held out the brown glass vial to my brother, who took it from me. Then I brushed the air with my fingers, sending Gilbert away, hoping he would discover the significance of the little vial forgotten by Charlotte, or belonging to someone else, now in his jacket pocket. Whether the contents were a harmless elixir, an effective remedy, or a poisonous concoction—all such things were easily attainable. Deadly plants grew along roadsides and in cultivated gardens. Opium, ipecac, arsenic, mercury, and many other substances lined the shelves of the pharmacy—to heal or to harm. The danger lay in the dosage.

Chapter Nineteen

Gilbert asked a chemist he knew at the hospital to help him analyze the dark liquid in the vial, then shared the result with me when he returned to his clinic. "Tincture of opium, for the most part," he said. "Mixed with alcohol, a trace of arsenic, a flavoring of sloe syrup."

Nothing out of the ordinary, if taken in moderation. Indeed, laudanum was a common enough prescription for nerves and sleeplessness. A little arsenic freshened the complexion, although, sometimes producing other, less fortunate results, as well.

"If Charlotte drank too much of it—" I inclined my head towards the little bottle in Gilbert's hand—"that could account for her insensibility at Testament."

"She was at Death's door," Gilbert said.

A door that might have been opened by ingestion of a dangerous substance, by suffocation in the pine box, by injury in the fall down the embankment, by loss of blood with the miscarriage. Charlotte's survival was a miracle, even as Gilbert mused over other explanations.

"The mixture in the vial could have been added to the tisane after it was brewed," he said, "ingredients of one intensifying or mitigating or interfering with toxic effects of the other. Then, she was sick to her stomach after the wreck, purging herself of poison taken in the teacup."

Had she drunk and seen the spider? That chilling image from *The Winter's Tale* lingered in my mind. Meanwhile, Gilbert spoke of Charlotte's lingering infirmities—her frequent headaches, thirst but little appetite, weakness and languor. Ella and I did what we could for her, following his recommendations, relying, too, on our own experience and commonsense.

"Charlotte was drugged," Gilbert said. "Poisoned. I believe she was. And if I had the contents of that cup, which Mrs. Duvall whisked away, I could prove it."

"But could you *disprove* that Charlotte poisoned herself?" I said. "Whether knowingly or accidentally, we can't yet rule out the possibility." Much as I knew my brother would like to—and cast Victor Eden as the villain of the piece.

Over the past months, whenever Gilbert had spoken to me of Charlotte, he intimated her unhappiness with her husband. Sensing the attraction that Gilbert felt for Charlotte, I thought him biased against Eden—still did. But now that I had seen Charlotte's bruises and witnessed her despondency, I, too, was concerned for her safety—whether she, herself, or someone else posed a danger to her.

Gilbert rose from his desk chair and commenced pacing and muttering around his office, while I kept still and quiet in the upholstered chair. He was expounding on Victor Eden's shortcomings—a subject on which he had obviously been ruminating for some time: "Eden is exacting and punitive—I've sensed that and seen the evidence. Certainly, the man is capable of selfishness, and his selfishness has led him to cruelty. Even if his intent were not cold-blooded murder, he is still culpable for endangering Charlotte."

"Gilbert—"

"Don't you see, Lenore?" Gilbert spread out his arms as he strode past me as if displaying a scene—and not simply revealing his emotions. "When Charlotte collapsed at Testament and Eden believed her dead, he wanted her away, interred before anyone had time to pause and suspect him of wrongdoing. That explains his hurry. And Mrs. Placide's delicate nerves gave him the excuse he needed to push through his scheme with the judge's full support."

"But why?" I asked him, pointing out that Eden would have nothing to gain by disposing of his wife.

Gilbert had slowed his pacing as I spoke and at last came to a standstill. "Eden's ambitious," he said, "ever advancing his career, seeking favor with the powerful. You've told me so, yourself—told me weeks ago that you'd heard he is entertaining political aspirations. He may have decided that a wife of simple beginnings is a hindrance to him."

"Oh, Gil, if that were true—" A shiver crossed my shoulders at the thought of the coldness of ambitious men. "Let me sound out Charlotte on what's troubling her—after she recovers herself," I said. "You may be right. But then again, the problem could be as ordinary—and misery-making—as infidelity."

"I wouldn't put that past him," Gilbert said.

"But suppose that Charlotte," I said, watching my brother's face for any change in his determined expression, "mistreated by her husband, found solace elsewhere?"

Gilbert's set jaw dropped. Not a sign that he was caught out and embarrassed, I surmised, but dumbfounded.

"What are you suggesting, Lenore?—that Eden suspected her of infidelity, then fed her poison? That's absurd. They aren't a pair of tragic characters in one of your friend Mr. Parr's theatrical productions." Gilbert shook his head in disbelief—but of what? My absurdity? Or the possibility that someone other than himself had been a comfort to Charlotte? "No," he said. "Poison signifies premeditation, not the passion of the moment. A jealous husband would strangle his wife with his bare hands. Or, if he found her with a paramour, he would execute them both with a pistol."

127

"So you make a distinction," I said, rather piqued. "A crime of passion calls for violence, and a crime of ambition calls for deviousness. Is that right?"

Gilbert didn't answer me.

I asked him another question: "Why do you think Eden would choose to commit the crime you accuse him of among his friends at Testament?"

"Because that's where he found an accomplice," Gilbert snapped back at me.

At that moment, I might have wished Gilbert and I both sunk in a swamp rather than mired in our current predicament. Rising and picking up the ring of cabinet and drawer keys from the desk, I sorted through the keys to find the smallest one. With it, I unlocked a shallow cabinet mounted on the wall, where Gilbert kept opiates and such. "I don't know what happened to Charlotte that night at Testament—or who is responsible," I said, measuring my words to calm myself, even if not my brother. I took the vial from him and placed it on the lower shelf, then closed and locked the cabinet door. "I believe she's frightened and distressed—possibly, in some sort of trouble. And for that reason, I'm willing to keep her a secret a little longer."

✛ ✛ ✛

Ella's perturbation with Gilbert stemmed from his decision—the one in which I had agreed to join him—to conceal Charlotte's whereabouts. She and I were in the kitchen that night, she preparing the roux, which required more culinary skill than I possessed, and I peeling shrimp for the étouffée, when the subject came up between us.

"It's just until we sort things out," I said. "Gilbert and I hope to discover the circumstances of her near-death experience and make sure that Charlotte is safe before she returns to her home." That sounded reasonable when I said it aloud, when I didn't think too far ahead about what our keeping her here entailed.

But perhaps not reasonable enough to Ella, who frowned her disapproval before giving voice to it: "Of all the cockamamie notions, Miss Lenore, this is the limit. This morning, when Mr. Gil tells me we're hiding Miss Charlotte from her husband—well, I think, sure enough, you'll talk him out of his crazy scheme."

"Oh, Ella, I ask only for your discretion."

"No, ma'am, you are asking for more than that. If this mess has anything to do with the folks at Testament—I'm telling you, it don't pay to rile up Judge Placide."

"Surely it won't come to that—riling the judge," I said, as if lightly uttered words could deflect the possibility. "If, as I suspect, Charlotte has fallen prey to melancholia and harmed herself—well, Gilbert and I will appeal to Mr. Eden's better nature to comfort his wife and find her the proper treatment. Even though Gilbert thinks there was another cause for her collapse."

Ella, who had tasted the roux while I spoke and adjusted the seasoning with a dash of pepper sauce, now held up her spoon and stared at me until I answered the question in her eyes.

"Gilbert believes Charlotte is the victim of a poisoner." There, I'd said it aloud to Ella.

"Lord have mercy."

I went on: "But regardless of what happened to her, whatever happens now and whatever we must do, Gilbert and I take full responsibility. No blame will be attached to you—I won't permit it."

The sincerity of my assurance to Ella matched that given to me earlier by brother. While mulling over what he had begun and speculating on where it might lead, Gilbert had grown concerned that the authorities, Judge Placide among them, might consider his actions, however well-meant, to be in some way criminal. "If that should happen, I will swear on my life," Gilbert told me, "that you had nothing to do with my—not my perfidy, no—with my temporary misdirection of fact and circumstance." But how temporary? And did he or I have any power to control—or protect anyone else from—the repercussions of our actions?

While Gilbert had endeavored to secure my cooperation with his plans, however they developed, I had weighed events and his impressions of them in a balance with what I suspected, or already knew, about Eden's patron. Even if I saw through my brother's effort to persuade me—how Gilbert deliberately played upon my aversion to Judge Royce Placide and those revolving in his sphere of influence—I had already cast myself as Paulina to Charlotte's Hermione. Easy enough for me, at Gilbert's suggestion, to perceive moral turpitude in Eden's character by his association with the judge. Through Ella, I had long ago learned of the judge's reputation for shoddy treatment of his servants, a few of them Ella's kin who were sold away or ran away, disappearing before the war. Then, when Bartholomew had taken me to Testament, I had experienced for myself the discomfort of the Placides' milieu. As soon as Bartholomew passed, I requested my attorney to withdraw my inherited funds, as far as possible, from any business ventures my late husband had entered on with the judge.

Before my thoughts were completely bogged down in past unpleasantness, Ella recalled me to our current situation. "You could take Mrs. Eden to the shelter after she rallies," Ella said. "Keep an eye on her there, same as you do for other women in a bad way. Charity be one thing, Miss Lenore, getting yourself tangled up in other folks' troubles be another."

Ella might be right. She often was. I could offer her suggestion to Gilbert. Yet I felt more inclined than otherwise to maintain a personal interest in Charlotte Eden. She mattered to my brother, sure enough, and he mattered to me. Then, as Ella and I finished the cooking, filled plates, and prepared a light portion on a tray to take up to Charlotte, I found myself recounting to her the plot of *The Winter's Tale*, remembering how Ella—my own Paulina—had soothed me in the wake of a husband's ire, imagining how I could do the same for Charlotte.

✦ ✦ ✦

We had truly undertaken keeping Charlotte's presence secret from anyone coming near the house—my charity guild and study club ladies arriving at the front door, Gilbert's young patients and their parents coming to the side gate, the washer woman and peddlers passing through the alley to the back door. I confined the daily maid, who was not in our confidence, to duties downstairs and in the kitchen garden, while Ella and I assumed all upstairs chores. Keeping occupied distracted me from fretting in those early days of Charlotte's sojourn with us.

Charlotte's bodily health improved, little by little. But Ella believed something was wrong with Miss Charlotte's spirit that broth and bed rest weren't fixing, which worried me, even as Ella and I assured Gilbert that he was not needed in a professional capacity.

In her first week of convalescence, Charlotte kept to her bed, saying little. She was polite but vague with me—as vague as I with her about when her husband might come for her. And she refused to be led into an explanation of old bruises beyond saying she was sometimes clumsy. But Charlotte was more at ease with Ella, who had a knack for winning confidences without seeming to pry—while I might rely on more circuitous means, myself, such as eavesdropping.

One afternoon in the parlor, leaving off playing a tune on the spinet, I heard Ella's voice floating down the hall, rising and falling in a sing-song cadence. I glided towards the sound, approaching the half-open kitchen door, to observe a scene within the room. Ella, not looking in my direction, stood holding a towel, twisting and blotting the wet rope of Charlotte's luxuriant hair, lifting it from off her neck. Charlotte in a white shift, her arms exposed, one still bandaged, sat in a cane chair, head tilted back and eyes closed. Humid air and the smoky scent of vetiver soap encircled them. Ella had helped Charlotte downstairs and washed her hair, perhaps given her a sponge bath, all the while I had been crooning to myself, one melody after another, ending with Ambrose's favorite, *Plaisir d' Amour*. And now Ella was crooning one of her familiar stories to Charlotte, who murmured her responses—so companionable were they.

Ella was winding up her story, something about bygone days of Master This and Mistress That, who married whom, who bought and sold whom, who was willed away when Master or Mistress died. "Oh, I be in a good place now—not like I was, thank the Lord," Ella said, her voice growing a little louder as she ended with her old quip: "In them days, we was ruled by the 'ators, Miss Charlotte. Imagine that. Speculator bought us in bunches, selling us up and down the river, breaking up families, raking in the money. Then Numerator counted us—how many field hands, gardeners, drivers, cooks, house servants, and such. Numbers was always changing. And last of all, Alligator—out for the ones that run off across the bayou."

Charlotte, unaware that an alligator had, supposedly, made off with her body, offered a rueful laugh at the tale's conclusion—the sort of response that storytellers expect to hear after they have made light of what has broken their hearts.

"Let's have a look at that arm," Ella said, and then I heard a hissing intake of breath, indicative of sudden pain. I peered around the door. Ella had peeled away the bandage on Charlotte's arm and was sponging at the exposed abrasion. "There, there," she said, "it's healing up nice. You going to be just fine."

"Fine enough to see my children?" Charlotte's voice sounded suddenly tremulous.

"In time," Ella said. "Just give yourself a bit more time, Miss Charlotte."

"Ella, do you know why I'm here? Why I'm really here?"

"Yes, ma'am, you're here to get well."

"But don't you find it strange that Mr. Eden hasn't come for me? Strange that Dr. Crew and Mrs. James want me to stay here?"

Ella did not answer right away. I heard her footfalls crossing the kitchen, the sound of a cabinet being opened and shut, the clink of glass against glass, and then Ella saying: "Just sit tight for a while, Miss Charlotte. Drink this up. Go on, it's blackberry cordial—do you good. We got to get your strength up, you being such a wobbly little thing." Ella was changing the subject, but Charlotte changed it back.

"Have you been with them a long time, Ella?"

"What?—oh, with Miss Lenore for years and years."

"Do you trust her?"

"Miss Charlotte, what a thing to ask," Ella said in that ambiguous tone of hers, not strictly scolding, nor quite teasing. "I trusts her almost as much as she trusts me."

"And Dr. Crew? What do you think of him?" Charlotte asked.

A pause, then Ella drawled: "Hmm, what do I think? He's all unsettled one day, then fixes on something the next and won't let go *no matter what*. So I hope—" She broke off, then called to Gilbert, who was opening the back door: "Hold a minute, Mr. Gil."

Ella was helping Charlotte on with her dressing gown, easing a sleeve over her freshly bandaged arm, then quickly closing the gown with its sash, as I entered the kitchen from the hallway and then Gilbert from the yard. From the moment Charlotte saw us, her expression and posture altered, and she seemed no longer so comfortable as she had been when thinking herself alone with Ella. Whether Charlotte were shy of us, or wary, I tried to draw her out with pleasantries, remarking on the healthy color in her cheeks.

133

Gilbert, possibly startled to see Charlotte up and about, said nothing, only gazed at her. Ever since his bringing her here, he had persisted in a sort of dream state. Although he spent little time with her—I didn't encourage him to linger in her bedroom—he would ask after her or look in on her, confessing to me that he simply liked knowing she was in the house.

Ella, quicker than I to notice how fatigued Charlotte looked, said, "I do believe Miss Charlotte's wore out. Mr. Gil, best you help her upstairs."

Charlotte, casting a grateful eye on Ella, pressed her hands on the table and pushed herself up from the cane chair. Coming quickly to her side, Gilbert placed his right hand at the small of her back and extended his left hand to steady hers, as if he would lead her in a dance. She walked well enough with him from the kitchen, through the dining room and parlor, and to the foot of the staircase. Following them out, I thought his offered support was overdone. But then Charlotte released his hand to place her palm upon the newel post and had no sooner taken the first step up alone, than she rocked backward. Gilbert caught her by her shoulders as the back of her head dropped against his chest, the crown of her hair brushing against his mouth—his mouth on her fragrant hair. I saw it happen. And, in the next moment, Gilbert had lifted her off her feet, surprising her, I surmised, from the sound of her sudden intake of breath.

Much had changed since Gilbert had carried a cold, limp form into the house on the night of the wreck. Charlotte had, indeed, come back to life—one warm cheek pressed against my brother's shoulder, one hand clutching the lapel of his frock coat. Through the gathered fabric of the skirt of her dressing gown, Gilbert must have felt the backs of her bent knees and the slight weight of her legs draped over his forearm. He took the stairs as if he were a groom carrying a bride to the bedchamber. I was right behind him as he crossed the threshold with her, then passed him, reaching the bed before him. I smoothed the rumpled sheets and fluffed the pillows—before Gilbert gently laid Charlotte on the bed, and she slipped her bare feet beneath the counterpane, out of his sight.

Chapter Twenty

Gilbert called often at Widow Eden's apartment to inquire after the welfare of Amy and Wilfred, then bring back reports of the children to comfort Charlotte. "I live for news of them," she said to my brother. With each visit, he also confirmed—to my relief and his—that the children's grandmother had yet to tell them what she believed of their mother's fate.

While at first Widow Eden had been reserved with Gilbert, she had warmed to him with the frequency of his visits, so he told me, and his expressions of concern for the children. Still, I decided to see for myself and accompanied him on his next visit, despite my discomfort with the entire situation. Our concealing the truth of Charlotte's whereabouts was like a stone dropped in a mill pond, causing ripples to spread out over the surface of the water, concentric rings of deception forming and expanding from the center of the lie.

At the beginning of the visit, I was taciturn, unusual for me, while Widow Eden was not. Gilbert and the young maid Narcisse were playing with the children on the hearth rug, helping Amy construct block towers, which Wilfred then gleefully knocked down, when Widow Eden took me aside. In the window alcove where we sat together, she explained—without my asking her—why she delayed telling Amy and Wilfred of their mother's passing. "What could they really understand about death? Better I tell them she is away for a rest. They are very young. Their memories of her will fade," Widow Eden told me. I had seen too many sad children brought up in a state of perpetual mourning not to appreciate her desire to shield her grandchildren. "It's different for a parent losing a child to illness," she added, "or a mother losing a son to the War. There's no forgetting that—ever."

My sympathetic murmurings moved Widow Eden to continue and tell me of her private sorrows, of losing her two elder sons at the siege of Vicksburg, when her youngest, Victor, was just a boy of thirteen, fourteen at most. "Then and there, I vowed to do anything to keep my one remaining son from going for a soldier," she said. "Some women couldn't sacrifice enough for the Cause, but not I—I already had. I would not give Mr. Jefferson Davis my last darling boy."

Then, what had she done in the final desperate throes of the war, when young boys and wizened old men replaced the ranks of men cut down in their prime? Had she hidden her youngest son, as some mothers had, or sent him away? Away, I understood, with assistance from Eden's paternal uncle, a great friend of the influential. "It was during Victor's sojourn in Europe that an interest in architecture took hold of him. And we see where that has led, don't we?" Widow Eden said with satisfaction. "His fine career. His excellent associations with the Placides and their circle and any number of commissions. And he is generous to me."

"Indeed," I murmured, all the while wondering: Was supporting his mother the reason, the only reason, that he had been stinting with his wife?

Then, with little prompting on my part, Widow Eden shared a few words with me concerning her daughter-in-law.

"I never really knew Charlotte, never understood her—not the way a mother understands her own," she said as if to preface, perhaps to excuse, what she would say next. Widow Eden, sitting near me, close by the bay window, leaned forward from her chair, her small head on its crane-like neck tilted and turned from me to

138

her grandchildren and back again, before she resumed speaking: "You see, Mrs. James, when Charlotte and Victor met, I thought the girl had seen her chance and seized it to out-marry herself. But now, I don't know. Suppose she truly was a romantic little thing who fell in love? My son, bless his heart, was so taken with her—why, he wouldn't listen to a word I had to say. And, I must admit she tried to better herself in ways beyond the pecuniary, reading from Victor's books and asking me any number of questions about the niceties of housekeeping. And Charlotte was a good little mother."

Her words echoed her son's sentiment, which had given Gilbert pause: *Charlotte was a good mother—I'll give her that.*

Widow Eden's pale-eyed gaze traveled again to her grandchildren, then slid back to me as she dropped her low voice to the merest whisper: "But now, don't you see, Mrs. James, my son has the opportunity to make a more advantageous second marriage." She patted my hand.

✢ ✢ ✢

In the course of my brother's work—treating patients in the clinic, making house calls, visiting patients at the hospital—Gilbert had accumulated bits of news about Charlotte's disappearance, which we recognized as mostly gossip and speculation. The search for her body, followed by a perfunctory inquest, had only confirmed Helene Placide's assertion that the tender remains must have been devoured by alligators—a gruesome end written up in the newspaper in lurid detail. That Dr. Baldwin had declared Charlotte dead before her body went missing saved Eden from the awkward position in which many an uncertain war widow had found herself, with no husband and no confirmation of his fate. Victor Eden, believing he had escaped that kind of purgatory, had actually set a date for a memorial service to be held by the Eden family tomb. The swiftness and finality of the man's decision shook me. While Eden's mother allowed Charlotte to remain alive for the children, Eden, himself, intended to finish her off by publicly assuming the role of widower on the morrow.

My temples throbbed on hearing this news, which Gilbert had imparted to me over supper, and I vented my frustration: "You must prove something against Victor Eden—you know that, Gil—or, sooner or later, return his wife to him."

Gilbert met my words with stony silence, so I continued by summarizing the problem as I saw it. Something was amiss between Mr. and Mrs. Eden, but had Victor intended Charlotte's demise? "Can we really rule out a self-administered dose of insufficient poisoning—the dramatic gesture of an unhappy woman hoping to gain a man's attention? Think of her low moods and long silences, while she convalesces here, waiting for her husband to come for her. Although, thanks to us, he doesn't know to come. Mark my words, she wants him to be sorry for whatever he's done."

At last, Gilbert responded: "You may be right, Lenore, about her wishing he were sorry. But if we send her back to him—and Eden is unrepentant—then we have put her in danger all over again."

After that conversation, too distressed to remain at the table, I left my brother to his custard and took myself to the parlor with my pipe. While Gilbert might go up later to sit with Charlotte, or fetch down her supper tray and give Ella a rest, I required solitude. Of late, I mused on *The Winter's Tale*, the dramatic story sliding over sixteen years between one act and another—with a little help from the Chorus of Time. But what did Paulina and Hermione do in all those years? I struggled with mere days—running a household, concealing an imperiled invalid houseguest, while trying not to be as completely remiss in my charitable obligations as I had become in my social ones. I had not seen Mr. Parr since our night at the theater, only exchanged a few notes with him, and he had kindly sent me a copy of Mr. Shakespeare's script that I might relive our experience at my leisure. Oh, if not for that night with

Ambrose, would I ever have found myself so enmeshed in other people's problems and passions? And the longer the histrionics continued, the harder for me to find a line on which to make my exit.

Chapter Twenty-One

On the night before the memorial service, Gilbert was called out to attend a child with a broken leg, a case which he later described to me and the gist of which I will insert here.

Young Ralph, the patient, claimed to have been sleepwalking when he fell through his open upstairs bedroom window and snapped a bone. Aware of blustery weather and intermittent rain, his mother seemed to recall shutting the window at bedtime—although she might have been mistaken. Gilbert had his doubts, too, not about the window, but about how the boy came to fall in the muddy flowerbed below it. The boy had reached the age—I recalled Gil at nine or ten—when the excitement of slipping out after dark to prowl around with other boys outweighed the fear of being caught and punished by parents. When Ralph's mother questioned why he had gone to bed in his overalls, the boy claimed he'd been cold. And when her eyes narrowed at him, he set up a distracting howl—oh, his leg, his leg! Gilbert seized the moment to set that leg. Then, leaving his patient incapacitated in bed and the window securely latched, my brother found his own bed, falling upon it fully clothed.

At the same early hour of the day, I was rising, dressing in a dark frock, arranging my hair and choosing a hat, claret-colored with a black feather. Preparing myself for an errand I would rather accomplish before explaining it to Gilbert, who was bound to object, I believed time for my departure of the essence. But that proved untrue, for Gilbert slept on and on. Thus, I was able to linger long enough for Ella to finish making ahead a dish of andouille sausage and vegetables for our dinner—part of which she sent away with me on my leaving the house.

"This way, Miss Lenore, when you knocks on Mr. Eden's door," Ella said, "anybody'd suppose you come bringing a covered dish to the widower."

That notion might get me over the threshold—although, in fact, I would be there on another purpose: to put an end to the charade of a funeral. Half the night I had tossed and turned on the subject and resolved to take action. Oh, I had no intention of sending Charlotte back to face cruel treatment and would continue to offer her my home as a haven. But Ella and I knew how Charlotte ached for her children and so could not hide from her husband forever. How was I to ameliorate her plight? How was I to soften any blame cast on my brother? I mulled over those questions under my umbrella all the way through the drizzle to Dauphine Street, and still had no certain answers on my arrival.

Eden's townhouse was as Gilbert had described it to me—a narrow tower with two tiers of galleries above the banquette, plastered brick painted an overripe shade of plum, gray shutters, black door, on which I rapped, waited, rapped again. At last, no housemaid came, but the master, himself, tall and somber like his abode, opened the door. Victor Eden wore a well-cut black woolen suit, appropriate for the day's occasion. His moustache was neatly trimmed and his dark hair glossy with pomade, his deep-set eyes heavy-lidded. Oh, I suppose he looked tragically handsome—but rather haggard, too, those eyes slightly reptilian, in my opinion.

"Mrs. James?" Eden sounded surprised and looked wary. "To what do I owe . . ." He let the sentence trail away, for I had not interrupted him.

I delayed saying anything, still unsure how to impart my news to him of Charlotte's miraculous recovery from death. Instead, I thrust the basket containing the covered dish into his hands, then closed my umbrella and stepped past him, as if Eden had invited me across the entryway. This shadowy bricked passage to the inner garden of the courtyard was only slightly darker than the gloomy day outside, and my eyes soon adjusted to the dimness. I looked up at Eden's impassive face, his spiritless eyes, and then tried my voice: "Mr. Eden—"

"Mrs. James, the time is not convenient," he interrupted me.

"But, sir, I must speak with you before—"

"Victor?" A woman's voice, not my own, sounded from beyond the archway in the passage, beyond which a stairway rose. "Victor, has someone come calling?" The high, thin voice descended with its speaker, who soon appeared through the archway—Margaret Duvall, looking starkly blonde in her black bombazine.

Indeed, the time was not convenient, and the private conference I had sought with Eden would not take place this morning. For now, Margaret took charge of the conversation and of the basket, whisking it from Eden's hands. "A covered dish," she said. "How nice." And she set it aside on the brick floor, showing appreciation for neither the dish nor my presence. Indeed, as she chatted on, neither drawing me further into the house nor shooing me out of it, I realized she saw me as a potential rival for Eden's attention. As well she might, for I had already beguiled and out-lived three husbands and, unlike Mrs. Duvall, was fancy-free to ensnare a fourth—if I were so inclined. On top of that, his mother had given me the impression when I called on her that she would welcome me as an advantageous match for her dear boy.

All the while Margaret prattled, Eden stood dumbly beside her—as if he were not hearing every word out of her mouth: "Oh, Mrs. James, there's so much to be done when a gentleman loses his wife. Don't you agree? So many details best left to a lady—the clearing up and sorting through the departed's things and so forth. . . Of course, some things might go to charity, mightn't they?

Haven't I heard tell of your good works, Mrs. James? Perhaps you know of a poor woman in need."

Finally, Eden came out of his stupor and shut her up with a sharp: "No. Charlotte's things are for Amy." So he was not insensible, after all, and now Margaret was the dumbstruck one.

I turned to Eden, asking after the children and was reassured to learn that they were still with their grandmother, still innocent of their mother's fate. Then I took my leave.

✛ ✛ ✛

Opening my front door, I saw Ella descending the stairs with a tray and heard Gilbert's raised voice coming from the upper hall behind her, my brother, himself, out of sight.

"How long has she been gone? Why did she go to him?" Gilbert demanded to know.

Ella responded with a tsking sound, catching my eye before she continued on towards the kitchen. Then Gilbert appeared at the top of the stairs, a stricken expression on his face. Gripping the banister rail, he descended. Upon reaching me, he spoke again, his voice lower now, but still fraught with agitation: "What have you done, Lenore? What did you tell Eden?"

Had Gilbert not discovered where I had gone—perhaps he had guessed and then received an honest answer from Ella—I might have avoided distressing him. Not accomplishing the purpose of my errand, I might have failed to mention it. But he knew and was upset with me.

I felt out of sorts with both of us. Without answering him, I turned towards my reflection in the mirror above the hall stand and fumbled with the removal of my gloves and the unfastening of my cloak. Gilbert, standing close behind me, lifted the cloak from my shoulders while his reflected eyes watched mine in the glass.

"Lenore," he said.

My eyes shifted from my mirror image to his as I withdrew my hatpin, then removed my hat. "It's all right, Gilbert," I said.

146

"How is it all right—if you've told him? Why did you go there?"

"I brought the man a covered dish. True to custom. Nourishing but light on the seasoning. Unlike some ladies, I have no desire to bewitch Mr. Eden with my culinary magic. Or, more rightly, Ella's," I added, giving credit where credit was due.

"But what did you say to him?"

"I might have offered him my condolences," I said.

"Your condolences. Then you didn't—"

"No, Gilbert, I didn't. I should have, but I didn't."

Gilbert hung my cloak on the rack, then linked his arm with mine. "Thank you," he said.

"Don't. I intended to tell him—at least, some version or other of the truth to prepare him," I said. But the moment had not been right for revelation, I thought, to excuse myself. Surely, in concealing Hermione for a lapse of sixteen years in *The Winter's Tale*, Paulina had more than once resorted to subterfuge.

I entered the parlor, seating myself in an armchair a moment before Dulcie jumped down from the windowsill and onto my lap. Gilbert remained standing just inside the parlor archway, some inner debate clouding his brow. Then he said, "Has Eden told the children there's to be a service this afternoon?"

"No. They continue as much in the dark as their father," I said. "While he believes Charlotte dead, they believe her alive—which is for the best, if we can find some way to restore her to her family before the little ones are thoroughly distressed. The man feels something, Gil."

"Guilt, shame, remorse, perhaps? We know he mistreated her, even if she won't say. Isn't that what stopped you telling him that she's here and alive when you called on him?"

"Mr. Eden was not alone when I called," I said. "Mrs. Duvall was there."

"Ah," Gilbert said, "such a comfort to the widower."

Chapter Twenty-Two

What do we say on hearing of a loved one's sudden passing? *No, it cannot be true.* Gilbert had said those words more than once to no avail. Only for Charlotte, his denial had become the truth, even as words and a date on a bronzed plaque on a tomb claimed otherwise. *Charlotte Eden, beloved wife and mother,* birthdate and death date, and nothing more.

Gilbert stood apart, under a dripping cypress, watching the mourners, who formed a half-circle, a dark crescent made of the domed black circles of their umbrellas. The umbrellas tilted and turned with the dispositions of those who held them—some attending to the muttered words of the priest, who stood uncovered in the drizzle, some slanting away, or inclining towards other umbrellas, the fabric of one rubbing against that of another in whispered communion. Who, sheltering here, would whisper, if he could, to Charlotte? Who among them would call her back?

Not those who had congregated within the opulent parlor of Testament, so quick to send her off. Not those who now clustered nearest the tomb of plastered brick, a windowless cottage with a rounded roof so low only a child or dwarf could stand beneath it. Of course, no one stood inside, where corpses were shelved, crumbling to dust, and nothingness was stored, awaiting judgment. As a clap of thunder sounded, a slender, black-gloved hand clutched at the arm of Victor Eden, the widower. Gilbert saw the movement the moment it happened and noted how quickly the hand had slipped away. Beloved Charlotte, already slipping away.

How willing some ladies were to offer solace. A few years ago, such ladies had followed Gilbert from the cemetery to his empty house, bringing him their inedible stews, patting his shoulder, cooing to him, as if he would welcome their fulsome condolences the moment his wife was interred. As if he would not see the calculations in their comfort, their plans to fill his loneliness as each appraised his furnishings and estimated his income. Now Eden was the object of such attentions—although, Gilbert's sister had only played the role of such a solicitous lady, calling on Eden to see how he fared, while other women had other designs.

In a cemetery, how could Gilbert not be reminded of Estelle and their child, buried in the ground in Baltimore? Might they have preferred the tombs of New Orleans? If Gilbert's son had lived past the hour of his birth, how old would he be now? Four—almost five—of an age to explore. A boy with the run of such a place as this could dash along the pathways, flit among the urns and monuments, startle mourners from their grief—like a little wraith on All Hallows' Eve.

A child could learn things here, as well, about the workings of the living world. Tombs, arranged along narrow paths and broader lanes, served much the same purpose for the horizontal as the city's houses did for the vertical. Grand tombs, ornamented with celestial statuary, rising to heaven, gated and locked, shone over all, displaying their occupants' wealth and status. The late Bartholomew James was interred in such splendor. While simpler, carefully tended tombs, their doorways swept clear of dry leaves and wilted flowers, some adorned with fresh wreaths and satin ribbons, glowed with the pious devotion of bereaved good housekeepers.

And what did the Eden tomb reveal about its owner? Indifference to his forebears, including the uncle who had been his benefactor, Gilbert later remarked to his sister. The rising architect housed his family's bones not in a grand structure, nor even a tidy one, but in something drear, on the edge of genteel poverty. The tomb's whitewash had long ago weathered to gray. Bits of plaster crumbled from the ruddy brickwork underneath. Cracks and fissures in the mortar had collected bits of soil from which sprouted weeds and wildflowers from seeds carried by wind or washed down by rain. Tenacious life asserted itself over decay.

Out of the corner of one eye, Gilbert glimpsed more life, this time not taking root but ranging over the cemetery ground—a flock of sparrows, pecking for worms. One moment the sparrows' brown feathers had been indistinguishable from the withered leaves through which they sifted, and in the next, their wings lifted clear in a gust, stirring the air in their upward passage before they reconfigured themselves, like a cluster of autumn leaves miraculously returned to the branches of an oak.

By the time Gilbert had turned his full attention to the ceremony, it was near conclusion. The priest, no longer able to turn the mist-dampened pages of his prayer book, which clung together and would not be separated, murmured on from memory. Then, with voice if not memory fading, he shut the book with a final *Amen* just as the drizzle turned into rain.

The *tableau* before the tomb shifted and reshaped itself—a fluid thing, able to fill the vessel that contained it, as it had filled the parlor on the night Gilbert had called at Testament. A fluid thing, now dispersing into the spaces between the rows of tombs and flowing into the watery afternoon. The widower preceded the others, taller than they, with his umbrella held high above his top hat, the peak of a moving black canopy sheltering them all—controlling their progress. Or was he impelled forward by those who came after him? Judge Placide struggled at Eden's back, wheezing with the effort of keeping up with a younger, leaner, longer-limbed man. More corpulent than lame, the judge jabbed the gravel with the point of his cane with every other step. Then came his wife moving with effortless indolence, as if sure the world would adjust its turning to the pace she set. Helene Placide, rustling in her black silk, held an umbrella over herself and a portion of her husband with one gloved hand and clinked her strings of jet beads with the other. Colonel and Mrs. Frank Duvall followed next, the husband limping but without a cane, stretching out the arm that held his umbrella in an attempt to cover his wife. But as Eden disappeared behind a tomb, Margaret quickened her pace, outdistancing the colonel. Dr. Baldwin, the last of their group and walking behind the others, looked back for a moment at Gilbert, and they exchanged an obligatory nod. Gilbert made no attempt to catch up with them.

Instead, he watched the others in the cemetery, those on the periphery, who had come to mark Charlotte's passing and now trailed away. He recognized a small, elderly woman with a dowager's hump as the milliner, Madame Joubert. Her elaborate mourning bonnet rivaled Mrs. Placide's own, and she had probably designed them both. The few young women with her were likely her apprentices or shopgirls. One of the girls—just one—sobbed into a handkerchief. Gilbert was not the only one to observe them. As they passed by, all of them fell prey to the scrutiny of a coarse, overfed man, wearing not black nor gray but brown tweed and a dingy bowler with a grease-stained hatband. Anyone could see he had no place at Charlotte's funeral, Gilbert later reported to his sister. Nor had another man—younger, thinner, with a drooping sandy-colored moustache, shadowed eyes, and pallid face. This man hung back until the others moved along, then shuffled forward between a pair of stone urns, angling towards the Eden tomb. When he must have thought he was unobserved, he reached his three-fingered right hand into his shapeless coat and pulled something from the inside breast pocket. But Gilbert saw him drop a little bunch of purple flowers at the base of the tomb, before vanishing around a corner.

Alone in the cemetery, Gilbert approached the Eden tomb and regarded the bronzed plaque on its wall, spattered with droplets of rain. Then he picked up the bunch of violets dropped there by another man, who, in Gilbert's estimation, appeared enervated and shiftless—a lotus-eater, a lost soul, nothing to do with Charlotte. The violets were artificial, cut from purple velveteen, the gray-green stems from a stiffer fabric reinforced with thin wire. They were the sort of flowers to be pinned on the crown of a lady's hat or on the lapel of her coat, not left at her tomb. Gilbert pocketed them and walked away.

Chapter Twenty-Three

In the late afternoon, when Gilbert returned from the cemetery, he entered the house quietly, passing the parlor doorway without speaking to me. Perhaps he assumed I was dozing in the armchair, my head lolling on the antimacassar, my stocking feet crossed at the ankle on a foot stool, and Dulcie draped over my lap. But I had seen him through slitted eyes as he paused on the threshold before proceeding up the stairs. To his room or Charlotte's? And if he intended the latter, what had he to say to Charlotte—while believing me out of the way of hearing him?

I rose, lifting Dulcie and then resettling her on the chair, before moving to the parlor doorway. Gilbert was already nearing the top of the staircase, without a backward glance in my direction, and thus I watched him, without his knowing. Despite a slight limp, for his sprain still pained him, Gilbert deftly avoided the creaky floorboard in the upstairs hall—evidence of furtiveness—as he approached Charlotte's room, its door ajar.

I, myself, had looked in on Charlotte a little while ago, she in the narrow bed paralleling the window, which was opposite the door. Unaware of my presence in the doorway, she had slowly raised herself from the pillows and leaned slightly forward, her hair fallen loose down her back and one of my crocheted shawls slipping from her shoulders, as she squinted at the window. What was she trying to see? The window overlooked the garden and side yard, not the street. Then, she had lifted one hand, her fingers caressing the shadowy air as if tracing the pattern of the lace curtain, perhaps imagining how she would render it in a drawing.

I approached the foot of the stairs. Gilbert now stood by her doorway and tapped a knuckle against the door frame to announce his presence, then waited. I imagined Charlotte nodding towards the ladder-back chair at the bedside, between bed and window, indicating he might sit with her. As he disappeared from my view into the bedroom, I ascended the stairs.

Reaching the upper hall, avoiding the tell-tale floorboard, I stood outside the room and, through the gap between door and door frame, took in the scene before me. Gilbert was saying something to Charlotte, or she to him, he leaning over her, inclining his head. Then he straightened up and moved the chair beside the bed, positioning it so that when he sat his back was to the door, his face to Charlotte. I might have announced my presence then and joined them. But I hesitated, waiting to hear the tenor of their conversation in progress.

Charlotte murmured, but still I heard her say: "The scent of rain clings to you."

More than the scent—the rain, itself, would cling in various stages of dispersion along his coat sleeves, the newest drops holding their spherical shape another moment before breaking open and spilling their contents into the weave of dark gray wool. Gilbert had walked to and from the cemetery without an umbrella and with his usual indifference to rainy weather. But now he must have become aware of its penetrating chill, for a shiver passed over his shoulders. A sign of someone walking over one's grave—wasn't that the superstition?

Charlotte shifted her eyes from Gilbert to stare past him, whether vacantly or attentively, I couldn't tell, at the drizzle streaking a windowpane. Gilbert followed Charlotte's gaze. "Is there something particular outside?" he asked. "A bird on the sill?"

"No, nothing." She focused again on his face, without so much as a glance in my direction.

I moved aside from the gap at the doorway to the sliver of space between the hinges and the frame of the half-open door. So far, Charlotte had been reserved with me in our conversation while less guarded when alone with Ella—and Ella was plainspoken with me. But how intimate were Charlotte's exchanges with Gilbert? I didn't know, for he was as evasive as Charlotte was withdrawn. Here was an opportunity for me to listen and assess their communication, observe their demeanors, however narrow my view, while I remained unobserved. Thus, I might put my mind to rest regarding the extent of their attachment, whether one-sided or mutual.

"Have you spoken with Mr. Eden?" Charlotte asked Gilbert.

"I saw him today," Gilbert replied. "But we hardly spoke."

"Will he come for me?" Her question, omitting *when*, implied the possibility that Eden might not come, even if he knew she were here.

"Not yet," Gilbert answered vaguely.

"I suppose he's very busy with his work for Judge Placide. Did he mention that to you?"

"No, he didn't say."

"Mrs. James tells me Amy and Wilfred are well, still with my mother-in-law. Behaving themselves, I hope." Her words sounded forced, but when she spoke again, saying, "I miss them so," I heard the catch in her voice and understood she was stifling a sob.

Perhaps Gilbert sought to distract her, to cheer her, as he told her about our last visit to Widow Eden's apartment, seeing the children playing with a Noah's ark. Sister and brother had taken turns speaking for the brightly painted wooden animals, inventing a story as they went along, something more to do with a riverboat adventure than a catastrophic flood. Other toys and a ragdoll dressed in blue gingham—not, to my relief, in a remnant of

Charlotte's old dressing gown—had lain scattered on the hearth rug near where Amy and Wilfred played under the patient supervision of the young maid.

"The girl's good with them, very careful and attentive," Gilbert told Charlotte, "although she's not far past childhood herself."

"Narcisse," said Charlotte.

The girl had a name. That was her meaning, wasn't it? Widow Eden's servant had a name, just as Charlotte had a name, even when she had worked in a hat shop, where clients looked past her to the milliner, saying: *Madame, tell your girl I want more silk roses on my bonnet,* or *I don't like the shade of this ribbon—tell the girl to change it.*

"Narcisse," Gilbert repeated the name, "is very kind."

A minute of silence passed, in which he failed to find anything else to say, before Charlotte spoke again: "Something's come back to me, Dr. Crew. At Testament, Mr. Eden and I had an argument."

"So it's true," Gilbert said in quick response, recalling, I assumed, Margaret Duvall's assertion, which he had shared with me, that the Edens had quarreled.

"Did he tell you?" Charlotte asked.

"Not exactly."

"I thought we would smooth it over. We had before. But we didn't, not this time. We couldn't have, not if he packed me off, instead—with you. Although you and Mrs. James have told me I was ill. I don't understand. And then—" Her words trailed away.

And then, there was the accident on the road, I finished her sentence in my mind, and her miscarriage—and Gilbert's misdirection.

"He was very angry—I remember that." Charlotte's voice sounded a trifle hoarse. "And he still hasn't come for me."

If Eden knew to come, would he finish what was begun at Testament? I shuddered.

"Could you tell me the cause of your disagreement?" Gilbert asked in a low, unhurried voice—though if he did not snatch at her answer, I would.

I peered with one eye, closing the other, the better to focus my view through the narrow gap by the door hinge. Charlotte's lips parted, and her breast rose with a quick breath. She was on the verge of saying something, I was sure, revealing something. Then the color in her cheeks suddenly deepened, and she pressed her lips closed, remembering something, I'd swear it, but saying nothing. She let the moment pass.

Gilbert leaned from his chair towards Charlotte, placing one hand on the quilted counterpane, as if his nearness would urge her to confide in him details of the discord between her and Eden, how serious it was, how dangerous to her. But she only watched him, warily, it seemed me. He lifted his hand from the bed clothes and ran it through his rain-damp hair, shoving the matted locks back from his forehead. He was nervous in her presence. How could he not be, when he had, that very afternoon, attended a service carried on by those who believed her dead? Those he had deceived. Gilbert ground the heel of one hand into the palm of the other, then rose and moved to stand at the foot of the bed, caging himself behind the brass bedstead.

Charlotte sat up further, straightening her back, the sheets rustling as she pulled up her knees and wrapped her arms around them. Was Gilbert sparing a thought for the warmth of the bed sheet, where her feet had rested a moment ago? His hands gripped the bed rail as if he might snap it in two.

Charlotte's face was upturned to Gilbert, whose back was to me, and I watched her gaze sweep over the man before her and fix, not on my brother's face, but on his left arm—on the mourning band encircling his sleeve, the black cotton cloth a shade darker

159

than the charcoal wool of his frock coat. Intent on going up to Charlotte, while he thought me unconscious in the parlor, he had forgotten to remove the band.

"You've been to a funeral," Charlotte said.

Gilbert flinched at her words, his right hand moving to clasp the band on his left arm, as if he could, belatedly, conceal it.

"Is that where you saw my husband?"

"Yes," he said.

"But you hardly spoke."

He nodded.

"Who has passed away?" Charlotte asked. "A mutual acquaintance?" When Gilbert remained silent, her brow puckered. "Oh, please, not one of your young patients?"

"No."

"You look so sad, Dr. Crew. Was it someone close to you?" Her voice was sweet with sympathy and persistence.

"Yes."

"Tell me."

Oh, brother of mine, what have we done?

Gilbert cleared his throat, then spoke: "The funeral ceremony was to honor someone not actually interred. The body was not there—has not been found."

"Oh? Oh, yes, that's very difficult for the family," Charlotte said.

"It can be," he agreed.

"I know," she said. "My father—my father's remains were not recovered. Although one of Father's comrades told my mother that he'd seen him fall at Vicksburg. Very bravely, of course. That's what people say to ease a loss, isn't it?"

"Yes," Gilbert said. "That's what people say—he fell courageously on the field of battle, she passed peacefully in her sleep."

160

Never he collapsed in camp with the dysentery, dying in his own filth. Never she writhed on blood-soaked sheets until the end, her stillborn baby torn from her body. We spin the truth and weave the lies.

"What can I say to ease your loss?" Charlotte asked.

Gilbert bowed his head. "Nothing."

"I don't understand you, Dr. Crew."

"I haven't lost her," he said. "In truth, I should ease your feelings, but I don't know how."

Listening to my brother, I nearly forgot to breathe.

"Mrs. Eden," he said, "your husband didn't send you off quite the way you thought he did. When you fell ill at Testament, it seems you fainted. You were in a sort of coma."

"As ill as that?" Charlotte shook head. "But Dr. Baldwin was there, and then you arrived—two doctors in the house. Why was I on the way to town? And what does that have to do with—with your seeing my husband at a funeral?"

"Before I arrived at Testament," Gilbert said, "Dr. Baldwin had already declared you dead." My brother's voice sounded flat, dead, itself, in the still air.

"Dead?" Charlotte whispered her incredulity in the single word.

"He thought you were. Your husband, they all said you were."

"But I wasn't. I'm not." Charlotte's voice was tremulous yet determined. "Even if that's what anyone thought—or anyone wanted— how could they have been so mistaken?"

"I've wondered the same thing," Gilbert said. "They were all so sure, so insistent that I take you back to town that very night. Then we were run off the road. The pine box fell from the wagon, down the embankment—" He broke off as Charlotte lifted a trembling hand.

"*I was in a box*," she said, her words charged with the horror of their meaning.

"Which broke open, and there you were—alive," Gilbert said. "And I brought you here."

"But you've told them. Surely, you've told them how wrong they were." This time, her words were almost lost amid her shallow breaths—as if she were in the midst of panic in a tight enclosure—fighting for air.

"I intended to," Gilbert said. "The next morning, I rode back to Testament, intending just that—to tell Mr. Eden. But when I saw him with the others, all of them together, something was wrong. Something *is* wrong. You were poisoned, I'm sure of it." As Charlotte's eyes widened and her breath quickened, he tried to change direction, reassure her: "You'll stay here, Mrs. Eden. You'll be safe here."

Was she listening to him? Hardly. Charlotte moaned and rocked herself to and fro, her eyes magnified with tears. Gilbert came to her side, falling over his words, failing to find any to undo his blundering. He extended a hand towards her shoulder, but she shrieked and slapped him away.

I took a quick step back from the doorway. Drawing a deep breath and clutching up a handful of skirt, lifting the hem above my ankles, I prepared to make an entrance from the quiet wings of the hall into the bedroom—the scene of commotion. But pushing the door aside and stepping forward, I very nearly collided with my brother shooting towards me, his eyes wild and face flushed as a fever patient's. Catching me by my upper arms, saving his balance and mine, Gilbert pivoted around me. And, in that instant, I would swear that his startled expression at my sudden appearance changed as we passed one another to a look of relief that his sister had arrived when most needed to calm Charlotte's hysteria.

162

Act II
Crossing Over

Chapter Twenty-Four

Gilbert stumbled halfway down the stairs before momentum deserted him. Pain fired in his legs, as if his ankle were injured anew in a reprise of his tumble down the riverbank.

The staircase, a straight shot, provided no turns nor landings on which to gather composure for further descent; he simply stopped on the middle stair, pressed his spine against the wall, and caught his breath.

Charlotte's wailing had propelled him from her bedside in search of his sister—who had been remarkably quick to respond, going to Charlotte, shutting the door behind her, muffling the lamentation within the bedroom. For an interval, his part was done, and Gilbert had escaped a distressing scene. Yet, for some time, he moved no farther in one direction or the other, but remained in his particular purgatory, between one floor and the other, neither here nor there. Betwixt and between—the fascination of a staircase, so he had told his sister when he was a boy.

This narrow staircase was the conduit, running slant from near the back bedroom, Charlotte's room, to near the front door, the porch and street and outside world. It ran along the interior east wall of the house and had a single, smooth banister rail, with no jutting ornament atop the newel post. It was the sort of banister down which boys launched themselves at bullet-speed, flying on, unimpeded, continuing airborne over the newel post to strike the floorboards in landing, perhaps to bash their foreheads or snap their forearms. Boys who lived in similar houses—Greek side-hall cottages—with similar staircases were sometimes Gilbert's patients.

Such a boy and his mother waited for him that very moment. Gilbert had forgotten they were coming in the late afternoon, nearly evening, after the service at the cemetery, which had been more on his mind. Only when he bestirred himself to finish his descent of the stairs and cross from the back of the house into the rectangle of garden, did he recollect the appointment. The mother of his patient frowned on the threshold of his clinic, the little boy behind her cheerful enough, amusing himself by marching back and forth on top of a bench, his sound arm extended, waving a palm frond he had snapped off in the garden.

Stepping into the clinic, Gilbert assumed his professional manner, no time to dwell on his botched conversation with Charlotte or how he might make amends to her. Instead, he focused on the removal of the splint and examination of the boy's arm, not really attending to the child, himself, nor to the mother. Not Gilbert's usual way, which was to treat the patient as much as the ailment and endeavor to allay fears and advise parents on safeguarding their children's health. But on this occasion, it suited Gilbert that the boy simply wanted the task finished and to return to playing, and his mother, who made clear she had waited quite long enough for the doctor to do his job, was ready to whisk her son home.

Moments after the pair of them departed through the side gate, Helene Placide, followed by her maid, entered there, the lady still dressed in her mourning regalia. By her ropes of jet beads and mourning bonnet, Gilbert recognized the judge's wife, without seeing her face behind her veil. And what was the meaning of her arrival? Helene had no little children. His sister had mentioned to him that Placide had offspring—a daughter or two, married off, and a son—but they were by the judge's first wife. The son managed

Placide's business in some other state, possibly Alabama, something to do with mining or railroads or both, if recollection served.

Gilbert's glance darted from the new arrivals upward to the gallery. Might Charlotte see Helene and her maid from the back bedroom window, which overlooked the little garden between house and clinic? But Charlotte's view from the bed was of the gallery railing and the baskets of jasmine and ferns hanging from the eaves. Only if she had left the bed and come to the window could she have seen the new arrivals crossing the brick path to the clinic door. The lace curtains, parted at the bedroom window had moved, and someone had looked down at him—his sister—and then had drawn the curtains.

Through the shadows of early dusk, Gilbert followed mistress and maid into the clinic, forming a quick impression of Helene's servant, whose name he had yet to learn. Her presence reminded him of Narcisse and his intention to take more notice of her, as he had told his sister, and commend the girl when next he called on Widow Eden. Helene's maid looked to be in her early twenties, born before the war, and a decade and a half younger than her mistress, and comported herself according to her station. She stayed back, head bent, eyes slightly averted—the eyes not dark but watery gray-green. Her smattering of freckles across light brown cheeks and a rusty tinge to the dark hair escaping the confines of her *tignon* evinced she was the offspring of a slaveholder and a slave, some ruddy-faced planter and his dusky concubine. Of course, Gilbert, like his sister, had heard men of the South hold forth in outrage—real or feigned—against racial impurity and miscegenation. Landed gentlemen, including the once ginger-haired Judge Placide, who years before had raped slave women with impunity, now threw up their hands in horror at the very idea of the superior white race fornicating with the black one, or with shades of black or brown or *café au lait* or cream with one drop of Negro blood.

165

Gilbert nodded the maid towards a cane chair in the waiting area, an unexpected courtesy that might have prompted the quick clearing of her mistress's throat. Then he pushed back his office door for Helene to enter the room, and as she passed him, her perfume swirled around her, lingering too heavily on the air. Some spicy blend of patchouli and sandalwood, Gilbert guessed. His sister had told him that he could have been a perfumer with his nose for scents. Of course, a discriminating sense of smell was also useful in his profession for distinguishing the safe from the toxic, the sweet from the sickly sweet, and the merely foul from the putrid and gangrenous. Gilbert left the office door open, not wishing to presume any sort of intimacy with his uninvited guest, but Helene circled back and shut it, an indication that what she had to say to him was not for her maid's overhearing.

"What brings you here, Mrs. Placide?" Gilbert asked, as suspicious as he was curious.

"Mr. Eden," she said. "*He* is the reason. I am greatly concerned about him, 'deed I am."

Gilbert waited for her to elaborate, but Helene appeared in no hurry to do so. She approached him, and he offered her the wing-back chair, the one he offered to parents of his young patients, upholstered in faded blue velveteen, the nap worn away in patches on the armrests. Helene declined, instead, removing and tossing her cloak on the chair. She, herself, remained standing too near to Gilbert, where he had stopped with a hand on the back of the chair. Slowly, with black-gloved fingertips, she lifted her black veil and folded it back over the brim of her hat—a gesture reminiscent of a bride's when the time has come for her to receive the groom's kiss. No, Gilbert was mistaken; when the time came, the groom would lift the veil. Helene's proximity disconcerted him, as did the pursing of her rouged lips in preparation—ah, in preparation to impart a confidence. Indeed, she was whispering, although the meaning Gilbert caught from her words did not bode well: "My husband has no idea that I have come to see you, Dr. Crew. We are meeting in secret—you understand?"

His position would allow him only one step backward, and if she took a step forward, his back would be against the wall, indeed, with the chair hemming him in on one side. Gilbert settled for leaning slightly to the opposite side, not wishing to appear repelled by her nearness, nor wishing to encourage it. Helene mirrored his movement, leaning the same direction as he, while reaching out to touch his hand that still gripped the top of the chair.

"You, sir, are chivalry personified," she said. "I sense that about you, Dr. Crew." Such flattery was bound to be followed by the request of a favor, or the demand for one. But first, Helene paused to lift her hand from his and arrange the strings of jet beads across her bosom with that gesture women use to draw attention from face to figure. "I know you will assist me—you simply must," she said, and when he did not ask how, trusting she would tell him, Helene went on: "You see, I have a particular ability, my dear sir, which my husband only appreciates when he fancies it under his control." Her lack of deference when speaking of the judge echoed her snappishness towards the man, himself, which Gilbert had noted in their parlor at Testament; although, their discord was none of his business, nor did he wish it to be.

Already discomfited by Helene's sudden appearance at the clinic—she having just come from the supposed widower's side and Gilbert having recently left the wife-presumed-dead in tears—he was further disturbed by the apparent direction of the lady's conversation. Helene Placide, while not appealing to Gilbert, was not bad looking—although what was what about a woman could be difficult for a man to discern, he had remarked to his sister, especially, if a woman were given to extremes of lacing up, padding out, rouging and powdering, and pinning on of false curls. Whatever her enhancements of fashion, the way Helene comported herself created an impression of glamour, if not of beauty. Men noticed her, even if they were not attracted to her. Gilbert was not attracted. Gentlemen would show her respect, which he endeavored to do despite a certain repellant presumptuousness in her demeanor, her calling him *dear sir* and touching his hand with her gloved fingers. While speaking, she had lowered her chin, as well as her voice, and looked up at him from beneath her lashes in a way designed to exaggerate the difference in their relative statures. Such maneuverings his sister could interpret for him—the way a lady created the illusion of her vulnerability to convince a gentleman of his power to aid her.

Helene spoke again: "In truth, Dr. Crew, the judge scoffs at my special gift when it brings him too close to what he fears."

"Which is?" Gilbert asked the question expected of him.

A smile lifted one corner of her mouth as she answered: "For all that man's power over the living, I do believe he fears the dead."

The dead—not Death, itself, which anyone might fear, but those who had died. Yet Judge Placide had told Gilbert that his wife could not abide a body in the house. *No talk about dying,* the judge had said, *don't set her off.* The Placides were a pair. Gilbert's own half-smile came with an exhalation and a shake of his head, as he wondered aloud: "But isn't it you, ma'am, who find the dead so alarming?"

Helene compressed her lips, and from her throat came that brief staccato sound of private amusement. Then, she said: "My husband told you that, didn't he? But what gives us the shivers—" here Helene chafed her puffed sleeves as if she were reacting to a chill—"might also kindle the blood. Don't you agree?"

Gilbert clenched his jaw and said nothing.

"Oh, most of us are a trifle disturbed by the sight of a corpse," she continued. "Only natural, the reminder of our own mortality. But I forget myself. You, sir,"—here she patted Gilbert's lapel—"would find a lifeless body fascinating." Her hand lingered on his jacket front. Had she detected a lurch in the rhythm of his heart? "From a medical standpoint." A smirk appeared, then vanished from her lips. "Wouldn't you, Dr. Crew?"

"I was asked to remove Mrs. Eden's body," he said, with perhaps a hint of defensiveness in his voice. "Judge Placide ordered it done—for your sake."

"Ah. And you were most obliging."

Feeling a touch of lightheadedness, Gilbert gripped the back of the chair with both hands. Then, when Helene moved away from him and began circling the rug, his equilibrium returned. Twice she covered the circumference of the braided rug. If earlier he had missed the fine sweep of her black silk skirt and the contour of her bustle, here was his second chance to take in the effect before she stopped, facing him, standing with her back to the oak desk. Her arms stretched out and behind her until her fingers just touched the desk's edge, her spine arched, her breast and chin lifted—Helene striking the pose of a figurehead on a sailing vessel, preparing to subdue the waves. What a repertoire she possessed for simpering, preening, insinuating.

"Dr. Crew, how you do look at me."

"I beg your pardon, ma'am." Gilbert looked away.

"Oh, I'm not offended." Although she might have been if, in fact, she had sensed so much about him, realized how unimpressed he was with those things on which she prided herself—her elevated status and her richly appointed person. "I suppose you are wondering how I came to be paired with such a venerable mate."

Gilbert wondered no such thing, but stopped himself before uttering the thought. Society easily accepted that a gentleman who survived—or avoided—the dangers of military service and other perilous masculine pursuits and lived to ripe old age might marry any number of wives, each in turn, as the one before her died in childbirth or simply wore out. Moreover, it was not unusual for each new wife to be younger than her late predecessor, so that the aging gentleman, looking on each new bride, might believe himself living in eternal spring. The same pattern was not socially acceptable for a lady, he had been assured by his thrice-widowed sister, for whom each husband had been suitably older than the last—and the last one considerably wealthier.

"You understand, I was just a slip of a girl before the War broke out. So young," Helene said—although not quite the infant she would have had Gilbert believe. "Daddy wanted me safely married off before he died, so he settled my future by turning me and Testament over to his old friend, the great Judge Royce Placide—bride and house, slaves and land, the living and the restless dead." She paused, regarding Gilbert, measuring her effect on him.

Not knowing where he was being led, Gilbert said the first thing that occurred to him: "You believe Testament is haunted?"

Helene smiled, this time with both sides of her mouth, and raked him with her eyes. "Every inch of it," she drawled, then wagged her forefinger at him. "Oh, I heard your dubious tone, Dr. Crew. But I will let it pass. You weren't raised around here, so you can hardly guess at my experience—at what an education I received from a very tender age." Advancing towards Gilbert, she paced off her words: "Social graces, dinner conversation, dancing, parlor games." The breathy emphasis she gave the last two words suggested something other than her solving metagrams or playing puss-in-the-corner. Helene stopped in front of him, a hair's breadth away. "And there was all that time," she said, "that I spent with the house servants, my daddy's slave women. There I was, just an itty-bitty girl, sitting on a stool by the kitchen hearth, nibbling pie crust and listening and learning all about spells and trances and phantasms."

"Voodoo?"

She chuckled as if in deprecation of the very idea. "But I should come to the point of my visit." Indeed, she should. "Dr.

Crew, at times I feel there is a chasm between my husband and myself nearly as wide as that betwixt this world and the next."

What would Gilbert have felt—not irritation—if Charlotte had said such a thing to him?

Helene continued: "Oh, the judge was delighted when my little forays into spiritualism netted him useful information. You see, there was a time when I would conduct a séance in my back parlor—" here she offered her sly hint of a smile to prepare her audience for something a shade naughty—"and, sure enough, the spirit-seekers would reveal more than the medium. Very helpful for those, such as my husband, who are interested in business, law, and politics, and like to have a little something to hold over their associates. But it was all a trifle tedious to me." She paused and tapped a forefinger against her temple. "Hmm. Now I come to think of it, Lenore and her last late husband participated a time or two in one of my gatherings, so perhaps she has already told you . . ." Wisely, Gilbert did not respond. "No? Well, what started as a sort of diversion, with some clever guessing on my part, has lately opened a door for me to realize my genuine sensitivity. I have discovered that I truly do have the gift."

Helene stopped then long enough for Gilbert to realize she required a response.

"Ah. Please go on, ma'am, if you will."

Evidently, that satisfied her, and she spun on: "I am attuned to the unseen, Dr. Crew. I have a power that is beyond ordinary control, even the control of my husband, which infuriates him no end. The judge is determined that everyone, including the dead, stay in their place. But the spirit world is quite literally free of his constraints. Oh, you look doubtful, but I'll convince you yet. You see, I was born with a caul over my face, a sure sign of clairvoyance. And I have cultivated my perception of the in-between . . ."

As she spoke, Gilbert fleetingly envisioned a scene that he later described to his sister: a midwife lifting with trembling fingers the fetal membrane, the caul that veiled the newborn's features—then, the midwife starting back from the cradle in her alarm at sight of Helene's shrewd ice-blue eyes snapping open in the infantile face.

"This fascinates you," Helene said, bringing his attention back to her. "I know it does, Dr. Crew, for in truth, I'm something of a mind-reader. I tell you for sure—you and I both know what it is like to long for someone who is, seemingly, beyond our reach. I can feel that in this very moment, read it in your thoughts and in your face. Oh, don't be alarmed." She raised one hand as if to stay him from taking flight, which might have crossed his mind. "Dear sir, it is a bond we share. You can't tell me I'm wrong."

What was she implying? That she knew of his dead wife and child? Someone might have told her that. And everyone in her generation had lost someone to the War.

"Victor Eden"—Helene drew out the name—"is disconsolate since his wife's demise."

Or overwhelmed by a guilty conscience.

"But I believe he would recover himself," Helene said, "if he could be sure, beyond all doubt, that there is nothing for which he need reproach himself and that she is at peace. But her sweet soul had barely left her tender body before her remains were snatched at the riverside."

Her words, like Gilbert's own blood, pounded in his temples: *Charlotte, sweet and tender.*

"Devoured by a beast," Helene continued.

Would she not let the image go?

"Why, Dr. Crew, how troubled you look."

"You said you came here for my assistance," Gilbert said, ready for her to be done.

"Yes, I did. And you are beginning to understand what that might entail—I know you are. But before I proceed, let me ask you a question to confirm a little suspicion of mine." *How convoluted her conversation was, twisting one way and another.* "You sensed something unusual about Charlotte Eden's passing, did you not?"

Gilbert's throat tightened, but he managed the words: "It was sudden."

"Only sudden? Nothing else? You don't think it could have been, shall we say, intentional?" Suicide?—as she and Dr. Baldwin had discussed in her grand parlor.

"Not on her part," Gilbert said.

"Oh." Apparently, his reply had surprised her. Would she read his mind and realize the implication laced in his words that any intentionality must be coupled with foul play? For a moment or two, Helene appeared thoughtful, her eyes distant, as she tapped a finger to her lips. Then she said, "You don't think she was melancholy? Despondent?"

Gilbert didn't answer.

"Dr. Baldwin said heart failure. Do you disagree with your colleague?" Helene persisted.

"I agree with you, ma'am—there was something odd about Mrs. Eden's passing. But I don't believe it was caused by a weak heart or by despondency."

"By what then?"

Gilbert refused to speculate for her.

"If only you could have examined her body before it disappeared," Helene said. "Charlotte's body did disappear. Did it not?"

Was the woman suggesting that Gilbert would have kept the corpse for himself? If he had kissed Charlotte at the riverside—and hadn't he?— surely, he had believed her alive.

Helene sighed. "So, Dr. Crew, we are left with a mystery to consider—when you come back to Testament."

173

"Ma'am?"

"Yes, indeed," she said. "You must come. Victor Eden is a shadow of himself and needs our help to recover from his loss, however that loss occurred. You were there—that night—dear sir. You were there at Testament and on the river road, the last living, breathing soul to be near Charlotte's mortal remains. For that reason, I ask, no, I require you to join us—all of us who were present on the night of Charlotte's passing—for a summoning of her spirit."

"A séance."

Had a draft entered the room then—a current of air slipping through the gap under the closed door, or through a crack in an otherwise snug window casement—creating a well-timed cold spot?

"Has Mr. Eden agreed to this?" Gilbert asked. "And the others?"

"Arrangements are in hand, Doctor. You will make six at the table."

"But I'm a skeptic."

"An earnest one, I'm sure," she said, "and that makes all the difference. I only ask that you be there, go through the motions, keep a receptive mind, and we shall see what happens."

Was this what she had done with the others?—told them each whatever she believed would bring them to her table. There they would be, the house party, reassembled. And through her supposed gift, Helene had handed Gilbert a gift: the chance to observe Victor Eden, the Placides, the Duvalls, and Dr. Baldwin, to interview them together and separately around the event of their calling to Charlotte's spirit, to watch them entangled with one another, one of them tripping on his lies. Then Gilbert might discover who among them would sincerely call Charlotte back—and who would only pretend.

Helene hummed on: "We must reach out to her that she may reach out to Victor and give him her blessing to go on without her—as he must. And to that end—I believe you have her things, Dr. Crew, the things she brought to Testament, don't you?"

"I beg your pardon?" Gilbert's mind might have wandered.

"Charlotte's personal effects," Helene said. "You haven't yet returned them to Mr. Eden, have you? Don't be alarmed, I'm not accusing you. I'm sure you've been very busy with your work. Such worthy endeavors—the healing arts and helping little poor children. Of course, you meant to return her things. But time slips away." Helene smiled. "You admired Charlotte Eden, didn't you? Quite natural. She was far prettier than her original lot in life should have allowed her to be. But all turned out well, for a while, at least. She came up in the world, married a gentleman, bore him children . . ."

Was poisoned at Testament.

Helene went on patronizing Gilbert: "I do understand your fondness for the little lady, that you would cherish some reminder of her." While Helene might not possess powers of extrasensory perception, she was intuitive. "You have the finer feelings—of that, I'm sure," she said. "Why, don't we all miss her? And your possession of her things is really to our advantage."

"What do you mean, ma'am?" Gilbert spoke calmly, making no acknowledgement of her suggestion that he was fond of Charlotte.

"Why, your delay in returning her belongings has saved us the difficulty of asking Mr. Eden to choose something, himself. Instead, I rely on you, kind sir, as I know I can, to bring to our gathering something of Charlotte's—intimate, hers alone. Perhaps her hairbrush, strands of her hair still caught among the bristles." Helene touched one of the tight curls that edged her forehead, tracing its spiral with a fingertip. "Or her perfume bottle with the tiny glass stopper that has so often touched the hollow of her

175

throat." Her fingers slipped to her own throat, covered by a high black lace collar. "Or an item of her clothing, imbued with a trace of her scent. You decide, Dr. Crew."

And when Gilbert made his choice and placed the intimate object in the spirit medium's hands, how much of Charlotte would Helene sense from it, how much of him?

In an effort to bring the interview to a close, Gilbert took up Helene's cloak from the chair, opened the office door, and gestured the lady towards the threshold. He placed the cloak on her shoulders just as they stepped into the empty front room. Seemingly unconcerned by her maid's absence, Helene talked on about her séance and then, as they continued into the courtyard and to the gate, she commented on the medicinal plants in the garden.

"I see you've fenced in the dangerous ones," she said, waving a gloved hand towards the ironwork surrounding castor bean plants and the like.

"Yes, ma'am. Little children will put anything in their mouths. And what's helpful if properly mixed may be deadly if misused."

"Indeed."

Gilbert glanced around for the maid, even if Helene did not. Then, in the shadowy covered walkway between the house and clinic, he discerned shapes of a pair of women, one tall and thin, the other diminutive but erect, in animated conversation—Ella and the maid. With a glance towards her mistress, the maid moved away from Ella, changing her posture as she did so, dropping her shoulders and lowering her head at the sound of her mistress's snappish voice calling her name: "Tansy!" Then, Tansy emerged from the shade as slightly less than what she had been only moments ago, the trick of those who survive by not giving offense.

Chapter Twenty-Five

Charlotte had not expected to die at Testament. That much had become clear to me as I witnessed her reactions to Gilbert's revelations—her shock that she had been pronounced dead, her horror that she had been laid out in a box, then her despair that she had been so soon accorded a memorial service, sans cadavre. No, Charlotte could not have intended to do away with herself, I now believed, even if she had knowingly imbibed a dangerous concoction for some other purpose.

Her hysterics continued for some time after Gilbert left her in my care, and I could get little sense out of her. Naturally, her overwhelming concern was for her children—to rally herself and return to them—while she wept afresh at any mention I made of Testament and its denizens. At last, I gave up questioning her and brought the decanter of medicinal brandy from my room. We each drank a glass before Charlotte settled down, exhausted with emotion, and I left her, promising to send in Ella with tea and buttered toast and Ella's own pacificatory presence.

Then I headed straight downstairs to extract from Gilbert the details of his tête-à-tête with Helene Placide. Oh, I'd seen that woman from the upper window, all bust and bustle and fluttering black veil, sashaying across the side yard and into the clinic. I knew a thing or two of her character, and I would know her business with my brother.

On my way to the back of the house, I encountered Ella coming in the kitchen door and shared a few words with her about Charlotte's care before I located Gilbert. Helene and her maid were gone, but Gilbert still stood by the garden gate, banded by shadows of the loquat boughs. He looked utterly bemused, so I linked my arm with his and brought him inside, all the way to the deep-cushioned sofa in the parlor, and there we talked.

First, I assured him that Charlotte was calming down, then prompted him to recount his conversation with his uninvited visitor. When he was possibly nearing the crux of his story, he suddenly asked me: "Is it true that you attended Mrs. Placide's séances?"

"Why, yes," I replied. "Years ago. When Bartholomew was alive and connected with Judge Placide, he expected me to humor the judge's wife by participating in one of her after-supper gatherings. Is that what she's on about now? A séance?"

"To summon Charlotte's spirit," Gilbert said.

"My stars and planets! What next?"

Gilbert told me of Helene's request of him to bring an intimate possession of Charlotte's to the gathering, then asked what he should expect if he joined the circle.

"I hardly know," I said. "But, of course, you must attend and observe—and not let yourself be hoodwinked. The night of my participation, so long ago, the circle was ladies only, while the men smoked and argued politics elsewhere. The ladies' request to the spirit world was for a glimpse of lovers lost. And while our spirit guide obliged us with old paramours tapping and moaning from the shadows, old secrets and scandals came to light."

"Even yours?" Gilbert said, lifting one brow.

I tsked at him. "Really, Gil—you think I'm foolish enough to give Helene a name to hold over me? No, I made up a lover out of thin air. But Helene conjured him anyway. As I suppose she will Charlotte."

✢ ✢ ✢

The next day, Gilbert returned to work with his usual earnestness, with a steady progression of patients filing through the clinic from morning until late afternoon. Then a book he had ordered arrived all the way from Scotland, the subject nutrition and diseases of childhood, which he said he looked forward to delving into—although not before making a visit to the hospital to look in on a patient.

My brother was not yet formally on staff at the hospital but maintained a cordial, professional relationship there with a surgeon, Dr. Clarke, whom he admired. A veteran of the Confederate surgery tents, experienced in the horrors that had taken place within them, Dr. Clarke was now a strong advocate for surgical innovations, particularly methods of anesthetizing patients. Whenever Gilbert's patients required surgery, he sent them to Dr. Clarke, who allowed Gilbert to observe procedures, assist with some, and discuss cases with him—to learn beyond the limits once circumscribed for him by his father-in-law, Dr. O'Brien.

The patient of concern to Gilbert that afternoon was a little girl admitted to the hospital two days ago for an appendectomy. Gilbert had been called in late by the child's desperate parents, after the great-aunt had exhausted her supply of plasters and purgatives and the child's appendix was on the verge of rupturing. In the nick of time, Gilbert had whisked the girl away to Dr. Clarke's operating theater, and she was now making a satisfactory recovery, so my brother told me before he shared details of an encounter outside of the hospital.

✛ ✛ ✛

At dusk, just as Gilbert departed the hospital and stepped onto the boardwalk, Colonel Frank Duvall approached him. "Glad I ran into you, Dr. Crew," he said, although he offered no reason for his being near the hospital, and his implication that he had encountered Gilbert by chance had not quite rung true. They walked together until they reached a shaded square with a vacant bench. Both of them welcomed the rest, Gilbert for his mending ankle and Duvall, for the thigh that maneuvered the weight of his wooden leg within its boot.

"Your limp is not so bad today," Duvall said.

"Nearly as good as new."

"Wish I could say the same." Duvall tapped his knuckles against trouser-covered wood.

"Are you satisfied with the fit?" Gilbert asked. "If not, I could recommend someone who does excellent work." And for a few minutes they discussed artificial limbs, two men speaking straightforwardly about a problem affecting one of them, as if that were the purpose of their meeting.

Still, Gilbert's sense that Duvall had tracked him down with another intention persisted. As the conversation on the bench turned away from amputations and towards the accident on the river road, his suspicion proved right. Duvall's posture changed, and he sat up rigidly, inches away from Gilbert on the low stone bench, his boots planted firmly parallel to each other, his hands with fingers splayed on his thighs, his whole being projected outward, away from Gilbert, who had angled himself towards Duvall, engaged in their conversation, attempting to draw him out. All of sudden, Duvall swiveled his neck, turning his face towards Gilbert, and fixed him with bloodshot eyes.

"Something has been heavy on my mind, Dr. Crew, ever since the night of Mrs. Eden's passing. I speak to you now in strictest confidence. You understand?"

We are meeting in secret—you understand? Helene Placide had said to Gilbert only yesterday. His sister, teasing and truthful, had told him that he had the face of a confidant: attentive, earnest, and a trifle ingenuous. The first two characteristics were a boon to him in his profession, the last one an occasional impediment. Although slight and likely to lessen with age, it sometimes cost him in respect from colleagues, sometimes caused others to underestimate him.

Gilbert offered Duvall an encouraging nod, and the colonel continued speaking: "I think you know, or have guessed, that it was my carriage that collided with the wagon."

Gilbert nodded again.

"The story's bound to come out. And I'd rather you hear it from me. Yes, I am responsible for the accident, and I'm here to apologize for bringing about your injuries."

"I appreciate that, Colonel Duvall." And Gilbert was surprised. Perhaps Duvall was not as arrogant as some of the company he kept.

"As for Mrs. Eden's remains . . ." Here, Duvall raised the palm of one hand to his forehead and slowly shook his bowed head.

"It was an accident, as you say, sir. My injuries were hardly mortal. And Mrs. Eden is—well, she is out of harm's way."

"And therein lies the irony." Colonel Duvall sighed.

"Sir?"

"I was in such a swivet to catch up with my own wife that I didn't spare a thought for Eden's wife." Duvall lifted his face and looked out towards the street full of passersby.

"Can you tell me why you were in a hurry to reach Mrs. Duvall that night?" Gilbert asked, as if the answer would surprise him. "In confidence, of course, sir."

Duvall nodded. "In confidence, as you say. The trouble began the day before, you see, when my wife and I had a spat. I was prosecuting a case that Judge Placide had sent my way, and I wanted Margaret to wait and go with me to Testament the next day. But she insisted on traveling with the Judge and Mrs. Placide. I knew Eden would be there, too." As the colonel spoke, he drew a metal flask from his inside breast pocket. "I wanted to arrive that night, though she was expecting me the next day. I wanted—" He paused and took a swallow from the flask as if not quite aware he was doing so, then put it in a different pocket from the one he had taken it out of, slipping it into an outside jacket pocket. "I wanted to catch her off guard. And before that, I wanted to observe her."

Certainly, at Testament, Gilbert had glimpsed the familiarity between Victor Eden and Margaret Duvall, supposing it all of a piece within the coterie to which they belonged or aspired to belong. But Gilbert could not imagine Eden actually preferring Margaret to Charlotte—although some men took whatever was offered, or whatever flattered their vanity to possess. He recalled how Margaret had angled herself beside him in the Placide's drawing room, offering him a brandy and exclaiming over his narrow escape from the jaws of an alligator. A show of regard had many uses. Familiarity was not always coupled with tenderness of feeling.

Again, Colonel Duvall took out his flask, sipped from it, and put it away in a third pocket. Gilbert pulled a dry biscuit from one of his own coat pockets, which he had stuffed there at breakfast. He tore the biscuit into bits and tossed a morsel to a solitary nearby pigeon. Immediately, it was joined by a dozen more, and he went on dividing the biscuit among the birds until he had no more to give.

"I'm beholden to Judge Placide," said the colonel. "In my profession, he's a good man to know. I wouldn't risk offending him. But something about Helene Placide unsettles me."

Gilbert, following Duvall's line of talk regarding the man's suspicions about his wife and Charlotte's husband, wondered about this new direction, the Placides.

"My wife is very much under the influence of Mrs. Placide," Duvall said, with a drawling relaxation of speech under the influence of whiskey.

Gilbert mulled a response to elicit further confidences, without voicing any disrespect for a lady. He brushed the last crumbs of biscuit from his hands, and the pigeons scattered, then reformed into a cooing mass, pecking again among each other's clawed feet in search of morsels already devoured. "Mrs. Placide is certainly a personality," he ventured.

"She controls my wife. And they both fawn over Mr. Eden." Duvall's bleary eyes suddenly narrowed. "Margaret was introduced to him under Mrs. Placide's roof. They've played cards together with Dr. Baldwin as a fourth. All the while the judge and I are in court, Mrs. Placide holds court, herself, with her house parties and soirees." He sounded as disgusted as a Methodist preacher describing an orgy. "Shuffling and discarding cards and people, that's what they do." Duvall's hands had begun to shake before he clenched them into fists.

"Will you attend the next gathering at Testament?" Gilbert asked, wondering if Duvall knew of Mrs. Placide's proposed séance.

"Oh, yes—that. I'll be there," he answered, fumbling for and locating his flask, taking a long drink, and stowing the flask back in its original place, his inside breast pocket. "But not at the table for the séance. According to Mrs. Placide, the dark circle must be composed of the ones who were near Charlotte Eden when she passed. And you, of course, who transported her remains. But don't you worry, doctor—I won't be hiding behind a curtain, rapping out messages from the next world. I'm not Helene Placide's confederate."

Gilbert appreciated Duvall's bitter humor, and they parted on cordial terms. The colonel even gave Gilbert his card, scrawling on it the place, date, and time of a gentlemen's meeting in town to which he issued an invitation, saying to show the card at the door for admittance. Not to a séance, Duvall assured him, but something else Gilbert might find of interest.

Chapter Twenty-Six

I had just stepped out of Charlotte's room and was standing at the top of the stairs when Gilbert came in, looking rather weary as he set his medical bag on the hall stand. Ella met him at the door and relieved him of hat and coat.

"You back mighty late, Mr. Gil," she said. "Had your supper?"

He nodded. "At the gumbo shop."

"Then you best go on up. Mrs. Eden be asking to see you soon as you come in."

"She wants to see me?" Gilbert's tone mixed surprise with relief. He had not spoken with Charlotte since yesterday's burst of tears.

"No accounting, is there?" Ella replied with a shrug.

Ignoring the rhetorical question, Gilbert gripped the bannister and started up the stairs, his face lifted—at which point his eyes met mine. I came forward, meeting him halfway on the staircase, telling him Charlotte wished to ask him some questions about the memorial service. He responded to me with a jumble of words about his not knowing what to say to her and what to hold back, but was quiet when we entered her room.

With a nod to Charlotte, I turned up the bedside lamp, and the shadows faded within the range of lamplight that circumscribed the little oval table and the upper end of the bed. Near the lamp was a cut-glass bowl filled with pale pink roses, which Gilbert had sent from a flower shop earlier in the day—his apology to Charlotte for having upset her. Beside the bowl lay a few pencils and sticks of charcoal and a crumpled handkerchief

185

smudged with charcoal. In the afternoon, I had brought Charlotte her supplies, encouraging her to draw to pass the time of her convalescence, although her sketchbook was not in evidence. Perhaps she had tucked it away when I had come in to sit with her half an hour ago.

With the sweep of one hand, I directed Gilbert to take the ladder-back chair, in which I'd sat earlier, so that he could face Charlotte while they conversed. I took the rocker on the other side of the narrow bed, sitting a little removed from them in shadow—a sympathetic chaperone.

Charlotte had suffered a bad night after learning her husband now called himself a widower, and I feared a weakening of what strength she had recovered. But I was heartened now to see her sitting straight with pillows stacked like rungs behind her back, as she regarded Gilbert with interest and spoke to him with a lilt of irony in her soft voice: "Dr. Crew, you must understand how alarmed I was to learn of my own funeral."

Indeed, Charlotte was much changed from yesterday.

She nodded to me, then continued speaking to my brother: "Mrs. James was very helpful, explaining to me the need for caution. I do appreciate your concern for my welfare." Charlotte's tone and serene expression seemed to soothe Gilbert, for his brow smoothed and his fingers ceased fidgeting with a loose jacket button. "Please tell me how I'm mourned," she prompted him. "What was the ceremony like? Who was there?"

How kind she was to him, resolving his dilemma of what to offer or withhold, giving him a subject on which to focus. If one could call Gilbert focused on anything, save Charlotte. Here was the complication for which *The Winter's Tale* had not prepared me, for Paulina had not hidden and housed Hermione under the same roof with an admirer—at least, as far as we know from Shakespeare's play. But under my roof, Gilbert gazed at Charlotte, hardly answering her questions, instead, rambling about the pearl gray sky of early afternoon, the sheen of light rain on the black umbrellas gathered by the Eden tomb, the bronzed plaque flecked with water droplets.

"What does it say?" asked Charlotte.

"Your name and dates. *Beloved*—" Gilbert lingered over that word—"*wife and mother.*"

Was that a shiver, that ripple of movement across the shoulders of her nightgown?

"And who stood beneath the umbrellas?" Charlotte asked.

"Mr. Eden," Gilbert said, "Dr. Baldwin, Judge and Mrs. Placide, Colonel and Mrs. Duvall—the ones who were at Testament."

"And sent me away," Charlotte said.

"Do you remember how you felt before you fainted?" Gilbert asked in his gentle bedside voice. "Was anyone with you? Did you really faint, or did you fall into a sleep mistaken for—"

"For death," Charlotte finished the sentence. "I don't recall fainting, I might have fallen asleep. I remember feeling light and heavy—lifted and blown about like a paper doll, then dropped like a stone into the pillows."

When the servants had dressed her, I thought, when they lifted her to pull a shift over her head and robe her in the fancy dressing gown and lay her out upon the bed.

"That was after you drank the tisane that the servant—Tansy, was it?—brought you." Gilbert was guessing, including about who had brought her the drink.

Charlotte considered his statement and, without contradicting it, said, "I'd been feeling unwell." Then she shut her eyes, the lids flickering, searching a scene in her memory. "I drank something sweet—and bitter," she said. "Someone was in the room, then someone else, milling about, whispering. I couldn't open my eyes. Someone shook me by the shoulders, very hard, but I couldn't wake up. I—I couldn't move. I thought—or dreamed—my hostess was vexed with me because I couldn't go downstairs to make six at table."

Gilbert flinched at the last phrase, *make six at table*—Helene's words to him, issued with her summons to the séance.

Charlotte opened her eyes. "That was why Victor insisted on bringing me to Testament. I hadn't wanted to go and leave the children. I wasn't well, was I? I told him so, urged him to go without me, but he said no, I owed him this for ruining his plans."

This was new information to me, as well as Gilbert, who asked: "What plans?"

"His architectural design, I meant to say. I'd spilled ink on it, and he had to start again or risk Judge Placide's anger—or lose the commission entirely, so he said." Charlotte went on about her husband's livelihood depending on Placide's favor, but I was thinking of her husband's ire and the bruises Ella had found. "Mr. Eden says we must not offend them," Charlotte finished.

Oh, hadn't I heard that same admonishment from Bartholomew James? Perhaps I huffed my breath a bit, for Charlotte darted a glance in my direction before she spoke again.

"Mrs. Placide requires a multiple of three for her parlor game. We were to be six in a circle, holding hands, holding conversation with those on the other side. She's made us do it before." Charlotte paused, then added, "And now, for all they know, I am on the other side."

Should Gilbert tell her that Helene had already set plans in motion to communicate with her spirit? No, not yet. Charlotte was speaking to Gilbert, her voice hardly above a whisper.

"I beg your pardon," he said.

"How did Mr. Eden appear to you—at my funeral service?" Charlotte enunciated her question more clearly this time.

Gilbert hesitated, then muttered: "Very solemn."

Charlotte gave him a curious look, as if she expected him to enlarge upon the subject, but he said nothing. Gilbert glanced towards me with the blank aspect of an actor who has forgotten his lines and, when I did not prompt him, returned his focus to Charlotte.

In the awkward silence, Charlotte brushed back a lock of hair behind one ear, seemingly absently, but then her fingers stopped and lingered over the place where another lock had been cut off close to the scalp—Margaret's doing with her shiny little scissors. Charlotte lowered her hand to her side. At last, she asked him, "Were there others?"

Gilbert nodded and named a few mourners he had recognized, parents of children he had treated, then added, "Madame Joubert came with a group of young ladies."

"Milliners and shopgirls. You know I trimmed hats for Mrs. James." Charlotte offered me a fleeting smile, which I returned, then added, "I met Mr. Eden in the hat shop when he came in with his mother."

And Victor Eden had been taken with her at first sight, so Widow Eden had told me. Drawn to her, as Gilbert had been, before he knew what was happening to him.

"Dr. Crew, was there anyone else?" she asked.

Whom else was she expecting? In my mind's eye, I saw the gathering in my memory of Gilbert's account and watched it disperse.

"There were two men," Gilbert said, "who obviously didn't belong there."

"Oh? You mean they didn't look like my husband's clients?"

I heard that sardonic note in her voice, belying her benign expression. There were layers to Charlotte's character—of this, I was certain.

"What were they like?" she asked him. "These men who didn't belong."

"The older one was portly, one might say—fat, really, grossly so, in mustard brown tweed and a bowler hat with a stained band. No, he didn't strike me as anyone with whom Mr. Eden would do business, or with whom you would have any acquaintance whatsoever. I think he came expressly to leer at the shopgirls."

If Gilbert had meant to choose his words carefully, he had become reckless at once. I shook my head, but Charlotte exhaled a short laugh, the sound signifying both disgust and amusement. Yes, she understood the man was appalling. But then, disgust must have outweighed amusement. Fleetingly, she winced—rather with the expression of a patient refusing a dose of bitter medicine, remembering its foul taste from another time.

"I've upset you, Mrs. Eden. Forgive me, please," Gilbert said.

"He doesn't matter," Charlotte replied.

"But you know who he is?"

"You've just described Mr. Keogh, the landlord of the building on Toulouse, where I lived with my mother. And after she died, until I married, I lived there alone."

"He came to the cemetery, to your—" Gilbert began.

"As you said," she broke in, "he came to leer at the shopgirls. What of the other man?"

"Well, I wonder—do you have a much older brother you've not mentioned? A cousin, perhaps, who would have been there?"

"No. No one left, no one like that."

Gilbert described the man who had left the violets: "Younger than the man in the bowler, but not so very young. Or, perhaps, ill-health has aged him. Thin, sallow, with a sandy-colored moustache that hung over his mouth."

When Charlotte made no comment, Gilbert asked if she knew the man. She shook her head, looking away from Gilbert and down at her hands folded at her waist, and I guessed Charlotte had just told my brother a lie.

"His hands," Gilbert said, "one of them was damaged—missing a couple of fingers. He was there alone, waiting until the others had all gone before dropping a little bunch of violets by the tomb. That's when I noticed his hands."

In her face, I saw a start of surprise, which she failed to conceal.

"You know him now, don't you?" Gilbert said.

But Charlotte did not acknowledge the question, nor name the man, nor offer any explanation for his being there, lagging behind to leave his offering in secret. Instead, she rubbed her fingertips together, as if between them she touched flower petals. The man meant something to her. I sensed as much, sure my brother sensed it, too. Gilbert was jealous of a stranger with a connection to Charlotte—that was evident to me, as well.

"I picked them up," he said to Charlotte. "The violets. Would you like to have them?"

If Gilbert were watching to see if her reaction would give away her feelings, he was not thinking how his actions gave away his own feelings.

Charlotte looked up and into his eyes. "You took them? Why did you do that?"

"I—I don't know," Gilbert said. Then he stood and thrust a hand in his pocket.

A silence ensued while Gilbert fumbled through the contents of his pocket with one hand, extracting various objects and transferring them to his other hand—a few wrapped peppermints, a stub of pencil, a small notebook, a pen knife, and door keys. At last, he withdrew the crumpled velveteen violets and set them on the table beside the lamp. Charlotte's eyes barely glanced across them before she turned her face away from the light and from Gilbert towards me. I saw her mouth begin to tremble.

Rising from the rocking chair, I came to sit on the edge of her bed and patted one of her hands, murmuring comfort.

Time to change direction of the conversation. I had no sooner thought as much than the way opened to me. As Charlotte shifted slightly on the bed, I discerned an object lying beside her: her open sketchbook, the flat page covered with a charcoal pencil drawing that, a moment ago, had seemed a part of the rumpled bed sheet on which it lay, until Charlotte had moved and the sketch caught the light. She had drawn the bed clothes, the ripple of cotton sheet folded back over the quilted counterpane—another of her studies in the drape of cloth.

"Why, I mistook your sketch for the bed clothes," I said. "How did you do this?"

Charlotte lifted and lowered one shoulder. "It's nothing, Mrs. James. I don't draw the lines, just start with darkness and shade towards the light," Charlotte said. "Draw the shadows, and the shapes will appear."

"You're an artist," I said.

"If I could draw Amy and Wilfred," Charlotte whispered. "I need to see them." She let her head fall back on the pillows and shut her eyes—no, not quite, only half-closed, and tears slid from the outer corners.

"Your children expect you any day now and—" Gilbert began, but she stopped him.

"How can they be?" Charlotte said. "If I am dead to their father."

Gilbert resumed his seat at the bedside. "They've only been told you are away for a rest."

"Charlotte," I said, "we call on them nearly every day. We promise you we'll do everything we can—" not knowing what that might entail—"to keep you safe for them."

"I want to take care of you and Amy and Wilfred," Gilbert said—my brother would voice his thoughts without thinking.

Charlotte stared at him with widening eyes as she raised herself from the pillows.

"I'm sorry," Gilbert said, then risked making matters worse: "Your husband has hurt you, struck you, hasn't he?"

She flinched at the question but did not answer it. "We live in a wicked city, Dr. Crew," she said. "So Mr. Eden has told me, time and again."

"As if that were an excuse for more wickedness," I said under my breath.

"The city is built on the sediment of old vices, he told me, layered over with new." Charlotte's words, the wisdom of her architect husband, echoed a line from *The Winter's Tale–It is a bawdy planet.* "I believe him," Charlotte said and chafed her shoulders as if to ward off a sudden chill. "I must keep my home a sanctuary for my children. I must."

Her face had puckered, and her eyes filled with tears. I grabbed up a shawl from where it hung on the bedpost and wrapped it around her. Gilbert pulled his handkerchief from his breast pocket and offered it to Charlotte.

"I'm going back to Testament," Gilbert told her, "Mrs. Placide's arranged one of her gatherings. I'm not a believer in séances, but Lenore and I do believe something is wrong, unnatural, and I intend to find out what happened to you. They are all coming, everyone who was there on that night."

Charlotte had begun to sob, and Gilbert dropped to one knee beside the bed and touched her shoulder, and this time she did not strike him away. Rather, she sank into the curve of his arm and against his chest, her teeth chattering, her body shuddering. With one hand, Gilbert pushed back her hair away from where it had fallen across her wet face, and then he cradled her cheek in his palm.

Chapter Twenty-Seven

The day before the séance, Gilbert apparently pictured himself as Poe's Monsieur Dupin, setting off to follow various lines of inquiry. Over breakfast with me, he compared an investigator's analysis of evidence and testimony, which leads to the solution of a crime, with a physician's analysis of symptoms, which leads to the diagnosis of a disease. Gilbert would be in his element, fitting investigations in between and around work in the clinic, visits to the shelter and hospital, and house calls, if summoned.

"Scattered but focused—the only way for me to get anything done," said my brother, tossing down his napkin and departing the table.

Fortunately, Gilbert scribbled notes throughout his days to review at odd hours of the night—aiding him to assemble fragmentary thoughts. And lately, so he had remarked to me, in reading over his medical notes, he had begun to see them less as a dry record of cases and more as little stories—his glimpses of patients' lives, along with descriptions of symptoms, treatments, and outcomes. What was reported to him did not always match what Gilbert observed; he was wise to record the patients' circumstances, even conversations and conflicts he noted in their surroundings, and write up what he surmised to be true of their lives, side by side, with the facts of their illnesses and injuries. He had resolved to do the same for Charlotte.

To that end, Gilbert required more journals, for he had filled his last the previous night. Since a clinic full of patients awaited him that morning, I offered to visit the stationer's shop on Royal Street, myself, to purchase three new books for him, two to be devoted to patients and one devoted to Charlotte. There was a particular type of blank book carried there that Gilbert preferred, the lined pages bound in heavy cardboard covered with red and brown marble-patterned paper and with a plain white square pasted on the book front for recording subjects and dates. I would get one for my own jottings, as well, and order another box of my embossed letter paper for writing to the twins. Arabella was owed a reply to her recent missive, and Allan had yet to answer mine regarding his activities.

Entering the stationer's, I was startled from personal thoughts by the sight of Victor Eden, completing his purchase of large rolls of paper and bottles of ink. He did not strike me as *a shadow of himself*, as Helene had described him to Gilbert, but as a well-nourished man going about his business.

Eden tipped his hat to me, offering a subtle smile. Was he recalling the flavor of Ella's covered dish? Or revealing the smugness of one who believes he has gotten away with murder? Time might tell.

"Why, Mr. Eden," I said. "How are you keeping? And Amy and Wilfred?"

"Well enough, ma'am—they're with their grandmother," Eden replied in his coolly toneless voice, confirming what I already knew. "I see little of them." Again, he confirmed what I knew from Widow Eden, who excused her son's absence when the children asked for him by saying their papa was terribly busy, such an important man.

Eden tucked the rolls of paper under one arm and took the parcel of ink bottles from the clerk. He was a tad awkward in his movements, so I held the door for him on his way out of the shop, for which he thanked me.

I nodded at his purchases, remarking: "More work for Judge Placide?"

Eden inclined his head. "He wants his construction in Alabama well along before winter sets in. I may have to go myself to see the project through."

"Ah," I said, that noncommittal utterance. Eden offered me no elaboration on his ventures in another state, but I supposed them more lucrative than his sketching plans for summer houses—if they were a furtherance of Judge Placide's private prison scheme, from which my attorney and I had withdrawn my inheritance from Bartholomew.

✦ ✦ ✦

Around midday, Gilbert joined me and several ladies for a committee meeting regarding the shelter we had opened—a small haven, tucked away on a back street, for women and their children who were no longer safe at home or had no home or needed a respite from husbands or fancy men. Sadly, most of the women would eventually return to the situations they had fled, pulled back by ties of affection or habit or monetary dependence—or fear that worse would befall them if they stayed away too long. My brother must have been as aware as I of the parallel with our sheltering of Charlotte.

Another doctor, the committee chairwoman's husband, served as primary medical consultant, but Gilbert had agreed to fill in, as needed, to treat and advise. After the committee meeting, I accompanied Gilbert as he made the rounds among shelter residents, stitching one woman's split lip, which she had received in a beating, cauterizing the chancre of another as part of her treatment for syphilis, then moving on to the residents' children.

One of them, a twelve-year-old girl, he treated for chancre, as well. While Gilbert could cure most of the children with doses of pleasantly flavored remedies for diarrhea or constipation, others he, or any physician, might treat without ever curing—ghosts of children whose lives had been stolen by the venery of adults. For them, there was tincture of mercury for disease and salves and suppositories for injuries, including vaginal tears and anal lesions. When I succumbed to weeping over such miseries, Gilbert was a comfort to me by his doing what he could for the sick and injured on any given day, practicing his art and controlling his countenance. He was right when saying that patients would not be helped by the sight of his despair or revulsion at what they had suffered. And Eden had been right, too, about the layering of vices.

As Gilbert and I departed the shelter, he told me of his intention to visit the tenement where Charlotte had grown up. Disturbed by his impression of her former landlord, Gilbert speculated that our gaining insight into Charlotte's past might lead us to insights about her present. While he chose to walk the three blocks towards Toulouse Street, I road home in my carriage, driven by the fellow I employed, off and on, from the livery stable. On my arrival, finding Charlotte and Ella in conversation in the kitchen, I joined them. Like my brother, I intended to learn more about a man whom Gilbert had seen at the cemetery, to lead Charlotte towards some explanation of that man, not Mr. Keogh, but the one she had not named, who had left the violets. Had this fellow been a source of conflict between Mr. and Mrs. Eden?

✠ ✠ ✠

Along a row of dilapidated apartment houses, Gilbert inquired after the whereabouts of Mr. Keogh among the residents. One of the tenants, before dashing into an alleyway, pointed him in the direction of a man stepping from a doorway onto the banquette. Gilbert recognized the landlord, wearing the same mustard-brown tweed suit he had worn at the cemetery. Red-faced and winded, Keogh panted through an explanation to Gilbert that he had been up and down stairs and hallways half the day collecting rents from dodgy tenants, but soon all would be squared away, giving the impression he believed Gilbert was a debt collector or a bank clerk in pursuit of him. Then, when assured he was mistaken, Keogh quickly jumped to another erroneous conclusion—of course, such a fine-looking, well-dressed gentleman would want an apartment, not in this building, oh no, but in another property Keogh managed, a block over.

"Something real nice, just the thing for you, on the side street, not far from here. Very private." Keogh winked. "You know what I mean?"

Gilbert guessed he was being offered a trysting place, wherein to keep a mistress or rendezvous with a married lover. Keogh's assumption that Gilbert was prosperous enough to rent a hideaway might be owing to his sister's being in town. Colleagues, friends, and even some young patients' parents had commented that Dr. Crew's appearance changed with his sister's comings and goings. Indeed, he was better dressed and better fed when she was at home, becoming rumpled and lean and careless of himself when she traveled for long.

Suddenly, Keogh's eyes narrowed, peering up into Gilbert's face. "I've seen you before," he said. "T'other day in the cemetery." That was it, then—any pretense finished that Gilbert was a libertine from whom Keogh might profit and, therefore, with whom he might engage in chit-chat. But, instead, Keogh's recognition of Gilbert increased his loquacity. "So you know Mr. Eden, sir. Recommended me, did he? A true gentleman. Doesn't forget a favor."

Gilbert flinched, which Keogh may have interpreted as a nod of agreement.

"Knew that little wife of his, too, didn't you?" he continued. "I just bet you did."

"Mrs. Eden, yes," Gilbert said.

"Mrs. Eden, my eye! Why, I knew that little minx when she was no such thing. Just a ragamuffin child, hiding in her ma's skirts—thinking she could disappear in them pleats. But I'd always find her."

Keogh wet his lips with a roll of the tip of his tongue, and Gilbert caught a whiff of garlic and onion. The man took his arm and steered him under the arch of the apartment building's doorway. There, they stood with their backs to the door, both looking outward, Keogh tracking with his eyes the passersby along the banquette and in the street, and Gilbert avoiding looking at him as the landlord imparted vulgar confidences.

Still, Gilbert forced himself to listen as the man held forth, sounding very pleased with himself to have captured a listener. Charlotte's father never came home from the War, he told Gilbert, so Keogh had, for a little consideration—"just a bit of kindly attention in return, you catch my drift"—made life a little easier for Charlotte's poor mother. "A lot of lonely women in them days. Yes, sir. And she understood on which side her bread was buttered."

But the widow had not lasted long. "One day she just up and died," Keogh said. Gilbert heard an echo of Judge Placide speaking of Charlotte: *just up and collapsed.* "And then there was her daughter—all alone in the world."

Gilbert willed his stomach not to heave as Keogh went on with his insinuations.

"That little gal was a peach," he said. "I tell you for sure, I would have moved her out of that attic room and into the place I'll be showing you, sir. Hadn't I brought her candy and trinkets when her mother was alive?"

And sent her off to play elsewhere while her mother treated him kindly.

"Little Miss Charlotte," Keogh said, "all of sudden, a big girl of fourteen or there about. So grown up, working in a hat shop. But not too big to sit on my knee. No, sir."

Gilbert felt a sudden jab of Keogh's elbow hard against his ribs, the pain of it eliciting a groan, which Keogh ignored as he droned on. How could Charlotte, small and delicately made, have fought off the landlord's attentions?—trapped in a dingy attic with

200

the bestial Keogh grabbing her around her waist with one arm and pinching her face with his other hand, each of his fingers as thick and greasy as the sausages he'd had for supper. His thumb and forefinger squeezing her cheeks, forcing her lips to pucker, as he moved in, his slab of tongue flicking from his foul mouth, like a viper's, tasting the air. Charlotte kicked him—she must have done—hard with her heels, with the full force of her disgust driven into his shins until he doubled over in pain, forced to release her.

Charlotte had not being as accommodating as her mother, Keogh admitted to Gilbert, then spat out the words: "But I showed her what's what. Called in a carpenter to divvy up the attic with more walls and moved in two more paying tenants. Left her nothing but a closet for her cot and slop jar."

"Show me," Gilbert said, possibly too abruptly.

"What? You serious?" Keogh's tone was suspicious.

"Yes, I am. You . . . you've intrigued me, Mr. Keogh." Gilbert counterfeited the cool tone of one impressed by petty revenge on a saucy girl. "I'd like to see for myself just where little Mrs. Eden came from."

Keogh snorted, eyed Gilbert as if he were a tad eccentric, but led him up the two steep flights of stairs to the attic, divvied up, as the landlord had said, by flimsy panels of thin board. Keogh caught his breath at the landing, before informing Gilbert that the current tenant of Charlotte's old room was out working at the cigar factory. "Slips me a cheroot now and again when she's short of the rent." He patted his breast pocket, where the cheroots were stashed. "And now, sir"—opening the door with a flourish, revealing a sliver of space under the rafters—"the lady's boudoir."

There it was—the cell that had been Charlotte's punishment for offending Keogh, hardly long enough for the cot or wide enough for the small wooden chest beside it, which served for storage and table. The unvarnished floor was bare of rugs, a dark patch of rot eating at the planking in one corner beneath an equally dark patch of water-damage spreading through the ceiling shingles. After the partitioning, the room had retained part of an undraped window with three grime-covered panes and a northern exposure. The still air was sour with the smell of unwashed bedding and pungent with mouse.

Keogh talked on, this time tossing out a backhanded compliment of Charlotte: "Even after I cut her down to size, little missy kept her things nice and clean—not like this piece of work renting from me now. But I can't say no to the tobacco."

Gilbert would recount his thoughts to his sister: Charlotte had slept in this tiny room, waked in it and dressed for work, and returned to it at the end of the day, again and again. At night, she had lain on that cot and listened to the shuffling and murmuring of tenants on the other side of the partition—perhaps to sounds of their arguing or lovemaking. And had anyone listened to her? She would have been alone with no one to talk to, but she might have sobbed into her pillow, and someone have might heard her.

"Does her husband know what you did?" Gilbert could no longer stifle his disgust.

"Well, now . . . that was a few years ago," Keogh answered, tripping over the words, as if suddenly realizing he had been carried away by the bitterness of rejection and revealed too much to a stranger. "Besides, I didn't know Mr. Eden in them days."

"And since then you've done him a favor that he hasn't forgotten," Gilbert said.

"That's right. As for the other—well, I just taught the girl a lesson," Keogh said, quickly recovering his confident and confidential tone, chuckling before going on. "She thought she'd gotten back at me when she took up with one of them new tenants, the one who moved in on the other side of her wall. No, sir, ain't likely she'd have told her husband about her little-bitty room and what she got up to in it."

"Oh?"

"The fellow was a veteran of the Lost Cause, don't you know. Gloomy sort. Worked as a clerk or some such. They were right close for a while. Miss Charlotte had that way of catching a man's interest, haunting his mind."

Gilbert turned away from the room—drop its ceiling a few feet, and it would have been no more spacious than the Eden tomb. He moved down the dimly lit passage towards the darker staircase. Keogh bustled after him, catching up and crowding Gilbert on the stairs.

"Weren't long before the fellow threw her over," Keogh said when they reached the landing. "I heard the pair of them going at it, right here, right on this spot, just before he moved out. Her crying that he'd promised to marry her, him answering back—war's over, men are dead, and forlorn women come cheap."

"Was he at the cemetery?" Gilbert asked.

"Yes, sir," said Keogh. "Surprised he's still breathing. Simon Langley—that's the name.

"He didn't forget her," said Gilbert.

"Didn't I say that gal was a peach?"

Gilbert nodded.

"Well, now, let me show you that property I mentioned."

But Gilbert begged off seeing the trysting place, saying he might return later, depending on circumstances, leaving Keogh to assume negotiations with a mistress were still in progress.

✝ ✝ ✝

Later, comparing Gilbert's account of his interview with the landlord to Charlotte's confidences to Ella and me, I appreciated how Charlotte might have seen Victor Eden as her Ivanhoe. And if he had proved less than chivalrous, she was, nevertheless, bound to him.

Describing incidents of her bleak beginnings, Charlotte had said to Ella, "Nothing on Toulouse Street could match the misery of your time before the war."

And Ella, ever the generous soul, replied, "We ain't talking about that time. Your troubles, here and now—that's what needs fixing."

Ella poured us each a glass of her blackberry cordial, and after we had all taken a few sips of that elixir of truth, I lifted the bunch of velveteen violets from the bedside table. "Were these yours, Charlotte? You knew the man who left them, even if you didn't want to say in Gilbert's presence."

Charlotte nodded and, with a little encouragement, told Ella and me how she had lost the violets to Simon Langley, who had sometimes given her a kind word. "That day he nodded to me, coming down the stairs as I was trudging up after work. I'd taken off my bonnet as he passed me and noticed the violets I'd pinned on the band were gone. *Did you see them fall, sir?* I asked, and he stopped with me on the landing to look for them. *Could have come unpinned and caught on your dress,* he said, making a show of looking for them—turning me around, then bending to study my skirt, even dropping to one knee and running his hands through the pleats of my hem. I felt embarrassed, even as we laughed together, muffling the sound so as not to disturb other tenants. Then, Mr. Langley got very quiet and opened his empty hands, one of them damaged, with scarred stubs where two fingers should have been."

"But he found those violets—and kept them, himself," Ella said, as certain as if she had caught him in the act.

"I suppose he did—or took them with his three-fingered sleight-of-hand when we passed on the stairs," said Charlotte, ruefully. "Later I saw him take a cigar right out of Mr. Keogh's breast pocket. He made a joke of it to me. But more often, he was sad."

"You two got close?" Ella suggested.

"I think we were sorry for each other. And I think he had the Soldier's Heart." Charlotte spoke of the affliction of countless veterans, the wounding of the spirit.

"Poor man," I murmured. Then, gently, I asked if her husband were aware of Mr. Langley's existence.

"I never told him," Charlotte said. "He wouldn't have been pleased."

Langley had moved on, so I gathered as we talked—taking the violets with him but leaving Charlotte, a girl in her teens, behind at Mr. Keogh's tenement. Then, no time at all after that, Victor Eden and his widowed mother had come to town and into Madame Joubert's Hat Shop. And Charlotte's life had changed.

Chapter Twenty-Eight

Before finishing his work day with a visit to the hospital, Gilbert took a brief detour to Madame Joubert's Hat Shop. A shiver of tiny copper bells strung along the top of the door announced his entrance, bringing him to the attention of the elderly milliner and her staff of young women glancing up from their work. They eyed him, a man alone, with interest—if only his sister had been with him to lend legitimacy to his appearance in a ladies' shop, for she was a frequent customer. As it was, he used her as the excuse for his presence, approaching Madame Joubert at her counter and saying he wished to surprise his sister with a new hat. Madame Joubert lifted her pointed chin and straightened up as far as her dowager's hump would allow her. Looking at him over the pages of a ledger, she widened her pale eyes, and her pince-nez dropped from her nose and dangled from its black satin ribbon pinned to her shirtwaist. Madame cleared her throat, and then inquired in a reedy voice: "But are you quite sure, young man, that Mrs. James wishes to be surprised?"

One of the shopgirls tittered, setting in motion a ripple of amusement among the other young women that traveled the length of the shop. Then, the copper bells jangled again, and a trio of fashionable ladies entered, a new source of interest. Madame Joubert replaced the pince-nez on her sharp nose and turned her attention to the more promising customers. And Gilbert took the opportunity to browse—as Victor Eden might have done when newly arrived from Baton Rouge, escorting his widowed mother into the shop. He would have caught the eye of all the shopgirls, but only Charlotte had caught his eye.

Perhaps, while Madame Joubert guided Widow Eden towards the purchase of an expensive hat, Eden had ambled towards the back of the shop, running a gloved hand along the countertop, as Gilbert did now, past the shy glances and tentative smiles of various apprentice milliners, until he reached Charlotte, sitting by herself, trimming a bonnet. Eden might have stopped as near to her as Gilbert was to a tawny-haired girl arranging darkly speckled feathers in the band of a green felt hat. Eden might have turned away then, as Gilbert did, to face the wall of shelves, a honeycomb of spools of ribbon and lace, then removed a glove to finger a length of brown velvet ribbon dangling over the edge of its tiny boxed shelf. Not wishing to appear forward, he might have spoken without looking at her, asking matter-of-factly which trims and colors were popular with the ladies of New Orleans—easy enough to start the conversation.

"So you were just telling Madame a tale," the tawny-haired girl said to Gilbert, a trace of a humor and an Irish lilt in her voice. "You're not shopping for your *sister*, are you, sir?"

"No, miss, I'm not."

The girl smiled, showing neat white teeth, and cut him a glance as she held up the hat she had been trimming, turning it one way and another. "You gentlemen come in asking what the ladies want in a hat. I'll tell you true—they want a hat that turns the heads of the gentlemen." She set the hat aside on her worktable, then spread her hands in a gesture of display over an assortment of trims. "So which is it for you, sir? Feathers or flowers?"

"Flowers."

"Ah, but then which ones?" Her fingers flicked through the piles of silken roses and velveteen leaves and violets—violets gathered and tied in a little bunch, like the ones Simon Langley had dropped by the tomb.

"I've changed my mind," Gilbert said. "Feathers."

"Feathers it is, sir." The girl picked up a full saffron-yellow plume, extended her arm, and brushed the plume across his cheek, then quickly brought it to her own cheek at the same time as she lowered her lashes.

In that moment, Gilbert recognized her as the only one who had wept among all the shopgirls at the cemetery. "You were Charlotte Eden's friend," he said.

She set aside the feather and, with it, her coy expression. "What makes you say that?"

"You were, weren't you?"

"If you know already, why are you asking me?"

"I beg your pardon. I noticed you at the cemetery. You see, I'm her children's doctor."

"I know who you are." She straightened up from where she had been leaning forward over her work table. "You're Mrs. James's brother, Dr. Crew. And I don't believe you're here to buy a hat for anyone."

"But you almost had me persuaded," he said. "May I know your name?"

"Miss Jeannie Rutherford to you."

Gilbert repeated her name, adding, "A pleasure to meet you. Our friendship with Mrs. Eden gives us something in common."

"Could be." Jeannie slid her eyes away towards the front of the shop, where Madame Joubert stood by a mirror, adjusting the tilt of a hat on the head of one of her customers, then looked back at him. "You're right, sir," she said, lowering her voice as one of the other girls peered at them over her own work table. "I was Charlotte's friend to the end, even after she got above the rest of us."

"By marrying Mr. Eden?"

"Yes—well, that is, I would have been. I hardly saw her after she left here."

"Mr. Eden liked to keep her close to home, do you think?"

"All to himself, alone," Jeannie said, a blush rising in her cheeks. "Oh, I shall never forget that first day he walked in the shop with his mother. Just arrived, they were—I overheard his mother telling Madame, and going on to say Mr. Eden had joined an architectural firm." The girl pronounced her words carefully but had managed to lodge an extra syllable somewhere in *architectural*. As if realizing the word hadn't sounded quite right, she cocked her head for a reflective moment, then as quickly returned to her story. "Well, sir, while his mother looked at hats, he wound his way back here, stirring up whispers as he passed, the heels of his boots striking the floorboards with quick, sharp clicks. I listened and watched him out of the corner of my eye, for I hardly dared look at him, he was that handsome." She paused, then added, "Rather like yourself," and Gilbert smiled at her flattery. "Then Mr. Eden stopped, right there, where you're standing now, sir, and spoke to Charlotte—who was sitting at this very work table. She was sewing a yellow silk butterfly on a straw bonnet and missed a stitch and jabbed the needle into her thumb. Must have hurt something awful, but she didn't so much as whimper. Even so, he gave her his handkerchief to staunch the bleeding. The decoration was spoiled with spots of blood. But you know what? Mr. Eden bought that little bonnet anyway, and wouldn't let Madame or his mother or anyone say another word about it."

So taken, Widow Eden had said. Yet something had gone wrong, hadn't it?

"It was hard for Charlotte after that, she being such a shy one and singled out for attention by an educated gentleman," Jeannie said. "The other girls were jealous, and Madame said he'd never marry her. But he did, didn't he? Such things can happen, and in a church and all. Though now she's come to a sadder end than even Madame foretold."

Madame had concluded a sale and was easing her customer's selection into a tissue paper lined hatbox when she took that moment to glance with arched brows in Gilbert's direction. Had he still not made a choice? He smiled at her, nodded, and picked up the first item that came to hand—a coil of pink satin ribbon, saying to Jeannie, "I'll take this."

"Not Mrs. James's color, sir."

"For Charlotte Eden's little daughter."

"Ah, poor little mite—very kind of you." Jeannie Rutherford left her work table and led him to the front of the shop to complete the transaction under her employer's gaze. Handing Gilbert the small parcel, she said in a clipped shopgirl's voice, "Thank you, sir. Do come again."

✝ ✝ ✝

Now with hair ribbons to bring Amy, Gilbert realized he must find something for Wilfred, too, before calling at Widow Eden's apartment that evening, for the boy possessed a keen sense of fairness. After completing a house call on Chartres Street, Gilbert had the good fortune to spot a toy vendor wheeling his cart and bought a pair of little carved wooden pelicans, another mated couple to board the Noah's Ark.

Widow Eden had retired early with a headache, Narcisse told him at the door, and she, herself, had tucked the children in bed. Gilbert apologized for calling so late and asked to leave the parcels with her, but she urged him to come in and present them to Amy and Wilfred.

"Maybe you'll have better luck than me, sir, getting those children to settle. They been fighting sleep for an hour, and Mrs. Eden say I better never shut my eyes when theirs are open."

Although Gilbert's appearance in the children's room and presentation of gifts created a brief flurry of excited energy between

Amy and Wilfred, he was soon able to quiet them, as the weary Narcisse had hoped. Sitting at their bedside, he yawned exaggeratedly, triggering the children's yawning with his, then began reading to them in monotone from a book of edifying verse for young people. In minutes, Wilfred was snoring, and Amy snuggled in the nest of bedclothes. Then, just as he closed the book, he heard a dry rustling and a whisper.

"Dr. Crew," Amy said. Her hand moved under her pillow, and then she withdrew a tri-folded sheet of paper and held it out to him. "It's a letter for Mama. I wrote it by myself. Will you send it for me?"

Gilbert nodded, taking the paper and slipping it into a pocket of his top coat. He could not go on keeping Charlotte from her children, her children from Charlotte. He kissed Amy's forehead and waited at the bedside until her eyes closed in sleep.

✝ ✝ ✝

I waited up for Gilbert, meeting him in the front hall as he came through the door with a draft of chill night air. "You look exhausted," I said, lifting the hat from his head and prying the medical bag from his cramped hand—he carried that bag around as if it were an extension of his arm. After setting his things on the hall stand, I aimed him towards the kitchen, urging him to finish the cassoulet and pecan pie. "You've a long day ahead tomorrow. But we should talk, Gil, before you make the trip to Testament." And talk we did on the subject of Charlotte.

That she had been seen by some people as a poor, shy girl swept off her feet by a successful gentleman surprised neither of us. That she had ever been a fortune-seeker, as her mother-in-law intimated, I doubted and Gilbert disbelieved. That she had been a little minx and an easy companion for another man—her former landlord's estimation—Gilbert called absurd.

"Nothing but a figment of Keogh's lascivious imagination," Gilbert said, "colored by her rejection of him."

Yet both Mr. Keogh and Mr. Langley had come to the cemetery, one drawn by curiosity, perhaps, and the other by remorse, returning the violets he had taken long ago. A vile man, whom she had refused; a troubled man, whom she had lost; an ambitious man, whom she had married—I listed them in my mind—adding my brother, whom she had entranced, whether by her nature or design or something betwixt the two.

We discussed her escape from Toulouse Street by marriage to Eden, and I gave Gilbert my impression. "Eden desired her, no question there. But something has gone amiss since they wed. Charlotte says she disappointed her husband—that he regretted marrying her."

"Then he's a fool," Gilbert said. "And worse."

"Gil, you've gathered Mr. Keogh has somehow become acquainted with Victor Eden," I said. "Suppose that spiteful landlord has told him of Charlotte's previous attachment—to punish her all over again for refusing his advances by poisoning her marriage."

"And then Eden poisoned her," Gilbert said. "If only she could remember—"

"She does." I had to tell him. "Ella and I couldn't draw her out about the caning, if that's what it was—she simply looked miserable, then wept for her children." I rose and took Gilbert's empty cup and plate to the drain board, turning my back on him to compose myself, before facing him again. "But Charlotte remembers her husband holding the cup to her lips." Gilbert stared at me with an expression, at once, stricken and hopeful. "But that doesn't prove he mixed poison in the cup—only raises suspicion a little higher. Whatever you get into at Testament, Gil—do be careful. Careful of what you eat and drink, sure enough. I worry about you."

And I went on worrying half the night in my room. For a time, after Gilbert had brought Charlotte in from the storm, I had hoped that if he could help her through her tribulations, he might also exhaust his fascination with her—begun at first sight of her. To that end, I had offered my aid and Ella hers. But could any of us help Charlotte through her ordeal if Gilbert complicated matters further, behaved more impulsively than he already had?

Chapter Twenty-Nine

Before dark, Gilbert arrived at Testament and turned his horse over to a groom in the stable. As no one was standing watch on the verandah to urge him into the house, he left his bags on the steps and took the opportunity to wander over the yard and into the garden, on the off-chance of encountering someone or observing something of interest there. After days of cold and drizzle, this evening was mild, and anyone might be abroad.

Elongated shadows of live oaks fell across the lawn, brick walks, and gravel paths. Scattered among the large trees were low-growing dogwoods and azalea bushes, not in flower this time of year, but somewhere nearby, sweet olive bloomed, its tiny white flowers barely visible on the branches, yet their scent hung in the air. And here and there, among the shrubbery were little white figures, half-concealed in leafy shadows—not ghosts nor goblins, but fauns and cherubs carved in stone. Gilbert followed a high evergreen wall of pyracantha, with its clusters of blood-red berries, to a break in the hedge. This was not the path that led to the listing gazebo. No, that was on the other side of the garden. Here he found a zigzag pattern of trimmed boxwood enclosing beds of herbs, surrounding a ring of gravel, which itself surrounded a circular walled lily pond constructed of tabby concrete embedded with broken oyster shells. From the center of the pond rose a white marble water maiden, not diminutive and tucked away like the cherubs, but as tall and well-formed as a living woman. Her carved garment skimmed her body like sheer muslin, gathered and clinging across her thighs, slipping away from one shoulder, exposing a pale breast. The statue's head titled back, eyes closed, her face sculpted in an expression of ecstasy, as if she were inhaling the garden's perfume—as if she were Hermione returning to life before Leontes. And surrounding her were sweet herbs and medicinal plants—lily, mint, lemon grass, cassava, bloodroot, and nightshade. How could Gilbert not think of Charlotte?

Charlotte, who had wept in his arms. If Gilbert had been reckless in his headlong rush to save her from peril, still he would not turn back—not when he might discover at Testament how she had been given up for dead and why.

When he entered the Placides' mansion at nightfall, the atmosphere so akin to that on the night of Charlotte's near-death, uneasiness overtook him, and his body threatened to rebel against his reason. The back of his neck prickled as he climbed the stairs to the room Helene had assigned him, the very bedroom where Charlotte had been laid out. On the way, his sweating palm slipped along the balustrade's railing. At the doorway of the room, his voice cracked like a boy's when he thanked the servant who had carried up his valise and black bag. Gilbert did not linger in the bedroom. Instead, he pocketed the object he had brought for the séance, then started downstairs to join the others—by an intentionally circuitous, exploratory route.

Throughout the downstairs rooms of the house, candles and lamps illuminated only portions of rooms, never the whole. They lit a circle of carpet, a square of blotter on a desk, a triangle of curtain tied back with a tasseled cord—flames casting more shadows than they dispelled. Each time someone moved, a dark shape darted up the wall. It was the same in any house at night, though it was more so at Testament.

Moving along a narrow back hallway, approaching its intersection with a wider corridor, Gilbert heard somewhere ahead the scraping sound a chair makes against floorboards when it is being pushed in or out from a table. Out, he found, upon reaching the abandoned chair, positioned a foot or so from an escritoire in a windowed alcove. A lamp burned atop the little desk, the light doubled on reflection in a windowpane, illuminating the objects beside it: a Holmes-style adjustable stereoscope made of polished wood inlaid with a geometrical design in mother-of-pearl and perhaps a dozen two-dimensional pictures printed in pairs on flat rectangles of cardboard, which would appear three-dimensional when viewed through the stereoscope's twin eyepieces. The optical effect had never ceased to fascinate him and his sister, who owned a collection of the double images. Gilbert glanced over the array scattered on the surface of the escritoire, all photographs of wartime, a popular theme—battlefields, corpses in a common grave, a body slumped against a split-rail fence, and then, behold, General Lee astride a pale horse. Gilbert lifted the stereoscope to see the picture still in the device, the one last viewed by someone else, expecting more of the same subject matter but finding something different.

Peering through the lenses, Gilbert beheld the image of a woman, resting on her side, nude on a striped divan. Although her back was to her viewer, she had turned her head and gazed seductively over her shoulder, her arm draped along her side accentuating the line of waist and hip. Her knees were slightly bent and angled away from her viewer, the better to expose her curvaceous buttocks and offer the suggestion of a glimpse of her pudenda. Gilbert's footfalls in the hallway must have interrupted someone in his entertainment and prompted his sudden leave-taking just before Gilbert arrived. While still looking at the image, himself, he considered that its subject was not entirely unrelated to the others, after all, for it was the sort that soldiers might have valued, gambled for, even fought over. He replaced the stereoscope exactly as he had found it on the escritoire and left the alcove.

Somewhere off the main hall, Gilbert approached an open doorway that framed the glow of a fireplace opposite the door.

217

There were so many rooms in a mansion—hard to know what to call them all. The warm lair where he found Judge Placide, Colonel Duvall, and Dr. Baldwin gathered by the hearth might be the judge's office with its broad desk at one end, or his study or library with its walls of leather-bound books, shelved from floor to ceiling. Gilbert heard the mumble of the men's voices, then their hearty laughter over something to which he was not privy. Their laughter ceased when they noticed him crossing the threshold from the dark corridor into the room.

For a moment, each man peered in Gilbert's direction, Placide and Baldwin from where they sat in high-backed, over-stuffed chairs on either side of the fireplace, looking like a pair of outlandish andirons, and Duvall from where he stood leaning one shoulder against the mantel, taking his weight on his sound leg. Gilbert felt sure these men had been at ease in each other's company for some time, that one of them had not suddenly arrived, moments ahead of him from the alcove. That left Eden as the likely viewer of stereoscopic pictures. As Gilbert approached the firelight, the three men acknowledged him with slight inclinations of their heads and resumed their briefly suspended conversation. Even if their banter were not for sharing with the widower, they showed no particular concern about Gilbert's joining them as they pursued the topic he had walked in on—Helene Placide's spiritualism.

"She is a spirited lady, no doubt about it," Judge Placide said with an air of toleration. "Let the wife be a queen in her home, I've always said, and she will indulge her husband—and forebear his amusements." Here the judge chuckled, Baldwin and Duvall echoing him, but the doctor's chuckle soon became a nervous cough and the colonel's an irritable snort.

Judge Placide continued, his comments confirming some of what his wife had already told Gilbert. At first, Placide had found Helene's pastime useful for furthering his own interests.

218

"Everybody lost somebody in the War—or somewhere along the way. Helene plays go-between for those who want to call somebody back and say what they failed to say." He directed the statement to Gilbert, who was the newcomer, for the others were familiar with Helene's practices. "Though some folks might be better off keeping things to themselves," the judge added with another throaty chuckle, this one shared only between himself and Duvall. Maybe Rufus Baldwin was one of the folks who had revealed something better kept private and now could not join in the other men's jocularity. Gilbert understood the judge's implication—as did his sister from her own experiences at Testament—the value to Placide of one more method, among many, for gaining knowledge of his associates' weaknesses, through the men or through their wives, thereby, increasing his control over them.

"However," Placide said, "there is a slight problem. My lady wife has played so long at mumbo jumbo that now she *believes* in her own power."

"Judge, we can't entirely rule out the possibility," Dr. Baldwin said in tentative defense of his hostess. "There could well be something more than the lady's intuition at work."

"And what might that be?" Colonel Duvall asked.

"Never mind," the judge said. "Dr. Crew, the colonel here thinks my wife has been unduly influenced by her upbringing."

"Sir, I never said—" Duvall began, but Placide cut him off.

"You don't have to say, Frank. I understand, I understand. Those black witches in the kitchen, mixing up spells and potions. You ever hear such stories, Dr. Crew, where you came from?"

"I've heard them since coming here, sir."

"Judge, your wife does, indeed, enter a trance state," interjected Dr. Baldwin, Mrs. Placide's champion. "I have confirmed this, as you are my witness. Now admit it."

"I'll grant you that, Doctor—aggravating as her trances may be," Placide said.

219

"And more than once, she has summoned the uncanny. Even I, Judge, a man of science, must acknowledge the unseen realm." Baldwin waved a crooked forefinger in Gilbert's direction, saying, "Don't you acknowledge it, too?" He waited for a reply.

"Some things are inexplicable," Gilbert ventured, and his colleague looked satisfied.

✦ ✦ ✦

How did a man behave after he had killed a woman, or believed he had, and believed he had gotten away with it? At the supper table, Gilbert tried to observe Victor Eden's every gesture, to listen for every intonation in his voice, anything that might betray him. But there were moments Gilbert was forced to miss. Judge Placide, downing vast numbers of oysters and glasses of wine, ever expanding in girth and garrulousness, demanded his audience's attention. If Helene Placide were queen of the house, the judge was king and determined to prove it.

Host and hostess faced off at opposite ends of the rectangular table, each seated on a mahogany throne. Along the two rows of more modest dining chairs, Baldwin sat on the judge's right with Duvall next to him, Eden on Helene's right with Margaret next to him. Spoiling the symmetry, Gilbert sat close on Helene's left, the better to catch sight of a pained expression that occasionally crossed her face. But she, like the others, submitted her attention while the judge held forth opinions, swore, sucked his teeth, berated the servants—whatever he felt like doing beneath the sparkle and glare of his cut-glass chandelier.

At one point, Placide tried to engage Baldwin and Duvall in some old argument they had had during the war years, though the colonel, who had been quietly out-drinking his host, put forth little effort to defend his own stance. Gilbert was surprised to learn that the judge, unlike the other two men, had never favored secession. But he was not surprised to hear Placide's reasoning: "If we'd stayed in the Union, I tell you for sure, our institutions would

220

be intact to this day—and for my lifetime. Which is *my* concern."
Here, he snorted as if he had amused his listeners. "Oh, I know, I
know, Duvall. We should have won, but we weren't going to win.
Not that way. Tie it all up in Congress with the know-nothings and
the do-nothings. That's the way to win. Then, nothing would've
changed, not here, not in the *real* South. I never gave a red-hot
damn what happened in Missouri."

When Duvall would not spar with him, the judge moved
on from politics to the personal. He admonished Eden to keep
himself occupied and hurry up with the planned renovations to the
Placides' houses. "You'll soon be back in fine form to complete our
grander plans. Am I right?"

Eden nodded on cue. "I'm already back at work on them,
Judge."

"Excellent!" And Placide drank to his exclamation.

Gilbert gathered from a further exchange between Placide
and Eden that the grander plans included Eden's designing
housing for men in various sorts of labor camps. Gone were the
days of the kindly master looking out for the welfare of his field
hands, Placide declared—surely, the judge was not referring to
himself—and changing times had forced the master's hand from
benevolence to practicality. While Placide might no longer own his
laborers outright, he had found ways to get them cheap and make
them profitable.

"This young generation of black bucks is going to learn to
miss the quarters where they were born," said the judge. "No
mistress of the plantation knitting them socks for the wintertime,
eh, Helene?"

Ignoring the question, Helene sipped her wine. She made
no effort to rein in her husband, even when he went on to offer
Eden advice on choosing a second wife—"Get yourself a rich widow
woman with experience in the boudoir and the ways of the
world"—even when the widower spilled burgundy on the tablecloth,

and Margaret was quicker than the servants to mop it up with her white napkin.

Gilbert's hostess simply slid her eyes towards him. *There, you see,* her eyes said, *this is what I have to put up with.*

As for Eden, he composed himself, if his clumsiness had, in fact, betrayed an emotion. "I appreciate your advice, sir," he said to Placide. "Of course, I will do what is best for the children." Then his glanced skimmed from one to another all around the table, as if he were gauging his audience. Who was impressed by his paternal devotion? Who admired him, who saw through him? The concern Helene had expressed for Eden when she had come to the clinic still puzzled Gilbert. Eden did not appear to be suffering from his loss so much as measuring the impression he created and calculating its gain to him.

✛ ✛ ✛

So Gilbert relayed the story to me on his return home, revealing, as well, an odd impression he had formed of himself as a poseur, much like Eden or any of the others there that night at Testament.

"I dismissed Dr. Baldwin's question regarding an unseen realm," Gilbert said. "But suppose I were only pretending to be skeptical of what I can't see because I lack sufficient magnification?"

Didn't we all feel that lack, some time or another? Gilbert's notions about the spiritual and the occult, like mine, were colored by our personal inclinations—mixtures of rote indoctrination, rational thought, and human need. Gilbert accepted that his wife and infant son had passed, yet he admitted imagining them still in existence, just out of his line of sight, in the next room, or at home while he went to work. Such thoughts, once a comfort to him, had lately come to disturb him, for he worried that Estelle and their child were not at peace, that his moving from Baltimore to New Orleans had disrupted them. But I believed it more likely that my brother, himself, was not at peace.

"We cannot choose whom we will survive," I murmured, my thoughts veering towards the phantom memory of a long-lost lover.

"Unless we, ourselves, take their lives." Gilbert's words returned me to the sensory world of parlor sofa and fireside, the scent of smoke and taste of brandy—and the subject of our speculation.

What had influenced the guests at Testament to gather for a séance? Was the answer anything beyond their indulging Helene or ingratiating themselves to her? Judge Placide, who had owned, controlled, and disposed of countless lives, despite his bluster, still fretted over his own mortality. Gilbert had heard the worry jangling in the judge's throat while the old man prodded Gilbert for information about a neighboring planter. *You do the doctoring for Pritchard's field hands, don't you? How many did he have working for him this harvest? Not so many as last time, I'll wager. And a sickly bunch, too. Old bastard's in trouble. Duvall, you find out about that lawsuit hanging over his head. Don't delay. I'll buy him out before the New Year.* On and on, as if the more Judge Placide acquired, the more he owned, the longer he would live, the longer he could delay leaving his soul to the mercy of his wife's psychic powers. Everyone at the dining table—the dissipated judge, the aging doctor, the drunken colonel, the restless wife and the vain one, the would-be murderer—and Gilbert, himself—all of them indulged in wishful thinking, wanting something to be true that could not be. World-weary or gullible or sick with longing, are we not all tantalized by what lies beyond our reach? Therein, that night, lay the allure of the in-between, therein the opportunity for Helene Placide to reign supreme over the next table. I urged Gilbert to continue his tale.

Chapter Thirty

Like animate shadows, the servants had peeled themselves from the dining room walls of Testament and come forward to the lighted table to clear the remains of the blancmange. Helene rose, and all the gentlemen, respectfully, did likewise, her husband more or less leaning forward from his chair. After such a feast, his full levitation required the aid of a manservant at each elbow. Then, as Helene glided from the table and towards the door, the freckled young maid, who had accompanied her to Gilbert's clinic, caught up to her, bearing a lamp to light her mistress's way. All evening the servants had anticipated and fulfilled the unspoken requirements of the Placides as smoothly as if the one were the familiar of the other.

In the doorway, Helene paused to address her friend: "Margaret, give me a moment to compose myself before you bring in the others."

When the moment had passed, everyone prepared to go with Margaret, except Colonel Duvall, who resumed his seat at the dinner table with a tumbler of whiskey and a cigar. Margaret looped one of her arms with Eden's and one with Gilbert's, and they preceded Dr. Baldwin and Judge Placide out of the dining room through the wide double doorway and across the lavish grand parlor. But, as they approached the narrow doorway leading into a small adjacent back parlor, or withdrawing room, Margaret released the gentlemen's arms, so that they passed through single-file—the lady, Eden, and Gilbert.

The room was dense with furniture too large for the space—a round mahogany pedestal table with six matching chairs, the seats upholstered in a velvet redder and darker than the wood. On the table, burned three candles in a low, branched brass holder. On the long, ornately carved sideboard against the wall, just behind where the hostess in her black silk gown sat at the table, a silver candelabra held three more burning candles, whose light, reflected in the mirror above the sideboard, created a golden aura behind the lady's upswept henna-colored hair. The flames, themselves, flickered and fed on the air, as if combining efforts with the heavy furnishings to suffocate the life out of the room.

Just beyond the pools of candlelight, the four corners of the darkly paneled room were blackened by shadows of the backs of chairs and of heads and shoulders as the guests took their places. As before, Eden sat at Helene's right hand, Gilbert at her left. Judge Placide, whom Gilbert had steadied when the man took his chair, was on Gilbert's left, Margaret next to him and exactly opposite Helene, then Dr. Baldwin between her and Eden. Full circle. Helene had determined the pattern as if she were arranging tokens on a game board. Then she asked the others to be silent and settle themselves for what would follow.

As the others prepared themselves—or pretended to—for communion with the other side, Gilbert adjusted himself slightly forward in his chair to catch a glimpse beyond Helene's profile of Eden's expressionless face, his gray eyes that met no one else's eyes. If Eden thought he had gotten away with murder, why had he come to a séance, where his victim might speak through the medium and accuse him? Likely, he was not in a position to refuse his hostess, the wife of his patron. If he were a disbeliever of the supernatural, Eden would sense no particular threat to himself. But only Gilbert, of all those gathered, knew for certain that Charlotte's ghost would not cross over nor materialize nor speak through the spirit medium to name her poisoner.

"We have come together this night to call Charlotte Eden back again to our world." Helene's voice was even more euphonious than it had been when coaxing Gilbert at his clinic to bring some personal item of Charlotte's to the table. "Dear friends, before we join hands to summon the departed, I ask Dr. Crew to place on the table an object that belonged to Charlotte, something that was close to her when she passed."

All of them watched him as he slipped a hand into his pocket and drew out the item, which he kept concealed in his palm while placing it near the candles centered on the table. Gilbert observed the others in turn, Victor Eden sitting rigid with mouth pinched and jaw set, Dr. Baldwin leaning in and squinting through his silvery-rimmed spectacles, Margaret Duvall half-arched from her chair, Judge Placide scowling and tapping a fat finger on the tabletop. Beside Gilbert, his hostess appeared serene until he withdrew his hand from the object, leaving it in view. In that moment, he heard her sharp intake of breath and sensed a current running through the others—perplexity, fearfulness, recognition —but was unsure to whom he should assign the responses circling the table.

"Well, what is it?" Dr. Baldwin asked. "It's so dark in here."

"A little medicine bottle," Margaret said. "That's what it looks like."

"Or a perfume bottle," Eden murmured.

"Or a vial of poison," said Judge Placide, his upper lip curling high above his teeth as he pronounced the word *vial.*

"Royce!" Helene started, her composure momentarily disturbed.

The judge snapped back: "That's the talk—why her spirit is so damned restless."

"Restless, indeed," Helene said, recovering herself, though not her honeyed tone.

Despite the brief flare of heat between the Placides, and despite the closeness of the chamber, a chill descended on the table, like a draft of air traveling over ice—which it might have been. Margaret shivered and rubbed her shoulders.

Dr. Baldwin cleared his throat before defending his medical opinion. "Now, we're not saying Mrs. Eden took poison. Nobody's saying that, judge. It was her weak heart. Victor, I tell you, it was her heart."

Eden nodded to Baldwin.

Helene took up the brown ridged-glass vial, stoppered with a bit of cork, and slowly turned it in her fingers, holding it up to the candlelight. Gilbert had emptied its contents into another bottle and refilled the vial halfway with cold tea. She tilted the little bottle one way and the other before replacing it on the table.

"We will join hands," she said.

In Gilbert's right hand, Helene's palm was cool, smooth, dry, a contrast to her husband's damp paw in Gilbert's left hand. Helene's gaze fixed on the candles burning in front of her, and she took her time over her words: "I asked Dr. Crew to choose an object from among the departed's things, something personal. But I tell you all, this object, this little vial, was new to Charlotte Eden. Oh, she may have taken it from someone, or someone may have given it to her—but it was not intimately hers. We will ask Charlotte to tell us the truth about her passing and to say her farewells to her husband. And we must not frighten her"—here Helene shot a glance at the judge. "We must welcome Charlotte."

As Helene's grasp tightened over Gilbert's hand, the stone in one of her rings cut into one of his fingers. Over the knuckles of his other hand, the judge's weighed like a slab of lard. Helene, as spirit guide, closed her eyes and let her audience wait. In time, her head and neck began to sway in a tiny orbit above her shoulders. When she spoke again, her voice floated from her, but not towards anyone in the room: "Come to the warmth and the light. Come to us, dear Charlotte. We invite you."

"Yes, we invite you," Margaret echoed Helene. "Come to

the candlelight."

A little time elapsed in which nothing happened. Even a single minute of nothing can seem long. Gilbert combatted his growing restlessness and a desire to pull his hand free of the judge's to push back the hair fallen across his forehead, strands of which had begun to tickle his left eyelid, by listening to and concentrating on the breathing of the others at the table. Judge Placide's somewhat labored respiration caught, now and again, in combining an exhalation with a low, rumbling belch. The air whistled faintly within Dr. Baldwin's sinus cavities, creating a hollow sound. Margaret's breathing hinted at congestion, as if she were coming down with a cold. Eden's breathing remained inaudible, while Helene's deepened with her trance, her nostrils flaring and her bosom rising and cresting with each inhalation.

Tapping sounded somewhere near Helene, but Gilbert could detect no movement on her part, no rustling of her skirts or shifting of her feet. The circle of clasped hands remained unbroken, even as the judge's hand shifted and cuffed Gilbert's left wrist. Helene's fingers curled over Gilbert's right hand and stroked his palm. "Charlotte, I feel your distress," she said. "Be calm, be calm," she chanted. "Oh!" Helene doubled forward as if in sudden pain. Then, she arched back against her chair, drew in her breath, and exhaled with a moan. "Oh, Charlotte, what troubles you so? Tell us, that we may help you find peace."

A scratching noise began, as of fingernails against a hard surface. Whatever contrivance produced the present sound, Gilbert tensed, imaging what it would have been like for Charlotte if she had waked within the pine box and clawed desperately at the closed lid, inches above her face. Eden, like Helene, had shut his eyes. Was he, too, picturing Charlotte, poisoned and trapped in a coffin? Baldwin stared at the candle flames, his mouth quivering as much as they. Placide frowned. Margaret had darted her glance from one to another, as had Gilbert, until their eyes met, and she almost smiled at him before looking away.

A muffled tapping sound replaced the scratching. Helene groaned, then parted her lips and thrust her tongue to the roof of her mouth and out, in and out, she repeated the motion. Truly, she must have been in a trance to allow herself to be seen doing such an inelegant thing. Gilbert, on her left, turned his face to watch her, and just to her right, saw Eden watching her, too, his eyes now wide open with an expression Gilbert interpreted as disgust.

Helene's tongue retreated from sight, and she swallowed. "Bitter. Oh, so bitter . . . I am cold and wet," she mewled. "I am pulled into the water, tangled—caught! No, I can't cross over. They're all around me, all around me . . ." Her voice had risen with the last words, and the tapping grew louder and faster until it pounded with the rhythm of a galloping horse.

Helene called out: "Charlotte! Can you hear me? Have I lost you?" Then she answered herself in a voice not quite her own: "No, ma'am, Miss Charlotte can't hear nothing. We's crowded on the bank. So many of us." Shrillness rose in the voice. "Miss Charlotte can't get by. Too many, too many in the way!"

The low, steady sound of galloping reverberated around the room. Eden shifted his eyes from side to side, Baldwin leaned back for a furtive peek under the table, while Margaret continued transfixed by Helene's performance. Placide scowled, his face turning a malignant shade of purple.

"We's all here, sir," Helene's spirit voice piped. "All around you, and Miss Charlotte can't get by."

"Who has surrounded her?" Eden said, his voice oddly level, as if he expected a reasonable reply.

The galloping sound ceased. Then, the spirit voice, this time whispery thin, answered: "No one. Gone. All those bare, brown legs running for the riverside, crossing over Jordan."

Judge Placide shoved Gilbert's hand away, then Placide gripped the table edge, tilting the table as he rose, causing the candle wax to spill and run towards him and the brown vial to topple and roll. With Gilbert's newly freed hand, he caught the bottle and dropped it in his pocket.

"Enough," the judge declared. "Helene, wake yourself up, you hear me."

"Oh, now, judge." Margaret was on her feet beside him, patting his arm. "Careful—Helene is in her trance," she whispered. "You heard her. She called Charlotte, no one else. But she can't control who answers."

The circle had come apart. The judge, breaking out first, huffed his breath and bumped into chairs on his way out of the dark little parlor, followed by Margaret, speaking to him in placating tones, and Dr. Baldwin, coughing into his handkerchief. But Helene took her time, keeping hold of Eden on one side and Gilbert on the other, while she returned from wherever she had gone. She blinked and shook her head and looked convincingly surprised. The mind could play such tricks.

Slowly, Helene turned to Eden, saying: "Victor, did she answer? Did she? Has Charlotte found peace?"

"I don't think so," Eden replied, "any more than I have."

Chapter Thirty-One

Did any of them truly believe in Helene's power? Possibly Dr. Baldwin and Margaret Duvall. But of what did that power consist? Of something more material than spiritual, I was sure, which had brought them to Testament to humor their rich and eccentric hostess, wife of the eminent Judge Placide. A good thing Bartholomew passed when he did, for I had not the disposition for socializing with such friends of his.

As Gilbert continued his account of the séance and its aftermath, he recollected with a trace of amusement: "Watching the Placides, I was reminded of the story that sent a pair of little boys I treated for measles into fits of giggles. You know the one, Lenore. The emperor in his fine new clothes, who was really *naked*—how the boys squealed over that word—and nobody would tell the emperor the truth."

✝ ✝ ✝

Gilbert had hung back in the little parlor while the others moved into the next room, the grand parlor, peripherally aware of them on the other side of the open doorway, milling around, talking among themselves. Then he went to the long sideboard, ran a hand over the carved cabinetry, lightly drummed his fingers on the polished top.

"Come along, Dr. Crew."

Looking up at the sound of his name, he met his own face in the mirror above the sideboard and, behind his reflection, that of Helene. Gilbert turned and approached her, offering his compliments on her sensitivity to the unseen.

"It is a gift and a curse," she said, looking pleased. "Voices and images from beyond, all competing for my attention, to speak through me. Oh, I am quite exhausted." She laid a bejeweled hand on his sleeve, as if for support.

Margaret, who had just rejoined them in the little parlor, chimed in: "Of course, you are, dear Helene. You called up a host of spirits. Why, their racket filled the room. We all heard them. You must get some rest now. I'll help you up to bed."

"Yes, do." Helene sighed. "And tell me all about what happened during my trance."

The ladies departed the room, linked arms and crossed the parlor's expanse of thick, vine-patterned carpet. The men, including Gilbert, who had followed the ladies out, watched them pass. Then, just as the pair of them reached the frame of the open pocket doors, Helene tilted her head over one shoulder and called back: "Victor, we shall make another attempt. Rest assured."

Colonel Duvall removed the stub of a well-chewed, unlit cigar from his mouth and muttered close to Gilbert's ear: "Horseshit." Then the colonel limped off in the direction in which his wife and their hostess had disappeared.

Soon, Placide and Baldwin were on their way as well, the good doctor soothing his dyspeptic host and offering to bleed him for any number of conditions—angina pectoris, gout, irritable bowel—whatever ailed him. For Dr. Baldwin, the leech never went out of fashion.

When Eden and Gilbert were alone in the parlor, Eden was the first to speak, although without committing himself in any way: "What do you think of séances? Anything to them?"

Gilbert could be equally evasive. "My first experience with one. Before now, I might have said a séance could provide a little comfort to the bereaved."

"But there was no comfort here tonight," Eden said, pausing before his reflection in the mirror above the mantel and

234

smoothing his moustache with a fingertip. "I'm in a bind, you see. Mrs. Placide wishes to help me in her way—and a strange way, it is—and Judge Placide has already helped in other, more tangible ways. Introductions, contracts. I understand Dr. Baldwin has been similarly helpful to you in your profession."

"When I was new in town," Gilbert said. And the old doctor had taken a sizable percentage for a few referrals.

"I've learned that anyone not born in New Orleans is always new in town," Eden said.

Gilbert agreed with him, then searched for something else to say to draw him. But before he settled on a question, Eden spoke again.

"Dr. Crew, I'd like you to call at my mother's apartment to examine the children," Eden said, revealing that he was unaware that Gilbert or his sister called there nearly every day. "My mother sent me word they're a tad poorly."

"I'll go tomorrow." Here was Gilbert's opening. "And yourself, how are you keeping, Mr. Eden?"

Eden hesitated before answering: "In a way, I rather miss her—Charlotte." His tone seemed to indicate the thought had taken him by surprise. "We didn't see much of one another. Separate spheres, you know. But I was accustomed to her being there when I came home."

"You were often away," Gilbert said—leaving unsaid that he thought Eden took her for granted.

"A gentleman needs a wife and children," Eden said, "but they are not all he requires."

What else, then? Stereoscopic pictures? A bevy of fawning women? A mistress in a rented room?

"Then you're not entirely bereft without your wife," Gilbert baited him. "Mrs. Placide told me you were disconsolate." Eden almost smirked at that, so Gilbert believed.

"I may have given Mrs. Placide that impression," Eden replied vaguely.

"I beg your pardon?"

"She takes such an interest in my affairs, makes plans for me. A period of mourning buys me a little time, you see. But I'm bearing up."

"So you seem," Gilbert said.

"What was in the bottle, Dr. Crew?" Eden asked without a flicker of inflection.

"Don't you know, sir? It was among your wife's things."

"A lady has so many things in bottles and jars—perfumes, creams, powders. We don't see all that, do we?" Eden said. "A man sees a woman."

Yes, a man sees a woman. In that moment, what had been more abhorrent to Gilbert—the thought that this man, who had lived intimately with Charlotte, had harmed her? Or the thought that, given the chance, he might take her back for his use?

"Poison," Gilbert said, stretching the truth, for the contents of the vial could have been meant as a sedative. "As Judge Placide suggested. A botanical mixture."

Eden stared at him. "Then she—"

"Or someone else," Gilbert interjected, "who wished to make it appear that she had, leaving the bottle to be found among her personal effects."

"Surely not." Eden shook his head. "If not her heart—well, Charlotte was melancholy."

"With reason?" Gilbert asked.

"I don't appreciate your tone. Dr. Baldwin said her heart failed, and that's the end of it."

Eden left the parlor while Gilbert remained a few minutes longer, giving the other man time to go upstairs and to his room before Gilbert attempted to retire for the night.

Chapter Thirty-Two

I had misgivings about going to the theater on the same night that Gilbert attended the séance. Events at Testament and on the road—on the night I had been lost in *The Winter's Tale*—were too recent. But, at last, I had allowed Ambrose Parr to persuade me to accompany him, after having demurred on several occasions to his invitations. And Ella had urged me to enjoy myself while she would spend the evening with Charlotte, who was partial to Ella's companionship. Thus, on the night of Helene's performance in her back parlor, I found myself tucked beside Ambrose in a cramped theater box, viewing the production of a rival company that he wished to appraise.

The melodrama's hero displayed relentless combative skills, dispatching nearly every other man in the cast with his sword and dagger. "I'll steal him away, if I can," Ambrose whispered in my ear, "for a production of *Titus Andronicus*." But to my way of thinking, the leading man strutted and fretted too many hours upon the stage below us—skewering too many pouches of stage blood concealed in other actors' costumes. Laundering and mopping the mess he made would be the real drama after the final curtain.

I found the leading lady more diverting. "Of the teapot school of elocution," Ambrose remarked, and I took his meaning. With the hand of one arm placed on an ample hip, elbow sharply angled to form her handle, and the other arm extended, with hand palm up, to form her spout—the lady poured forth her lines, steaming with innuendo. Oh, how that image of her posing came back to me when Gilbert continued his tale of what transpired in the wee hours at Testament.

✠ ✠ ✠

The supernatural was seductive. Even the suggestion of it was seductive—even to sensible people, for it played on their hopes. When the object of desire was beyond reach, did we not reach out anyway, on the merest chance that we had mistaken what was impossible?

At Testament, such notions might have crossed Gilbert's mind, induced by the inclination of the evening, the calling to Charlotte's spirit. And now some essence of her seemed to linger in the bedroom where she had been laid out for dead. Gilbert's sister speculated that strong emotion might make the unseen palpable, and Ella vowed that spirit was strongest in places where souls had suffered—a slave market, a battleground, a sick room. Although Charlotte had not died in this room, Gilbert had suffered here, fearing her lost.

He paced the room, stopped, touched the delicately curved back of the dressing table chair, as Charlotte must have done when pulling out the chair before seating herself in front of the oval mirror, unpinning her hair, brushing the dark sheaf of it over one white shoulder. Gilbert went to the bed and lay fully dressed on top of the counterpane, his head on the feather pillow that had cushioned Charlotte's head, his hands crossed on his breast, as her hands had been crossed on her breast. But instead of passing into a sleeping death, he kept his eyes open, surveying the room, seeing what Charlotte might have seen in lamplight and shadow before her eyes closed. The foot posts of the canopy bed loomed like a pair of gaunt sentries. Against the wall opposite the bed, an armoire stood, topped with wing-shaped crests on either side of the finial, the shapes repeated in silhouette above the furniture itself, shadows spreading up the wall and folding into the ceiling. When unconsciousness had overtaken Charlotte, carried her beyond the whisperings and rustlings in the room, the servants must have lifted her like a doll, removing her clothing, pulling the sleeves of the dressing gown over her limp arms, smoothing the sheet folded at her waist, spreading her hair across the pillow. Had either of them sensed the life remaining in her and said nothing—and only done what they were told to do?

The room was different now. Charlotte's toiletries were all gone from the dressing table, and the cup and saucer were gone from the bedside table, where the lamp now burned low. What had she drunk from that cup, so close at hand, that Eden had held to her lips? Drops from the vial mixed in the tisane? Gilbert tried to conjure the scent of the dregs in the cup, turn scent into taste, as if a ghost of bone china could linger in a room and give up its secret.

Sleep in that room seemed impossible for him. Gilbert turned up the lamp and propped himself with pillows to pass the night somehow—forcing his attention away from Charlotte and towards reviewing case notes he had brought along, then reading a new volume on the treatment of fevers. For a few hours, he lost himself but was recalled by—of all things—a tapping sound. The book he held jumped in his hands and fell to the floor. Surely, he had dozed off at last and been startled awake by a dream. No. The tapping came again, soft but distinct at the door.

The sound grew sharper, more insistent as Gilbert crossed the room, ceasing abruptly as he placed his hand on the door latch. Should he call out *who's there?* to something he lately dreamed, or pull open the door to an actual visitor waiting? Neither. He felt the handle move against his palm, moved by pressure from outside the room. He let go, stepped back, and watched the door swing open towards him. The lamp on the table within the room shone its light on the figure in the doorway, on the powder-white face of Helene Placide. In a forest green dressing gown, with hennaed hair loose about her shoulders, she disconcerted him even more than she had on her arrival at his clinic in her black silk and mourning veil.

"Praise be, you're up, Dr. Crew. I saw your light over the transom." She had come without a candle, herself, without a light of her own, knowing her house in the dark.

"Is something the matter, Mrs. Placide?" Gilbert asked, taking a step forward, blocking her entrance into the bedroom, at which moment she snatched his arm and pulled him with her into the corridor.

"Oh, yes, indeed," she whispered. "Come with me."

"Where is the judge?" Gilbert darted a look up and down the passage. "Is he unwell?"

"Dead to the world," Helene replied. "While the dead may well be stirring."

"What—"

"Oh, the man's snoring, fit to shake the walls. I gave up trying to sleep and was up, looking out my window, when I saw something—a pale shape flitting across the lawn."

"A person?"

"I couldn't say. It was so very quick—then disappeared into the garden."

That was the way with revenants, wasn't it?—shying from light and from close inspection. Nothing to hold onto. Nothing that could be proved or disproved.

Helene conducted Gilbert towards the back stairs, continuing her whispering: "What if it's Charlotte trying to get back, to reach Victor, communicate with us? I called her. Perhaps she has made her way, after all, through the veil. Oh, you must come and tell me what you see."

Tactfully, Gilbert objected: "But Mrs. Placide, if you couldn't make it out, when you are far more experienced than I in perceiving visitors from the spirit world—"

"In my trance state, yes, but this is another matter. We must investigate this phenomenon. And you must be with me. I rely on you, sir, to be my witness—my strength if I should faint."

240

His hostess, who hardly seemed on the verge of a swoon, knew her way over the expanse of her shadowy grounds as well as she knew it through her darkened labyrinth of corridors and chambers. Stirred by curiosity and suspicion, Gilbert accompanied her in the middle of the night through the back of the house and across the damp lawn. Avoiding the gravel path, they traveled silently over the grass, Helene clinging fast to his arm, making him uncomfortably aware, even through the drapery of her dressing gown, of her uncorseted contours pressed against his side.

They entered the main garden through an arbor covered in wisteria—a different approach from the one Gilbert had taken in the afternoon past the live oaks, shrubbery, and dimpled cherubs. Suddenly, Helene stopped and pointed ahead of them to a pale, irregular shape, floating above the ground but making no progress in any direction. Gilbert asked her to wait while he intended to go forward without her to discover the meaning of the shape, but she would not leave him. They took another few steps, and then Gilbert was sure, if he had ever been in doubt, that the thing was no apparition suspended on the night air but a length of cloth. A lady's fringed shawl, he decided on closer examination, draped over or caught on the dark hedge of pyracantha.

Gilbert had no sooner detached the silken shawl from the hedge branches that had snagged it than Helene snatched it from him. She ran the length of it through her hands, then shook the material with such violence that he wondered if she were not only assuring herself of the shawl's tangible qualities, but also attempting to shake out any little goblins hiding in its folds. At last, she laid the empty shawl over one of her shoulders.

"Well, then," Gilbert said, his words both vague and final, indicating the foray into the garden had reached its conclusion. He took hold of one of Helene's elbows, careful to maintain some distance from the rest of her, intending to turn them both back towards the house, but Helene, instead, turned abruptly into him,

241

her pendulous breasts swinging into his ribcage, as with her free hand she grasped his lapel.

"Oh, no," she whispered into his sternum, with which her face was level, "we must go on. There may be more to discover."

In the uncertainty of darkness, and in the suddenness of her turning, Helene may have miscalculated where she would arrive. Gilbert ingenuously chose to assume so. He released her elbow and retreated from her, but one end of the pale fringed shawl that lay over her shoulder clung to the rough wool of his jacket, and the fabric was, momentarily, suspended between them.

"Mrs. Placide, I will go on, but you must wait here."

"But I insist on—"

"No, ma'am. I insist. Wait while I go up ahead. If the shawl's owner has met with any harm, then I, not you, should be the first upon the scene. Wait here—for your own safety."

When he was some distance from her, Gilbert glanced back to make sure she had stayed put but could hardly make her out—only the dangling length of the light shawl indicated where she stood. As he progressed along the hedge, various explanations for the shawl in the garden darted through his mind. It might have been left there by anyone at any time, not necessarily that night. Or if tonight, it could have been planted, perhaps by a practical joker among the guests, to excite, then disappoint Helene on her quest for spirits. Could Colonel Duvall be the culprit with a secret sense of humor, or enough drink in him? Then again, Gilbert's warning to Helene, that someone might have met with an accident or foul play, could be the truth. Or what if Helene, herself, had tossed her own shawl into the hedge and then come to him with her story? To what purpose? Had she, in want of attention, come to his room in her dressing gown, in the middle of the night, to lure him into the garden? And then—Gilbert stopped before a break in the hedge.

From somewhere ahead of him, came a low, steadily grinding sound. He took one more step, just far enough to see past the last shrub in the dense hedge. By the half-light of a half-moon, Gilbert saw what he already knew to be in that particular part of the garden: the marble water maiden and the curving wall around the lily pond, encircling the statue and encircled by a path of crushed stone and oyster shells. Only then, he saw what had not been there on his stroll in the afternoon. On the rim of the low wall, feminine hands were braced, slender fingers splayed, supporting a woman who was bent far forward from the waist. Her fair hair swayed and swung loose over her bent head. Her white nightgown, bunched above her waist and fallen towards her shoulders, left exposed her pale legs and buttocks. Behind her, stood a tall man, his dark suit in some disarray. He gripped the woman by her waist and pounded himself against her in an earthly act no spectral being could perform. The man's boots were the source of the grinding sound, the soles churning the gravel, as the man thrust himself into the woman.

When a black gauze of cloud covered the moon, obscuring the pair by the lily pond from view, still the night hardly muffled the sound of them. Their panting quickened in the darkness, their moaning rose to its crescendo and died away. Then the clouds slipped by. Moonlight shone again briefly on the woman's nakedness before the nightgown fell over her legs as she straightened her back. The man offered her no lingering caress. Finished with her, he simply turned away and was buttoning his trousers.

How fortunate that Helene had asked Gilbert, not Duvall, to escort her into the garden. Fortunate, too, that he had gone alone to discover Eden, who claimed to rather miss his wife, finding consolation with the obliging Mrs. Duvall. But, as Eden had remarked, a wife and children were not all he required. Eden's coupling with Margaret confirmed how little Eden had regarded his marriage, how little he mourned, and how easily he could use a foolish woman, discontent with her own husband. Gilbert was disgusted by Eden. Perhaps appalled at himself, too, for an undeniable feeling of arousal at that brief glimpse of Margaret's pallid body, not wanting her—yet reminded of his wanting. He would never confess as much to his sister, but his flushed face and his faltering over telling details of the night would speak volumes to her.

Chapter Thirty-Three

Gilbert withdrew along the hedgerow, the way he had come, dreading his next encounter with Helene. The night had grown cooler, a light wind stirring through the upper branches of the live oaks. Helene had wrapped the shawl around her and shivered as Gilbert approached her.

"Oh, I thought you were never coming back," she cried. "What did you see?"

Panting to hear his answer, she darted at him, but Gilbert avoided a collision, catching her by the shoulders and holding her at arm's length. "We should go back to the house, Mrs. Placide," he said. "Please, ma'am, if you will, lead the way." With a slight pressure of his hands on her shoulders, he rotated her counterclockwise towards the house, lifting his right arm over her head as she passed under it, then releasing her. The memory of a dance pattern his sister had taught him long ago flared like a firefly of the mind, then disappeared. Helene hesitated after he let go of her, but when he did not come forward to take her arm, she complied with his request.

Following her across the dark lawn, Gilbert wondered what to say when they reached the house, when she would demand to know what he had seen in the garden. Not an easy situation for him, for Gilbert had been strictly brought up by respectable parents. Mother had been a schoolteacher before her marriage to

Father, who had held to meticulous standards in both his profession as pharmacist and his role as head of the family. Gilbert's boyhood had been a series of lessons, chores, and reprimands, fortified by Sabbath-day sermons, a perpetual reeling in of his disorganized energies, and then a careful spinning out of them in what Father and Mother deemed constructive endeavors. Not an exciting household by any definition, not until the war came, and his elder sister's exploits—eloping with a soldier, running off to nurse the wounded—had been a revelation to him. Then, in the years since the war, his few years of medical study and practice, Gilbert had certainly witnessed the multifariousness of human nature. He was not so much shocked by the scene in the garden as taken aback by the brazenness of it. Hadn't he witnessed the pantomime of Eden's private exchange with Margaret in the gazebo? Hadn't he seen how familiarly she had laid her gloved hand on Eden's arm at the cemetery? Of course, intimacy existed between them. But for how long, and was Charlotte aware of it?

Gilbert intended to tell Helene nothing, only calm her nerves and bid her goodnight. But inside the house, with no assistance from him, his hostess recovered from her shivering and breathlessness with remarkable swiftness and asserted her control by gripping one of his hands and pulling him after her through a maze of hallways and rooms. With his free hand, he groped for a wall, a door frame, any fixed object, disoriented by darkness and by their hurried pace, uncertain of where she was leading him. As they passed through a narrow doorway, Gilbert bumped his shoulder against the door frame, and Helene released his hand, moving ahead of him. Soon he heard clinking and rattling sounds, then a scraping, and he inhaled a whiff of sulphur as the match she struck caught fire. Helene lit a single candle in the three-branched holder, and its light confirmed that she had brought them to the back parlor, the scene of her séance.

This time, Helene seated herself, not at the table, but in a corner on a darkly upholstered settee. Looking up at him, she patted the space beside her and waited. Since the day he had piqued her interest with his story of the wreck on the river road, Helene had taken more notice of Gilbert than he ever would have invited. She patted the cushion again. He joined her on the settee, not as close as she had indicated, but angled towards her in a posture expressive of polite concern—meanwhile, wracking his brain for a civil way to extricate himself from her presence.

The candlelight shone on Helene's face. Her eyes widened and her fingers fluttered at her throat as she spoke: "Now you must tell me, Dr. Crew. Exactly, what did you see?"

With the scene still vivid in his mind's eye, Gilbert wisely said nothing—certainly not that he had seen Margaret fornicating in the garden with the man possessing, of all surnames, that of Eden. The name's connection to the book of *Genesis*, and Adam and Eve realizing their nakedness, led Gilbert to the recollection of another biblical story that had titillated him in his youth—and for which he had turned to his sister for a fuller explication of its meaning.

"You found no lady in need of rescue? Did you?" Helene leaned towards him. "If you had, you would not be here with me now."

"No, ma'am, I would not." But here he was, alone with Mrs. Placide, as awkwardly situated as Joseph with Potiphar's wife.

"You saw something. You mustn't withhold it from me," Helene said. "You've been changed by it, I sense that. Alarmed? Yes, your tone and your manner towards me are clearly changed." Her own tone was an odd mixture of chiding and wheedling, indicating Gilbert was a brute not to satisfy her curiosity. "Tell me everything, Dr. Crew." She laid her hand over his hand, which rested on his knee.

"Ma'am, I cannot."

"Oh?" She drew out the little word. "Was what you saw so strange—so *unearthly*? But if you can't describe it, sir, at the very least, share with me how it has affected you, the feeling aroused in you—for my researches, you understand, into the nature of the incorporeal."

Helene peered into his face, an expectant expression on her own. Gilbert set his jaw and refused to blink. Her histrionics irked him, and he was tempted to make up something to put an end to the interview—*Oh, Mrs. Placide, you stirred the spirits tonight. Yes, ma'am, indeed, you did. Why, I saw a dozen ghostly dancers performing high kicks on the rim of the fountain*—but one rash statement, one lie, could so quickly beget another and another. He might only intrigue her more. No, Helene would not be satisfied until she had taken possession of every detail of his supposed encounter with the uncanny and made it her own. "Mrs. Placide, I assure you, there was nothing in the garden that need concern you," Gilbert said with truthful conviction.

Helene withdrew her hand from his. "I don't believe you." Her voice carried as much conviction as had his own.

"Ma'am, I saw no ghosts, no phantasms, no— "

"You saw *something*," she accused him.

Gilbert did not respond.

"You saw somebody." This time she whispered.

A realization struck him then: he had not been her first choice of escort into the garden. What other man alone in his room had she gone to first? Surely not nearsighted Dr. Baldwin, however much devotion he professed for her. She had gone to Eden's room, hadn't she?, and not finding him there, had come to Gilbert. Gilbert could tell her that he had seen Eden by the fountain, and that Eden—in solitary contemplation, with only the marble water maiden for company—looked as if he did not wish to be disturbed. Although Gilbert had waited a bit too long to offer such an innocent explanation, he tried it anyway, no sooner beginning than Helene huffed, yanking the fringed shawl from her shoulders and wringing it in her hands.

"I know who this belongs to," she said. "It was mine before I gave it to Margaret."

"Who might have left it along the hedge, accidentally, at any time," Gilbert said with minimal inflection.

"Or left it as a signal of her whereabouts for a rendezvous," Helene snapped back. "You saw her with him, didn't you?" Helene had been very quick to reach that conclusion, but then, she knew both of them better than he did. "Why are you shielding Margaret?" she demanded. "Has she offered to meet you, as well?"

Gilbert got up and stepped away from Helene, the better to collect himself, to control the anger her words had sparked in him. "Mrs. Placide, that is uncalled for."

She rose from the settee, flinging down the shawl behind her. "They were together." Her voice dropped into a smoldering register: "You don't have to say, Dr. Crew—that much is written on your face." So Gilbert said nothing and let her read his face, if she could, in the shadows. She took a step towards him, and he immediately moved away from her to the far side of the round table, putting distance and the solidity of the tabletop, with the candle burning in its center, between them. "Well," Helene said with an exaggerated sigh, "I suppose you thought you were protecting me from—oh, from something unseemly." She paused, then added, "I appreciate that." Which was as close as she was likely to come to an apology for the offensive question she had thrown at him. "We shall say nothing about this, Dr. Crew, nothing about what you saw tonight. How can we? Colonel Duvall would *murder* Margaret."

"And Mr. Eden?" The question escaped Gilbert.

"I shudder to think. Call him out under the oaks. Challenge him to a duel."

And thereby, if the colonel's aim were true, rid Charlotte of her faithless husband.

"No, sir." Helene said. "We must be discreet, even if my houseguests are not."

"But the colonel already suspects his wife," Gilbert said.

"Oh? Did he tell you that?"

The heightened note of interest in her voice made Gilbert cautious in his reply: "It's my impression that he keeps a close eye on her."

"Oh, yes—when he isn't drinking," Helene said. "But tonight the colonel was well on his way to a stupor, so there's a chance he won't find out."

"About this occasion, but—" Gilbert stopped himself, even before Helene interrupted.

"But you don't understand, Dr. Crew. You don't know Mr. Eden as intimately as I do." Helene placed one hand on one hip. "Of course, Victor is a *man*—a man of appetites. But he is not himself just now, so recently bereaved." She extended her other hand, palm up and arm slightly bent, affecting the appearance of a teapot, as she served a drop of spite: "And Margaret can be such a ninny. Not the sort to inspire a grand passion, don't you agree?" Helene offered a pitying smile, then added, "I wish I could be shocked. I truly do."

"I thought you were shocked, Mrs. Placide."

"Upset—naturally, with the strain of the séance, disturbances in the night, knowing what you must have witnessed outside." Helene placed both her hands, palms down, on the tabletop. "But I tell you, I have seen things . . ." Here, she closed her eyes as if returning to her trance. "When Margaret and I went upstairs, she told me about the voices that came to me when we were gathered in this room. I know who they must have been in life. No wonder, Charlotte couldn't get through to us, couldn't get past them. They would have trampled her."

"With their galloping?" All that knocking and clattering within the sideboard. "Who were they?" Gilbert asked, dutifully, when he might have asked: who was Helene's accomplice? Was it Tansy, shut in the cabinet, a tighter fit than the makeshift coffin that had held Charlotte? And was she not content with simply making a rapping sound on cue with her knuckles, but she must kick her heels against the wood?

Helene's eyes snapped open. "Who do you think! All those brown legs in white stockings. They were my husband's fillies and, before that, my daddy's. You know I'm not talking about horse breeding." She made a low chortling noise deep in her throat, without parting her lips, a scornful sound.

The trance, the racket during the séance, had all been for effect. And now Helene expected him to believe that lost souls had crowded into her little parlor. Gilbert wanted no intimate knowledge of her family's shameful past. As she droned on to him, he ground the heel of his hand against his temple, as if he could rub out a pain starting there.

"I tell you, Dr. Crew, right here in this very room, they pranced for the gentlemen's pleasure, for the master and his guests. Round and round the table, they strutted—in nothing but those white silk stockings and garters. The special ones, you understand, who were never whipped. Master's orders. Oh, no, they must be unblemished, tender. They were raised like veal for his table, and he devoured them."

As Gilbert gripped the back of the chair nearest him, it must have bumped against the table edge. The burning candle's liquid wax sloshed, spilling over the rim of the cooler wax that had contained it and puddling on the table's surface. Gilbert was aware that slaveholders had been able to do what they liked with their property. He had heard and read accounts of exploitation and cruelty that had not ended with the war, but had altered and assumed other forms. Still, what Helene had just said to him was beyond anything he had ever heard from a lady of brief acquaintance. He wanted to ask her if she had ever intervened on the servants' behalf to spare them humiliation. Although she might not have done so as a girl, faced with her father's excesses, as a wife, could she not have had some influence on her husband? Gilbert could pity her if she had pitied those women. If her nerves were delicate now, if she were eccentric, unbalanced, he would understand that. How could any woman have grown up and lived in such a world as Helene had inhabited—first, with her father and then with her father's contemporary, who became her husband—and not have been affected by it?

Helene returned to her place on the settee and folded her hands in her lap. "The judge doesn't like to be reminded of what he can no longer get up to," she said. "Puts him in a foul temper, don't you know? But he had his day."

That was all? After conjuring a scene of debauchery in this very room, she had no more to say. Placide had had his day of raping the women he had owned and shared with his guests—as easily as he had passed around the whiskey decanter and the humidor—but now, an impotent old man, he had slowed down. Not quite the same thing as respecting another person's humanity.

Helene exhausted him, and he was tempted to walk out of the room, but forced himself to stay and remain quiet. Let a person ramble, and the person revealed more than if the listener interjected remarks. In Gilbert's profession, the speaker was usually a patient or patient's family member, but he was beginning to perceive the value of his method of listening to investigations of other sorts. However, in the immediate circumstance, fatigue had become an obstacle to his concentration. He leaned against the back of the chair, unwittingly fading in and out of awareness as Helene talked on and on, himself falling into a sort of trance, when he caught the sound of his name: "Dr. Crew?"

Gilbert blinked.

"Dr. Crew, I asked you a question." There was the tone, familiar from his schooldays, indicating he had not been paying attention. "Tell me, did you ever own a slave?"

"No, ma'am," he answered.

"Oh, but you were a little boy in those days, weren't you? What about your father?"

Gilbert shook his head.

"Didn't you ever want one of your very own?" Helene persisted.

"No, never."

"But you had a wife . . ."

Close as the room was, Gilbert felt cold, only cold, for weariness had dulled all other sensations. He could no longer keep Helene's face in focus, or quite catch all the words in the rise and fall of her voice, or formulate objections, spoken or not, to her remarks. She had become a dark, murmuring shape, sinking into the cushions.

". . . husbands may betray their wives with impunity," she said. "That's just how it is—while the wives suffer the shame of it. Suffer far worse than that, if they ever dare betray their husbands. So unfair, isn't it?"

Was Helene sympathetic to Margaret for reckless behavior? Not quite.

"My husband and the colonel are close, so I oblige Royce by taking Margaret as my friend. Still, I see her for what she is—the sort men trifle with, don't you agree? No better than she should be. We can't really blame Victor—a man who has lost his wife but not his appetite. You're a widower—haven't you ever filled a lonely hour?"

"Excuse me," Gilbert said.

"Come now, Dr. Crew. I asked you a simple question, and you tell me nothing. At the next séance, I'll have to call on the late

Mrs. Crew to learn anything at all about you. Here I am so open with you—baring my soul—and you keep yourself a secret."

"Ma'am, we were hardly acquainted before—"

"Charlotte's passing. But now you and I share a common interest in her sudden departure. We've formed an alliance, haven't we? And at the next séance, we may yet discover how Charlotte came to vanish."

Chapter Thirty-Four

At last, Helene took up the sputtering candle and led the way upstairs. Gilbert followed at some distance to avoid stepping on the trailing hem of her dressing gown. They encountered no one else in the passage. Eden and Margaret had already returned to the house, Gilbert supposed, retiring to their respective bedrooms, while he and Helene had still been closeted in the back parlor. All was quiet, so it seemed Margaret's return had not disturbed her husband's slumber, as Gilbert hoped Helene's would not disturb the judge's. Before they separated outside the door of his room, Helene turned to Gilbert and touched the tip of her forefinger first to her lips, then to his—a gesture signifying the shared bond of a secret between them, he chose to think, not the transfer of a kiss.

Alone, Gilbert threw his clothes over the dressing table chair, burrowed deep into the bed covers, and slept until daybreak. He woke hungry and curious about what might transpire at the breakfast table. How would Eden and Margaret behave towards one another under the watchful eye of Colonel Duvall? Would Duvall find confirmation of his suspicions in his wife's over-solicitous manner towards the widower, or in Eden's studied indifference to her? Would Helene let slip her knowledge of the garden rendezvous or Gilbert bear witness with his readable face?

Gilbert's appearance was hardly fit for scrutiny. The dark gray suit he wore again that morning was as rumpled as it had been when tossed aside a few hours earlier, and his cheeks were rough with stubble. He had forgotten to pack his shaving gear—or a comb and brush, he realized, upon rummaging through his valise. Raking a hand through his hair, then gathering up the few belongings he had remembered to bring, Gilbert started downstairs, careless of what his hosts and their guests might think of him. After all, he had come to Testament with the purpose of observing them, not being observed.

Entering the dining room, Gilbert found, to his disappointment, the only member of the *dramatis personae* present to observe was Judge Placide, the only other early riser who was not also a house servant. Nevertheless, Gilbert took a moment, standing just within the doorway, to study his host, seated at the far end of the room. He'd had his day, his wife had said. And had it brought him pleasure to demand and possess whatever he wanted from whomever he lusted after? It had if his pleasure were derived from power. And the judge still wielded power, if not prowess. Yet, in spite of Placide's controlling vantage point, his position at the head of his long table, his adiposity filling his throne of a chair, the judge might be unaware of any number of goings-on under his roof or out in his garden.

The judge looked up from his steaming platter of food, waved his laden fork, and called out to Gilbert, "Not leaving so soon, are you? Eat something before you go." He sounded in good spirits, quite the generous host this morning and none the worse for last night's bluster.

Gilbert set down his bags by the door and joined Placide at the table. Within moments, a stoop-shouldered servant appeared from a side door that led to a warming kitchen, bringing a hot plate of soft-cooked eggs, cheese grits, smoked ham, and feather biscuits, placing it in front of Gilbert. The man poured Gilbert a cup of coffee, too, and refilled the judge's cup before the judge waved him out of the room.

"Glad it's just the two of us," Placide said, continuing his meal. "Something I want to discuss with you, Dr. Crew."

Gilbert's first thought was that his host somehow knew about his nocturnal encounter with Helene and that Placide's seemingly amiable demeanor was his way of keeping Gilbert off guard before springing a trap. Had she told him, perhaps embellishing the tale? Or had someone else secretly observed them, even as Gilbert had observed Victor Eden with Margaret Duvall, and then reported back to the judge?

"Sir?" Gilbert said and waited.

The judge took his time, speaking through a mouthful of partially masticated ham and egg: "You interest me, young man. My lady-wife tells me that you show promise."

Gilbert took a swallow of coffee. The judge's words had been delivered in a confidential tone, and he followed them with an urging for Gilbert to dig in before his breakfast cooled. Placide hardly sounded as if he were about to accuse anyone of overfamiliarity with his wife. But a judge could toy with other people, if he so chose. Gilbert waited to hear more of where his host was leading before giving in to satisfying his appetite.

"Oh, Mrs. Placide will have her little gatherings and such, and who am I to say no to her?" The judge smiled benignly, the very model of an indulgent husband. "You called it, yourself, young man—some things are inexplicable." He gave Gilbert a knowing wink.

For a minute or two, the judge concentrated on breakfast, and Gilbert did the same.

Then, Placide started up again: "As I was saying, my wife's spiritualism is only one of her many talents—and not her most reliable. I tell you for sure, she has herself a real sense about flesh-and-blood folks. And she has brought you to my attention. Bright, vigorous young man, one to watch, so she told me."

As Judge Placide continued, he showed a surprising knowledge of Gilbert's professional and charitable work, his interests in preventative care and improvements in the compounding of medicines. Gilbert had not thought Placide's friend, Dr. Baldwin, particularly interested in his pursuits and wondered aloud how the judge had become aware of them.

"Oh, folks talk, tell me things," Placide answered vaguely. "I heard how you fixed up my far neighbor Morrison's field hands with some tonic of yours."

"I treated them for dysentery, sir."

"And didn't lose a one, and those hands didn't miss a day of harvest. Now *that* interests me." The judge explained that years ago, among his other wartime activities, he had grown crops of poppies for the Cause and, from that experience, had come to appreciate the art of concocting remedies of various sorts. "Patching up soldiers and getting them back on the battlefield was what mattered to the Old South," he said. "Patching up laborers and getting them back to work—in fields and factories, mines and lumber camps, and on the railroads—is what matters to the New South." Placide capitalized the last two words with his tone, as if he were speaking of the transformation of a separate country, distinct from the Union, and so it was for men of his ilk.

Gilbert buttered another biscuit, glanced towards the door, where still no one else entered, and waited to learn where Placide was leading.

"Your interest in the health of little children is all very noble—if not particularly lucrative," the judge said, dragging out the first syllable of the last word. "But I have a notion of using your talents on a new project of mine that you will find—shall we say?—enriching." Again, that dragging out of a last word. "After all, there is the possibility that you might want to marry again, set up a household of your own."

Gilbert lifted one brow to indicate his attentiveness but said nothing.

"Your late brother-in-law,"—Gilbert's third late brother-in-law, to be precise —"he and I had embarked on a business venture

258

about the time his cantankerous old heart gave out." Placide smiled, as if taking Gilbert into his confidence—both men sharing an understanding that Bartholomew James had been irascible. "But I," the judge went on, "have continued with those plans, which have proved rewarding, though they could be more so. Bringing you in now is a way of sharing part of the profits with my late partner's family, don't you see?"

"Does this mean my sister is not, at present, realizing any profit from her husband's final venture?" Gilbert asked.

"Now there's a shrewd question," said the judge, without answering it. "I didn't like to trouble Mrs. James when her bereavement was fresh upon her. And later, well, she appeared to think our project a bit too indelicate for her involvement. No doubt the lady had her point. After all, the business I speak of pertains to matters involving the criminal elements." Gilbert must have looked askance, for the judge next offered his wry assurance: "Oh, nothing illegal at our end, young man. Absolutely not!"—followed by an avuncular chuckle. "The venture includes the building and maintaining of new private prisons in our fair state and away in Alabama. I tell you, Dr. Crew, it is no small thing, housing and feeding a slew of lawbreakers. Damned expensive—allowing men to sit around the jailhouse, loafing at taxpayers' expense. But now, while we make the miscreants pay for their crimes, we make them work, and we make a profit doing it. That's where you come in—to patch them up and get them back to work."

"You want me to treat the prisoners, sir?"

"Indeed, I do, in a manner of speaking," said the judge. "And I am very interested to know how we can perk them up, get more work out of them. You make me a tonic for that and I'll—" He broke off, his attention diverted towards the doorway, through which Margaret Duvall had just passed.

Rising, Gilbert held a chair for her at the table. Her light, lusterless hair was neatly coiled and pinned on top of her head, and she was fully clothed, her brown pleated silk rustling as she crossed the room. Long, tight sleeves encased her arms, and a high collar with a cameo brooch covered her throat. Any awkwardness Gilbert may have revealed, looking at her in daylight while recalling her appearance by moonlight, went unnoticed by Margaret and the judge. They seemed more interested in exchanging pleasantries with each other—Placide abandoning whatever he had been saying to Gilbert, and Margaret remarking that, no, the colonel was not yet up, and she had seen no one else on her way downstairs. Then she stifled a little sneeze behind a dainty handkerchief. Perhaps she had caught a chill last night.

Gilbert, thanking Placide for his hospitality, left the table and took up his bag and valise by the doorway.

"We'll talk in town," the judge called to Gilbert. "Pity you'll miss the itinerant preacher this morning, coming to save my tenants' souls. Sermon's on the Tenth Commandment—*thou shalt not covet thy neighbor's*—oh, you know the rest."

Thy neighbor's house, wife, manservant, maidservant, ox, ass—*nor any thing that is thy neighbor's*. Yes, Gilbert knew the rest—including thy neighbor's land and crops and field hands. Judge Placide enjoyed his little jokes.

"So nice to see you, Dr. Crew," Margaret murmured, without looking in Gilbert's direction. She had buttered a biscuit and was holding it out to Placide, who bit into it directly from her offering hand.

Gilbert departed for home.

Chapter Thirty-Five

I combined my recollections of Testament with Gilbert's account of his time there among the Placides and their intimates—that peculiar, uncongenial circle—and felt my skin creep. Perhaps I was feeling again Judge Placide's breath on my neck as he had seated me at the card table for a game of faro in his grand parlor. And now Gilbert had experienced Helene Placide's back parlor game, her calling to inhabitants of another world—or to a servant who had something of a mind of her own. While Helene's spiritual powers might be based more on self-delusion than on psychic gift, my brother and I agreed, her protean nature, apparent to Gilbert in their late night conversation, had a force of its own. And by her coming to him in the night, she had led him to the garden and confirmation that Eden's knowledge of Margaret was carnal.

Charlotte wished to hear the outcome of Gilbert's trip to Testament on his return. Thus, in late afternoon, he and I came to her room, intending to tell her of the séance, nothing more.

We found Charlotte intent on a drawing, abrading the page with her pencil, deepening a shadow. Other sketches were everywhere around her—scattered on the nightstand, across the counterpane, and on the floor. All of them were variations of the theme in her sketchbook, depictions of curtains and bed clothes. Even so, lifting a page and turning it to the light at the window, this time I glimpsed other shapes, which I'd not noticed before in her drawings: the roundness of a shoulder within the pleat of a drape, the impression of a hand on a pillow, the contour of a leg in the ripple of a sheet. Even if I were only imagining the secrecy and sensuality within them, Gilbert need not see them. I gathered the

261

drawings, Charlotte's landscapes of the bedroom, and stacked them on the night stand, placing the top one facedown.

Then I urged Charlotte to put aside her sketchbook and move from the bed to the rocking chair, where I arranged a quilt over her lap. I seated myself in the ladder-back chair, while Gilbert remained standing. He took a moment to collect himself and checked his breast pocket, perhaps to be sure he had a clean handkerchief folded within, which he could offer Charlotte if she were brought to tears by anything he said.

Gilbert began with who had been present and who had participated in the séance, Charlotte giving him her full attention. Then he spoke of each person's deportment: "Mrs. Placide takes herself very seriously, and Dr. Baldwin and Mrs. Duvall have cast their lots with her. Judge Placide ended up aggravated by all the tapping and carrying on that night, but this morning he seemed to have dismissed the whole event. And Colonel Duvall, who didn't join in, is a thorough skeptic. No, the séance was not a success."

"How could it be?—if Mrs. Placide intended to call me back from the dead." Charlotte made perfect sense, her voice pleasantly mellow—but I heard its sardonic undertone. "Dr. Crew," she said, "you haven't mentioned my husband."

"Haven't I? Mr. Eden was accommodating enough to Mrs. Placide. However, in private, he admitted to me that his obligation to the judge is behind his humoring the judge's wife."

Charlotte nodded, and Gilbert looked thoughtful. I wondered if he would tell her what else her husband had said to him in private. I hoped not. What did a man like Eden mean when he said he rather missed his wife?—that he missed her services, the use of her, or simply noticed she was gone? Knowing what he had done later in the night to relieve his loneliness, I was offended for Charlotte's sake.

Charlotte gave Gilbert a speculative look. "Did he confess anything else to you?"

"He denied knowing anything about the bottle of poison," Gilbert said.

"Oh," she said. "He might have been telling you the truth."

Yet, if Eden were the man I took him for, with the forethought to keep the bruises he inflicted out of sight—well, poisoning, too, was an act of forethought.

"Do you still have no recollection of how the bottle came to be among your things?" Gilbert asked.

Charlotte looked away from him and towards me, and I saw her fingers curve over the arms of the rocking chair. I had asked her the same question in various ways, wondering if her answer would ever change. "That question again," she said, setting the chair in motion. "Did I know what was in the vial? How did I come by it? What of my frame of mind that evening? Had I looked forward to the trip, enjoyed the company?—before collapsing. You think I don't know where those questions lead?" The rapidity of her rocking increased with the sound of perturbation in her voice, and I put a hand on the arm of her chair to slow her down.

"We want to help you, Charlotte, and restore you to your children. And to that end, anything you remember, anything you know or suspect happened to you—tell us."

"Do you think I chose to drink poison, Mrs. James?" she said. "What good would I be then to my children?"

"The night Gilbert brought you here, we didn't know what had happened. I talked to him in generalities—not about you, in particular—but about women who, for various reasons, might take an elixir, or even an abortifacient, and end up *accidentally* poisoning themselves."

Charlotte shook her head.

"Or wives so unhappy that they momentarily forget all else, except a desire to put an end to their distress," I said.

Charlotte laid a hand over her heart.

"I told Lenore none of that pertained to you," Gilbert said, "that you would never—even if you knew for certain that your husband—" He stopped too late.

"That my husband what?" Charlotte stared at Gilbert.

He delayed answering her, crossed to the window and parted the curtain, revealing dappled sunlight through the loquat boughs. The longer he hesitated, the more tempted I was to intervene—was taking a breath to begin when Gilbert gently spoke to Charlotte: "I know you would never harm a child."

"Or myself, for that would harm my children. Even if my husband—*what*, Dr. Crew? Beat me?" At last, she had said it.

"Yes," Gilbert said. "Or if he broke your heart."

"How do you believe he would do that?"

"The usual way, I suppose," Gilbert said. "If he became entangled with someone else."

Charlotte fell silent. I thought of Helene's words, repeated to me by my brother: " . . . *husbands may betray their wives with impunity . . .That's just how it is—while the wives suffer the humiliation of it. But they suffer far worse than that, if they dare betray their husbands.*" Had Charlotte suffered Eden's infidelity, alone? Or had she ever given him cause for jealousy? Or had Eden only suspected that he had *drunk and seen the spider?*

"I'm so sorry, Mrs. Eden," Gilbert said.

"Then you know for certain. Is that the other thing my husband confessed to you?" That Gilbert had withheld from her earlier—I heard the implication in her question.

"He said nothing. I saw them together." But before Charlotte could ask him for details, if she intended to, Gilbert asked her if she had known of the affair before going to Testament.

"Maybe I did," she answered without intonation. "Maybe I expected as much sometime in married life."

Gilbert looked ill-at-ease, his glance darting towards me and back to Charlotte, before he spoke again, this time in seeming generalities of an unnamed wife and mother, devoted but in terrible despair. Mistreated by her husband, she might forget herself, might act against her better judgement. If such a thing were true of Charlotte, though she denied it, Gilbert was attempting to help her feel safe enough to confess it to us. "No one could blame her," he went on, "for she would not be responsible in the moment that despondency overtook her."

I understood him, for Gilbert had spoken to me of case histories that haunted him—a mother of four children who gave birth to a fifth and, shortly after, lost her mind; a father who came home from the foundry, ate supper with his family, then stepped into the alleyway behind the house and put a bullet through his head. Were these moral failings? My brother didn't believe so. Lungs could congest and cease to breathe, blood vessels could close and cease to carry blood, and brains could cloud and cease to reason. There had been a time when Gilbert, himself, had been nearly overtaken with melancholia.

"Is that what you think of me, Dr. Crew?" Charlotte said, and I was taken aback by a hardness in her voice. "Do you think that I am so weak and so simple that I could not see my way—for the sake of my children—past a man's infidelity?"

"No. No, of course, not," Gilbert said. "I only meant that if you had, temporarily—"

"Gone mad," Charlotte finished the sentence, perhaps not quite as he would have worded it. "And I will without my children,"—her voice fell as she looked past him, towards the fading light at the window.

I took Charlotte's point. In *The Winter's Tale*, Hermione did not know that her daughter had survived, but Charlotte knew her children needed her and she them. Gilbert and I could not hide her indefinitely—until little Amy grew to womanhood like Perdita—even if we were guarding Charlotte from a would-be murderer. Thoughts whirled in my head, one question chasing another. What had Eden to gain by the loss of Charlotte if, with no penalty, he were already enjoying his double life? Could Margaret, alone, have poisoned her lover's wife? Margaret was loose, possibly rather stupid, but was she also cruel? And where was her gain? Even if Eden were a widower, Margaret was Colonel Duvall's wife, so she and her lover would still carry on in secret. How were Gilbert and I to extricate Charlotte—and ourselves—from the morass we had now played a part in deepening, if not creating?

I felt Charlotte's glance flick across my face and then caught the last words of her sentence: ". . . strange, Mrs. Placide calling my spirit to cross over from the other side, when I'm really in between one place and another. I think of Ella, whose life's been far harder than mine."

"You're close to Ella," I said.

"I like her. When she tells me her stories—and I know she's making light of sad memories for my sake, she's that kindhearted—" Here, Charlotte smiled. "Even so, she contradicts my mother's teaching that black folks were better off under the old system. What a thing to tell me, to tell anyone—how could Mother have believed it? But she had."

"A lot of people did, still do," Gilbert said.

Charlotte looked at him. "Yes," she said. "My mother told me slaves didn't have to worry about food, shelter, clothing, or medicine—that was all taken care of for them by master and mistress. Not true for us in our little room in Mr. Keogh's building. She said that after the war, while the freedmen were bemoaning their loss of a sure thing and the gentry were pining for the loss of their elegant way of life, it was she—Mother—who was left weeping for what she never had. Not the essentials nor the niceties. She was widowed by the war, burdened with a daughter, reduced to sewing piecework until she went near-blind and starved—I must never forget her sacrifice." The last words sounded as if they had been forced past a stifled sob. She swallowed and went on: "I wanted to help, I told her, and she asked me how I was going do that. *Could I raise the dead?* she wanted to know. No. I could only raise myself, hardly that."

"I'm sorry," Gilbert whispered.

"All of a sudden," Charlotte said, "Mother died. I was away at work when it happened, when she brewed her last cup of tea. I guess you would say, Dr. Crew, that Mother forgot herself in a moment of despondency."

If Gilbert could have taken back those words he had said to Charlotte. He came towards her and dropped to one knee. "Charlotte," he called her by her given name, "I had no idea." The tears that had welled in her eyes while she spoke of her mother spilled down her cheeks. Gilbert offered his handkerchief, and as she took it from him, he repeated: "I had no idea."

"I know you didn't," Charlotte said, her tone holding an intimation of tenderness.

I rose from my chair, blinking away a sting of tears in my own eyes, and came to stand close by Charlotte, placing a comforting hand on her shoulder. Then Gilbert came to his feet and backed away towards the window.

Charlotte dried her tears, then spoke again: "I've told you this because I want you both to understand. When Mr. Eden came along, I was nothing but a poor, ignorant fool of girl."

"You are too hard on yourself," I said.

"No, Mrs. James. Victor took me as I was, even when others advised him not to. I don't know why he did—maybe I caught his fancy one particular afternoon—and then he was too gallant, or too stubborn, to take back his proposal. He gave me a home and the means to better myself. How could I not be grateful to him for such an opportunity? Who was I to have misgivings? Lord knows, I wanted to believe in improbable fortune."

The fortune in the palm of her hand and in the tarot cards—Charlotte had told me the same story she had told Gilbert

267

on the night he met her. How she had longed for a home and a family. For most of her childhood, she had been without her father, who was gone to war and lost to it. Then her mother lost, as well, and Charlotte, without guidance, barely sixteen, had married Eden—who had married her perhaps on a whim, as she suggested. Or as a show of independence from his patrons, which had not lasted. Although, I could also believe he had been charmed by her, even if he lacked the capacity for love.

"If we were ill-suited," Charlotte said, "he was still my chance to leave the attic on Toulouse and the hat shop on Royal. That shotgun house in Faubourg Marigny looked like Paradise to me. Four rooms, imagine that?"

Not a closet in Mr. Keogh's tenement.

"I'd walk up and down the hall counting them," Charlotte said. "Sitting room, bedroom, nursery, kitchen. The rooms were full of things to do—I polished furniture, swept floors, made beds, mended and ironed, baked and cooked. And every chance I could find, I read and read from books on Victor's shelves—my first learning beyond prayer book and primer." She paused, looked up at me, then said with more deliberation: "And I did what other women do to get by—to live—they trade with men."

Yes, they traded with men—traded their beauty, their fecundity, their labor for whatever the men decided these commodities were worth.

Charlotte set aside the quilt from her lap, rose from her chair, and walked to the window, her movements more than steady—graceful. Ella had told me Charlotte spent time pacing her room, sometimes the upper hall, building her strength.

"Victor wouldn't be the first man to regret his choice of a wife," Charlotte said.

Gilbert shook his head, and I heard him mutter *fool.*

"Victor wanted—expected—" She broke off, then began again, a different thought: "What you say you know about my husband—that you saw him with her—I want you to know what you discovered is such a little thing to me."

"How can that be?" Gilbert sounded incredulous.

"As long as my children are safe and well," she said, "the other is such a little thing."

Yet little things can grow, like monsters under the bed, more terrible for being out of sight.

"Surely, his behavior upsets you," I said. "You quarreled with him at Testament."

"But not about *her*," Charlotte said, without naming her rival for Eden's attention.

"He frightens you," Gilbert said. "I've felt it when I'm with you. He's mistreated you."

"What do you call mistreatment, Dr. Crew, of a wife by her husband?"

"If he were unkind," Gilbert said. "If he struck her. Made unseemly demands upon her."

"Tell us about your quarrel with Mr. Eden," I said to Charlotte. "What you remember."

Night had fallen as we talked, the lamps in the bedroom still unlit. Only the glow from a sconce down the hall entered through the open doorway, casting a band of soft light just over the threshold without reaching us. Darkness had moved from the corners of the room, settling around us, obscuring our faces from each other's views—the room shadowy as a confessional.

"I was on the staircase," Charlotte said, "when Victor came out of the parlor into the hall. He called up to me to fetch his rolls of plans from the bedroom and bring them to the judge's study, saying I'd better be careful with them, and I obeyed. Then, when I came to the study door, Victor was already with the judge and the colonel. Judge Placide asked me to step in, sounding friendly, but I felt embarrassed—shy of them, thinking they might be making fun of me."

269

"Would they?" I asked.

"The judge invited me to look at the plans—for a prison, hundreds of tiny cells. I was a little dizzy in my condition. And I thought about my old room and Mr. Keogh, and I could hardly breathe. You understand?" She was breathless as she spoke.

"Yes," Gilbert said, and I came to stand close by her at the darkening window.

Charlotte continued: "I said to the judge *couldn't the convicts have a little more space, sir?*, and the colonel said *whatever for?* But the judge chuckled. And then—then he said something about my husband being an expert in tight places and at boxing up things, saving him costs and materials. If the judge meant that as a compliment, Victor didn't look pleased. There was something vulgar, too, in the judge's tone. I excused myself and got out of there."

Charlotte drew breath to fill her lungs, then let it go. I found myself doing the same.

"I went out to the garden for some air," she said. "In a little while, Victor came out, too, and caught up with me, pulled me into the gazebo and told me I had no right to question his plans, especially to the judge. He said Judge Placide didn't care what I thought or what I felt. I was to bite my tongue and not say another word." Charlotte's voice broke off.

And then Eden had made sure his will was done. He had silenced her and boxed her up.

Chapter Thirty-Six

Later that night at the kitchen table, Gilbert and Ella shared a supper of red beans and rice while I shared only their conversation. Mr. Parr would call for me soon, and I was saving my appetite for oysters and champagne with him at Antoine's.

Gilbert was curious to learn more about the Placides, and Ella obliged with tales heard or overheard during her time as a cook at Testament and from gossip gleaned from one servant or another after she had left to run my household. "Discord at Testament go way back," Ella said. "Miss Helene's mother died young, and that gal grew up wild and willful. Got herself into trouble when she was maybe fifteen. That's when Judge Placide—forty-five, if he was a day—stepped up and married her, making sure her father deeded him house and goods, land and slaves, in the bargain. Her old daddy stayed on the place but didn't last long after that."

"But Placide should have married her if the child were his—" Gilbert said.

"Which it weren't. No, sir, Mr. Gil. Judge told outsiders the baby come early and died, but the house servants knew different. He put that child, a girl, out somewhere, maybe to another family. Must be about twenty or twenty-two by now, if she lived—and never knowing her kin."

Like Ella's own lost relatives, sold away before the war—the ones she and I had never been able to trace. Or like Perdita, abandoned in the wild, before she was reunited with her mother, Hermione.

"Judge Placide wouldn't be caught dead raising another man's child," Ella said, "nor none of his own that was mixed blood." So, in exchange for protecting Helene's reputation, the judge had taken control of everything her father had accumulated and then brought her a brood of stepchildren to raise, who were nearly as old as she. "To take her mind off losing her love-child," Ella added, "if you can believe that, sir."

"She had no children by the judge?" Gilbert asked.

"I heard she miscarried a time or two. And then that friend of hers, Mrs. Duvall, didn't want to show up the judge's wife having babies and spoil their little circle. Or spoil her figure. Ain't that right, Miss Lenore?" Ella turned to me.

"So Margaret intimated," I said, "back when Mr. James required me to socialize at Testament."

"And how did the flirtatious Mrs. Duvall manage that?" Gilbert asked me, but I nodded for Ella to answer.

"Oh, she told Miss Lenore just how," Ella said, "in case she was interested in the same—Dr. Baldwin kept Mrs. Duvall supplied with pessaries."

"Ah," Gilbert said, casting a sideways glance at me.

The door chime sounded, and I was on my way.

✛ ✛ ✛

"Ideas rise in your imagination like bubbles ascending a champagne flute," Ambrose said with a smile at me and a nod to the waiter replenishing our glasses.

Indeed, while my mind whirled with the secrets and suspicions I harbored regarding Charlotte's fate and her husband's actions, I had spent the evening spinning for Ambrose my notions for stage plays, asking his opinion on characters and scenes—breathing nothing to him of actual events. And while we lingered over our supper at a corner table, my charming companion did not burst my effervescent creativity. On the contrary, he encouraged me.

When I described the scene of a poor young girl nearly suffocating in a tiny garret, her hopes raised, then dashed by a

272

brooding lover, Ambrose exclaimed that he could see it all before him as a tragic opera. "With arias to break the heart in twain," he said, drawing my hand to his breast. I carried on, suggesting a ghost story performed behind a murky scrim, then followed with a drama of depravity and poisoning.

"Swordplay and stabbing, too," Ambrose said, "to excite and appall the audience. And, when I produce your masterpiece, I'll employ your brother as theater physician to attend the ladies when they faint."

Conversation with Ambrose was a respite for me from my worries over Gilbert and Charlotte and from all the bits and pieces of conversations with them and Ella that disquieted my mind. I had been struck by the coincidence of Helene marrying Placide when she was about the age Charlotte had been when marrying Eden. And Charlotte was now about twenty-two, the age Helene's lost daughter would be, if the girl survived. Could Charlotte be that daughter, given away to Mr. and Mrs. Varcy—or found by them—in a Shakespearean twist of fate? Hermione's baby daughter had been found and raised by a shepherd in The Winter's Tale. Suppose Helene suspected, or had discovered, Charlotte's identity?—which would explain Helene's interest in reaching across to contact her on the other side. A flight of fancy on my part, perhaps—and Helene was far from my notion of a Shakespearean heroine—but the idea might be worth jotting down in my notebook.

"Twins are a marvelous device for confusion, comedy, romance," Ambrose was saying as he signaled the waiter for another bottle of champagne. "You may well find inspiration, Lenore, in those twins of yours for one of your convoluted plots. Characters at cross-purposes, masqueraders, mistaken identities—" Ambrose held up his linen napkin, hiding his face, then whipped it aside, with the pronouncement: "The Curtain of Concealment drawn back by the Recognition of Truth! The stuff of theater, my dear audacious lady, and you will pen the script."

With that goal in mind, I sought Ambrose's advice about a complicated scene, the climax I envisioned for my play-in-progress on a stage crowded with actors. "How does one direct the attention of the audience to the essential action while they are taking in the breadth of the spectacle?" I asked.

To illustrate his explanation, Ambrose arranged and rearranged a cast of actors—represented by items of cutlery, the cruet set, silver napkin rings, and champagne flutes. Thus, I learned how an actor might be set apart by himself, or grouped with other actors set apart from the crowd, and moved down stage—in this case, a crystal flute and a dessert fork to the edge of the table—to captivate the audience's interest.

"Movement and countermovement," Ambrose said, "may balance or disrupt the balance of the scene"—here, a napkin ring suddenly rolled between the featured players—"and one creates a sort of dance with dialogue."

And while the audience might be guided artfully to focus on the words or gestures of a particular actor, something else might be happening on the stage at the same time, right in front of the audience's eyes, and go unseen until the deed was done—until it was too late.

Chapter Thirty-Seven

Gilbert, who had been skimming the *Picayune,* as he did daily for news of the upcoming presidential election, set the paper down beside the remains of his breakfast as I entered the dining room.

"I've been thinking," I said, joining him at the table. "Charlotte is much recovered and, despite all our assurances that Amy and Wilfred are safe, she's bound to go to her children. If they were not in Widow Eden's care, Charlotte would be with them right now—no matter the consequences to her safety."

I had not said anything that Gilbert did not already recognize, only what he preferred not to face, judging from the twist of his mouth before he spoke: "Then I'd better concentrate on uncovering the truth about Eden—all of it—posthaste."

"But if the worst you find is that he's a selfish brute—"

"Which he is," Gilbert interrupted.

"Once upon a time," I said, "not so very long ago—Victor Eden was Charlotte's rescuer, her way out of poverty."

"She fears him now," Gilbert said.

"And does she see you, Gil, as her next escape?"

My brother stared at me. "I brought Charlotte here for her protection—she isn't calculating."

"She has learned to be expedient," I reminded him. "Admitted as much, doing what other women do to get by. They trade with men."

Gilbert pushed back his chair from the table and rose. "Well, you know more about that than I," he said—not in heat, but with cold reserve.

While he had refrained from making any mention of my third husband and what I'd traded with Bartholomew James, I heard his implication. Gilbert was defensive of his feelings for Charlotte, I sensed that, too. In his shading of truth and circumstance, he must believe in her purity of heart to mitigate his guilt for so desiring her. Which he did in that way that makes the beloved all lovable and any fault in the beloved excusable or invisible.

I drew a calming breath, then said gently, "I'm concerned for you, Gilbert. Whatever any of us does next, I can't help feeling concern. I've seen her effect on you. For the past year, I've seen it. And I can't believe Charlotte hasn't seen it, too. Women know."

The ripple of discord between Gilbert and me did not immediately dissipate, but we managed to move along through the morning.

Only a few patients with minor ailments required Gilbert's attention in the clinic. Meanwhile, Dr. Clarke sent word that the two patients Gilbert had referred to him in the last week had been discharged from the hospital—no need for Gilbert to call in there. Thus, my brother found himself far ahead of the schedule he had sketched out to me. And I found myself with time before my afternoon plans to accompany him—first, to the shelter, where I lent him a hand with treatments for an hour or so, and then on to see Mr. Keogh, who might let slip something useful in our investigations of Eden's doings.

With my face concealed behind a heavy veil and figure beneath a voluminous cloak, my voice limited to murmurings, I allowed the boorish landlord to take me for the mystery woman with whom Dr. Crew was in negotiations. And Gilbert allowed himself to be taken for a young man not yet over fool's hill—not so far from the truth, I sighed inwardly.

After Gilbert let on that he and a certain lady were close to reaching an accord, Keogh offered a tour and the benefit of his opinions. He led us along the corridors of his better apartment building, a palace of luxury compared to the squalid tenement described to me by Gilbert, in which Keogh had crammed Charlotte and her mother. I hung back, behind my brother and the landlord, as if shy and unheeding of the men's conversation, but I caught the drift. The more Gilbert played the role of an affable young man embarking on an illicit affair with a married woman, the more forthcoming Keogh became. "Not at liberty to meet in your own place, eh?" he said with a wink and a nod. "Oh, I can help you there, sure enough."

The landlord rattled off a variety of services that he or fellows he knew and swore by might provide: delivering food and liquor to the room, running messages back and forth, keeping a lookout, keeping secrets. Dropping his voice, though not below my hearing, he went so far as to hint at services of a darker nature, of arranging for problems, small or large, to disappear. "No one the wiser," said Keogh. Of course, there were fees attached to every transaction. With so many possible expenses here, no wonder Eden had been stingy at home—demanding strict economy from the wife he deceived while pampering his mistress.

"Nothing out of the way about any that," Keogh said. "Paying for services rendered. Just ask the police and the lawyers—and the almighty judges, levying their *sin tax* on certain activities. The pleasure professions—know what I mean?" He tapped a forefinger to the side of his bulbous nose.

"Not sure I do," Gilbert said, widening his eyes ingenuously, prompting Keogh to elaborate on a convoluted system of graft, a sort of fascia supporting and binding the private underbelly of the city to its public body. But, of course, both my brother and I already knew that the city was constructed on the strata of old depravity paved over and over and over with new.

With a smoothness that surprised and impressed me, Gilbert led Keogh towards the topic of their mutual acquaintance. "I've the impression, sir, that Mr. Eden is very satisfied with your extra services." Having an impression was vague enough, I thought, and could be modified or retracted, if necessary, depending on how Keogh responded. In their first conversation, Keogh had asked if Eden had recommended him to Gilbert—and for what could Eden have recommended him if not for his rental properties and his discretion?

"Ah, he's a deep one. Him and his veiled lady." Keogh's volume increased with those words, which he cast in my direction. "Or does he have himself more than one? I haven't got a peek yet under the cloak and draperies—more's the pity." Keogh followed his speculation with a chortle. By this time, he had stopped outside a door at the end of an upper hall and was fumbling with a ring of keys, mumbling again to my brother. "If I'd had the chance years ago to give that gentleman a piece of friendly advice—and he'd taken it . . . ." Keogh tried several keys, unsuccessfully, in the lock before chancing on the one that fit. "Yes, sir, if Mr. Eden had listened to me, he would've married himself a rich lady with family connections. And he'd have set up little Miss Charlotte in a room like this here." The landlord pushed open the door on its creaking hinges to reveal a trysting chamber, the last he had available, so he informed us, and in high demand. "Damned lucky you stopped by today—this would've been gone tomorrow."

I didn't believe him. While Keogh remained in the doorway with Gilbert, telling him a tale about the room's former occupants giving up the place two days ago—falling out, so he said with a chuckle, over one or the other's peculiar appetites—I stepped inside. By a sliver of moat-filled light cutting in between the dark window curtains, I took in the condition of the chamber, certain it had been unoccupied and unaired for months. Silently, the stale atmosphere and dust-coated furniture contradicted the landlord's claim that the premises had just been vacated.

I wondered if the room in which Victor Eden kept assignations with his mistress were anything near as gloomy as the one I surveyed. Here, the wainscoting's black lacquer was scarred where a chair back or the iron bedstead had scraped against it, uncovering a pale gray undercoat. Gilbert's description of the gash marring Colonel Duvall's glossy black carriage door darted before my mind's eye.

Above the wainscoting, red and black vertical-striped wallpaper barred the walls almost up to the chipped crown molding, although, at that point, the paper had begun to curl away, surrendering to the city's perpetual damp. There were dark furnishings around the periphery of the room, shadowy things—a dressing table, chairs, washstand, chiffonier. And, on the opposite side of the bed from where I stood, there was the elongated oval of a framed mirror on a stand and, within the dingy glass, a mottled image of myself obscured in dark draperies. On the bed between me and my reflection, a counterpane lay over the contours of lumpy pillows and twisted sheets that hinted at the shapes of embracing lovers. I thought of Charlotte's sketches, her shadings from which the shapes appeared. And I imagined the tangle of hidden bedclothes, unwashed, stained and soured with the couple's dried sweat, the man's semen, perhaps the woman's blood. The counterpane's faded gold fringe hung crookedly over the edge of the mattress, partially concealing a pale something, a nightshirt or a shift, where it had fallen and been kicked away, halfway under the bed. All around me within the room, I sensed a lingering abandonment that was more than sexual.

Silence fell. Keogh had ceased his blathering to Gilbert, something about rents and terms. Even with my vision somewhat impaired by my veil, I had the impression that Keogh was waiting for my brother to answer a question. The landlord had cocked his large head and extended his right hand, palm up, adding emphasis to whatever he had just said, to which Gilbert had yet to reply. Perhaps taking Gilbert's hesitation as an attempt at bargaining, Keogh might have thought he were sweetening his offer by adding: "Tell you what, spend one night here with your lady-friend, just one night, sir—for a slight consideration." He rubbed thumb and fingers together as if feeling a bank note. "See how the two of you get on—you know what I mean? Then we'll see about longer terms. More than fair, don't you agree?"

With a low tsk, I registered my distain for that arrangement, and Gilbert stepped to my side. "Thank you for your time, Mr. Keogh," he said, then escorted me past the landlord and down the corridor towards the stairwell. We had both had enough.

Keogh labored to keep up with us, panting in pursuit in his attempt to seal a bargain. "Hold up now, hold up. I know about you young gents getting yourselves in too deep, falling short of ready money. I know a lender or two. And I can work with you, myself, on the rent, same as I've done for other gentleman. Take me an hour or two in trade, now and again, with your little lady-friend—wouldn't I just? I wager she's a real peach!" The disgusting man had spoken to Gilbert, as if I were nothing but a piece of stage property.

I was tempted to step aside at the end of the hall, perhaps to see Keogh trip on the frayed carpet and bump his way down to the bottom of the stairs—but Gilbert gripped my arm and whisked me away.

✢ ✢ ✢

My brother had hated the play-acting with Keogh, as had I—and to what end? What information had we actually gleaned from the garrulous landlord, for all his lewd insinuations? A late night walk in the gardens of Testament had given Gilbert the proof of Victor Eden's licentiousness. What we needed was proof that Eden had poisoned his wife, attempted to murder her, after their argument. Or, failing that, we needed his confession, whether he gave it through our designs or his folly. And then what? Gilbert and I walked briskly away from Keogh's properties, as if by accelerating our pace we could outdistance revulsion and frustration—leave them in some back alley traveled by Keogh's tenants.

As we neared our next destination, Widow Eden's apartment, I lifted my veil in time to catch sight of Amy and Wilfred, accompanied by Narcisse, in the small fenced park nearby, and pointed them out to Gilbert. The children, intent on rolling a red rubber ball and chasing after it, did not notice us, but Narcisse came to the open park gate.

"Sir, ma'am," Narcisse said with a nod to us, "Miz Eden be having one of her headaches. So I brought the children out to tire them out while she takes her lie-down."

"They look well. News of your good care will be a comfort to—" Gilbert stopped himself before saying *Charlotte*, substituting Eden's name at the last moment.

"If you think he be interested, sir," Narcisse replied.

Then, Wilfred, spotting Gilbert, squealed and ran towards my brother with a toddler's amazing mixture of forward propulsion and side-to-side motion. On arrival, he threw his arms around one of Gilbert's legs in the instant before the child would have lost his balance. Amy approached me, although with more reserve. With one arm wrapped around the ball, holding it to her, she slipped her free hand in mine. We all shared small talk and a few peppermints—to whet the appetite for supper, not to spoil it, Gilbert assured Narcisse.

Gilbert and I walked with the maid and the children to the door of the apartment building but did not go inside, only promised to call again tomorrow.

"Please, Dr. Crew," said Amy, "will you go to Father's house, too, and make sure Sergeant Hunter is catching mice for Mama?" So the stray cat Gilbert had brought them now bore a rank as well as a name.

"Bring him to play with me," Wilfred added, his eager smile and bobbing head a contrast to his sister's solemn mouth and earnest demeanor.

My brother looked thoughtful as we went on our way. Then, as we were near to parting, I for an afternoon musical gathering at home and Gilbert for a house call along the Irish Channel, he remarked: "Children lose it in stages—that spirit of playfulness, hopefulness—if they're ever allowed to have it."

"Yes," I said, "little by little."

Children embraced or surrendered to what they were taught or learned from observation, and, if they survived long enough, took up their tasks and accepted their disappointments. Of course, Amy and Wilfred were on Gilbert's mind, as were the Dunleavy girls awaiting him, I surmised. Gilbert had told me about his earlier visit to Widow Dunleavy's address along a street of blighted row houses, where he treated her girls, ages seven and eight, for mumps. Routine cases, nothing to worry over, he had told mother and daughters with confidence. As usual, he had offered advice regarding proper rest and hygiene, nourishing meals, and, when the girls were completely well, healthful exercise—prescriptions easier said than fulfilled in a household of scant resources. Widow Dunleavy made shirts by the dozens every week, working at home to support her daughters and keep them close. "My girls already sew on buttons and are learning to sew a straight hem. Bright as buttons, themselves—when they're well. Such a help to me," she had told Gilbert, "threading needles and tying off the last stitches when my eyes wear out."

Little time to be little. No wonder that Charlotte, who had worked throughout her own childhood, treasured the time she had found to paint and garden and play with her children.

Chapter Thirty-Eight

Returning home barely half an hour before my guests, who included Ambrose Parr, were expected for the afternoon's musical program, I was relieved to find preparations nearly complete. Ella and the daily maid had already arranged chairs in rows before the parlor spinet, laid out china and silver on the dining table, and were now in the process of setting out refreshments. Ella waved me away upstairs to change my dress, saying I wouldn't be needed until the doorbell chimed.

Hurrying along to the top of the stairs, I ran my gaze over the wall that paralleled the railing of the stairwell. There hung the portrait in oils of my youthful self with my precious little ones, Allan and Arabella—an idyllic composition of us sitting placidly on the grass under a willow, a picture book open on the lap of my billowing skirt and the children nestled in the folds of it on either side. Children were on my mind. As they were on Charlotte's. I'd seen her most recent sketches—glimpses of wide-eyed, childish faces peeking from the folds of curtains.

I had changed from my day dress to more aesthetic draperies—a tea gown of rippling emerald green silk—and freed a few curls from their hairpins to tumble over one shoulder, when a thought struck me. While Charlotte listened to the concert from upstairs, unseen by the guests, she might still find some pleasure in dressing for the occasion. From the back of the armoire, I took out another tea gown, one I had kept for sentiment's sake, having worn it after my second husband, Samuel, passed. I had designed it myself during my Pre-Raphaelite period. A vine pattern of gray-green velveteen leaves twined over the lavender fabric of the bodice and across the rounded neckline, finishing at one shoulder with a cluster of tiny purple velvet wisteria blossoms. A bit snug for me now at the high, gathered waist, but Charlotte was of slighter proportions, and the colors of the paneled skirt, watery blue-violet and dove gray, would suit her—those soft shades that ladies wear as they emerge from deep mourning into half-mourning—as they, themselves, gradually rejoin the world of the living.

Bringing the gown to her room, I found Charlotte dressed in her skirt and blouse and in the process of folding her other clothes, packing her carpetbag.

She turned to me. "I'm sorry, Miss Lenore. I must go to them. You understand?"

Yes, I understood. A woman without children could disappear, begin again elsewhere—but not a woman with children, whose heart was never again her own. However dastardly Eden had behaved towards Charlotte, a matter still in question, she would not abandon Amy and Wilfred.

Charlotte had thought to slip away during the afternoon concert, leaving a note for me. But what would she say to her husband?

"I plan to tell Victor that I was stunned and wandered away after the wreck," Charlotte said, "but have recovered myself."

"And if he harms you again?" I asked, standing there before her, the tea gown laid across my extended arms as if I were holding a fainted form—or the remains of a woman.

"I will ask for his mercy," Charlotte said. "I would live as a nursemaid in Victor's house to be near my children." Was this an overstatement spoken with the sincerity of motherly devotion? No, she meant what she was saying. "The others wouldn't notice me as a servant. Victor could do as he pleases. The widower. I wouldn't trouble him." Charlotte paused, perhaps reflecting on where her odd solution might lead. "He could divorce me, secretly," she said, "and I would stay in his house, as secret as I am here, and take care of Amy and Wilfred."

I could hardly begin to raise my objections: she had already lived as maid-of-all-work in Eden's house. If he divorced her, her position would become even more precarious than it had been, and her proximity to her children could be gone at any moment at his choosing. Wife and children were the man's property.

"If only I can bargain with him," Charlotte said.

"Wait," I said. "I beg you to wait—give me time to think of something." Which I did, on the spot, with no idea if I could accomplish it. "I'll go to Widow Eden first thing tomorrow—yes, that's it. I'll invite the children here to give her a rest, I'll take them with me right there and then and bring them to you."

"And when Victor finds out they're here?" Charlotte said.

"Oh, we'll worry about him day after tomorrow."

With Charlotte's assurance that she would delay her flight, and my promise to deliver the children, I left her. And I left the tea gown for her to wear, suggesting she sit in the upstairs hall to hear the concert. Music, art, poetry, beauty of all sorts have a way of enhancing one's imagination—stimulating ideas for extricating oneself from difficulties, so I firmly believe.

✝ ✝ ✝

My guests arrived, and the concert began with Geraldine Ivy singing a few parlor songs while accompanying herself on the spinet. As she trilled her way through the lyrical affairs of ardent beaux and saucy belles, I was aware of Ambrose casting an admiring glance in my direction. But, as a conscientious hostess, I would not allow myself to be too distracted. I kept an eye open for the needs of all the guests, providing refreshments and pleasantries, and kept an ear trained to murmured conversations around me—half-hearing, as well, other goings on in the house. Thus, I heard the kitchen door open and softly shut.

Ella and the daily maid were replenishing the punch bowl, and Ella could act in my stead, looking after the guests while I slipped away to the back of the house. There, I found not Charlotte leaving against my advice, but Gilbert returning home. He looked done in.

Gilbert set his medical bag and his hat on a kitchen chair and was about to remove his coat when I drew him back outside and under the shelter of the gallery overhang, for light rain was falling. Out of earshot of the daily maid returning to the kitchen and of the guests' carriage drivers chatting and smoking under the dripping eaves in the alleyway, I urged him to tell me what troubled him. Had something transpired concerning Mr. Eden?

No. It was a case. As Gilbert had finished his scheduled house call, Widow Dunleavy had told him she was worried about a neighbor child, the Macready girl, whose father and brothers worked at the fish market, and Tilly, too—until some days ago. One of the boys had told Widow Dunleavy this morning that Tilly had cut her hand shucking oysters and couldn't work until she mended. "There's no mother," the widow said, "and that man won't ask for help, but won't you look in on her, Dr. Crew?" So Gilbert had, finding Mr. Macready and his sons just home from work, smelling of fish and preparing to pan-fry some odds and ends left over from a day of gutting and filleting.

"He looked suspicious of me and said he couldn't pay," Gilbert told me. "Don't even think of it, I said to him."

"Suit yourself," the man had replied, with a jerk of his head towards the far corner of the room, farthest from the stove. There, Tilly lay on a pallet on the floor, its moss-packed mattress ticking grimy and flattened with use—she had lain there all day, alone, Gilbert surmised, with a tin cup of water and a heel of bread untouched beside her. No more than five or six years old, she wore a soiled, out-grown pinafore over a brother's shirt, her little bare feet and ankles exposed beneath the hem. Her hair, a tangled mass

286

of coppery curls, formed a sort of nest around the pale circle of her golden-freckled face, in which her eyes flitted beneath closed lids, perhaps watching a dream. Otherwise, she was perfectly still. Her sound arm lay across her waist, and her injured one at her side, the hand wrapped in a bloodstained handkerchief. I could see it all as my brother spoke, and I shivered in my silken gown in the misty chill of the late afternoon.

Gilbert had asked if the child had had a fever, and Macready shrugged, saying: "Might've done, day or so ago." Not looking at his daughter, keeping busy at the stove, he had snapped an order to one of his sons before adding an afterthought: "She perked up a bit this morning."

But that hadn't lasted. Gilbert knelt beside the girl and touched her forehead, which was cool—past fever. He opened his bag and made sure clean bandages and antiseptic solution were at hand. "There now, Tilly, I'll be so careful," he had said to no response. When he unwrapped her darkened hand and wrist, the pungency of gangrene shot up his nostrils, momentarily causing him to turn his head. But, as quickly, he turned back and examined the child's hand resting in his, the ragged-edged puncture wound in her palm, imagining how Tilly must have come by it—seated on a high stool in her father's stall at the fish market, little feet swinging above the ground, while she did a big girl's job. She was prying open the hinge of an oyster shell when the short-handled, sharp-bladed knife slipped in her grasp and jabbed into her palm—and she had screamed with sudden pain and fear at the sight of her own blood. But Tilly had been quiet as Gilbert brushed his fingers across her cheek, as a last little puff of air escape her parted lips. The movement beneath her eyelids slowed, ceased, no more dreaming—no pulse at her wrist or her throat, the poisoned blood quiet in her veins.

"If days ago, I could have dressed her wound. Or if her father had seen the danger and brought her to Dr. Clarke, who

287

might have taken her hand but saved her life," Gilbert said. "I felt her last breath, Lenore—here." And he held up his hand for me as if in evidence of the unseen—the last breath given up as the body expires, the spirit, which is the soul, spirited away. He and I had been brought up to believe in spirit without physical manifestation. Although, Gilbert had once professed to me that he better understood spirit as distillate—meaning more than spirits of hartshorn or *aqua vitae*—rather, the essence of what is and what stirs us and may be lost in a moment and forever.

"She's gone," Gilbert had said, looking up over his shoulder at Tilly's father, whose mouth twitched for a moment, then set in a thin line. Macready, his sons gathering behind him, had left off frying fish and come to stand behind where Gilbert knelt. The three boys darted their eyes from father to sister's body and back again, as if gauging what their father expected of them, and saying nothing.

"If something like this ever happens again," Gilbert had begun, with a quick glance towards the boys, "please send for—"

"For you?" Macready had stopped him. "For a saw-bones to finish the job? Better not happen again, I'm saying. How's anybody going to earn his keep with not but one hand?" Hard words, but Gilbert told me he had heard the agony in the man's voice.

Gilbert had handed over the modest fee he'd received from Widow Dunleavy to Macready, who accepted the money without acknowledgment. "I wanted to help with arrangements for the child," he said with a break in his voice. Then, he asked if I might suggest something more to be done for the Macready family, some assistance—or interference, depending on the recipient's point of view—from a benevolent society to which I subscribed. I would see what I could do—and loved my brother all the more, knowing that no matter how long he practiced his calling, he would never become inured to the death of a child.

As Gilbert mounted the back stairs to the gallery and upper hall, I returned to the parlor, where a fire burned in the hearth and a violin joined the spinet. As Ambrose came to stand beside me under the parlor archway, I felt sure the current of warm air and sweet music surrounding us also rose and travelled the staircase to keep company with Gilbert, perhaps lifting him from his dispirited state. And Charlotte would be with him, too, wouldn't she? I thought of going upstairs right then, but Ambrose had linked his arm with mine and was humming in my ear. Only when the musicians' melody ended, did Ambrose release his hold on me to join the round of applause, and I was able to excuse myself from him—with a promise to perform *Plaisir d' Amour* on my return.

Halfway up the stairs, I paused betwixt the first and second stories, allowing my eyes a moment to adjust to the dimness of the upper hall ahead, illumined only by the fading light passing through the panes of the French doors leading to the gallery. Then I spied Gilbert, not with Charlotte but alone, silhouetted against the glass doors. He sat in a ladder-back chair, head bowed, shoulders slumped, elbows on knees, and face in hands, covering his eyes.

Gilbert did not see me, even when he slowly lowered his hands and lifted his face. He must have caught the scent of sweet olive, as I had, lacing the air, preceding Charlotte as she moved through her open doorway and came to stand before him. Her back was to the stairs, my vantage point, her dark hair, unpinned, flowing to her waist. Gilbert, looking up at her, did not glance past her and still did not see me—he saw only Charlotte in that fanciful tea gown, in the hazy light, appearing like a water maiden draped in a swirl of blue-violet.

Gilbert started to rise in her presence, a reflex of manners instilled in him in youth, but Charlotte shook her head and put out her hand, palm down, almost touching his shoulder, indicating he should not move.

"What is it?" she whispered. "My children—"

I barely caught the sound of her voice, but Gilbert spoke more clearly. "Amy and Wilfred are fine," he said. "I saw them today, playing in the park with Narcisse."

Charlotte must have sighed her relief, her breast rising and falling before she spoke again. "What troubles you then?" she asked. "Tell me."

"A case," Gilbert said—saying nothing more than that.

But Charlotte, inclining her head towards him, looking into his eyes, I felt sure, said, "I'm so sorry," as if he had told her everything. Another song commenced downstairs, and if she said more to him, I didn't hear it. With her fingertips, she touched his forehead, brushed back his rain-matted hair from his brow. When she drew her hand away, he rose from the chair, standing inches from her without breaking his focus on her now upturned face. *Women knew.* Charlotte knew how vulnerable he was to her, didn't she? And she had not stepped away from him.

I completed my ascent, clearing my throat at the top of the stairs, and the pair of them turned to me—Charlotte with a gentle countenance and Gilbert with a startled one. His hands, which in another moment might have clasped Charlotte's, he stuffed into the pockets of his top coat. And then, his right fumbled in its pocket and a curious expression crossed his face as Gilbert withdrew a folded paper. Recognition of what it was dawned on him, and he offered the paper to Charlotte, saying: "For you. From Amy."

Amy's letter to her mother, which Gilbert had mentioned to me but failed, until this day, to deliver to Charlotte. How could he have been so thoughtless? Had he, and I with him, been so distracted by the theatrics of Helene's séance and its aftermath? But Charlotte had her missive now, unfolded it and looked at it a long while before holding it out for me to see. In pencil, Amy had drawn a woman and a little girl, side by side, with round faces, wavy outlines of dresses, and straight stick-arms, and had precociously labeled them *Mama* and *Amy*.

"Thank you, Dr. Crew," Charlotte murmured, then refolded the drawing and pressed it to her breast. "And thank you, dear Miss Lenore, for my children." Whom I had promised her.

Charlotte retreated from us, moving silently along the runner of carpet, nimbly avoiding the creaky floorboard on the way to her room, the hem of the fluid skirt swirling just above her bare feet. Gilbert watched her go.

Then I took hold of his arm, drawing him with me down the stairs to the parlor. Gilbert could turn the pages for me as I played and sang of love's vicissitudes.

Soon enough, he would be out of the house again, on his quest for something with which to condemn Charlotte's husband. Colonel Duvall expected my brother that night at a clandestine assembly, where Gilbert hoped to observe Eden with him. Would Gilbert witness the two men in comradery that transcended either's marital discord? Or catch the pair of them in confrontation? Even if Gilbert did not confirm his own suspicions of Eden, he might confirm Duvall's suspicions.

Such was the nature of entanglements—pleasures fleeting, heartaches lifelong.

Chapter Thirty-Nine

At daybreak, Ella woke me with her *Lord have mercy!* and bade me follow her to the clinic, which I did, forthwith, my dressing gown flapping around me and my hair a hoo-raw's nest. Ella had come early to the clinic, intending to sweep before patients arrived, when she had discovered Gilbert. "Passed out or sleeping like the dead, Miss Lenore. Can't say which," she told me as we crossed the garden. Then, opening the door to the consulting room, she pointed at my brother, who lay motionless under a cotton sheet on the examining table.

"Gilbert?" I said, my hand to my heart. Then I sighed with relief when he moved, slowly swiveling his head towards me and half-opening his eyes.

On the floor near the table, Gilbert's mud-caked boots and outer clothing lay in a heap, reeking of some foul effluvia. With the handle of her broom, Ella elevated the coat above the other garments and said to my brother: "Blood, Mr. Gil?"

Gilbert was hard on his clothes, a hazard of his profession—still, the dark red streaks on the cuffs of his coat sleeves gave me pause. I feared some violence had occurred in the night and asked him for an explanation. As he came to fuller consciousness, realizing he was not warm in bed but shivering in his union suit atop a table, Gilbert sat up, swinging his legs over the table's edge and pulling the thin sheet around him. Then, at my repeated request, he began his tale of nocturnal events.

✛ ✛ ✛

As Gilbert had headed for the address Colonel Duvall had given him, he found himself retracing a stretch of Toulouse Street not far from Mr. Keogh's properties. A fresh light rain had commenced, dampening down the accumulated street odors of the day emanating from the usual refuse and rotting matter, urine and animal droppings. The covered banquettes were already crowded with pedestrians, so he trudged along the muddy street, avoiding horses, carts, and carriages. Gilbert rarely rode in the heart of town, saving his horse for trips to outlying areas, preferring the exercise and freedom of movement, sometimes the lack of forethought, that foot travel provided. With his coat collar turned up, the collar points shielding his face on either side like a pair of harness blinders, and his hat brim pulled low over his eyes, he had some difficulty seeing and just missed the entrance to his destination but retraced his steps to the door. It was a drinking establishment, noisy and congested along the length of the bar in the front room. The secret society, according to Duvall's instructions, met in the back room.

Gilbert shouldered into a crowd of men whose heads were overhung by a billowing cloud of cigar smoke, then made slow progress across a floor slick with tobacco spittle. Nearing the far end of the room, he saw a powerfully built man standing in front of a closed door, arms crossed over barrel chest and square chin lifted, as if defying anyone to get past him without his permission. Of course, a secret society must have a sentry. Some men—Gilbert's father-in-law, who had tried to recruit him into a particular society, among them—apparently believed that covert rituals and arcane trappings could dignify any amount of nonsense or wrong-headedness.

Gilbert watched one man approach the sentry, speak to him, and gain admission. Then another man was refused, displaying frustration by rising on the balls of his feet and wagging his forefinger under the sentry's nose. The sentry shoved him down with a single thrust, then re-crossed his arms. After the man had scrambled up from the slippery floor and exited the saloon, Gilbert tried his own luck.

"Who sent you?" The sentry cocked his head, presenting a heavy-lobed ear into which Gilbert might deposit his answer.

"Colonel Frank Duvall," he said, then held up Duvall's card for good measure.

Although the colonel's name worked like the "Open Sesame!" of *Arabian Nights*, one of Gilbert's boyhood escapes, no glittering treasure cave lay across this threshold—only a crowded room lit by an oil lamp with a dirty glass chimney. That single lamp on the table cast more shadow than light on the men's features and barely illumined, not a cloud, but a spectral haze of tobacco smoke hovering above their heads. The room sweltered with men in heated conversations, and Gilbert wished he had removed his top coat and hat before entering, for he found no space to maneuver here. Pressing his back against the wall, he scanned what he could make out of the faces, the fleshy and the gaunt, shifting and segmented, as the side of a nose or the ball of a chin or the ridge of a brow emerged from the dark, catching the lamplight.

And he listened. The talk was political, not surprising, given that tomorrow was Election Day. All the men around him vehemently favored General Winfield Scott Hancock for president over General James Garfield, Gilbert's choice, better kept to himself at this gathering.

As his eyes grew accustomed to the dimness, Gilbert caught sight of a familiar pattern of motion. Beyond the two men closest on his right, another man raised a flask to his lips, lowered it, tucked the flask in his breast pocket, started to reach for it again. "Colonel Duvall," Gilbert called out, and the man looked his way, then pushed past the other men to reach Gilbert's side and slap his shoulder.

"Glad you joined us, very glad," Duvall declared heartily and with a slurring of words.

Duvall took hold of Gilbert's arm, as if they were old friends, and pointed out Mr. Turnbull, the leader of the assembly of the Crescent City Regulators. Turnbull sat at the table in a high-backed chair, proportioned and carved to resemble a throne, designating the man's importance. Pounding his gavel, nearly upsetting the lamp, Turnbull called the meeting to order. The few other men seated in cane chairs, one of them with a long black beard with an odd white streak running through it, and all the rest of the men, standing and circled around the table, gradually grew quiet. Of all the oblique features on all the shadowy faces in that packed room, Turnbull's was most sinister—pale domed forehead, taut skin, black brows shading deep-set eyes, if eyes existed in those sockets, which were dark as if worms had already done their work—his face, a veritable Death's Head. Indeed, he opened the meeting with a mortal threat, drawling each syllable: "Strange fruit. That's what the tree bears when we are crossed."

Murmurs urged him on, and Turnbull, in his sepulchral voice, laid out plans for Election Day to his followers. Their charge and duty was to exercise their rightful influence, make sure undesirables did not presume to vote, and generally stir up things at the polls as they deemed necessary. That last point led some men to bragging about various humiliations and cruelties they had already meted out to those who had crossed them, those they considered uppity or felonious. As Gilbert listened to tales of beatings and brandings, the sweat collected on his brow trickled down the sides of his face and under his collar. Anyone who offended these men might find his life changed or lost at their will. In Ella's stories, river reptiles were not the last 'ators to torment her people, after all—no, she must add the Regulators to her litany.

As the meeting wore on, Gilbert tried to contain his visceral reaction to what was said and to Duvall's mutterings of approval. On occasion, the colonel might be a pleasant enough fellow, but he was not benign. Gilbert kept to the wall, watching the faces around him, peering towards the door each time someone opened it, wondering when Eden would arrive to join the assembly. Head aching and eyes stinging with smoke, Gilbert grew dizzy. As if the colonel had sensed a wave of sickness were washing over Gilbert, Duvall offered his flask. Surprised, but not ungrateful, Gilbert took a swig of bad whiskey that burned going down, then left a too-sweet aftertaste that coated his tongue.

"Come on, man," Duvall said, pulling Gilbert after him to the door and out of the back room, into the relative openness of the saloon. "You look done in." He found them chairs, and Gilbert dropped onto one, at last letting go of his black bag and wedging it between his feet.

"Thank you, sir," Gilbert said. "It's been a long day."

Duvall was hard to make out—inviting Gilbert to a meeting where men whipped themselves up to the verge of violence, and then, outside of the back room, showing solicitude, offering Gilbert a peaceful drink. From the bar, Duvall bought them each a smooth bourbon and clinked his glass against Gilbert's before they drank. "I'll introduce you to Mr. Turnbull before we leave tonight," Duvall said, leaning close to avoid being overheard by men nearby, who were not Crescent City Regulators. "Be glad to sponsor your induction."

"That's very generous of you," Gilbert said. "Bet you did the same for Mr. Eden."

Duvall drew back and cocked his head. "Yes. I did that for him."

"But he didn't attend tonight," Gilbert observed.

"Not unusual these days for him to miss a meeting," Duvall said.

Here was an opening. Gilbert considered giving the colonel the address of Keogh's better properties. But Duvall, red-eyed and rather drunk, was in no fit state to tear through alleyways, as he had down the river road, in pursuit of his wife.

"Well, Colonel," Gilbert said, "a gentleman in mourning—"

Duvall held up a hand. "Has no time for politics," he finished the sentence with a note of sarcasm.

They talked another few minutes, Gilbert buying a second round of bourbon, before the colonel admitted he only tolerated Eden to please the judge. "Royce and I go back before the war, before ranks and titles—sure as hell, before scalawags and carpetbaggers. The judge brought Eden in late on our ventures, after we lost one architect to yellow fever and another to the pox. Not our first choice, but the judge got him cheap. Eden had troubles in Baton Rouge."

"Would you elaborate?"

The colonel drained his glass before replying: "Let's just say, Victor Eden cut corners a little too tight on a design—and it wouldn't hold up the paper it was drawn on."

Suddenly, Duvall stretched his neck and looked over Gilbert's shoulder to something or someone catching his eye. "Pardon me a minute, Dr. Crew," he said, pushing back his chair, stumbling slightly as he rose. He laid a hand on Gilbert's shoulder, regaining his balance, then moved around him and towards the outer door. Gilbert twisted in his chair, watching the colonel limp away, swerving between tables, to meet up with a man in a loose raincoat and slouch hat, who stood in the doorway. Briefly, they conversed, Duvall appearing to grow agitated, shifting his shoulders and peering beyond the other man, out towards the street. Soon after, the other man left, and Gilbert turned back to his drink, expecting Duvall to rejoin him at the corner table. But he did not. When Gilbert looked again across the room, Duvall was nowhere in sight.

The colonel did not return—not in the minute for which he had excused himself, nor later to introduce Gilbert to Turnbull, as he had offered. A few men emerged from the back room and came to the bar. Likely Turnbull and others had left by a rear door.

Still, Duvall did not reappear.

As the rain slackened to a fine mist, Gilbert left the saloon and walked along the banquette, not so congested at the late hour. He had not gone far, however, before meeting with the sight of a crowd gathering at the entrance to an alley and the sound of screaming.

Gilbert ran towards the screams—a woman's sharp staccato cries of "Help!" and wails of "Murder!" But a wall of backs of men blocked the way into the alley. Using his sturdy medical bag as a wedge to drive between two men ahead of him, Gilbert forced his way forward.

"I'm a doctor," Gilbert shouted into the crowd. "Is someone hurt?"

Those who heard him picked up the cry: "He's a doctor—let him through!" And others, the concerned and the curious, shifted enough to allow him entrance to the alley. Two policemen were there ahead of him, standing side by side, one of them holding up a lantern. Their backs to him, they obscured his view of the woman beyond them, whose shrieks had now quieted to sobs. Then the policeman with the lantern stepped back a pace and shone the light into the passage. Here was the part of the men's professions that they shared—policemen and physicians—they stepped into other people's nightmares to discover the quick and the dead.

In this case, the quick was Margaret Duvall, sunk down amidst her crumpled skirt and cloak and keening on the rain-soaked earth. The dead—for, most likely, he was dead—was a man whose head and upper body Margaret cradled in her lap. Her hat and veil lay on the ground beside her, and her loosened hair fell over the man's face. The lantern light glinted on the hilt of a knife, protruding from the man's abdomen, while all around the hilt spread a dark stain—blood soaking the man's buttoned-up waistcoat and thrown-open jacket, spilling over the front of his trousers and down between his splayed legs onto the ground. Blood—staining

Margaret's skirt and the edges of her cloak and covering her gloved hands as she attempted to draw her own her garments over the wound. Too late to staunch the bleeding.

Gilbert exchanged quick words with the policemen, and together they set to work. The one with the lantern shone the light as required, as Gilbert bent over the man. The other circled behind Margaret, taking hold of her shoulders and moving her back and away, while Gilbert relieved her of her burden, taking hold of the man's head and shoulders, easing him back and laying him flat on the ground. In that moment, even before looking at him, Gilbert darted a glance at Margaret's face, into her horrified eyes. Then, as swiftly, he cast his gaze downward, into the fixed eyes that did not belong to Margaret's lover. No, the man was not Victor Eden, not Charlotte's husband, whose incapacity, if not his death, would have simplified a number of difficulties. Instead, it was Gilbert's drinking companion, Margaret's husband—now the late Colonel Frank Duvall.

Gilbert could do nothing for him, save what he had vowed to do for Charlotte when believing her lost to the world—he would be Duvall's witness, recording, within the limits of his observations, the malicious injury done to the colonel, giving testimony, if called, at an inquest.

Around Gilbert, discussion and speculation rose and hummed: *Who was the dead man?* A gentleman. Colonel Duvall. A hero of the Cause, wasn't he? *What happened to him?* Shot. Bludgeoned. No, sir, stabbed. *Robbery?* Don't know. *The woman? His mistress?* His wife. *Anybody see who did it?* I saw a fellow high-tailing down the alleyway. *Chase after him?* Naw, not me. *How about you?* Didn't see nothing—just heard that caterwauling woman.

As Gilbert bent to examine the body by swaying lantern light, one of his feet slipped in thickening liquid. Momentarily, he dropped to his knees before regaining his balance, time enough for rank dampness to seep into the wool of his trousers. Then, someone in the crowd called out that he saw one of Duvall's leg's twitch—as likely to be the wooden one as the other, for the colonel was far past reviving. Someone else said, no, it had just been a rat running over the dead man's boot. Gilbert shot a glance around him, then went on with his work.

"Back off, fellows. Give the doctor room," said the policeman who still supported Margaret Duvall. "Give the lady some air."

Give the dead man's soul free passage.

Gilbert sensed movement behind him, a coolness of space opening up, then heard a few snatches of talk concerning Mrs. Duvall and what was to be done for her. But he missed the conversation's outcome, for he was intent on what examination of her husband's body revealed.

Colonel Duvall had been stabbed just below the last button of his waistcoat. With a single, deep thrust, his assailant had sent a blade up to its cross guard and hilt into a low-slung paunch of fat, penetrating the bowels. No razor slash to the throat, nor dirk through the heart to bring a quick end. The location of the wound fitted with Duvall's prodigious loss of blood and told a story of slow death. Withdrawing the knife, Gilbert saw that it was, indeed, designed for thrusting, with its narrow, rigid blade, triangular in cross-section, tapered to a needle-sharp point—perhaps a parrying weapon that a swordsman would brandish in one hand, his rapier in the other. Back in Baltimore, Gilbert had seen the like on the stage in a production of *Hamlet*. And in his profession, he had seen the resulting wounds, accidental or intentional, of any number of dangerous instruments. He gave the weapon into the keeping of one of the policemen.

When had Margaret found her husband? If Eden and Margaret had spent the evening together, wouldn't he have escorted her at least part of her way home? How had she and Duvall come to be together in the alleyway? And, while gradually bleeding to death, had Duvall strength to speak to her? Here might be a parallel to another play, one that Gilbert and his sister had attended just after his moving to New Orleans—Antony, falling too low upon his sword, wounding himself through the bowels, and languishing through any number of lines of dramatic dialogue with Cleopatra before he expired. What parting words had Duvall for Margaret? Gilbert looked around to find her, but she was gone.

Chapter Forty

Ella had let Gilbert's blood-stained coat slide from her broom handle and back to the floor beside his boots. Then, she and I had both sunk into cane chairs to hear him out as Gilbert had told his story of murder in a hollow voice, his own words giving him pause, even as they shocked Ella and me.

"My stars," I murmured, but Ella's utterance was more to the point.

"You think Mr. Eden got something to do with it," she said.

Gilbert nodded. "Given his relationship with Mrs. Duvall."

Ella snorted at that, then spoke with firmness: "We can't be upsetting Miss Charlotte, fragile as she is. See that husband of hers locked up and then tell her—that's what I say."

In the space of the next half-hour, Gilbert and I both made ourselves somewhat presentable, then conferred again with Ella at the kitchen table. Not a peep yet out of Charlotte, which was a mercy, since we three had much to discuss. Gilbert brought out a pencil and his journal of case notes pertaining to Charlotte's brush with death, now adding observations on Duvall's murder, scribbling in questions and speculations as we conversed.

"Colonel Duvall must have come upon them in the alley," I said. "As you suggest, Gil, that man he spoke to at the door of the saloon could have been his spy—following Margaret to her assignation with Victor Eden and reporting back to the colonel."

"That would explain Duvall's rushing off—if he knew his

wife and Eden had just left the apartment and were nearby," Gilbert said.

"So the colonel confronted the pair of them on the street," I said. "But if he were threatening them, why, on earth, would they follow him into a dark alleyway?"

"They was mortified," Ella answered my question with conviction. "There they was—caught out by the husband. But Mr. Eden's not one to air his dirty laundry on the public street. Oh, no. I can picture the whole thing, plain as day."

Gilbert and I gave Ella our full attention as she continued: "Mr. Eden is never wrong, in his opinion—" Something she'd learned from Charlotte "—and he tries to put off the colonel with some excuse about chancing on Mrs. Duvall, offering to walk her home. Just pulling some yarn out of thin air. But Colonel Duvall ain't having none of it, and he shoves Mr. Eden into the nearest alley. Or, t'other way 'round, and Mr. Eden shoves the colonel—'cause, like I said, he don't want no talk about his business on the street. Anyways, the colonel's the one armed and spoiling for a fight, so he whips out his knife. But Mr. Eden won't be bested. He grabs the colonel's wrist with both hands and twists his arm." Ella demonstrated the maneuver with an imaginary opponent. "Next thing you know, that blade be buried in Colonel Duvall's innards."

"And what was Margaret's part in the fray?" I asked as if Ella had been an eyewitness.

"Oh, she's still fussing and fluttering on the banquette," Ella said. "Whilst Mr. Eden, he run off, out the back way. And then, when things quiets down, and all she can hear is one man moaning, she steps into the alley and sees her husband, blood pouring out of him. Well, guilty and sinful as she is—she be right sorry at the last. So she takes the colonel in her arms and hollers for help."

Ella's speculative account, dramatic as it was, had a certain plausibility—for Eden stabbing Duvall made more sense than Duvall stabbing himself in a crazed display of despair over Margaret's betrayal. A chance attack, an armed robbery, was even more improbable, for why would it just happen to occur around the time that Duvall encountered his wife with Eden? Of course, the colonel might have had foes of whom we knew nothing, who tracked him and killed him for reasons yet to be discovered—someone who knew Duvall, as we did not, and had something to gain, or something to prove, by killing him. He had been a prosecutor and could well have made enemies. Then another idea dawned on me: "What if Victor Eden wasn't there?"

"What?" Gilbert said. "What do you mean—not there?"

"Well, now, Miss Lenore got herself a point," said Ella, who had gotten up from the table to prepare a breakfast tray for Charlotte. "We just been assuming he was with her, that's all. Naturally, a gentleman such as yourself, Mr. Gil, would escort a lady-friend down the street at night. But, here, we be talking about folks who go slipping off, getting up to no good in secret."

"Ella's right, Gil. While what she described may well be what happened, without a witness who saw Mr. Eden there, we can't assume—" I broke off, then started again, as the notion of Margaret alone developed in my mind: "Women rarely commit murder and may be overlooked as culprits. Suppose only husband and wife were ever in the alley."

"But Margaret Duvall—really, she—" Gilbert seemed to struggle with my conjecture. "Could she be capable of such violence? Selfishness, vanity, pettiness—I grant you—but surely not murder. If she wanted her husband out of the way, wouldn't she have persuaded Eden to get rid of him for her."

"If she holds that kind of power over him," I said.

"Her persuasion wouldn't have been necessary—not if Duvall confronted Eden. The men fought and, in the midst of their fury, one killed the other," Gilbert said. "And, if Margaret's sorry about her husband's death, as Ella's suggested—" Gilbert cast a hopeful look to Ella—"she may tell the police exactly what happened."

"Well, sir, that just might tidy things up," Ella said on her way out of the kitchen. "But sorry be one thing, getting truth out of a deceiver be something else."

Chapter Forty-One

It is an ill wind that blows nobody any good. Hadn't I heard that a time or two during the war years and after? And now I saw an opportunity to parlay the sudden disaster that had befallen Colonel Duvall into a comfort—no, not for Margaret—but for Charlotte, to whom I had made a promise. I had tossed and turned half the night on how to keep my word, but no more.

Turning to Gilbert, who was busy jotting in his notebook, I said, "I have a plan to bring Amy and Wilfred to Charlotte." He set down his pencil on the kitchen table and urged me to continue, which I did, organizing my thoughts as I went along: "A couple of days ago, I met Dr. Baldwin as he was leaving Widow Eden's apartment, and I was arriving. He told me the lady needs a rest—stopping short of saying her grandchildren are wearing her out. I know you call him a quack, but he's right about her not looking well. What could be more natural than for me to take the little ones off her hands for a while?—especially, in light of my frequent visits to them, their ease with me, my growing fondness for them." I paused for breath—and emphasis. "And in light of what Mr. Eden is mixed up in."

"You'd accuse him to his mother's face?" Gilbert said.

"Of course not. I will go to Widow Eden at a polite hour this morning to offer my hospitality. But before that—just as soon as you can be on your way—you must to go to Victor Eden's office."

"And accuse Eden of murder to *his* face?"

"Really, Gilbert, if I could just put my plan in your head, without having to explain it. Victor Eden, whatever his part in the colonel's death, must be in a dither this morning. You'll catch him flustered and put his mind to rest about the children and his ailing mother, freeing him to console Widow Duvall." My brother smiled and nodded at me then. I went on: "If the children are here, Charlotte will stay—at least, for a little while longer—where they'll all be safe, allowing time for, well, for whatever happens next."

Here I have recorded what happened next to Gilbert, which forced me to reassess the value of ill winds.

✙ ✙ ✙

Gilbert met Eden at the moment of that man's arrival at his office, even holding the door for him as Eden entered laden with umbrella, briefcase, and rolls of architectural plans.

"Some pressing errand?" Eden asked, with a brow lifted in surprise, possibly suspicion.

"Yes, sir," Gilbert said, "Dr. Baldwin points out that your mother is in need of a rest. And, as my sister has become fond of the children, I've come to ask that you allow Amy and Wilfred to stay with Lenore. Perhaps for a week or two."

"My mother's girl looks after them well enough," Eden replied, "without taxing Mother's nerves too far."

Gilbert said nothing, giving Eden time to think a little more on the welfare of his mother and his children, if he cared to, but the man gave no hint of anxiety. He only looked tired. His jaw tightened and nostrils flared a moment as he stifled a yawn. But there was energy in his movements, a subtle current of excitement as, over the broad surface of his slanted drawing desk, Eden unrolled a large sheet of paper covered with plans, smoothed it out, and secured its curling edges with millefiori paperweights. Gilbert's sister had brought home the very same type after a trip to Italy, "a thousand flowers" design captured in heavy glass. Eden's paperweights were a colorful touch beside his drab pencil drawings of three rectangular buildings, or perhaps three floors of the same building, each cut into myriad tiny squares, like the plans for a monochromatic mosaic.

Eden regarded his work, added a line here, darkened another there. Then he tapped the tip of his pencil along a crowded row of squares, counting them, perhaps calculating how to squeeze a few more cells into his housing plans for prison workers.

"For the judge?" Gilbert said, still watching him.

"Hmmm." Eden jotted numbers along a margin. "Charlotte ruined the first set of plans—spilling ink." An edge to his voice indicated the mishap still rankled with him.

"Surely, an accident."

"You think so?" Eden lifted his face to Gilbert's. "Then you didn't know her as well as you thought you did."

Gilbert chose not to respond.

"If she could see the improvements I've made . . ." Eden took a step back from the slanted table, the better to admire his work, ignoring Gilbert.

Then, as if recalling Gilbert were in the room only to dismiss him, Eden said, "Tell Mrs. James that I appreciate her interest in the children. I haven't seen a bill from you, so I assume you aren't treating them for any illnesses—are you, Dr. Crew? Indeed, they seem to be in far better health than when their mother was here to summon you."

Eden's words were coolly spoken and finished off with a smile as narrow as his closely-trimmed moustache. He was judging his wife by himself, implying he thought Charlotte had used the children as an excuse to invite Gilbert in while her husband was out.

Now Gilbert chose his words: "Amy and Wilfred are in good health, Mr. Eden. But, you see, my sister and I—while hoping to relieve Widow Eden, as I said—also thought to relieve your mind of additional concerns—given what has befallen your friends, Colonel and Mrs. Duvall."

"Colonel and Mrs. Duvall," Eden echoed, his eyes admitting no understanding of what had happened to either of them.

There was not a mark on Eden's clean-shaven cheeks, nor a bruise on his square jaw, nor a scratch on the back of either hand. He had walked effortlessly into his office and around his drawing desk, without a catch in his gait or his breath that might have indicated a twisted knee or a cracked rib. Gilbert saw no obvious sign that the colonel had done Eden any injury before Eden took control of the knife—if that were what had happened. But, as Gilbert elaborated on the previous night's events, he watched Eden for other, subtle signs that would tie him to Duvall's death—signs of unease and of fear of being found out.

"You haven't heard the news then, have you?" Gilbert feigned ingenuousness. "Well, of course, it wasn't in the morning papers. Nobody sent word to you? No?" Eden did not respond, except with a twitch near the outer corner of one eye. "I was there last night," Gilbert continued, "just after it happened. Yes, sir, I saw the crowd by the alleyway and ran right over to discover that Colonel Duvall had been stabbed." Gilbert stopped himself from adding to death—letting Eden wonder another moment about the outcome.

Eden drew a quick breath, then exhaled as he sank onto a dark red leather chair. He clinched his hands over the armrests. A full minute ticked by, according to the wall clock, before Eden asked, "Did he—has Colonel Duvall survived the attack?"

Gilbert shook his head.

Suddenly, Eden came over ashen, looking as if he might be sick. Was he truly so taken aback by the news of Duvall's death—or shocked by the idea that Gilbert had nearly caught him in the act of murdering Margaret's husband?

"The colonel died in his wife's arms," Gilbert said. Eden looked up at him with an expression of incredulity, and Gilbert

310

went on, as if wondering aloud: "They must have been out for the evening together, when they were attacked, don't you think?"

"I . . . I wouldn't know. How could I know?" Eden stammered over his reply.

"There is some hope," Gilbert said, "that the killer will be brought to justice."

Eden blinked.

Gilbert continued: "The colonel died slowly, you understand, and he may well have had time to recognize his attacker and speak some last words to Mrs. Duvall."

This time, Eden shut his eyes and kept them shut.

"Naturally, as you are such a close friend, you will want to be of assistance to Mrs. Duvall in her time of loss," Gilbert said, omitting the phrase *as she has been to you*, for that might lead to a different conversation. Then, he reminded Eden of his sister's offer to relieve his mind of concern for Amy and Wilfred, expecting Eden to nod in acquiescence.

Still sitting rigid in the leather chair, Eden opened his eyes and looked at Gilbert, who stood in the doorway ready to take leave.

"No," he said.

"Mr. Eden?"

"No," Eden repeated. "Your sister need not trouble herself. Tomorrow I'm sending the children to stay at Testament."

Chapter Forty-Two

"I never heard any of this," I said to my brother on his return from Eden's office. "I shall call on Widow Eden and proceed—in all innocence—to offer my hospitality to the children."

Gilbert had intercepted me just as I was departing for the widow's apartment, and we spoke in near-whispers in the front hall. Charlotte, up and in the kitchen with Ella, was making gingerbread for Amy and Wilfred, knowing nothing yet of last night's murderous event.

I skewered the crown of my hat with a hatpin. "You never said a word to me, Gil."

"But there's more," Gilbert said anyway, following me out the door. "Whether you choose to hear me or not. Chances are, Mrs. Placide won't be going to Testament any time soon. And she may not want to take on Eden's children in town."

As Gilbert and I proceeded to the nearby livery stable for my horse and carriage, he explained himself. Indeed, he'd had a busy early morning, and the day was still young. Leaving Eden, Gilbert had hurried to cast his vote for General Garfield, keeping hat brim low and head down, for he had recognized a few Crescent City Regulators and had no desire to meet their eyes or engage with them in political discussion. Feeling a little freer on leaving the polls, he strode to the hospital for a brief consultation with Dr. Clarke. But first, in a hospital corridor, Gilbert had encountered Dr. Baldwin, the old man loudly blowing his nose into a handkerchief.

Greeting one another, Gilbert had offered sympathy to Dr. Baldwin, who had, according to his claim, caught a head cold from

Widow Eden. And from there, they swiftly moved on to the sensational. Yes, Dr. Baldwin already knew of the colonel's murder. "But you, young man, were on the spot!" He sounded positively envious that such excitement had passed him by. "Why, just suppose the villain had still been there in the shadows, or mingling with the crowd, looking on while you examined Colonel Duvall's body—oh, the audacity!"

Then Dr. Baldwin shared with Gilbert the news that Margaret Duvall was now staying with Judge and Mrs. Placide in their town home. "She can't be alone," he said. "Needs her friends after what she's been through, don't you know?"

"Last night, I had no opportunity to ascertain Mrs. Duvall's condition," Gilbert said. "Was she, in any way"—here a pause to indicate the delicacy of the matter—"was the lady physically harmed by her husband's assailant?"

"*Interfered with*, don't you mean? A mercy she was not! Terrible business. Cold-blooded butchery!" Then Dr. Baldwin had raised his handkerchief and prepared for another violent blow.

With the new knowledge of Margaret's whereabouts, Gilbert proposed that he and I call there first, before I went on to see Widow Eden. Gilbert wanted to interview Margaret while last night was fresh on her mind and before she spoke again with Eden. And Gilbert suggested I could manage Helene and the matter of Charlotte's children with my usual aplomb.

The Placides' mansion in town, while not as vast as their mansion at Testament, was even more ornate, to my mind—cluttered with countless fragile whatnots, china bric-a-brac, and gilt clocks crammed into beveled-glass display cases and littered over tabletops and along mantels. A housekeeper's nightmare, Ella would declare it.

A servant, who seemed uncertain where her mistress had got off to, led us through a series of over-furnished rooms and into the tropical jungle of the conservatory, where Margaret reclined on a wicker *chaise longue.*

"How good of you to come, Dr. Crew," Margaret said rather dreamily, extending a hand, which Gilbert was too late to catch before it fell onto her lap. "But Dr. Baldwin has already been to see me. I'm sure he has." There was no certainty in her voice. But I believed her, believing Baldwin had given her a sedative, which would account for her languid demeanor and mauve-shadowed eyes. The eyes gradual shifted in my direction. "Oh, Mrs. James," she murmured by way of recognition that I, too, had been good enough to come see her.

Gilbert and I took seats in wicker chairs that the servant—Tansy, as I now recalled her name—had found for us among the potted palms. Then, we offered Margaret our condolences for her loss, she seeming momentarily confused until Gilbert reminded her of his coming upon her last night in the alley.

"Oh, yes. Yes, you were there." Margaret brushed her hands across the front of her fresh dress, perhaps thinking of the bloodstained one she had worn last night. "Such a comfort, not to be alone," she mused. "People have been so kind." Again, she touched her skirt, running her fingers over the mustard gold wool. "I should be wearing black," she added, her tone contrite. "I will soon." Margaret looked at me, perhaps wanting another woman's acknowledgement that she would do the right thing.

"Of course," I said. "But you've hardly had time to think about what's customary."

"Yes"—a brief smile—"dear Helene will tell me what to do."

I nodded. "I'm sure she will."

"And Mr. Eden has called on you, no doubt," Gilbert said blandly, "to offer you his assistance."

"No. Not yet," Margaret replied in a small voice.

It would not be too difficult for her to feign the distress that I sensed emanating from her. Even if Margaret had played a

315

part in causing it— even if, or although, she had not been fond of Duvall or had been estranged from him—her husband had bled to death in her lap. A shocking experience for anyone to endure, and I sensed she was genuinely distraught. Gilbert believed Eden had been distraught, too, for his own reasons—likely worry over what Duvall's dying words might have been, or over how far Eden might rely on Margaret's devotion and discretion.

Gilbert drew his chair closer to the *chaise longue* and lifted Margaret's hands, holding them between his palms. "Mrs. Duvall," he began in the soothing tone of his best bedside manner, "please, tell me everything that you remember about last night. Unburden yourself. And allow me to be of service to you, if I may."

Margaret emitted a little sigh and nestled her hands within his before she commenced lying to him: "My husband and I were out together, just wending our way home, when we, well, when we paused on the banquette. Then, all of a sudden, he drew me just into the side street—the alleyway." Margaret hesitated, as if struggling over how to phrase what she would say next, how she might continue the fabrication of her story.

"The colonel took you into the alley—why did he do that?" Gilbert prompted.

"Oh, my husband is—was—very rash at times." She glanced at me, then back to Gilbert. "Very demonstrative in his attentions to me. You understand, Dr. Crew?" Here, even while gazing at my brother through a haze of sedation, Margaret managed a flutter of her lashes in his direction.

"Yes, ma'am, I do understand," he said.

Margaret smiled, only for a moment, perhaps believing she had achieved her desired reaction from Gilbert, that she had secured his sympathy with her charm, before going on: "We'd no sooner stepped into the alley for a private moment—what became our last embrace—when a killer came out of nowhere. Just cut us in two." Margaret's voice had dropped into the low, incredulous

316

register of one who could not quite believe what had happened to her, or, at least, could not quite believe the version of it that she was reporting. "The man pulled away, quick as he'd come on, and then—then my husband fell against me. I tumbled back, trying to hold him up. But I couldn't. We were on the ground. And, oh, the blood, the blood ran everywhere."

According to Margaret's account, Colonel Duvall had fallen facing her as she fell back, he sliding down the front of her gown to his knees before collapsing onto her lap as she crumpled earthward. Yet, when Gilbert had seen him, the colonel had been lying on his back in her lap, his head against her bosom, her hat gone and hair fallen from its pins veiling his face, and the knife handle jutted from his abdomen, centered in line with his waistcoat buttons.

"How could that be, Mrs. Duvall?" Gilbert said gently. "Surely, the colonel must have been facing his attacker, given the location of his wound."

"Oh." Margaret darted her eyes about as if she were, for a moment, lost. Then, she looked down at her hands between Gilbert's and slowly drew hers away. He settled back in his chair and waited, as I did, for her to explain. She laced her fingers together over her waist and drew a full breath before saying: "You're right, Dr. Crew. Everything happened at once—that's what confused me. My husband must have turned in that instant the man came at us to put himself between me and the danger. To shield me, that's what he did. So, when Frank was stabbed—" I saw her joined hands tighten and press against her waist—"he must have been facing the man, and I was behind him."

"Then you caught a glimpse of the man's face, didn't you?" Gilbert said.

Margaret shook her head. "No. I didn't see his face." She then laid her hands, one over the other, at her breast. "I have no idea who he is. Some vicious stranger, who did his dirty work and ran away. That's all I know." Margaret's voice had become plaintive, whining, like that of a child fighting sleep.

"You've been through a terrible ordeal, Mrs. Duvall. A shock, from which you will need time and care to recover." Gilbert sounded sincere, as if he'd been utterly taken in by her—if I didn't know better.

"So true," she said, puckering her mouth into a pout and furrowing her brow.

"I hope you find solace, Mrs. Duvall, in the knowledge of your husband's devotion to you—right to the end of his life," Gilbert said. "He died defending you—a hero's death."

"Why, so it is." Margaret allowed her facial muscles to relax, and a serene expression came over her features. She sighed and eased her head onto the cushion behind her.

"When you are ready, Mrs. Duvall, I hope you will share with me the colonel's last words to you. Perhaps, he knew—" Gilbert stopped, for she was no longer listening to him, her eyelids closed and her breathing deepened with sleep.

I nodded to Gilbert, and we quietly rose from our chairs, preparing to leave the conservatory. But we had only advanced a few steps when we both halted as a faint rustling sound caught our attention. Ahead of us was movement among the greenery, one long frond of a potted sword fern dipping and rising again with the light pressure of the hand of someone passing by it, parting the dark foliage with her bejeweled fingers and emerging into the hazy light at the bay window. Helene Placide had materialized from the depths of her cultivated jungle, smiling and holding up a watering can, as if offering us an explanation for her presence behind a screen of leaves—undisclosed, while we had been in conversation with her houseguest.

She glided towards us, glancing benignly at the sleeping Margaret. Then, setting aside the watering can, she ushered us away with her, through the rooms Tansy had led us earlier and into a small sitting room, itself a cultivated jumble of horsehair sofa and chairs interspersed with carved tables with marble tops on which dried flowers and dead birds were displayed under glass domes. A close, depressing room. We declined her offer of a seat, Gilbert saying he must be going soon. We remained standing near the doorway while Helene brushed past us, skirting the furnishings to reach and realign a pair of grim, possibly ancestral, portraits on the far wall. Then she turned to face us both, although her eyes were trained on Gilbert.

Helene began her discourse by complimenting him on his charitableness towards Margaret and finished with: "Of course, I know from personal experience what a comfort you can be to a lady in distress."

Her allusion to the night at Testament, the reminder of Gilbert's excursion with her into the garden followed by the awkward intimacy of conversation with her in the back parlor, must have brought a taste of bile to his throat. Gilbert swallowed and said nothing.

"Poor Margaret." Helene sighed and took a step closer to my brother, who took a step closer to me. "I simply cannot imagine what will become of her now." Helene half-smiled in my direction, as if sharing with me some womanly understanding of her friend's frailty. "Oh, I'll do what I can," she said. "But without the colonel to look after her, whatever will Margaret do with herself?"

"She might marry again," Gilbert said, prompted more by the imp of the perverse, I assumed, than by belief that marriage would be the solution to her future.

Helene's eyes widened. "And if she were willing, Dr. Crew, are you saying you'd be interested?" Her sly smile made clear she knew her question had caught him off guard—and embarrassed him. "Margaret's a trifle older than you are, that's true. Still, her experience in certain matters needn't be a disadvantage."

"But suppose her affections are already engaged elsewhere,"

319

I said sweetly.

Helene released a brief huff of breath before abruptly changing the direction of the conversation. "We shall have another séance," she announced.

"Oh. So soon after Colonel Duvall's passing?" I said.

"No better time," Helene replied.

While the spirit was still bewildered by the sudden loss of the body—was that her reasoning?

"We positively must—after the funeral," Helene added. "Although, forgive me, Mrs. James—I must leave you out. Only six at the table, you know. While your dear brother must attend, for he is closely associated with both of the departed, indeed, with each one within the hour of death. Then, there's myself as spirit medium, the judge, Margaret, Mr. Eden, Dr. Baldwin, who so expects to be included. You understand? "

I nodded, and Helene went on, saying she had changed her mind about holding the next séance at Eden's townhouse; no, that wouldn't do. Now that they would be contacting Colonel Duvall, as well as Charlotte, the Placides' own parlor in town, where both spirits had been given hospitality in life, was the better choice.

"We have a duty," she said, "to reach out to both Charlotte and the colonel—two souls cut adrift under such unhappy circumstances."

"Both of them closely connected to Victor Eden," Gilbert said.

Helene acknowledged his comment with a lift of her brows. Would he dare pursue the connection further, suggest to her that Eden and Duvall could have fought over Margaret? Suppose he took her a little way into our confidence, she, who had the judge's ear, and see where that led? But Gilbert had chosen not to, or lost the opportunity as Helene prattled on, relaying to us what Judge Placide had relayed to her—matters pertaining to Colonel Duvall's demise. The judge would waste no time in making final arrangements for his friend and colleague. Helene gave us some notion of when the inquest—at which Gilbert would give evidence—would be held and when the funeral was most likely to take place. Yes, these new obligations in town would delay the Placides' going to Testament. And shouldn't they also delay Helene from playing hostess to the Eden children? Apparently, not.

"I promised Victor," Helene said. "Tansy can take them on to Testament and keep an eye on them. She would anyway, even if I were there."

"But I was so hoping to borrow the little darlings, myself, from Widow Eden," I said. "Just the other day, I told her my house has echoed like a cavern since my twins left, and I've been aching for children." I could prattle as well as Helene. "Yes, I insist, Mrs. Placide. Amy and Wilfred must be my guests. And, of course, you wouldn't want to be without Tansy when you hold your next séance."

The measured emphasis I gave that last sentence seemed to settle the matter. For all Helene's gifts, her conjuring of spirits might suffer without the presence of her handmaid.

Then, after I bid her good-day, she turned to Gilbert with parting remarks. "One more thing, Dr. Crew. I, not you, sir, will secure the objects once belonging to the departed. That little vial you brought to our last gathering was *not* a success," Helene said, half-scolding, half-teasing him. "But Colonel Duvall's pocket flask will be quite another matter, don't you agree?" She smiled primly, but a glint came into her eyes. "And I have great hopes for a very personal item, which I've just discovered, an item imbued"—Helene drew out the word—"with Charlotte's very essence. Sure to coax her into the light, into communion with us all."

321

Act III
Exhumation

Chapter Forty-Three

Into communion with Charlotte, Gilbert had no need for a spirit guide. His awareness of her was so heightened that his communion with her might occur at any time, wordlessly—even without her conscious participation. I reckoned he could blink and see her face, breathe and catch a whiff of her perfume, listen above the noise or beneath the silence around him and hear the throbbing of her pulse. I remembered the old conjuring tricks of longing, had practiced them once upon a time, aching for my young soldier, running away from home to find him and hold him again to my heart. I knew where longing had led me and worried for my brother, but lacking the gift of clairvoyance, could not say what future awaited him.

Gilbert, impatient to bring Amy and Wilfred to Charlotte, drove the carriage at a clip from the Placides' mansion to Widow Eden's apartment. Then, I left Gilbert holding the reins while I went in without him to see Widow Eden, the better to present the offer as solely my own to take the children off her hands. No mention of Gilbert and his meeting with Eden, not a word about Testament.

Widow Eden took her time considering my invitation before replying: "Thank you, Mrs. James. Very generous of you. I shouldn't like to decline a short respite." Which caused me concern that she would decline if I were not more persuasive. But then her brows angled downward from the furrow between them, like eaves above her eyes, in an expression of long-suffering. "My headaches," she said. "And now this head cold. Still, don't keep them away from me too long. I find myself growing fonder . . ." Her voice faded as she patted each child's head.

Understanding then that her grandchildren were free to come with me, I enlisted Narcisse to pack their things and help me bring children and luggage down to the carriage. The maid saw us off less regretfully, perhaps, than her mistress.

On the way from the Quarter to Faubourg Marigny, I simply told the children that they were coming for a visit, saying nothing of their mother. Both seemed accepting of the change, both sufficiently lulled by their recent mid-day meal, the rocking motion of the carriage, and the nearing of their usual naptime. When we arrived, Amy, yawning and rubbing her eyes, shuffled after me into the front hall. Gilbert followed us with Wilfred drowsing over his shoulder.

In the moment I stopped at the hall stand to hang up my cape, Amy stepped out from behind my skirt, rubbed her eyes again, and looked up the long, narrow staircase, the passage dimly lit by a single wall sconce on the cloudy afternoon. I followed her gaze to the topmost stair, over which spilled the hem of the blue-violet tea gown. Draw the shadows, and the shapes will emerge—thus, Charlotte, herself, emerged, the contours of her body suggested by the drape of the gown, the angles of her cheekbones and the curve of her cupid's bow mouth revealed by the glow of gaslight.

Amy tugged on one of Wilfred's dangling feet until her brother woke in Gilbert's arms and kicked against Gilbert's side to free his foot from her grasp. He looked down at his sister, then turned his head towards the direction she pointed, up the stairs.

Charlotte descended one step, then another, and Ella materialized from the dark at the top of the stairs behind her, there in case Charlotte needed a supportive arm. At clear sight of his mother, Wilfred squealed and twisted in Gilbert's grasp, punching his little balled fists against Gilbert's shoulder, trying to break his hold, so Wilfred could swivel and launch himself towards Charlotte. Gilbert restrained him just long enough to prevent his falling and to set him down at the foot of the staircase before the boy began scrambling upwards on all fours—a faster method of locomotion for him than Amy's deliberate step-together-step, one hand catching at every other baluster.

Charlotte met her children halfway on their journey. Then, she dropped down on the middle stair, and they wrapped themselves around her. Amy hugged Charlotte's neck and kissed her, again and again, and they each brushed tears from the other's cheeks. Charlotte encircled her daughter with one arm and her son with the other. But Wilfred, rowdy with joy, would not be still in her embrace. He climbed onto her lap, laughing and pulling at the cluster of purple velvet wisteria blossoms ornamenting one shoulder of her tea gown.

Moved as I was by the sight of Charlotte with her children, I spared a glance for Gilbert, who gazed at Charlotte as if seeing her anew. Indeed, he might never before have seen her so radiant with happiness, and his smile at her seemed rueful to me. I recollected the scene in The Winter's Tale when Leontes witnesses Hermione coming back to life, his joy tinged by his regrets.

As I ascended the stairs, Ella descended them, and we converged upon Charlotte and her children and shepherded them on upstairs. Gilbert would bring in the bags, see to the horse and the carriage—the usual things that he attended to—although, when I glanced back at him over the stairwell railing, he appeared fixed where he stood. Then Dulcie appeared in the hall, circled his feet,

325

butted her head against his shin, and, apparently, spurred him to action.

For the rest of the afternoon, while Charlotte and her children reacquainted themselves, Gilbert attended patients in the clinic, Ella went about household tasks, and I slipped away for an hour or so to the little escritoire in my room. I left my door ajar, however, the better to catch the sounds rising from the parlor—Wilfred giggling and Amy singing to her own random plunking of keys on the spinet, Charlotte joining her children in laughter and song. Some creative energy must have come into the house with the little ones, for I could hardly scribble down ideas fast enough, whole scenes for my stage play springing to mind. I even sketched arrangements of furniture and patterns of movement for the actors. Bits of stage business, wasn't that a term I had heard Ambrose use? What would he think if I not only offered him my play with an eye to his producing it, but also myself as artistic director?

When my literary fervor abated, an interlude of peace took its place, settling upon the household—for twilight had come with still no sign of Eden coming for the children. He might not know they were gone from his mother's apartment. But he would know. Time was precious.

The six of us gathered at the kitchen table for a light supper with gingerbread for dessert, then gathered again in the parlor, in sociable communion—Gilbert finishing case notes, Ella darning a stocking, I writing letters to the twins while Dulcie swatted a paw at my moving pen, all of us looking up from our tasks, again and again, as Charlotte, Amy, and Wilfred exclaimed over the stereoscopic slides that brought another world into the room.

Unlike the slides Gilbert had seen at Testament, which depicted martial and erotic themes, these slides captured the highlights of my Grand Tour, taken after my third husband's passing—Edinburgh Castle, the Palace of Versailles, boats on the

Seine, a bridge arching over the Arno, a gondola floating on a Venetian canal—all three-dimensional through the magic of the stereoscope. "As if we are there," Charlotte murmured, "as if we could be." But when Amy and Wilfred discovered the box of storybook tableaux, once belonging to Allan and Arabella, Europe gave way to *Gulliver's Travels, Hiawatha, and Ivanhoe.*

For the sixth or seventh time, Amy appeared at my elbow, requesting I look at a scene, too, and share her delight. But no, this time it was something else, something worrying her. "Mrs. James, is that a ghost in the picture?"

I looked at the image. A fingerprint on the lenses, a smudge on the cardboard slide, a trick of the light—all answers with which I could have dismissed her question. But she had asked in earnest, and Charlotte had seen it, too, the pale form hovering behind Lady Rowena as Ivanhoe takes her hand. With my handkerchief, I wiped the lenses and dusted off the dual images on the cardboard, but the inexplicable form remained until Gilbert intervened. With his lead pencil, he shaded the phantom from both pictures, bringing the lady into high relief. "Better?" he asked, and Amy smiled at the improvement.

When bedtime came, Charlotte took Wilfred on her hip and Amy by the hand, then whispered *thank you* to each of us in turn—Gilbert, Ella, and me. I followed them upstairs to make sure my guests had all they needed for a comfortable night. Already, Gilbert had moved a pair of children's cots from the clinic into Charlotte's room and Ella made them up with pillows and quilts—although, long before morning, Amy and Wilfred would likely be in Charlotte's bed, nestled beside her, making sure of her. Small children needed their mother, and their father must wait for his wife, particularly true in a household short of servants and nursemaids. Was that how it had been in the Eden house? Victor Eden, impatient in the doorway of the nursery, while Charlotte crooned a lullaby to the children. Her voice might have caught when she had seen him watching her, but then she had gone on singing until the children were asleep. She had tucked them in and turned to go, but one or the other woke and cried for her, and the cycle of tending and soothing began again. And her husband no longer waited in the doorway.

Chapter Forty-Four

At the close of our peaceful evening, after Charlotte and her children and Ella had all retired for the night, I began to droop, myself, when Gilbert decided to share with me what was on his mind. While Charlotte had been present, he had kept quiet about the news that agitated him, that now set him to pacing the parlor rug. Hours ago, while working in the clinic, Gilbert had received a summons to the inquest, set for day after tomorrow, to be followed by the funeral the day after that, and then—if Helene Placide had her way—another séance.

"If Eden can't be held responsible for the attempt on Charlotte's life, he might still be held for Duvall's murder," Gilbert said.

My brother had followed this thread of thought while out to return my horse and carriage to the livery stable, retracing the street to Keogh's buildings and then around to the saloon, where the Crescent City Regulators had held their meetings. Gilbert wanted to be clear about distances between places and where persons could plausibly have been in relation to one another—the better to recognize a lie if he heard one at the inquest. He had also stopped at the alleyway where Colonel Duvall had met his death and where the stain of his blood still lay like a shadow cast on the ground. Walking the length of the alley, from where Gilbert had entered it on the night of the murder, all the way to the other end, had lead him to the rear of Keogh's better property—the one in which Margaret kept her assignations with Eden.

"I wonder," Gilbert said, "if the two of them were ever on

the banquette that night, at all, or if they were only ever in the alleyway after leaving Keogh's building. And there Duvall confronted them. The man I saw speaking with Duvall at the door of the saloon told the colonel where to find them."

"He might have done," I said.

"And if that man could be found—if I could find him—and he gave testimony," Gilbert said, "surely, the pieces would fall into place."

The idea seized him, and I could not dissuade my brother from heading off that very night in search of some stranger in a slouch hat and ill-fitting raincoat. I could only wait up and fret until his return a couple of hours later—distracting myself at intervals by imagining upsetting scenarios and dashing off heated dialogue between characters in my play-in-progress.

Such pursuits, rather than wearing me down, had keyed me up, and by the time Gilbert shuffled wearily home, I was ready for a full report of his excursion. After I poured us each a brandy, he obliged me, and I, curled on the sofa with pipe and snifter, saw it all.

The street outside the saloon where the Regulators held their meetings was noisy with late night revelers—men's slurred voices rising above the racket of tinny pianos pounded upon in various establishments. Men crowded the banquette and staggered into the muddy roadway, grumbling or laughing or singing, some shouting up to the women who leaned invitingly from upstairs windows.

Inside the saloon, Gilbert navigated through a fog of tobacco smoke, around tables crowded with patrons, across a floor slippery with spittle to reach the bar. Ordering a whiskey, he attempted to strike up a conversation with the barman: "Terrible about Colonel Duvall. I had a drink with him here on the very night he was murdered, remember?" The barman did not recall. "He left in a hurry when a man in a slouch hat came for him. Not

330

so tall as the colonel, maybe a little heavier? They went out in the rain." The barman turned away, pouring a drink for another customer. "There was a meeting here that night. Remember that?" Gilbert said to no response. Men on either side of him pressed in for space at the bar, forcing him back from it. Gilbert snatched up his glass and moved away through the crowd to the far end of the room and the closed door, no sentry stationed at it this time.

As Gilbert tried the doorknob, which did not turn, he heard a gruff voice by his ear: "That's not the way out." The speaker had a full black beard with a jagged streak of white, like a lightning bolt, running through it—one of Mr. Turnbull's men.

"I thought there might be a meeting," Gilbert said by way of excuse.

The man's eyes narrowed to slits.

"In light of what happened to Colonel Duvall," Gilbert said. He could not catch the bearded man's short reply, which was lost amidst a burst of guffawing at a nearby table. "I have information," Gilbert shouted, relaying to this man what he had told the barman, growing hoarse trying to make himself heard above the din. Gilbert had hoped for some information in return, but received none.

"You with the police?" the man asked.

"No, sir, absolutely not. The colonel was a friend." Gilbert stretched the meaning of the word. "The man he left with could be a witness to his murder."

"Think so?" The man, whose name might have been Smith, if Gilbert had heard him correctly, sounded doubtful. Even so, Gilbert had handed over his card, asking to be informed if Smith came across any news that might be helpful in bringing to justice the murderer of their mutual friend.

But my brother would be unwise to pin his hopes on forthcoming information from one of Duvall's fellow Regulators.

✛ ✛ ✛

331

Next morning, as I entered the kitchen, Ella was informing Gilbert: "Miss Lenore give the daily maid a week's paid leave—mighty generous, I say. But I guess it had to be done. That gal's a gossipy little thing, and we don't need the world knowing we got houseguests."

Indeed, since Gilbert had brought Charlotte here, he, Ella, and I had made numerous adjustments to keep her presence secret. And with enough practice, I supposed, deception might become second nature.

As I gravitated towards the coffee pot, exchanging good mornings with Gilbert and Ella, sounds of activity in the upstairs hall reached us in the kitchen, the scurrying of feet across the floorboards and Wilfred's squeal of laughter when Charlotte must have caught him. Ella smiled a moment, setting a plate of poached eggs on toast in front of Gilbert, then, as quickly frowned.

"On the subject of gossip and nosing around," Ella said, "the judge's girl, that Tansy, been around here t'other day, wash day, saying Miz Placide sent her for cuttings from some of your shrubs, Mr. Gil."

"That's odd," Gilbert said. "Mrs. Placide didn't mentioned wanting cuttings to me."

Nor to me, when we spoke just yesterday in her jungle of a conservatory. More likely that we would be asking her for starter roots and seedlings.

Ella returned to the stove and stirred a saucepan of oatmeal. "If you ask me, Tansy just sniffing around 'cause that's what she does," Ella said. "I sent her home with a bit of thyme and curly parsley for her master's table—should've been water hemlock." Which Gilbert would never grow in his garden of medicinal plants, but he and I took Ella's point. She was not an admirer of Judge Placide.

During a lull in the afternoon, Gilbert took advantage of the kitchen for mixing medicines, before it again belonged to Ella for supper preparations. He was standing at the stove, stirring a simmering concoction, when I brought Charlotte in with me. Not having read a newspaper since her arrival, she knew nothing of Colonel Duvall's murder and its possible implications, and Gilbert and I had agreed we should inform her while Ella was upstairs minding the children.

Gilbert turned his head as we came through the doorway, his eyes focusing on Charlotte, who wore, not the eccentric tea gown this time, but her modest white shirtwaist and gray skirt.

"Smells like a candy shop in here," Charlotte remarked, and Gilbert smiled at her. "But you aren't making candy?"

"No, a tonic for stomachache," he replied. "Goes down more easily if it tastes like peppermint."

Charlotte returned my brother's smile, saying, "You've never forgotten what it's like to be a child."

"My patients remind me," he said. "Being sick or hurt is hard enough for them—so I sweeten the cure with mint or cherry syrup, licorice or sarsaparilla."

"Do you make all your own medicines?" she asked.

"Most of them." And Gilbert often improved on our father's old formulas much as Ella enriched the recipes coming down to her from her grandmother.

Gilbert took the saucepan of bubbling liquid from the stove and set it to cool on an iron trivet. Charlotte circled the table, surveying the several bottles of tonics and syrups and jars of salve that he had already prepared. She asked him questions about ingredients and uses, and he answered. They were making conversation—Gilbert, perhaps, to ease into or delay relating the grim news about the colonel. And Charlotte? She was aglow, of course, with her children in the house to lift her spirits. Happiness, which renewed one's interest in life in general, might account for fascination with particulars—such as I saw in Charlotte's careful attention to Gilbert's words and actions as he talked of remedies and poured the rose-colored liquid from the saucepan through a funnel into a series of clear glass medicine bottles.

I brought the chit-chat to a close. "Gilbert met with your husband yesterday morning," I said to Charlotte. "About Amy and Wilfred and other matters." With the change in subject, I perceived a change in Charlotte's demeanor, as if a shadow had fallen across the bright expression she had worn a moment ago.

"Oh," she said. "He had no objection to their coming here, did he, Miss Lenore?"

"They're here now," I said, not answering her question.

Charlotte darted a glance at Gilbert. "How did he seem to you?" she asked.

"He was—" Gilbert hesitated, then said: "At first, he seemed preoccupied with work."

"I see. And will he visit Amy and Wilfred here?" Charlotte's voice held a tremor.

"He didn't say," Gilbert replied without speculating that Eden might well have something to say when he found out where his children were being housed.

Gilbert pulled out a chair from the kitchen table for Charlotte, who seemed in need of sitting down. I pulled out my own chair and joined her, placing a hand over hers on the tabletop.

"Perhaps some of Ella's blackberry cordial," I said to my brother, who brought the decanter and three glasses.

"I don't know what to do," Charlotte said, looking into my eyes. "How to go on."

"We will find a way," I said with confidence I did not feel.

"What proof is there that Victor poisoned me?" Charlotte didn't wait for an answer, which neither Gilbert nor I possessed, but went on in some agitation: "And if he didn't, I must go back to him. Even if he did, I must go back. I've thought and thought about our every conversation, what he said, what he didn't say. The judge has a hold of him and works him—and is never satisfied. If only I could find a way to talk to Victor now, as I was never able to before—if he would listen, consider my plan to take care of our children, even as their nursemaid. You said that wouldn't do. But I don't know what else—"

"Something has changed," I said, then nodded to Gilbert.

"Something has happened," he said. But rather than explain, Gilbert reached into a trouser pocket, withdrew a folded piece of newspaper, opened and smoothed it on the tabletop, and offered it to Charlotte. Her hazel eyes widened as they lit on the bold headline—*Col. Duvall Cut Down!* "He was killed night before last," Gilbert said.

"Killed," Charlotte repeated in a whisper. She looked from Gilbert to me, then returned to the printed words, scanning them, running a finger along beneath certain lines, reading them again. The story, which my brother must have torn from this morning's edition, began as a panegyric for Duvall, calling him *a prominent citizen and respected attorney, a keeper of the peace and standard bearer of civilized society, a valiant soldier, wounded in service to the Confederate States of America,* and so forth. Then came a lurid account of his murder, written in the popular style: *As Colonel Frank Duvall escorted his comely wife homeward, the couple were set upon and brutally attacked. It is believed they were caught unawares on their nocturnal stroll by a depraved madman, who brazenly snatched Mrs. Duvall into the pitch-dark alleyway. Colonel Duvall, ever the hero, pursued his wife's attacker but was, tragically, stabbed to death.* Mention was made of the killer having fled the scene of his wickedness, followed by a description of Duvall's prodigious loss of blood, a river of it running from the alleyway into the street, alerting passersby to the crime, even before the horrified Mrs. Duvall found voice to cry out for help.

"*Colonel Duvall's final throes of agony were mitigated only by the knowledge that he had sacrificed his life for his wife's honor,*" Charlotte read aloud. *"With that final thought for comfort, the brave officer and gentleman expired in Mrs. Duvall's embrace."* Charlotte's forefinger stopped on the last line: *"The fiend is still at-large."*

Staring down at the piece of newspaper, Charlotte whispered in a voice devoid of irony, "Poor Mrs. Duvall. How shocking for her."

Even if Margaret had passed the evening fornicating with Charlotte's husband and making a cuckold of her own, I finished the thought in my head. That Charlotte held more pity than scorn for her rival said much about the generosity of her character.

"I'd met with Colonel Duvall earlier in the evening," Gilbert said, "and then he'd hurried off. I came upon the scene in the alley shortly after the attack."

"Gilbert is to give evidence at the inquest tomorrow," I said.

"Then you saw who attacked him?" Charlotte said, meeting Gilbert's eyes as she handed him the newspaper story.

"No. He was gone. And the colonel was already dead when I reached him," Gilbert said. "I examined the body."

Charlotte took another sip of cordial, then asked Gilbert if there were some particular reason he had met with the colonel.

"He had invited me to a sort of political meeting," Gilbert said. "I hoped to learn something useful, thought Mr. Eden might be in attendance, too, but he wasn't."

"Charlotte," I said, "it is possible that on that night, Colonel Duvall received some confirmation that his wife was keeping company with Mr. Eden and confronted him. The colonel already had his suspicions."

"The men could have fought each other," Gilbert said. "You know it's possible,"

Slowly, Charlotte nodded. There it was—Gilbert's second accusation against Eden of murderous intent followed by Charlotte's acceptance of the possibility. If Eden were found guilty

336

of killing his mistress's husband, he could go to prison, might be executed. Charlotte, like Gilbert, must have seen the prospects a conviction would open. I certainly did.

The door chime sounded, and I think we all flinched as that ordinary sound brought us back from speculations.

Gilbert rose, asked Charlotte to wait in the kitchen, then hurried along the hall towards the front door. I followed him, still some paces behind him when Gilbert opened the door to a tall, slim man in top hat and frock coat, one gloved hand poised on his walking stick. Mr. Parr coming to pay me a surprise call, I conjectured, for with the lowering sunlight behind him in the doorway, I saw, at first, only a silhouette and could not make him out for certain until he crossed the threshold. No, not Ambrose Parr. Victor Eden.

Chapter Forty-Five

Gilbert had taken a step back, Eden another step forward, as if presuming my brother had invited him in to vent his ire. He had expressly told Gilbert not to collect the children, so Eden claimed, yet Gilbert had gone against him and done precisely that. "Are they here, Mrs. James?" Eden addressed me on my approach, then back to Gilbert: "First, you lose my wife's body, then you take my children. Have you no scruples?" I wondered Eden didn't choke on the last word.

"When we spoke, sir," Gilbert said, "I might have misunderstood you."

Eden glowered, then raised his stick as if to emphasize whatever he would say next.

I intervened. "Mr. Eden, it was really I who misunderstood my brother." I cut my eyes in Gilbert's direction before turning back to Eden, smiling at him as if I hadn't a brain in my head. "Do, please, excuse my confusion, sir. I thought only to relieve your dear mother, who is suffering from a dreadful cold, as I understand." As I prattled on, explaining away my actions as based on a zealous desire to be helpful, not a disregard of Mr. Eden's wishes, Eden darted his glance from me to Gilbert and back again. If he suspected a conspiracy between my brother and me, I gradually persuaded him to accept my best intentions.

"I'll see them now, Mrs. James, if you please," Eden said.

I beamed as if nothing would delight me more—as if we had nothing to hide and Charlotte were not again in peril of feeling the force of her husband's displeasure. But my chest tightened with apprehension as I led Eden to the parlor to wait my return with his offspring. Gilbert stayed with him while I started up the stairs, taking only a few steps before hesitating. Should I go straight up to Ella and the children? Or hurry first to the kitchen and warn Charlotte to stay put? Had she overheard her husband, blustering in the front hall—as I was overhearing Gilbert in the parlor, attempting to make civil conversation with our unwelcome caller? Gilbert commented on the impending inquest, the funeral to follow, adding that he had the impression from Mrs. Placide that all plans for going to Testament had been postponed. I could not catch Eden's response, if he offered one.

With a hand on the banister, I leaned a little ways to peer from the staircase and down the hall towards the back of the house, still considering a dash to the kitchen first and then up the back gallery stairs to the children. And then I saw Charlotte coming towards me, head cocked at a questioning angle. What was she thinking? This was no time for her to encounter her husband—not until we learned the outcome of the inquest. I let go the railing and with both hands shooed her towards the hall door into the dining room. For the life of me, I could not remember if the pocket doors dividing dining room and parlor were open, shut, or somewhere in between. Still, if Charlotte stood to one side of the china cabinet, she might remain out of Eden's sight. She disappeared into the dining room at the instant I heard Eden's voice behind me from the parlor archway leading to the hall.

I darted a glance in his direction, relieved that he was not yet looking my way, but over his shoulder at Gilbert, I presumed, who was out of my sight. In that indolent baritone of his, Eden said something about his not having all day and what could be keeping me. By the time he did turn in my direction, I was all aflutter, bending as far forward as my corset stays permitted, while I patted the stair ahead of me. In that posture, swiveling my neck just enough to eye him, upside down, as he stepped into the hall, I told

Eden I'd dropped a shell comb—in my hurry to fetch the children. "There," I said, securing a comb already in my hair as I straighten my back. "I won't be a moment, sir." We exchanged smiles, and I didn't need eyes in the back of my head to know Eden watched my ascent.

Ella, having heard Eden's voice in the hall, had already prepared the children for a possible audience with their father, so he was not kept waiting any longer. Step-together-step, hand-in-hand, Amy and I came down the stairs, Ella behind us with Wilfred on her hip. Eden had returned to the parlor, and Amy greeted him there.

"Good evening, Father," she said with careful enunciation.

"Good evening, Amy," Eden replied.

"Papa?" Wilfred sounded doubtful. Then, at a whispered prompt from Ella, he said, "Sir."

"Good evening, Wilfred." Then to me, Eden remarked, "They look well."

With the formalities of greeting over, Eden seemed to have little else to say to his daughter and son, despite his having hardly seen them in weeks. I maintained a serene unobtrusiveness, and Gilbert held his tongue, while Ella filled the conversational void: "Little Miss Amy is a marvel at the piano, sir, singing and playing. A natural-born talent."

"Is she?" Eden said.

"And this here young man—" Ella gave Wilfred a bounce on her hip "—why, he is so smart, he just—"

"See Mama," said Wilfred.

I shot a glance towards the broad pocket doors between parlor and dining room, each pulled only halfway out of the walls. With Wilfred's announcement, I expected to see Charlotte standing in the gap. But no, I saw only a suggestion of her reflection in the leaded glass of the china cabinet, for she was just on the other side of one of the pocket doors. I drew a quick breath.

"I do so enjoy your children, Mr. Eden," I said while moving a little further to one side, so that Eden, turning to face me, turned his back on the dining room doorway. "They distract me, sir, from missing my own son and daughter, grown and gone."

Wilfred grinned and piped up again: "Mama play with me."

Gilbert sucked in his breath, but Eden took no notice, instead casting a severe look at his son, perhaps interpreting the boy's statement as an impertinent demand.

"Willie." Amy gave her brother a warning look, and I felt the warmth of kinship with her.

"Wilfred," Eden corrected her.

"These children just full of imagination, yes, sir, Mr. Eden," Ella said, giving Wilfred another, more vigorous bounce on her hip.

"I assume their bags are packed," Eden said, regarding Ella coldly.

"Oh, my stars," I said, "I thought you only wished to see Amy and Wilfred, not take them from me, Mr. Eden. Please, sir, do let me keep them—another day or two? While this sad business—" which I left unnamed—"is being settled." Assuring him of how obliged I'd be to him for indulging my motherly heart, I saw his mouth twitch and set in a hard line. But he acquiesced to me—on condition that he might call again to see the children in my tender care.

With that, Ella and I took Amy and Wilfred from the parlor, Ella taking the little ones upstairs, while I slipped away and through the hall door to the dining room to join Charlotte. Surely, Gilbert would show Eden out now. No one had taken his hat or gloves or walking stick from him, nothing to retrieve for him, nothing to slow his leaving. But still he lingered, speaking to Gilbert. I beckoned Charlotte closer to me, away from the reflective glass-fronted china cabinet, but still near enough to hear the conversation in the adjoining room.

"Your sister is a very lovely lady, Dr. Crew," Eden said.

Indeed, I liked to think I was, but his saying so irked me. Did he expect Gilbert to pass his compliment on to me? Become the go-between for his next conquest?—which would never occur. And what must Charlotte be thinking? I felt her sideways look at me, even as I thought I saw a cobweb on the chandelier.

The men's voices droned, words indistinct, and then Gilbert said clearly: "If my wife could come back—if such a thing were possible—I might do things differently." I remember his making such a statement to me, adding that, if he could go back in time and un-marry Estelle, she could be living happily without him, as her father's darling daughter and not his wife at all. "And you, Mr. Eden?—would you have done anything differently?" Share a confidence, receive a confidence—was that what Gilbert was playing at?

"If such a thing were possible," Eden said, "I'd teach Charlotte to see reason about my career—that fed and clothed her—about the important decisions a man must make in his profession, to further himself . . ."

His statement might not sound unreasonable, if Eden and Charlotte were like many other married couples, the husband devoting more and more time to the demands of his profession, the wife neglected. Or had it been the other way around, Charlotte giving all her attention to the children, Eden ignored? Discord might grow between a husband and wife, and the first wrong note never be found. But I doubted Eden deserved the benefit of the doubt as he droned on, disdainfully, not answering Gilbert's question but expatiating on how both his wife's presence and her loss had inconvenienced him.

"A dutiful wife keeps a man's domestic life in order," Eden said. "While her death leaves him open to the designs of other ladies. You see the position I'm in—it's not that a widower necessarily seeks out attention, but he may receive it, unsought." He was making an excuse for himself. "My wife could be too fastidious about some matters, too lax about others . . ." Eden's voice trailed on and away like his footfalls following Gilbert's towards the front door, but I caught his parting comment: "You heard my son, Dr. Crew—even Charlotte's spirit comes back to the children, not to me."

Then I heard the door close behind Eden and watched his wife shudder.

Chapter Forty-Six

At the coroner's inquest, Margaret Duvall gave every appearance of being distressed, with her face pale and eyes red, mouth trembling and hands fidgeting with a limp lace-trimmed handkerchief. The new widow wore an unremarkable mourning bonnet and lusterless black dress, perhaps on the advice of her dear friend Helene, becoming a shadow of her former self. Truly, she seemed to narrow and lose dimension, waning between her imposing companions—Dr. Baldwin in his dark frock coat on one side and Helene in her glossy black silk and jet beads on the other side, the ruffles and flounces of her gown taking up the remainder of the bench. Judge Placide sat apart from his wife, in an oaken armchair proportioned to his grandeur, at the front of the room and to one side, the better to keep an eye on all those involved in the proceedings—coroner, witnesses, and spectators—as I was doing from my seat and, near me, Gilbert from where he stood against the wall by a couple of newspaper reporters. Like them, he had brought pencil and notebook, prepared to record statements and events, although not as sensationally as they might. From my vantage point, I noted Victor Eden lurking at the back of the crowded room, far removed from his mistress and their mutual friends. But if this were his attempt at inconspicuousness, it had failed, for Eden's superior height and elegant apparel and whatever impulse caused him to lift his prominent chin distinguished him from the men around him and would not allow him to fade into the background, even if fading were to his advantage.

I was smartly turned out, myself, in a sleek basque and draped skirt in electric blue while, by contrast to me and Eden, my

345

brother was just presentable. He had been up much of the night, called out to assist in treating a family suffering varying degrees of burns in a house fire—his loss of sleep was nothing compared to that, he said when I woke him after his couple of hours sleep and forced him to full consciousness with coffee and a hot breakfast. He had shaved in a hurry, nicking himself along the jawline, but managing to avoid slitting an artery. Meanwhile, I laid out a clean shirt, selected a suit, and fussed over him: "The gray will do—somber, but not funereal. No plaid trousers today, Gil. And try not to bleed on your collar. You are giving testimony."

But when? I began to lose hope. The coroner called witnesses, seemingly, as the spirit moved him, while Gilbert had taken to leaning against the wall, looking as if my strong coffee would not sustain his clarity of mind much longer.

First, one of the two policemen who had been in the alley testified to observable facts, including the time at which he had come upon the scene, the position of the body, and the location of the knife wound. Then he described the weapon, itself, the thin blade and sharp point, adding that the knife had—according to private testimony on which the coroner did not ask him to elaborate—belonged to Colonel Frank Duvall. "Must have drawn his weapon, and the villain turned it on him." Or was it given to the attacker in advance by the woman who had access to it?

The policeman finished his testimony by listing off or pointing out anyone now in the room whom he recognized as being in the vicinity on the night in question. Surely, he would have noticed Victor Eden but made no mention of him.

"The other policeman," the coroner said, "will corroborate your testimony? Let's call him and see."

"Can't do that, sir," said the policeman who was giving evidence. "He's long gone. Took a job in another parish for real money." A smattering of comprehending chuckles from the spectators acknowledged how poorly paid men were who tried to make a living keeping the peace in New Orleans. Bribes might augment salaries, but not everyone took them, or was offered the opportunity. The coroner looked unamused and, after a glance in Judge Placide's direction, asked the policeman to step down.

Next, came a series of self-proclaimed eye-witnesses. One swore he had just stepped off the banquette by the entrance to the alley when he slipped in something slick and wet and his feet went right out from under him. "Stumbling drunk in his own puke," a man too near me said under whiskey breath. But others around the room nodded and murmured or gasped at the account of a river of blood oozing over the ground. Witness after witness reported seeing one thing after another, as if they had not all been looking into a dark alleyway but, instead, peering through a lit-up kaleidoscope of revolving images. Some claimed the attacker ran away down the alley: he was a big, heavy-footed fellow in a flapping overcoat; no, sir, a thin, wiry man with a slouch hat, leaping and darting like a white-tailed deer; oh, no, a pair of colored boys in overalls, for sure, one of them hollering and waving a machete. On and on, until the coroner finally looked as weary of them as I felt. Still, none of the witnesses had yet described Eden, and I would have bitten my tongue, slapped myself to stay awake, and listened to them all, if only one of them would point an accusing finger towards Eden at the back of the room. Then an investigation would follow, Eden's arrest and trial and imprisonment, all in a neat progression of justice.

Unfortunately, the coroner had heard enough and called a halt, even though more men and a few women were still eager to bear witness, false or true. Surveying the lot of them over the top of his spectacles, the coroner said: "If every one of you folks gathered here were, in fact, on the street that night—shall we say within ten feet or so of where the murdered man fell?—well, it looks to me like Colonel Duvall drew a bigger crowd for his stabbing than Marie Antoinette did for her decapitation. Now, let's get on with this."

347

The room quieted. Then, the coroner, recalling the widow's presence, followed his callous remark with: "'Beg pardon, Mrs. Duvall." Margaret turned her face into Dr. Baldwin's lapel, and the old physician patted her shoulder.

For another moment or two, the coroner made notes and shuffled through documents on his desk, without looking up and thus avoided Judge Placide's scowling countenance. But when the coroner raised his head, he exchanged a nod with the judge, perhaps an understanding passing between them that now was the time for a different approach. And so it was, as the coroner again addressed the assembly in his authoritative drawl: "Ladies and gentleman, we have heard a number of reports, differing in details, but all testifying to the shocking circumstances of Colonel Duvall's demise. The late colonel was a respectable citizen, a practitioner of the law, moreover, a war hero accustomed to meeting his foes in the light of day, face-to-face on the field of battle. But he was ambushed, attacked under cover of night and stabbed to death in an alleyway by someone—whether tall or short, heavy or slight, bearded or clean-shaven—" here the coroner swept his gaze over the various eye-witnesses "—by someone whom we all agree is a despicable coward."

From the murmurings around me, I picked out words of consensus that the killer was, indeed, low-down—along with words of dissension as witnesses defended their versions of the event to whomever would listen.

"No more meandering," the coroner called out, winding up his own circumlocution. "Time to get at the truth." Although how we would arrive at it, based on the next witness's testimony, was anyone's guess.

Leaning on Dr. Baldwin's arm, Colonel Duvall's widow came languidly to the fore. "Mrs. Duvall is under my care," Baldwin announced, then made a show of easing his patient onto a chair near the coroner's desk and asking her if she felt strong enough to answer a few questions regarding her husband's passing. Margaret nodded dreamily. Perhaps she could answer—if not too befuddled with laudanum, or too confused by details she wished to hide.

After the doctor had shuffled back to his seat on the bench beside Helene, Margaret's demeanor underwent a subtle but perceptible change. She straightened her back, blinked several times, and looked about her, as if waking to the realization that she was now the center of attention. When the coroner began to question her in a gentle, patient voice, a contrast to the one he had used with some other witnesses, Margaret responded favorably. "I do so appreciate all the trouble everyone's gone to," she said, "for the colonel's sake and mine." She smiled demurely, letting her gaze travel over the faces before her—Helene smiling back as if encouraging her, Dr. Baldwin looking important with anxiety writ on his brow, Judge Placide even more important with his grave visage, colleagues and associates of the colonel, members of the Crescent City Regulators, anyone who had been on the street, or claimed to have been, on the night of Duvall's murder. I looked them over, too, from the well-heeled to the downtrodden, following Margaret's line of sight all the way to the rear of the room.

She must have been looking for Eden, who was no longer standing by the far wall. No, he had taken a seat at the end of the last bench by the door. Ready, I supposed, to spring for a quick exit if Margaret, or anyone else, said something that he did not wish to hear or to be heard by others. Could he trust her to keep his secrets, to remember what all of them were and conceal them in their proper order? From the way Eden shot his glance to the ceiling, I guessed that Margaret had caught his eye. Then, looking back at her, I saw she had composed her hands over the handkerchief in her lap and tilted her head towards the coroner, poised to begin her tale.

For her present audience, Margaret shaped events of the fateful night much as she had shaped them for Gilbert and me among the potted greenery in Helene's conservatory. Vague about where she and Colonel Duvall had been all evening, leaving the impression that they might have had a little supper somewhere, Margaret wound her listeners along towards the alley, the turning point, where she was thrust into darkness.

"The colonel pulled you into the alley?" The coroner sounded doubtful. "Am I hearing that rightly, ma'am?"

"Oh, yes, my husband is—was—very rash at times. Very demonstrative in his attentions to me. You understand, sir?" The same words in the same thickened voice, the same flutter of lashes, she had used with Gilbert. Even the coroner's response was an echo of that previous conversation: "Yes, ma'am, I do understand." But then, Margaret's account diverged slightly from the one she had tried out in rehearsal. This time she did not claim to have been locked in an embrace with Duvall when the attacker struck. She had learned from her mistake and adjusted the story to fit the position in which she and Duvall had been discovered.

"Everything happened so quickly," she said. "My husband must have heard the man approaching, although I did not, and wheeled about to shield me from danger. That was when he was stabbed." Margaret pressed her clasped hands to her waist.

"With his own weapon?" the coroner prompted her.

"So quickly. He fell back against me, and I collapsed with the weight of him. His head fell against my heart." On the last word, she moved her hands upward and crossed them over her bosom. A convincing touch.

"So, Mrs. Duvall," the coroner said, "as I picture the scene, you, as well as your husband, were facing the attacker—which leads me to hope that you can shed some light on his appearance. Dark as it was, you might have noticed the man's height or bulk or whether or not there were two of him. Isn't that true, ma'am?"

Margaret shook her head. "No, sir. I can't tell you a thing about him, not a blessed thing. I was so terrified, I shut my eyes."

When Margaret first began her testimony, her lies had

sounded practiced, but as she continued, I heard an odd strain of sincerity enter her voice. It was there now. Of course, with enough repetition, a lie could transform itself into a memory. And then, even the liar who repeats it might not know the difference.

The coroner muttered some acknowledgment of what a terrible ordeal Mrs. Duvall had endured, then asked her if her husband had spoken any last words to her.

"No," Margaret answered abruptly, as if his question had startled her. "No," she repeated, looking towards Helene, "he said nothing about his killer—not who nor why." Margaret's gaze travelled on, to the back of the room. "I think Frank was amazed by what happened—as I was."

"But no last words?" the coroner asked again.

"He might have said goodbye," Margaret murmured.

"Ah. And then help arrived in the form of concerned citizens," the coroner said with only a trace of irony, "a slew of witnesses, a couple of policemen, even a doctor to examine the victim of this brutal crime."

"And my friends," Margaret said. "I was so stunned, sir, I didn't know what to do, when, all of a sudden, someone was helping me up from the ground and handing me into a carriage. And inside were my dear friends, Judge and Mrs. Royce Placide."

This was news to me, as I was sure it was to Gilbert, who shot his glance my way. Would Margaret's revelation lead the coroner to ask for testimony from the Placides? I no sooner wondered than dismissed the notion. Helene, with a subtle shake of her head, and the judge, with a jutting out of his lower lip, displayed their immediate displeasure with Margaret's linking them publicly to her misfortune, even though they had helped her in private—and, if Margaret were oblivious to their reactions, the coroner was not. He was the judge's man. I saw the look that passed between them.

"Dr. Gilbert Crew," the coroner said.

My brother blinked, as if amazed to finally be called, then pocketed his notebook and pencil, and stepped forward. I regretted that Gilbert had not been preceded by at least one of the Crescent City Regulators—someone who could have attested to Duvall's actual whereabouts that night and contradicted some of Margaret's narrative, so Gilbert would not be the first to do so. While she had told her story, Margaret seemed to gain confidence, only to lose it on returning to her place between Helene and Baldwin, becoming once again rather pathetic next to her elegant friend and vulnerable under the old doctor's solicitousness. I saw too clearly that Gilbert's testimony, by opposing a lady's, would strike the whole assembly as brutish. Worse than that, as unreliable—if Gilbert were to begin by calling Colonel Duvall's widow a liar.

My high hopes, shared by Gilbert, that suspicion, if not outright blame, would fall upon Eden, descended with my realization that casting suspicion on Eden now depended solely on my brother's testimony. He would need to establish that Margaret had not spent the evening with her husband but had encountered him, or been overtaken by him, around the time that he was attacked. Gilbert would have to expose Eden's affair with the murdered man's wife to reveal the source of conflict between Eden and Duvall—the motive for one to slay the other.

My head ached as I watched Gilbert scan his listeners' faces to gauge his audience, I reckoned, the better to modulate his answers when the coroner's questions came at him. Yet Gilbert looked exhausted to me, and I asked him when the day was over what he had actually seen through his bleary eyes. At first, he could not focus on a single face, he told me. Individuals' features ran together and forms overlapped, low voices stirred into a wordless hum, and odors mingled in an invisible miasma. Then, as he had slowed and deepened his breathing, Gilbert's acute sense of smell began to break the air into pockets of sweat trapped in wool clothing, oil in hair, tobacco on breath, a trace of perfume on skin.

With that whiff of perfume, simultaneously exotic and familiar, the sharpness of his other senses returned, and he saw Helene Placide's subtle smile and nod in his direction.

Gilbert turned to the coroner, who fixed him with eyes magnified by the thick lenses of his spectacles. If only Gilbert could manage to introduce the truth without appearing accusatory, influence the coroner's line of questioning, signal the man with expressive looks as the Placides had done, or as I sometimes did with Gilbert. But the frowns and lifted brows and drawn up postures that other people used to such effect had never come naturally to my brother. He would prefer to begin with facts, with his seeing Colonel Duvall alive and engaged at the meeting of the Crescent City Regulators, without actually naming the organization, of course. Then, some of the Regulators present in the room, perhaps Mr. Smith, would mutter their agreement just loud enough for the coroner to hear. Ah, yes, they would say, *we, too, spent much of the evening with the colonel, without his wife.* Then, the coroner would ask another question or two, and soon Gilbert would describe having a drink with Duvall, shortly before the colonel disappeared into the night. One question leading to an answer that led to another question, another answer . . .

"You just *happened* by the alleyway minutes after the murder was committed," said the coroner. "Is that true?" His tone seemed to cast suspicion on Gilbert.

"Yes, sir, I was nearby," Gilbert said, and hurried to explain his presence in the vicinity. "You see, Colonel Duvall had invited me to a meeting held that night in an establishment near the crossroads of Toulouse and Bourbon—"

"Young fellow," the coroner interrupted, "you are here in your capacity as a medical man." But skepticism in his tone, then Dr. Baldwin's dry cough, confirmed Gilbert as an upstart. The coroner continued: "Kindly limit yourself to medical testimony. We need hear no comments about how you spent the earlier part of the night along certain streets." A few chuckles rounded the room. "Confine yourself to the alley. What made you stop there? What did you see and hear? That's the sort of thing we need to know." *We need to know?*—he and the judge, I supposed.

"Yes, sir. When Colonel Duvall did not come back to finish his drink with me, I began to wonder what had happened and left the saloon to look for him," Gilbert said, and I admired his determination to make the point that Duvall had been in his company. No response to that from the coroner, and Gilbert went on: "I saw people gathering near the entrance to the alley, then heard a woman's voice screaming help and murder. I identified myself as a doctor—I had my medical bag in hand—and the crowd allowed me through to where I found Mrs. Duvall—"

"Cradling the lifeless body of her husband," the coroner finished for my brother.

Gilbert nodded, glancing towards Widow Duvall, then stared at a point beyond her, at Eden, who now stood in the rear doorway, I discovered in following the line of Gilbert's gaze. Then I heard Gilbert's voice gain strength as he described the angle and depth of the wound and estimated the length of time required for Colonel Duvall's life to bleed away. Watching Eden's stony face, listening to Gilbert's testimony, I barely heard the shifting and rustling that indicated movement somewhere in the room. "A quick thrust of the knife, a parrying weapon, sloppily done," Gilbert said, "if the attacker intended to kill his victim outright. Then a slow death. Which raises the question—" Gilbert broke off.

Margaret had risen and was standing in Gilbert's line of sight, her tall, thin body swaying as if it were a sapling tossed by a breeze. Dr. Baldwin had only half-risen beside her before she toppled and fell against him, sending them both back down to the bench. "Give her air! Give her air!" Baldwin cried out to encroaching onlookers. "Cut her laces," another man suggested, followed by Helene's quick response—"That won't be necessary."

354

She had already pulled a bottle of smelling salts from her reticule and was waving it under Margaret's nose.

Brusquely, the coroner announced that he had heard all he needed to hear from Dr. Crew. The widow's swoon had effectively ended Gilbert's testimony, the most salient parts of which had been either censored or ignored. I threaded my way through the departing crowd to reach my brother and link my arm with his.

The Placides' shielding of Margaret protected not only her, but also Eden. But even though the judge did business with Eden, even though he might call him a friend, Duvall had also been the judge's friend, a closer one of longer standing. That should count for more than saving Mrs. Placide's lady-in-waiting from public embarrassment and allowing Margaret to persist in her lies. Concealing an illicit affair was one thing, covering up a murder something else. Surely, Judge Placide would want justice for the late colonel, even if it meant some inconvenience to himself regarding the architectural plans for one of his ventures.

Murder by person or persons unknown, the coroner ruled.

Chapter Forty-Seven

Gilbert and I, attentive as we had been to proceedings at the inquest, also tried to keep an eye on Charlotte's husband, but we had both looked at Margaret on the verge of her fainting spell. Thus, I had lost sight of Eden, and Gilbert had caught only a last glimpse of him as Eden disappeared through the rear doorway. And wasn't that Mr. Keogh, short and stout in mustard tweed, following on his heels? Gilbert thought so—thought the landlord reached up to clap Eden on the shoulder. Neither my brother nor I had noticed Keogh earlier, but then there had been so many common-looking men present for the day's spectacle.

Helene and old Baldwin were guiding Margaret out between them when I heard Gilbert mutter more to himself than to me: "Let them go. I'll have a private word with Judge Placide." Although, not private from me. I stayed close to Gilbert as we threaded our way towards the judge, who had reached his carriage, the clerks attending him just depositing him on the seat inside as we caught up.

"Judge Placide," Gilbert called from the banquette. "May I speak with you, sir?"

Placide turned his florid face to size up the pair of us from the open carriage door. At best, I thought, he might allow Gilbert to make an appointment with one of the clerks, at worst, refuse to acknowledge the request. But the judge did neither. To my surprise, he invited us both to sit with him within his carriage, offering me some pleasantry about the fetching angle of my plumed hat. With a counterfeit simper, I pretended to be flattered, then let Gilbert do the talking.

After thanking the judge for his time, Gilbert plunged into his purpose—with some attempt at tact. "Judge Placide, I mean no disrespect to Mrs. Duvall, who has endured a shocking experience and may well be confused—but I must tell you that Colonel Duvall spent his last evening at a meeting of the Crescent City Regulators. He was not with his wife until very near the time of his death. I know this for a fact, sir. I was there, I saw him and drank with him."

The judge held up a hand. "So you indicated to the coroner," he said. "But surely, you knew when you accepted Colonel Duvall's invitation—which he and I agreed might be extended to you—that you were attending a meeting of a secret organization." Here he narrowed his eyes at me. "And whatever you know about the matter, Mrs. James, I expect discretion." I nodded, widening my eyes at him before he turned his attention back to Gilbert. "Members' names and activities are not to be bandied about in front of just anybody in a public gathering."

"An inquest?" Gilbert said.

The judge dismissed the interjection: "You know better than that, young man."

"But sir, Colonel Duvall was murdered," Gilbert said—a fact that ought to trump any rigmarole attached to a secret society.

"That he was." The judge nodded. "But not at the meeting. You understand me?"

"Someone came to the saloon and spoke to him, and then the colonel left. I think the other man told him where to find Mrs. Duvall and Mr. Eden, who were together that evening."

"And you know that for a fact?" Placide said archly.

"I know they have been together."

"But not for a fact that night?" The judge paused for an answer that Gilbert didn't give. "Well, now," Placide resumed, "that's none of our business. None of our concern."

"But if Victor Eden attacked the colonel—"

Judge Placide snorted. "What are you talking about? It's the cuckold kills the lover, not t'other way around. Way of the world." Here, he winked at me, then continued to Gilbert: "Let the law handle this, you hear? I will offer a reward for information leading to an arrest. Money will work its magic on somebody's memory. Just you wait and see. And no more of your casting aspersions, young man—you understand me?"

Placide pushed open the carriage door with the tip of his cane, ending the private interview. Then, as Gilbert stepped down and offered me his hand, the judge added for his clerks to hear: "Dr. Crew, you and I must talk again soon. Prison expansions are nearly complete, and I have a job waiting for you. Why, you'll make yourself a tidy sum." Placide nodded towards one of his clerks, saying, "Set an appointment, sooner the better."

But not before the colonel's remains were laid in the Duvall tomb.

✝ ✝ ✝

The inquest's ambiguous outcome thoroughly upset me and infuriated Gilbert. Neither of us knew what to say to Charlotte. Even so, that didn't stop Gilbert from blurting out to her that Placide was offering a reward for information. *As if truth were for sale*, I hissed as an aside to my brother. After which, Gilbert agreed with me in private to let Charlotte enjoy her children while he and I kept otherwise occupied—giving us all a little breathing room.

On the day of Colonel Duvall's funeral, a lowering sky threatened but did not deliver rain, only a fine mist that lifted before the final *amen*. The funeral cortege proceeded at a measured pace and with all the trappings of a glass-paneled hearse pulled by sleek black horses with midnight plumes rising from the crownpieces of their bridles. As the colonel's last earthly journey progressed, I recalled the scene Gilbert had described to me of Duvall tearing down the river road through a curtain of rain, his carriage hurtling out of the darkness towards the wagon, forcing

Gilbert's fall down the embankment and the breaking open of the makeshift coffin—the revelation that Charlotte lived. On that night, Duvall's rash action in racing to confront his wayward wife had led to Charlotte's rescue; on another night, rash action had led Duvall to his death. No rushing for him now, only the slow process of decay.

The funeral was well attended by the late colonel's friends and associates. Numerous veterans appeared in the uniforms of their past, or portions of uniforms—jacket or cap or medals from their glory days—some men with a crutch or a cane, some with an empty sleeve. Some of the men, Gilbert whispered to me, he recognized as Regulators, Mr. Smith among them. A few policemen stood by, as well, discouraging curiosity seekers, some of whom had given testimony at the inquest, from trespassing into the circle of chief mourners.

Gilbert had told me how close Margaret had stood to Eden, placing her hand on his sleeve, in front of the Eden tomb, comforting him as he faced the loss of his wife. Or reassuring him that he had gotten away with ridding himself of her. This time, in front of the Duvall tomb, the heavily veiled Widow Duvall was flanked by Judge and Mrs. Placide. Dr. Baldwin stood just behind her. But Eden kept his distance. Even after the colonel's body was entombed, he did not come forward to offer the support of his arm. Instead, Dr. Baldwin escorted Margaret away.

I wondered at Eden's aloofness. Gilbert speculated that, if Eden and Margaret had planned together to rid themselves of their spouses—or Eden had planned and Margaret had gone along—Eden now only pretended indifference to her to avoid suspicion falling on them. But would he remain so distant when they met again at Helene's next séance?

As the new widow and her friends departed, the other mourners dispersed, some leaving the cemetery straight away, some winding along the paths to visit other tombs and pay respects to longer-dead friends or family. Gilbert seized the moment to catch up with Mr. Smith and step from the path with him for a brief private word. I stayed back while they spoke, and then Gilbert returned to my side, discouraged. No news yet on the whereabouts of the man with whom Gilbert had last seen Duvall, but one of the other Regulators might have seen him, too, and might try to track him down. Where were we to go from here?

For a while, we simply wandered among the tombs. Or, perhaps, Gilbert was guiding me as subtly as one might guide a planchette on a talking-board, along the path leading to the Eden tomb. We were not the only visitors, for Eden was there ahead of us. Gilbert and I stopped under a cypress tree some distance from him and saw him run his gloved fingers over the bronzed plaque. Was Eden assuring himself that Charlotte would not return to reproach him for the past or impede his plans for the future? Or had his touch indicated a twinge of regret? As I contemplated what motivation I might ascribe to a character in my play-in-progress in a similar circumstance, Gilbert drew me back along the way we had come.

Our seeing Eden had reminded Gilbert of Simon Langley, Charlotte's former beau, alone by the tomb, dropping the little bunch of velveteen violets. And from violets, Gilbert's thoughts and my carriage, which he drove, turned towards Royal Street and Madame Joubert's Hat Shop. "I've a notion to buy a hat for Ella," he said, "in appreciation for her many kindnesses."

Then Gilbert should be the one to choose it, I told him, as we entered the shop, a girl at the front display counter greeting us. She smiled in particular at my brother, and her eyes twinkled when he explained his purpose: "I'd be obliged, Miss Rutherford, for your advice in selecting a hat for a grandmotherly sort of person to wear to church. Nice, but not too daring."

Glancing over the fanciful headwear on display, I saw nothing that fit his description. But Jeannie Rutherford determined to oblige my brother, brought forth hats from behind the counter and out of boxes, until they found just the thing. Then, she congratulated Gilbert on his choice, made under her influence and with my approving nod, of a moss-green hat with saffron and brown speckled feathers in the band, and a soft brim that could be worn at a variety of angles, as she demonstrated. Had Charlotte been so flirtatious with Eden when he had come to the shop?

As Gilbert chatted with Jeannie, she cast a furtive glance in the direction of Madame Joubert, whose distinctive silhouette—her dowager's hump, piled hair and sharp nose with pince-nez affixed—was visible through the glazed window of her corner office. Occupied with accounts and ledgers, Madame might not notice how long Jeannie took tucking Gilbert's purchase into a nest of tissue paper.

Gilbert guided the conversation with an ease I'd only recently realized he possessed, leading Jeannie to recollections of her friendship with Charlotte, including an admission that she knew of Simon Langley. Perhaps Gilbert had brought us to the shop simply to buy a hat, but he was not passing up the opportunity to gather tidbits from the shopgirl.

"It was over between them," she said, "just before I came here, and Charlotte and I became friends. But she told me about Mr. Langley—how he could be so kind, and then, all of a sudden, the Noonday Demon would shake him by the scruff of the neck. Some men were never right after the war, isn't that so?" She looked to both of us, and Gilbert and I agreed with her.

"Do you think Mr. Eden knew about Charlotte's previous attachment?" I asked.

"Well, if he did, ma'am, it didn't stop him marrying her."

"But it might have rankled with him," I suggested. Helene Placide's previous attachment had rankled with the judge, hadn't it?—but then she had been carrying another man's child.

"Oh?" Jeannie said. "But it's so long ago now."

362

Depending on one's perspective. This girl was barely out of her teens.

"Mr. Eden could have just found out about Mr. Langley," Gilbert said.

I considered the possibility that Keogh might have told him when they began doing business together. For spite, to stir up discord between Charlotte and her husband—another punishment for the little minx, who had not been as accommodating to Keogh as her mother had been. I imagined the landlord smirking as he said: *Cut your little wife's housekeeping money, Mr. Eden, and set your lady-friend up in style.*

"Are you saying there was trouble between them—Charlotte and Mr. Eden? Did you see that, Dr. Crew, maybe on a house call?" Jeannie had a taste for gossip, sure enough.

Madame's office door snapped open, and Jeannie darted a glance her way, but Madame did not emerged into the shop, instead summoning one of her assistants into her office. Jeannie closed the hatbox and tied it with a yellow grosgrain ribbon before she placed it in Gilbert's hands, eyeing him in the transaction.

"Poor Mr. Langley." Jeannie dropped her voice, and Gilbert and I leaned in to hear her. "He must have loved Charlotte more than he could say. Seems so to me, after what happened."

"What happened, Miss Rutherford?" Gilbert and I asked in near-unison.

"The night after Charlotte's funeral—that's what I heard from my uncle, who is a policeman. Mr. Langley stepped out into the street somewhere along Esplanade, fell under a carriage and died," Jeannie said. "But was it an accident? I'm thinking a broken heart."

"The soldier's heart that never healed," I murmured, and Jeannie nodded.

"Strange," she said, "him losing the will to live in a world without her, even though they'd parted so long ago. While her husband went on his merry way."

"I beg your pardon?" Gilbert said.

"Well, no time at all after Charlotte's passing—oh, but it must have been after you and I spoke that first time," Jeannie said, as if she were keeping a casual tally of their conversations. "Mr. Eden came in escorting Mrs. Placide and her friend, and he seemed different. But not in the way I'd expect for a grieving gentleman, all solemn, going about his duties. No, he was chatting away with the ladies as they tried on hats, practically preening, himself, for the shopgirls—bolder than he'd been with Charlotte. Full of himself, if you ask me." Jeannie was an astute young woman—no longer so impressed as she had been with Victor Eden.

The shopping excursion she described must have occurred before Eden's garden rendezvous with Margaret, before Helene had read in Gilbert's face what he had witnessed that night at Testament. Eden had been squiring the ladies about town—Mrs. Placide's friend Margaret enjoying the private thrill of being out in public with her paramour and Helene deluding herself that she enjoyed the full attention of her minions. Helene demanded attention. That was my impression when Bartholomew introduced us, and Gilbert knew it now. Others must admire her person, pay her courtesies, come when she summoned them to commune with disembodied spirits or search for ghosts in the night.

✝ ✝ ✝

The next summons from Helene came in the form of a letter delivered by her maid Tansy, who was there when we returned home, talking with Ella by the side gate. It was our household's washing day. The laundress, who did the heavy work, was already gone, and Ella had finished hanging clothes on the lines strung near the kitchen garden. As we approached, Tansy turned from Ella and regarded us rather slyly. Then she held out the letter to Gilbert, saying: "I's to wait for your answer, sir."

Shifting the beribboned Joubert hatbox under one arm, Gilbert took possession of the letter, broke the red wax seal, and perused the message. As did I, standing at my brother's elbow. The letter, written in flourishing style, began with Helene's premonition that she could persuade Duvall's spirit to reveal the identity of his murderer. Then came the date, time, and place of her séance, which could not be held too soon, considering a villain remained at-large, free to kill again—this last phrase underlined several times. Indeed, the séance was set for that very night, ten o'clock at the Placides' town mansion. From the lateness of the designated hour, Gilbert understood that he was not invited to dine, a relief to anyone with no desire to spend a protracted evening devoted to rich food and heavy drink in the company of the Placides and their guests. "Tell Mrs. Placide that I will be at her service tonight," Gilbert said, and Tansy departed.

Then Gilbert, Ella, and I came through the back door into the kitchen, where he presented the hatbox to her with his gratitude for her care of our guests and for her discretion.

Ella lifted the hat from its tissue paper nest, touched the long feathers secured in the band, turned the hat one way and another. "Mighty stylish, Mr. Gil. Yes, sir, I'll be proud to wear it. Thank you, sir." She had placed the hat on her head and held up a polished silver tray to examine her reflection when Charlotte, entering from the hall, joined us.

"In very good taste, Miss Lenore," she said, but I would not take the credit from Gilbert and corrected her assumption. "So you have an eye for ladies' hats, Dr. Crew," Charlotte said, an uneasy undercurrent in her voice that caused me to wonder if his having gone to Madame Joubert's shop had stirred a memory she would as soon forget.

"A Miss Rutherford assisted me," Gilbert said.

"Jeannie, yes," Charlotte murmured, "and her feathers."

After Ella left the kitchen to put the hat away in her room and look in on Amy and Wilfred, who would soon be waking from their naps, I invited Charlotte to join Gilbert and me in the parlor. My hope was that the three of us would discuss a course of action for Charlotte and her children, with the understanding that nothing had yet been proved against Eden—might never be. But Gilbert, at once, took the conversation in a different direction.

"Mrs. Placide has invited me to another séance," he said to Charlotte, holding out Helene's letter for her to see.

Charlotte glanced at the page but didn't touch it or read it. "Does she plan to ask Colonel Duvall who murdered him?" she said with a bluntness that surprised me.

"Yes," Gilbert said. "And if she knows the answer, maybe this is how she'll reveal it."

"Or if Tansy knows," I muttered, pouring myself a dry sherry, offering some to Charlotte and Gilbert, who both declined.

"Mrs. Placide can say anything she pleases in her spirit guide's voice," Charlotte said. "And I think she likes to shock."

Truer words were never spoken. I swallowed a sip of sherry, then another, recalling I'd not eaten since early morning, nor had Gilbert, who missed meals near as often as he lost sleep. Still, while we were in no state to discuss troublesome matters, Gilbert would not be deterred.

"Did your husband know about the man in Mr. Keogh's tenement—about Simon Langley?" Gilbert asked Charlotte.

What next, I thought, waiting like my brother for her reply. Would he ask if Langley had ever come to her house after she married Eden, or had Charlotte ever met him elsewhere while the maid worked her half day?

"Gilbert." Charlotte spoke his given-name for the first time in my hearing, freighting it with meaning I could not quite discern. Possibly, a warning. Staring at Gilbert, she took her time before she asked him a question of her own: "Who told you whatever story you've been told?"

"Mr. Keogh."

"You've talked with him?"

Charlotte had directed her question to Gilbert, but I answered: "We had occasion to, yes."

Her eyes darted towards me, then back to Gilbert as he said: "Mr. Keogh said there was an understanding between you and Mr. Langley."

"And you believed him?" Charlotte addressed Gilbert, not me. "Whatever he said to you, you believed him." She was offended, and I heard what she had not said to Gilbert—*you took the word of a greedy lecher, who made life as miserable as he could for me.*

Gilbert's face flushed while Charlotte's blanched. And I felt none too steady, myself.

"I'm sorry, Charlotte," Gilbert said. "I shouldn't have asked about him. I only thought—"

"But you did ask. Why does he matter to you?" She wouldn't look away from Gilbert. "Because you thought he'd been my lover? Is that it?" And Charlotte knew that would matter to my brother, she must have known.

"Wasn't he?" Gilbert's voice was barely audible.

Exhaustion, like wine, must have lowered Gilbert's reserve and left his tongue unguarded. But where was Charlotte's modesty now?

"He might have been," she said, "maybe even become my husband, if not for what the war did to him—and the laudanum."

"He couldn't forget you," Gilbert said, his voice betraying his meaning: *I cannot forget you.* "How could he?"

"My husband has," she said.

"And that's your husband's failing," I said. "Charlotte, you should know—that is, Gilbert and I have just learned that Mr. Langley met with an accident, a fatal one, falling under a passing

367

carriage shortly after—"

In my moment of hesitation, Gilbert finished the sentence: "After he left the violets by the tomb."

"Gilbert." Again, Charlotte said his name, this time with a slight change of intonation, a gentleness, as if she were trying out a different meaning of the word.

When had his regard for her, his gallantry on her behalf, changed—become something mutual? An invisible thread tightening between them. In the upstairs hall, Charlotte had brushed his hair from his forehead, not knowing I observed her. Charlotte had caressed his brow, and she would break his heart when she was gone. Then, would my brother wander with his sorrow into the path of death? My heart shuddered for him.

Chapter Forty-Eight

Late as the hour was when Gilbert arrived, the Placides and their guests had just concluded supper. Helene on Eden's arm and Margaret on Baldwin's were crossing the main hall from dining room to drawing room, the swaying hems of the ladies' black silk gowns barely skirting the bric-a-brac cabinets as the couples paraded past. Only Judge Placide was absent.

"Temporarily indisposed," Helene said with a moue of disgust.

Dr. Baldwin, after settling Margaret on the divan, approached Gilbert with more detail. "The judge suffers a touch of dyspepsia from time to time," he said in a confidential whisper. "And irritable bowel, too, don't you know? I gave him a purgative. Shouldn't be too long before the oysters and horseradish release him from their grip."

While they waited for Judge Placide to join them—to make six at table—Dr. Baldwin, who was quite at home, poured glasses of sherry for the ladies and bourbon for himself, Eden, and Gilbert. Margaret melted into the divan cushions, swirling the sherry in her glass and studying it with over-bright eyes, evidence she might already be under the influence of one of the old doctor's nerve remedies. Helene did not join her friend on the divan, thus leaving all the gentlemen to stand while she, appearing uncharacteristically agitated, tossed back her sherry and paced the carpet. Making no secret of her impatience, she glanced at the mantel clock and sighed with each of her turns around the room.

Finally, Helene announced she would go to her husband and hoped to find him sufficiently recovered. Gilbert offered to go with her to be of assistance, if needed. But Dr. Baldwin intervened, saying he would accompany Mrs. Placide and see to the judge, who was his patient, not Dr. Crew's. Relieved on that point, Gilbert was put on edge by another, being then alone with Eden and Margaret and the vivid memory of Duvall with a knife in his belly.

Margaret, likely more drugged than dangerous, shifted her dilated eyes from her lover to Gilbert and back, perhaps implying by her restless glancing that he should leave them alone, give them a moment. Then, Eden surprised Gilbert by excusing himself to go out on the gallery for a smoke.

"I wouldn't mind a bit if he smoked in here," Margaret said, her voice a trifle thick. "Helene might, but I wouldn't—I love the smell of tobacco." She stared towards the French doors, which Eden had closed behind him after stepping outside. Through the glass panes shone the brief flare of a match, then the glow at the end of a cigar. "Come and sit by me, Dr. Crew," Margaret said, turning her gaze on him. "I must tell you something, I just can't keep it in."

Curious, he joined her as she had asked, angling himself on the divan to see her face full in the lamplight, the high color of rouge on her cheeks and on her quivering lips.

Margaret began: "First, there was Charlotte's passing. Then my husband's. Oh, and that dreadful inquest and the funeral—everything happening lickety-split." Her breath caught between phrases, as if she were, even now, dashing from event to event. "But all of it happened for a reason, Dr. Crew. It was meant to be."

Meant to be? And what reason would Margaret offer for standing by while Eden murdered her husband?

"Victor will marry me now," she said.

Gilbert stared at her. Had she actually said the words? Admitted to a plan that had rid them of the spouses who had stood in the way of their happiness? Or had he misunderstood her?

Margaret's fingertips tapped the back of his hand, then her whispery voice sounded again, fraught with nervous excitement: "Oh, not tomorrow. But sooner rather than later. A widower with children needs a wife. I'm sure I've heard Victor say so." Then Margaret, delusional with opiates, rambled about her plans for sending Amy away to the convent school, putting Wilfred in the care of a nursemaid, and hiring myriad servants, whom she would order about. "Charlotte skimped so on the housekeeping, wasting her allowance on who knows what, not wanting servants too under foot. You catch my drift? That way, while Victor was at work and the babies napped, she could entertain her lover." Only in the topsy-turvy world of Margaret's mind.

"You can't be serious, Mrs. Duvall," Gilbert said, even as he felt a lancinating pain tightened across his brow. The brief rest he had taken prior to his arrival at the Placide's house had hardly revived him, and the headache would persist until he was home again.

"But I am serious, sir. Charlotte's behavior was worrying to Victor, and he confided in me." Margaret lifted her pointed chin as she spoke, looking determined, sounding petulant. She had to tell someone that she was needed and desired by Victor Eden. Perhaps she had guessed that Helene would scoff at her claims. *Margaret can be such a ninny,* Helene had told Gilbert, *not the sort to inspire a grand passion.* "Oh, she was sweet to look at," Margaret said, her dismissal of Eden's wife an echo of Helene's dismissal of Eden's mistress. "But they married in haste, I heard, that first baby born a bit too soon—and a girl, after all. Victor was a gentleman about it, but he was trapped, you see. Charlotte entrapped him."

The French doors parted, and Eden re-entered the room. Margaret smiled with pressed lips and inhaled deeply, no doubt relishing the scent of cigar smoke surrounding him. Of course, he had confided in Margaret, in bits and pieces, hinting at first, then telling her outright lies about his wife's alleged waywardness, her

371

breaking his trust, if not his heart. Margaret had been flattered by his intimate disclosures. She had sympathized. She had been so easily seduced. Duvall had said of Helene Placide, "She controls my wife," and Gilbert had taken him at his word before understanding that Margaret was capable of recklessness without prompting from Helene or anyone else.

The small parlor devoted to Helene's séances in town resembled its counterpart in the country—dark and crowded with mahogany furnishings, this time the six chairs circling the table upholstered in midnight blue, rather than blood-red velvet. Three candles burned in a branched candlestick on the center of the table and three on the sideboard, which was not as large as the one at Testament and would be a snug fit for Tansy. If she were not already secreted behind one of the closed velvet curtains covering the windows, hiding even the faintest glow of a streetlamp.

The guests sat as they had previously, Helene before the sideboard, Eden on her right, Baldwin on his right, Gilbert on Helene's left, Placide on his left, Margaret exactly opposite Helene in the circle. But this time, Helene did not open the séance with serenity. Before ever slipping into a trance and allowing a bevy of restless dead to compete for her voice, the spirit medium made evident she was still in a snit over the delay caused by Placide's overindulgence at supper and subsequent indisposition. He must pay for upsetting her, although indirectly, as Helene berated one of his manservants for being slow to bring her a box she had demanded.

From the box, Helene lifted two objects, placed them in front of her, and quickly covered them with her hands, her fingers distracting with their glittering rings.

"Two deaths," she said. "A widow and a widower sit at our table tonight." Her voice lowered and deepened, losing the snappishness that she had directed at the servant, and Dr. Baldwin, if no one else, appeared enthralled by the sound. "Colonel Frank

Duvall," Helene intoned, holding up one of the objects, the murdered man's flask—that migratory vessel, which Duvall had, in life, shifted from pocket to pocket between sips. Helene handed Gilbert the flask, instructing him to pass it along. The smell of strong spirits clung to the vessel and sloshed inside it as Gilbert transferred it to the judge's waiting hands. Placide accepted the flask with some reverence, cradling it for a moment in both his broad palms as if he were taking possession of a piece of his old friend's body.

"Charlotte Eden." Whispering the name, Helene lifted the other object, a tiny cloth doll, to the candlelight for all to view. After she had passed it to Eden, he rubbed the pale fabric of the doll's dress between thumb and forefinger. Familiar to him? Indeed, if it were made from a scrap of Charlotte's old dressing gown, the one Gilbert was told would be cut up to dress a doll. Then Eden touched the doll's dark hair, a swatch of human hair—snipped from behind Charlotte's ear? Helene had hinted of her discovery of an item *imbued with Charlotte's very essence.*

The flask moved clockwise and the doll counterclockwise around the table, somehow arriving simultaneously in Margaret's hands. Perhaps, she had held onto her husband's flask a little longer than the judge or Gilbert had. Then, Dr. Baldwin had given her the doll, just as Helene said in a faraway voice: "The colonel's flask was among Margaret's things when she came here to stay. A keepsake. Why not? But the little poppet—hadn't she sewn it for the Eden children after their mother's passing? A keepsake for them, made from their mother's gown and with their mother's hair. Yet it, too, lay among Margaret's possessions."

Margaret dropped both flask and doll on the table, darting a glance at Helene, who did not acknowledge it. Then Margaret looked down at the objects, shaking her head as if confused about what to do with them. The solution that came to her was to shove them away, the flask towards Baldwin and the doll towards Placide, who both shoved them on to Eden and Gilbert. Eden did not touch the flask, but Gilbert picked up the tiny doll, its features drawn in ink on the white cloth face, eyes no more than simple lines, as if the lids were closed in sleep or death. Margaret's effigy of Charlotte?—Helene was not the only superstitious one in the room.

When they joined hands, Helene shut her eyes and repeated the phrase with which she had begun the gathering: "Two deaths. How did they come to pass? Illness, accident, or suicide?" The choices for Charlotte, Gilbert assumed. "Murder or someone else's self-defense?" For Duvall. "How can we know? When will you tell us?"

Without moving his head, Gilbert shifted his gaze around the circle. He neither saw nor sensed the presence of the ghostly hovering nearby but felt a ripple of tension traveling among the living. The judge eyed his wife, Eden watched Margaret, who seemed unable to focus on anything, and Baldwin briefly caught Gilbert's eye, blinked, and returned his attention to Helene. Swaying slightly in her chair, Helene quavered on: "Come to the light, come to the warmth. Colonel and Charlotte, you who have crossed over, reveal to us your secret knowledge. Two deaths, your deaths. Death comes in threes. Who will be the third?" Helene cocked her head as if listening to a voice only she could hear.

Then the racket began, audible to all—not a tapping within the confines of the room, but a clamor beyond it of booted feet stomping in approach. The door swung open. Four men crowded near the doorway, towering above Tansy, who had not hidden in the parlor but stood outside it and in front of the men. She must have let them in the house and only now tried to slow their progress past her into the chamber. But she could not, for those men came in like Chaos.

Instinctively, Gilbert stood, anticipating some sort of confrontation. The men ignored him and Eden, who had risen, as well. Neither did they show any regard for the ladies

374

present—Helene, who gasped her protest, a hand flying dramatically to her bosom, and Margaret, who whimpered and shrank in her chair to be patted and protected by Dr. Baldwin. He sputtered his disapprobation at them—how dare they invade Mrs. Placide's parlor?—and the men ignored him, too. Instead, they closed around Judge Placide, two of them in police uniforms, one in a dark, well-tailored suit, and one in checkered trousers and a patched gray coat. This last man might have been a colleague of Colonel Duvall, one of the Regulators.

Remaining seated, unperturbed, the judge acknowledged all the men with a nod, then spoke to the one in the black suit: "Well, Mr. Nash, I take it you have news for me."

"I do, Judge," Mr. Nash replied. "A witness has come forward, his statement sworn to. We are here tonight, sir, to make the arrest."

At last, the judge registered surprise. "*Here?*" he said, giving the word an extra syllable.

"Yes, sir."

The judge's small eyes flickered in Gilbert's direction. Gilbert looked towards Eden, who had backed himself to the wall. Then, low-voiced communication passed among Placide and Nash and the other men, followed by one of the policemen escorting both Gilbert and Eden out of the room and into the hallway. Were they both to be taken into custody? Gilbert was alarmed. If someone had born false witness against him to collect a reward, what justice could he expect from Judge Placide?

"We'll wait here, sirs," said the policeman. He shut the door behind them and positioned himself in front of it.

"What's happened? What's going on?" Eden demanded to know, drawing himself up to look down his nose at the policeman.

"Not my place to say, sir," the policeman replied.

Thus, Gilbert waited with Eden in ignorance, trying to imagine what might be transpiring within the parlor: Mr. Nash and his men reporting some fresh evidence to Judge Placide, who had offered a reward for information leading to an arrest, Helene listening to every word because she was the judge's wife and would not be left out, and Dr. Baldwin hovering near Margaret, his patient, ready to revive her in the event of her fainting at the revelation of Duvall's killer.

Far from fainting, however, Margaret screamed as piercingly as she had on the night of her husband's murder: "No!"—a prolonged wail that crossed through the solid oak door and rang down the hall. Eden clenched his jaw, and a ripple of facial muscles tightened and twitched.

Soon, Tansy opened the parlor door. Gilbert had forgotten that she too was inside, hearing and seeing all, unnoticed until she was required to perform some service or other. The man in the gray coat stepped into the hallway, grim satisfaction written on his broad, whiskered face. Behind him, the Placides and Dr. Baldwin conferred hurriedly among themselves. Then, Mr. Nash and the policeman near him turned to Margaret and raised her from her chair. She appeared as limp as the tiny cloth doll she had made, which Gilbert had dropped into his pocket when the séance was interrupted. The men gripped her under her forearms, impelling her forward and out of the room. As Margaret passed through the hall, her head rolled back on her fragile neck, and she cast a pitiful look towards Eden.

Helene, coming to the parlor doorway, called after her: "Courage, Margaret—don't despair!"

Chapter Forty-Nine

I could not take it in. Nor could Gilbert, who woke me on his return around midnight to tell me the news. He brought a candle with him, placing it on my nightstand before he sat at the foot of my bed. I propped a pillow behind me, drew up my knees and wrapped my arms around them, and then, by the light of a single flame, I listened as Gilbert conjured every detail he could recall of the séance gone awry.

According to a witness who had come forward for his reward, Margaret Duvall, by herself—not Victor Eden, nor the two of them together—was the culprit, and now she had been arrested for the murder of Colonel Frank Duvall.

Dr. Baldwin, by his own admission, was flabbergasted, shocked, and flummoxed, in that order, he had told Gilbert. Then, at Baldwin's urging, Gilbert and Eden joined the doctor to be driven home by his coachman. After the three of them had settled in the carriage, Gilbert pulled a woolen lap robe over the old man's knees, for Baldwin had begun to tremble.

"Looking as if he might benefit from one of his own nerve remedies," Gilbert told me.

Then, Rufus Baldwin had rattled on: "Must be some mistake. Must be. That little lady could not have stabbed her husband. Margaret is high-strung—I'll grant you that—but murder! No, sir, I can't believe it. Too extreme! Even if she and the colonel were a mismatch—and we could all see that they were—but no more than some other couples, no more than—"

"Charlotte and I," Eden had said without a trace of emotion in evidence.

377

Dr. Baldwin had coughed, then said to Gilbert, more than in reply to Eden: "Margaret took a spin on the music hall stage before her marriage, don't you know? A real stunner. Judge Placide spotted her talents and no sooner introduced her to the colonel than he was besotted with her. And she cared for him in her way—surely. We've seen how distressed she is at losing him. And now this outrageous business. I don't know what to think."

"If it's true that Mrs. Duvall had something to do with her husband's murder," Gilbert had said, looking at Eden, not Baldwin, "I strongly doubt that she acted alone."

"My stars," I interjected, "you said that to his face."

"And Eden turned away," Gilbert said, "staring out the carriage window, before he said in that smooth way of his: *I'm sure Judge and Mrs. Placide will do everything possible to assist Margaret in her difficulties.*"

For Eden would not assist her—no alibi, no defense would be forthcoming from him. Her difficulties, Eden had said—not his, not theirs to share. Even if his composure were founded on innocence, which was doubtful, his indifference to Margaret in her time of need was founded on vice that he had proved he possessed. And his cold-heartedness, his sense of self-preservation, Eden coupled with an understanding of Judge Placide's power to manipulate the law for the sake of Placide's friends.

Gilbert refused to accept that Margaret's arrest exonerated Eden, but it could, I reminded him. If nothing were proved against Eden, then Charlotte must return to him with their children. "She can't remain our secret forever," I said.

"Would that she could," Gilbert said under his breath, then spoke up, telling me that he had an early appointment with Placide and hoped to prevail upon the judge to reconsider the idea that Margaret had acted with an accomplice.

✛ ✛ ✛

After passing the few remaining hours of the night in fitful sleep, Gilbert rose at dawn to walk along the fog-shrouded levee to clear his head before facing the judge. On his arrival at the judge's office, a clerk brought him and Placide fragrant coffee in bone china cups, the judge's looking out of place in his pudgy hands, as if his thick fingers would snap off the handle when he raised his cup. He made a sucking sound as he drank. Then, instead of immediately settling down to business on the subject of Gilbert's employment, for which the judge had summoned him, Placide opened with the subject that Gilbert had intended to broach.

"I have found a way out," Judge Placide said, "for our friend Margaret from the morass into which she has fallen. No easy solution, I tell you for sure."

"Then it isn't true, sir," Gilbert said. "She didn't kill the colonel." Of course, Gilbert reckoned, Mr. Smith and the Regulators would have gone to Judge Placide with any new information, not to Gilbert, for he was not one of them. "Someone else—" Gilbert began with hope, but the judge held up one hand and stopped him.

"I didn't say that, young man. A witness—a businessman in the vicinity—saw Margaret do in the colonel."

"Then why didn't he say so at the inquest?"

"Seems he hesitated, in conflict with himself about what he saw and what to say."

Hesitation based on finding out which paid more, keeping quiet or speaking up, Gilbert speculated. Speaking won out, and if the witness could be believed, he was having himself a quick one with a strumpet up against the wall at one end of the alley just before the colonel pulled Margaret in with him at the other end. "The tart was gone and the witness just buttoning up when he glanced down the way and spied the couple—didn't know then it was the Duvalls—locked in what he took for an amorous embrace—"

"The killer could have already stabbed him and run off by the time your witness—"

"Hear me out," said the judge. "He saw them slipping down to the filthy ground together. Not like my witness, who kept himself upright in the alleyway." Apparently, the judge could not resist a vulgar innuendo, even while discussing a colleague's murder.

"Surely, the colonel cried out," Gilbert said, "yet your witness didn't come to his aid."

"At the time, he misinterpreted the moaning."

"And since then, sir, has he received the reward you offered?"

Placide ignored the question, musing, instead, upon the weapon. "That knife—poniard, really—I gave it to the colonel. Never thought it would come to such a use. I bought a couple of them at auction, among some other Caribbean pieces, keeping one for myself. Picked up some Spanish gold and a few baubles for Helene, too—loot that might have belonged to Jean Lafitte. Pirate treasure." The judge relished the last two words, perhaps winding himself up for more tales of acquisition.

Endeavoring to steer the conversation back to Margaret and her lover, Gilbert asked the judge what he thought might have induced Margaret to stab her husband.

"Oh, she could be a *naughty* one." Placide's tone said he ought to know. "And my old friend Frank Duvall had his pride. I figure he was trying to scare her a bit." *By waving a poniard at his wife?—that would do it.* "Make her behave," the judge said, "after some little transgression. Yes, I know she wasn't with her husband all the evening. And then she panicked and turned the blade on him. Might not have been too difficult for her, depending on how much he'd had to drink. A terrible accident. No wonder she's blotted it out of her mind. *And out of her mind she is now.* Won't stand trial, no, sir—I have settled that with my man Nash, who was here this morning even earlier than you. Dr. Baldwin and I are sending

Margaret to an asylum. I'm not pleased with her, you understand, but I won't tolerate having a scandal around her sullying the colonel's name. He died a gentleman and a hero, and we'll leave it at that. Margaret should be damned grateful for my intercession."

"She had hopes for something else," Gilbert ventured. "Before the séance, Mrs. Duvall told me that, with her husband gone, Mr. Eden would marry her."

"Ridiculous!" The judge slapped his desk. "Hasn't been any time since Eden escaped from one hysterical little wife—doesn't need another."

With a log in his eye, Placide was pointing out the mote in Eden's.

Then, the judge turned the conversation to his repugnant prison works project, which involved his hiring out men arrested for loitering, vagrancy, petty theft, being black, being poor—any excuse would do—and forcing them to work on railroads or plantations, in lumber camps or mines. War and new law had not changed him; Placide must own other people.

"I like to have myself a finger in every pie," he said of his varied enterprises.

Then, when the convicts collapsed from their re-enslavement, Gilbert was to revive them and send them back to work until they dropped again—dead—if he and Placide could come to terms. Fortunately, their conversation was interrupted by a clerk reminding the judge that he was due in court. Thus, Gilbert avoided articulating his response to Placide's proposal.

✛ ✛ ✛

When Gilbert returned home after a series of house calls, he and I shared a few private words with Charlotte in the hall outside the kitchen. Inside, Amy sat at the kitchen table with Ella, who was teaching her to make marzipan rosettes to decorate a sponge cake. Wilfred sat nearby on the floor, drumming a wooden spoon on a set of overturned pots and pans. I had already shared with Charlotte the news of Margaret's predicament, and she and I both wished to hear the outcome of Gilbert's conversation with Judge Placide.

As we listened to him, Charlotte watched her children through the doorway. Only when he had finished, she looked at him. "Margaret might have done it," Charlotte said. "Even done it alone. But I can't help wondering if Colonel Duvall might still be alive if only Victor had broken with these people."

These people, not Margaret, in particular. I considered her choice of words.

"So Mr. Eden's affair with Margaret was not such a little thing, after all," Gilbert said.

"But it's over. And I'm still Victor's wife, Amy and Wilfred are still his children. I weigh my hurt in a balance with their happiness—" Charlotte looked towards Amy and Wilfred. "I know what I must do."

But Gilbert would not relinquish the idea that Margaret might yet be persuaded to implicate Eden.

Then, Charlotte said again: "Margaret might have done it. Some women will do anything to secure the man they want."

"A man might do anything, too," Gilbert said.

As my brother had done? His solicitude towards her children sincere, but coupled—was it not?—with his desire for Charlotte, then his accusations against her husband, plausible but slanted, again, by desire. Was that what he meant? Or was he thinking of future actions?

"Mama," Amy called, "come see my roses."

"Coming," Charlotte called to her, then to Gilbert, she said: "Will you be working for Judge Placide?"

Gilbert shook his head. "Nothing would induce me."

But something could.

Chapter Fifty

Dr. Baldwin gave his grudging permission for Gilbert and me to see Margaret the evening before her exile to the Magdalene Ladies' Lunatic Asylum. A facility for inconvenient women, Dr. Clarke called it, tucked away west of Baton Rouge on what had once been a plantation and where, according to him, the patients' every comfort had a price. Rather like Mr. Keogh's special apartments.

"Fortunate for Mrs. Duvall," Dr. Clarke said as we met him going into the hospital, "Judge Placide's willing to pay the fee to keep her there. He just might see his way to purchasing a few amenities for her—for the sake of his friendship with the late colonel." Nothing too lavish, I imagined, given Placide's opinion that Margaret should be grateful to escape prison for the madhouse.

For one last night, Margaret resided in New Orleans, in a closet of a room in the hospital, a constable posted outside the door. Before our going in, Dr. Baldwin had warned us: "She's in quite a state, not at all herself. Pay your respects, but don't agitate her."

I was taken aback by her appearance, which was no longer under her careful control and contrivance and was, Gilbert later told me, more disturbing to him than it had been on the night of Duvall's murder—for then she had been in the throes of high drama. Most of her pale hair was haphazardly knotted at the nape of her neck, the bits cut short for side-curls now hanging limp at her temples. Her face, devoid of cosmetic enhancement, was gaunt and pitted with shadows in a shadowy room, where a single lamp burned on a high shelf, out of her reach. Of course, Margaret could not have touched the lamp—never mind upsetting it—even if she had managed to balance herself standing on the three-legged stool on which she presently sat, for over her shapeless, unadorned dress Margaret wore a quilted restraining jacket that bound her arms across her body in a lonely embrace.

Silent and still, slow to turn her face towards us as we entered the room, as soon as Margaret recognized us, her attention fixed on my brother, and there was no stopping her chatter: "You came! As I prayed you would, Dr. Crew. You can tell them, tell everyone, I never stabbed my husband. You were there, you know. A stranger did it—stuck him through—and I thought, for sure, he'd do the same to me." Margaret cast a glance in my direction, then fixed again on Gilbert, whom she might delude herself that she could influence. "Rob me and ravish me first, sir, but stab me, too. I was wearing some nice jewelry. But he didn't take it. Ran off quick as he'd come, panting in his rush. And then you arrived and saved me. And you will again, won't you? Won't you?" She caught her breath, staring up at Gilbert with wet, imploring eyes.

The room was furnished with a cot and the low stool, which she occupied, nothing else, so Gilbert sat on his haunches in front her, face to face with her, no longer the looming figure above the supplicant. With his small patients, he did the same, sitting or kneeling to meet them eye-to-eye and, thereby, begin to calm their fears and gain their trust. Margaret was afraid, clear enough, and uncertain whom to trust—or she should have been.

I stood nearby, a witness to Gilbert's purpose—which was not to save Margaret, but to coax an admission from her, some word or phrase implicating Victor Eden, which would make Charlotte's return to him impossible. That was all Gilbert wanted. And I had come with him to hear the interview, myself, not wanting to rely solely on a second-hand account of it.

"Mrs. Duvall—Margaret," Gilbert said gently, "you know things didn't happen quite the way you say they did that night.

384

Maybe, if you tell me a little more about what really occurred, we can straighten out this tangle and you can go home."

"Could I?"

"You and I both know that Colonel Duvall was out at a meeting and with me for much of the evening, and you were with someone else."

"Oh. But he hasn't come to see me." Margaret's mouth trembled as she spoke. "No. Hasn't lifted his little finger to help me. I don't understand. I don't understand how he can do this to me—do nothing for me. After all I did for him, anything he wanted."

"You're speaking of Victor Eden," Gilbert said. Margaret did not contradict him, and he continued: "Mr. Eden was with you when Colonel Duvall confronted the two of you in the alley. Isn't that right?"

Margaret looked straight into Gilbert's eyes.

"Isn't that right?" he repeated.

"No, sir."

"Margaret?" Gilbert resorted to the tone a parent uses when warning a child not to lie.

"No, it's not right. I was alone." Margaret sniffed loudly. "He wouldn't walk with me."

"He wouldn't walk with you ever, or he wouldn't on that particular night?" Gilbert asked.

Margaret's brow furrowed and mouth twisted a moment before she answered: "He walked with me sometimes—part of the way—but not that night. He'd been warned, you see. Helene warned him that my husband was having him watched."

"How did Helene know to warn him?" Gilbert asked the question that had come to my mind, too. Had Helene suggested to the colonel that he keep a closer eye on Eden—or on Margaret? I wondered. What was Helene's real interest in their affair? Was she as good a friend as Margaret believed her to be?

385

"We might be seen, Victor said, and we couldn't risk that," Margaret said. "So he took another route—and I was alone." She rocked from her waist, back and forth. While admitting her liaison with Eden, she had also exposed his indifference to her after sating himself. Looking out for himself, not for her—leaving her to find her own way home along dangerous streets. "Since that night," she said, "I've been so muddled—" Drugged with laudanum, I thought. "At the inquest—I don't know what I said. But there was a man—not tall like Victor, but short, heavy. He pushed me, I think he did, and then Frank was there, and they tussled."

"He pushed you before Colonel Duvall reached you?"

Margaret blinked as if struggling from a daze, perhaps trying to retrieve a memory. Then she shook her head; she wasn't sure. "I smelled onions—what a thing to remember now," she murmured. "Then my husband fell against me and the man scuttled off. And I screamed."

"But you didn't scream right away, Margaret, did you? Colonel Duvall was stabbed low with a narrow blade, and it took time for him to bleed to death. You waited. Before you screamed for help, you waited to be sure he was dead." Gilbert's tone was gentle, but relentless.

Tears spilled from Margaret's eyes. "How can you say that to me?"

"All that blood," he reminded her. "You can't tell me you didn't wait."

"What if I did? You don't know what he was like—miserable and mean with drink. I lived with it." Margaret lifted her chin defiantly, but as she tilted back her head, tears ran down her cheeks. With her hands confined in the jacket, she could not brush them away. I thrust my handkerchief at Gilbert, who took it and dried her tears and wiped her runny nose. Then she went on: "Frank was always jealous, always watching me. But I didn't kill him, I wouldn't, I swear. Not even to be free of him for Victor's sake. I just waited—that was all. I just held him and comforted him—that's what I did. I knew he wouldn't last, so I patted him and soothed him, pacified him and . . . " Margaret's recitation of excuses for what she had and had not done for her husband, her twists and turns of mind as she struggled to escape the trap she had constructed, were both pitiful and repellant.

"You say you wouldn't harm your husband, even to be free for Victor's sake," Gilbert said. "But didn't Victor Eden do something for your sake?"

One corner of her mouth jerked upward in a grotesque half-smile, there and gone. "Charlotte." Margaret breathed the name. "Do you think so? Oh, do you think he—"

"Don't you?" Gilbert prompted her,

My heart pounded when I heard her answer: "For me?" Margaret actually sounded pleased when she said those words.

"Who else?" Gilbert said. "He gave her something, put it in her teacup. You thought so, yourself, that night, didn't you?—when you were clearing away her things. And he waited for it to take effect."

"Charlotte was sick—queasy," Margaret said. "Helene suspected another baby, but I knew that couldn't be true. Couldn't be his if it were. Victor didn't want Charlotte any more—he wanted me. Something else must have been wrong with her—she was in such a dark mood. Helene ordered Tansy to mix the tisane to set her right, but Charlotte added the poison herself, not Victor. From that little brown glass bottle, isn't that right? She did it, herself—that's what you're saying?—and Victor waited. And now . . . now all I have to do is wait again, and he'll come for me. Oh, I thought my friends had deserted me, the judge sending me away. But it's part of a plan. It's happening for a reason . . ."

Before we left her, Gilbert laid my handkerchief in her lap, as useless to Margaret in her bound condition as reason was to her demented mind.

Chapter Fifty-One

Gilbert and I returned to our quiet home in Marigny with our minds disquieted. If Margaret had finally told the truth, then Eden had not wielded the knife—even if he'd had a word with Mr. Keogh about arranging for a problem to disappear—no one the wiser, as Keogh had said when listing his special services. Nor had we proof that he had poisoned Charlotte; although, I suspected he had done more than wait for his wife to expire.

I watched my brother trudge up the narrow stairs ahead of me, the impending loss of Charlotte's presence weighing upon him. Reaching the upper hall, we saw Charlotte's door stood open and heard her voice, her reading voice, soft and rhythmic, and Gilbert and I peeked in the doorway. The lamp was turned up, the room aglow, and Charlotte sat on the floor between the children's cots, her feet tucked under her hem, a picture book lying open on the lap of her gray skirt. Amy, on her cot, held the doll I had given her, its porcelain-face with long-lashed eyelids that closed when the doll lay on its back, as it did now, while Amy's heavy-lidded eyes continued gazing at her mother, transfixed. But Wilfred, on his cot, thumb in mouth, had given in to deep sleep. For another moment, we observed them, mother and children. Then, Charlotte paused in her reading and looked towards the doorway.

As her eyes met mine, we exchanged a flicker of smiles. Then Charlotte fixed her dark gaze upon my brother, the gentleness I had seen in her expression towards her children vanishing, replaced by something I could not read. But following the line of her vision back to Gilbert, I saw the meaning of his look at her, his face masking nothing, not his longing, nor his love. If she had not already guessed, he was telling her now—without saying a word.

"Come along," I whispered to Gilbert and softly closed Charlotte's door.

With Charlotte and the children settled for the night, and Ella, too, I supposed, I went to my room to prepare for a late supper engagement with Ambrose, whom I had neglected for too many days. Attending to my toilette, exchanging the plain garb I'd worn to the hospital for a plum-colored silk gown, ornamenting my chignon with amethyst-studded combs, I felt a frisson of anticipation—coupled with a pang of guilt. My mood rising as Gilbert's fell, I felt sorry for my brother, even though I had warned him against setting his heart on the impossible.

As I entered the parlor, Gilbert laid aside the volume of Whitman's verse that had absorbed him, shifted his legs out from under Dulcie on the footstool, rose and approached me. Taking from me the purple velvet cape I carried, he wrapped it around my shoulder, at the same time, drawing a deep breath. "Oriental rose," he said, "with notes of vanilla-scented tobacco—a heady combination, Lenore. Mr. Parr will be at your mercy. Are you expecting his proposal tonight?" Gilbert's tone was light, but his smile was wistful.

"Possibly," I said. "And I might accept if Ambrose promises we'll take a long European tour with his theater troupe. A journey so restores the spirit." Although, it struck me, Gilbert was more in need than I of travel. I moved aside the curtain an inch at the front window to see if my suitor's carriage had arrived. No, not yet. Letting the curtain fall, I turned back to Gilbert and said what I believed needed saying, even if it meant my casting a pall over our conversation: "Of course, I won't go anywhere, Gil, until matters are settled here. As things stand, if Charlotte's to have any future with her children, her husband must take her back. You don't want to hear it, but I don't see any other way. We can hope that he won't mistreat her, but—"

"He already has," Gilbert said. "And Margaret refuses to implicate her lover, who is protected by the judge—belongs to the judge, as Charlotte and her children belong to Eden. That's the core of it."

"Property," I said under my breath.

"If I'm wrong about Eden, if he has not poisoned or stabbed anyone," Gilbert said, disdain in his voice, "if all his bruising is done out of sight and his only obvious sin is being a selfish bastard—"

"Gilbert."

"Then I've been wrong to keep his wife from him," Gilbert continued, moderating his tone. "Any number of decent women, lovely women, too, have married difficult men, yourself included, Lenore, the third time around, and lived with the consequences. If I'm wrong, I've made a mess of things for Charlotte, for you, for all of us. And I am sorry."

"You didn't do it alone," I said. "And whatever else you have or haven't done, you saved Charlotte's life. On that terrible night, you saved her from a foregone death."

"An accident of fate saved Charlotte," Gilbert said. "And I was on the riverbank to gather her up."

"Oh, Gil." I reached up with my lavender-gloved fingers and brushed the hair back from his forehead. "An accident of fate took Estelle and the baby," I said, "and there was nothing you could do about it. This time you could do something and you did by protecting Charlotte, giving her time to recover herself."

"You've done that, Lenore—you and Ella. For me, as well as for Charlotte."

I kissed my brother's cheek and, leaving him with his favorite Whitman, went to answer the rapping at the front door. There, Ambrose awaited me, offering a nosegay of cream and yellow hot-house roses, along with a paraphrase of Poe, my favorite poet: "For the rare and radiant lady whom the angels name Lenore."

Ambrose guided me through a swirl of fog into the plush interior of his carriage, where he moved close for a whiff of my perfume. I tilted my head as his moustache brushed across my throat, casting a backward glance through the carriage window into the darkness.

Just before Ambrose signaled his driver to move along, I saw the shadowy front porch of my house cut by a bar of light as the door opened and a shape appeared, delineated in the glow of the hall sconce. I recognized Charlotte only by her small stature, for her form was engulfed by a voluminous hooded cloak, probably borrowed from Ella. The hem trailed over the threshold, and she lifted it in descending the porch steps. At my request, Ambrose asked his driver to halt the carriage. Gilbert was coming after her, cramming hat onto head, thrusting arms into coat sleeves, then pulling the door to behind him and catching up to her before they were both obscured by fog. Ambrose followed my interest in the scene, peering out the window with me.

"Your brother had a visitor this evening?" he asked.

"My houseguest," I replied.

"Ah. Then, may I offer the lady and Dr. Crew conveyance?"

"Thank you, Ambrose, but no. Let's follow along after them, at a distance, just to see where they go."

"I sense an intrigue," Ambrose murmured in my ear before he instructed his driver.

If Ambrose only knew . . . Gilbert and Charlotte were somewhere ahead of us, the driver keeping track of them when I could not. Then the carriage came near enough for me to glimpse through the fog the pair of them arm-in-arm, to my relief. Alone, how could Charlotte have seen anything around her, even passersby under a streetlamp, or heard the creak of carriage wheels, the out-blown breath of weary horses passing near her, with her head muffled in the hood of the cloak? Gilbert would look about and listen for hazards, I thought, just as Ambrose's driver pulled his carriage up short, avoiding collision with a wagon at a crossroads.

Setting off again, the driver tried and failed to located the couple walking in the fog. "Never mind," I said to Ambrose. I took some comfort that Gilbert was not likely to be escorting Charlotte to her husband's house, for they were headed in the opposite direction when they had disappeared from my view.

What happened between them that night, while I kept company with Ambrose, I have since pieced together from the little either would tell me in the days following, from Charlotte's later confidences, and from one of Gilbert's letters to me after he went away on a journey that did not restore his spirit. But I record the night here as it may well have unfolded.

✛ ✛ ✛

Charlotte had left Amy and Wilfred asleep, Ella sitting with them. Then, she had entered the parlor in Ella's borrowed cloak, raising the hood to cover her braided hair, shadowing her features until they resembled those hidden in one of her shaded drawings.

"I would like to go out," she had said. "Will you walk with me?"

And Gilbert's heart had lurched, for he thought she meant to go to Eden's house that night. He was not ready for her to go, never would be ready.

"I'd like to walk to the river," Charlotte said, as Gilbert caught up with her outside the house. "Only to the river." She linked her arm with his, and they were on their way, Charlotte hidden within the drapery of the cloak, Gilbert with his hat pulled low and collar turned up against the chill. If an onlooker glanced their way, they were a couple, not a widower with another man's wife, strolling to the waterfront.

For a moment, Charlotte's hand tightened on his arm, then relaxed as she drew a deep breath and sighed it away. "Miss Lenore has told me about her travels," she said. "Suggested I might go away somewhere. But I know what that would mean for me—not really traveling, but stealing off with my children, our becoming runaways, being hunted. Ella has told me things, too. I'm tied here, that's how it is. A walk on a misty night will have to do for me."

For them both. Gilbert had proved nothing against her husband but his selfishness—and Gilbert admitted he had been selfish, too. How Charlotte would return to Eden, what she would say, he didn't know. Gilbert would do whatever she asked him to and, whether she asked or not, take all the blame he believed he had earned for his concealment of Charlotte's fate and worse. Then, while—or if—Charlotte and Eden reconciled their differences, Gilbert might seek a change of scene—if no one prevented him.

Charlotte drew closer to him, and Gilbert felt the tension coursing through her arm linked with his. "Victor must not send my children to Testament." Her voice floated out of the darkness of the hooded cloak that swallowed her. "Never to Judge and Mrs. Placide."

"I'll deal with the Placides," Gilbert said, his thoughts already churning. If it were possible he could explain Charlotte's absence and reappearance, mollifying not only Eden but also the judge and his wife, what then? Perhaps, Helene might not become hysterical, or lapse into a morbid trance, or whatever the spirits moved her to do. Judge Placide was the real challenge—how to circumvent his displeasure, as severe as a lesser man's wrath. What sentence might he pass on Gilbert? Gilbert had not considered the repercussions of his rashness when he had entered the grand parlor of Testament and felt menace in the room and had begun his deception—only to protect Charlotte.

For a while, Charlotte and Gilbert walked on in silent, separate contemplation.

By the clouded light of the moon, distant shapes of steamboats, moored, came into view, their looming smokestacks blacker than the deep night sky. Then, along the levee, a few men gathered by the orange glow of a brazier. And dark beyond them on the wharf were crates stacked and sacks piled high to be loaded aboard boats or onto wagons at daybreak.

Over the black water, fog drifted like a gauze veil on a moonlit breeze, a pale ghost following the course of the river. But as the fog rolled over the bank and into the streets, it gathered momentum and opacity. The men at the brazier disappeared within it. Even the glow of their fire disappeared. The sound of their gruff voices, followed by the passing banter between an invisible man and woman, the woman laughing, rose and receded in the mist through which Gilbert and Charlotte moved. Gilbert discerned only wisps of motion, bits and pieces—the flick of a coattail, the thrust of a walking stick, the sway of fringe along the edge of a shawl, and the flutter of ribbons trailing from a phantom bonnet. Suggestions of person or persons unseen—or apparitions drifting through a cloud on earth.

A circle of hazy light surrounding a streetlamp glowed across the way without penetrating the fog swirling around it. Someone brushed past Gilbert, stirring the air. Someone else bumped his shoulder, muttered, and vanished. Gilbert drew Charlotte towards the streetlamp, pressing her arm to his side to be sure of her. And Charlotte held firmly to him as she veered from collision with another couple passing between them and the lamppost, glimpsed and gone. Then they stopped close by a high plastered wall that smelled earthy with damp, possibly a garden wall, for vines grew over the top of it. The branches of wisteria dangled low and leaves brushed across the crown of Gilbert's hat.

Gilbert could not see Charlotte's face and wondered if her expression were as mild as her voice: "Victor was different when I met him. At least, he seemed so. We'd hardly begun to court when he took me on a carriage ride to Mr. Pritchard's plantation, where he was doing some work. Mrs. Placide was there, too, visiting Mrs.

Pritchard. Victor and I had been out walking over the grounds, and he took my hand to help me over the stile. Then, as I was standing at the top of the stile, Mrs. Placide came across the lawn, calling to him. Suddenly, he looked over his shoulder at me, squeezed my hand, and said marry me. Just like that. I was sixteen and smitten and did what he said."

Charlotte freed her arm from his, then raised her hands to push back the hood of the cape and let if fall to her shoulders. Gilbert sensed more than saw that she had lifted her face, perhaps wanting to feel the air and taste the mist and savor the anonymity of night. He did.

"Eden was smitten, too," Gilbert said.

"Or wanted to shield himself from the designs of other women."

"But Margaret Duvall?"

"Was proof he can do as he pleases. He wants that, too. And my carrying another child of his was proof, again, that he could do what he pleased with me, that he is in command and out of anyone else's control. But he isn't."

"Judge Placide controls him," Gilbert said.

"Before I met Victor, when he was just beginning his profession in Baton Rouge, it seems he made a mistake in a design," Charlotte said. "Victor would never talk about it. And then he went to work for Judge Placide."

"The judge told you this?"

"Not in so many words. Colonel Duvall said something to me this past year—when we were sitting out while his wife and my husband and Mrs. Placide and Dr. Baldwin were playing cards. He told me Victor was just the sort of architect the judge and his friends liked to employ for fitting up their big houses with peepholes and hidden doors because he had his own secrets to keep and—" Charlotte stopped.

The sound of footsteps grew louder, approaching them by the wall, then fainter, passing them by, the scent of cigar smoke trailing through the fog with the footsteps.

"That day at Testament, I didn't intend to argue with Victor, but he became angry, beyond all reason, to anything I said to him. I pleaded with him not to go ahead with those dreadful plans for the judge. Victor knew what Mr. Keogh had done to me—I told him. I told him about the landlord cutting my room into a closet as a punishment. I told Victor about my nightmares. But he didn't want to hear what I had to say. He didn't want to know that I'd ever been anything other than a doll in a shop until he took me home."

Her voice strained, she went on: "What we do for the least among us—and what we fail to do—matters. I learned that when I was a child and have never forgotten it."

Her allusion to the Gospel of Matthew brought to mind his sister's remark to him after one of her conversations with Charlotte: "Charlotte's her own odd mixture of Sunday school lessons, superstition, and commonsense. Sweet and bitter and a touch of something else."

"I asked him for a little kindness for the miserable," Charlotte said. "But he saw nothing wrong with designing cells so small that a sparrow couldn't build a nest in one. Nothing wrong with boxing up other people, for other people are nothing if it pleases the judge. And Victor must please the judge, as if that man were God Almighty. That's the example he would set for our children, our precious, innocent children. I had hoped he was better than that."

In the dark, Gilbert touched her cheek and felt the wetness of tears, reminding him of the rain on her face the first time he had touched her cheek, when she had lain in the broken, makeshift coffin. Gilbert had lifted her out, held her, kissed her.

"The judge expects me to work for him, too," Gilbert said.

397

"But you're free to refuse him," Charlotte said.

If Gilbert could remain so. Her husband, beholden for the judge's patronage, thought he was not, and Charlotte, chained to Eden, dependent on him for her livelihood, was not.

Charlotte's hand rested on Gilbert's coat sleeve. "When you first told me that I'd been given up for dead—then that my husband might have poisoned me—I was horrified," she said. "You know I was. But then I began to wonder—what if he'd just as soon have me out of the way? With Amy and Wilfred restored to me, I wanted a reason not to go back."

"You have a reason," Gilbert said.

"I have a husband, who is talented and proud and cowardly, all at once." Her voice was unguarded and weary, each word a weight. "And I am stubborn and moody and headstrong and will never give up my children. Do you understand?"

"Yes." Gilbert understood. It changed nothing that her respect for his profession had turned into her friendly regard for him—perhaps, turned into fondness—and his admiration of her had become desire.

"I must pray he will take me back," Charlotte said, "whatever bargain we strike, for our children's sake. I've troubled you and Miss Lenore and dear Ella for too long—and am so grateful to you all. Forgive me."

Chapter Fifty-Two

They returned from the borderless uncertainty of the fog to the familiar doorway of the house on Rampart, the boards of the porch firm underfoot and the door, swinging open, solid on its hinges. Gilbert took the mist-dampened cloak from her shoulders, Charlotte emerging from its dark folds in her white blouse and gray skirt. She had hardly spoken on the walk home and did not say goodnight to him then, only touching his sleeve before she started up the staircase. While Gilbert hung the cloak and his hat and coat in the hall, he aware of her ascent, her disappearing from the edge of his vision.

Gilbert removed his shoes and carried them, the better to move quietly up the stairs without disturbing the sleeping children. Then halfway up he paused at the sound of whispering. At Charlotte's bedroom doorway, Charlotte and Ella were changing places—Ella retiring for the night to her room at the back of the house, and Charlotte closing herself inside with her sleeping children for their last night together, here, down the hallway from Gilbert's room. She was going back to Eden, keeping her children.

Gilbert took the last steps up the stairs and then went along to his room, opened the door but did not shut it. Nor did he light a lamp. A low light from a sconce in the hall, a diffuse glow reaching his doorway, would do for him. The curtains he had drawn back early in the morning when looking out to gauge the chance of rain were still parted at the upper gallery windows, and beyond them, the fog settled low along the street while clouds blotted out moon and stars.

Moving slowly in near-darkness, Gilbert set aside his shoes and began to undress, hanging his jacket over a chair, then cravat and starched collar. He removed his pocket watch and chain from his waistcoat, and laid the waistcoat over the chair, as well. He dropped watch and chain, collar studs and cufflinks into a chipped saucer atop the bureau—the familiar clinking sound part of the nightly ritual that conjured nothing and no one. No shapes emerged from the darkness of the deep green walls, no ghosts retreated into the shadowy corners.

Gilbert slipped his braces from his shoulders, as if removing a pair of weights, and let them dangle from the waistband of his trousers. He unbuttoned his shirt and peeled it off, another layer, undershirt remaining. He laid the shirt over the other garments on the chair, then released the first button of his trousers.

Then, he stopped, unable to move for a time, trapped in his thoughts. This was the last night he would spend under the same roof with Charlotte, he, alone in his room. She had said as much. This was as close as he had come to his heart's desire—no closer—if it were only, purely his heart's desire. But he was consumed by wanting. Had he gone a little mad in pursuit of Charlotte? More than a little mad? And, if ever he had possessed her, would he not have been the one possessed? She would take his spirit with her when she was gone. But if he loved her, he must make it possible for her to live again with her husband, for the sake of her children.

Gilbert crossed to the bed and turned back the counterpane, folding it back to the foot of the four-poster bed. He ran the palm of one hand over the white cotton sheet, cool as a winding sheet. Even so, he ran his hand the length of the unwarmed bed as if it were the length of Charlotte's body. If desire could make it so.

Then Gilbert sank onto the edge of the mattress, just opposite the open doorway, and hung his head and stared at the floor, at the band of faint light that lay across the threshold. He heard the sighing of his own breath, the thrumming of blood in his temples, nothing else. His vision of what little he could see blurred, and the light at the doorway shifted and diminished, in part, replaced by a shadow. He raised his head. A pale form leaned against the door frame, which was nearly twice the height of the form, itself. Shape and shadow together—beloved Charlotte, conjured by longing.

Rising, Gilbert took a step towards the doorway. The illusion of her remained still. If she were really there, she would have said, straight away, if something were wrong with the children, if they needed his attention. But she said not a word. And he dared not speak, for if he did, she might vanish, leaving him talking only to himself. Charlotte could not be where he imagined her. And yet—a whiff of sweet olive blossom reached him, and then a touch traveled lightly over the back of his left hand, firmer as Charlotte took hold of his left hand in her right one and brought it around her to the small of her back and pressed it there.

"I'm not here," she whispered, her cheek against his shoulder, her breath warm on his bare arm. "This one night, I'm not here. You understand?"

Yes, Gilbert understood. They were not here together, as they had not been on the riverbank, Charlotte in his arms—and no one need ever know otherwise. Wasn't that what she had said? It was what he heard.

With the fingers of his right hand, Gilbert touched a pulse point at her throat and felt the throb of her blood. With the fingers of her left hand, Charlotte pulled loose the ribbons of her white cotton dressing gown and opened the gown at her breast to the thin shift beneath. Gilbert bent his head and pressed his ear to her breast and listened to her beating heart. He felt the rise and fall and rise of her breast in respiration. Then, Charlotte drew his face towards hers, he, still bending over her, his mouth finding and covering the cupid's bow of her lips. He embraced her and lifted her and carried her to his bed, to the smooth white sheet. The ruffles of her cotton gown fluttered like feathers, opening and falling away, revealing flesh softer and finer than swan's down, drawn over bones as delicate as those of a little bird.

Chapter Fifty-Three

Arriving home in the wee hours, halfway up the stairs on tiptoe, I caught an eyeful of Charlotte, slipping out of Gilbert's door, pulling her shift over her head on the way to her room.

How long had this been going on? I hardly slept, fretting and mulling when I should have been dreaming. For the past year, I had been aware of Gilbert's regard for Charlotte, witnessed his growing attachment, suspected his burgeoning desire. But I had trusted in his chivalrous sensibilities while, until recently, I had not known her well enough to guess what she would do, whether or not she would keep him at arm's length. I should have been wiser. Gilbert, mourning the loss of wife and child, and Charlotte, oppressed by her husband—my stars, they were as vulnerable to each other as tinder to spark. A woman could accept a man's attentions, keep him waiting for some reciprocal gesture for only so long before she must decide her course of action—to decline or encourage his further advances. I had come to such a pass last night with Ambrose and, with some reluctance, found myself sympathetically inclined towards Charlotte and Gilbert in the morning—despite my forebodings.

Time came for the clinic to open, and Gilbert was not yet down for breakfast—not even out of bed, I discovered, looking in on him. His door was ajar, curtains open to the daylight, and Gilbert was just then stretching and turning beneath the sheet. I saw him caress the indentation of the pillow next to his, where Charlotte's head had rested. I imagined him fighting sleep half the night not to

403

lose her to his own unconsciousness. And now he struggled to wake.

Taking a step back from the doorway, I called out to him as if only then approaching his room. "Gilbert, are you ever getting up?" As I entered, he sat up in bed, pulling the sheet over his bare chest. "Little patients and their not-so-patient mothers will soon be waiting for you," I said, sorting through the clothes tossed over the chair, then opening the armoire in search of a clean shirt for him. I was bustling, something I knew Gilbert disliked, as if my brusque manner might disguise my agitation.

"Leave it, Lenore," he said. "I'll get myself ready."

"Will you?" I snapped at my brother, my own restless night telling on me. I'd not even considered that he wouldn't get out of bed until I was gone. All his clothes were across the room, or nowhere to hand—undershirt and drawers might be under the bed.

"You must be worn out," Gilbert said, "after your night with Mr. Parr. Did he—"

"Propose?—yes, he did," I said. "Which is more than you can do for Charlotte." Gilbert regarded me warily, and I pressed on: "Was last night your farewell to her, or hers to you?"

"Let it alone, Lenore."

"I wish I could. But even once—there may be consequences to the meeting."

When Gilbert said nothing, only frowned, I blustered on: "My stars and planets, Gil—what now? This isn't wartime when polite society might glance away from a rash act or two."

At that, Gilbert glanced sideways at me. "Was that your excuse, Lenore?—that it was wartime."

I might have heard a teasing note in his voice and took heart from it. "Oh, Gil."

"Propriety wasn't always your first concern," he said. "And you can't tell me that your theatrical Mr. Parr is a prig."

"Of course, he isn't. And we may need him, yet—before this

imbroglio is over—to disguise us in costumes and float us out of New Orleans on a showboat." I flipped up a corner of the counterpane and let it fall.

Fleetingly, Gilbert smiled, perhaps envisioning the scene before he charted a different, more sober course. "Charlotte and I have no plan for escape," he said. "She won't have it. For another night, she's asked that Amy and Wilfred stay here. And she's asked me to take her back to face her husband this evening."

✛ ✛ ✛

Gilbert saw patient after patient in the clinic until the close of day, and I hoped his occupation spared him a little from the agitation that plagued me, intensifying as the night approached. I dashed off a note to Ambrose, asking his forbearance while I considered his flattering proposal, assuring him that I was not being coy—only that certain matters required resolution before I might be at liberty . . . Oh, the entire missive was an ink-splotched muddle, but I sent it anyway before Charlotte joined me in the parlor for a private word.

Charlotte was more on edge than I, understandably so, as she confessed to me what I already knew—that she had grown fond of my brother.

"And he of you," I said without revealing my insight into their intimacy.

"Gilbert has urged me to leave New Orleans with him, leave Louisiana," Charlotte said. "With the children, too—although, by law, they belong to Victor. But I've told him no, we would have no peace."

Charlotte said she would tell her husband the truth—"Not all of it," I warned her, "tell it slant." And she agreed that there were things Eden need never know. She would tell him she had believed he wanted her gone, that she was frightened and begged Gilbert and me to shelter her in secret. Perhaps that had become the truth to her. If Eden would allow, she would resume her place as wife and mother, hoping she might also reclaim the better part of Eden's nature.

While Margaret in a madhouse took the blame for sins beyond her own, I thought, Eden would keep his privileges and remain the man that Charlotte had married—nothing much to reclaim there, in my opinion.

That evening, Charlotte lingered longer than usual over bedtime stories and goodnight hugs with Amy and Wilfred—some children sense when their mother is uneasy and are loath to let her go, holding on for mutual comfort. Not until the children were asleep with Ella nearby did Charlotte join Gilbert and me in the front hall, where we prepared to be on our way.

I was determined to accompany Gilbert and Charlotte, believing my presence might temper Eden's reaction to his wife's return. Indeed, this was my purpose—as Paulina to Hermione, there to remind Leontes of the value and virtue of the lady he had cast aside. And if Charlotte were not quite the paragon of *The Winter's Tale*, if she had a past, if she were sadder but wiser for experience, was it not possible that she would come to shine brighter against the shadows from which she emerged?

Charlotte wore her russet-colored basque and draped skirt and her amber drop earrings. I stood back, giving Gilbert a moment to stare at her and say nothing, before I came forward with a simple gray hat for her to wear, a thick veil attached to the brim. Charlotte thanked me—for more than the hat, she said, kissing my cheek—then adjusted the angle of the hat on her upswept hair and drew the veil over her face.

This night beneath a waning moon, there was no rolling fog in which to lose track of each other, or to lose our way and prevent us ever reaching Eden's house. Only a fine mist laced the air. For a time, I walked just ahead of Gilbert and Charlotte, glancing back to see them walking arm-in-arm along the banquette, as they had last night. Then, when we reached the townhouse on

Dauphine—mournful with its plum-colored plastered walls, latched gray shutters, and black-lacquered door—Gilbert set down his medical bag, his appendage, which he had carried out of custom and with intent of appearing to Eden only in his professional role. As he raised his hand to lift the knocker, a heavy brass ring held in the teeth of a lion's head, Charlotte suddenly caught at his coat sleeve and stopped him.

"No," she said. "Not the street door." Charlotte tilted her head towards passersby, indicating no scene should be played for them. Had she seen through the veil a carriage and driver stopped across the street and a pair of young men in dark suits, standing idle and smoking near the steps of the next house, and felt a shiver of apprehension? We would go in the back way from the alley. She still had her keys, which had been among her things brought from Testament—which Eden had not bothered to claim.

We walked to the end of the block of townhouses, turned the corner, and continued to the entrance of the shadowy alley. I wished we had brought a lantern. Gilbert picked his way past refuse and rubbish bins stirring with rats, keeping Charlotte and me close behind him. At the back door of the townhouse, Charlotte came forward, fumbling the key out of her reticule. But even with ungloved fingers, she seemed unable to fit it into the lock and handed it over to Gilbert, who rattled the key into place. The release of the lock sounded as a soft click, but the door handle still resisted Gilbert's effort to turn it. No, not the handle, itself, he said—someone holding it on the other side of the door. He let go the handle and waited. Slowly, the door inched open, allowing a bar of hazy light to escape from the house.

"Who's that?" A woman's sibilant voice ran the words together.

"Dr. Crew."

"What you doing here?—sir," she said, the last word sounding like an afterthought.

I peered around Gilbert's shoulder and squinted at the outline in the doorway. Was this the daily maid who had shuffled through chores for Charlotte? I suspected not, and then heard Gilbert call her by name.

"Tansy?"

"Yes, sir."

Why was Tansy here? Had she accompanied her mistress on a late evening visit? We must retreat, for we would not want the complication of Helene's presence when Eden discovered his wife was still alive.

"Got some folks with you—sir?" Tansy craned her neck from the doorway, at the same time pushing the door wide open.

The glow of the lamp burning deep inside the courtyard of the house barely touched Gilbert and me and Charlotte, veiled beside us.

"Bring 'em on in, girl," a man's voice, but not Eden's, drawled.

The speaker sat in shadow under the arch of the loggia at the back of the house. A tall, three-paneled painted screen just beyond his own bulk blocked much of the view into the courtyard, but I spied part of a circular wrought-iron table there with lace-patterned, white-painted chairs tucked around it—six of them? I couldn't see them all. On the table burned a lamp with a frosted glass chimney. The night was mild for late November, but the breeze eddying down through the courtyard might have extinguished lighted candles.

"Come on in, Dr. Crew, and bring the ladies with you," the man said in a rusty whisper—the man being Judge Royce Placide.

As Gilbert took a step over the threshold, with Charlotte and me at his back, I felt a sickening sensation that we had that moment set foot inside the hidden workings of a séance. Gilbert set down his bag inside the doorway as Tansy pulled the door shut behind us, locking it.

"Come on, you all—get yourselves over here with me," the judge said, an undercurrent of excitement in his voice.

What was he playing at?—as if we were now part of his game.

Angling himself up from his chair just far enough to reach Charlotte, still cloaked and veiled, he closed one heavy hand around her wrist. "Tansy," he said, "fetch chairs for Mrs. James and little Mrs. Eden." Placide winked at me. "You can't tell me I'm wrong."

Gilbert caught Charlotte by her other arm, for she had swayed. Tansy brought two of the chairs from the table and positioned them for Charlotte and me near where the judge sat in another such chair, too small for him but sturdy, the narrow seat augmented by a wide cushion to accommodate the breadth of his posterior.

A chuckle rumbled in the judge's throat before he said: "I couldn't say for sure you'd bring her back tonight, but I knew she'd come if she heard there was a prospect of my wife taking Eden's children to *haunted Testament.*" He shivered the last words in a mockery of eeriness. "That'd tease their little mama out of hiding, sure enough." Placide had acknowledged Charlotte and then spoken about her as if she were not there—or no more than an object.

"Does Mr. Eden know about—" I began.

"Not yet," Placide interrupted me, another instance of his discourtesy. "But he might be pleased to see her."

I thought we had been careful—Gilbert, Ella, and I. How did the judge find us out? What did he know?

Placide turned his attention on Gilbert: "You're a perceptive young fellow about some things, but I have years on you. I read your face whenever Miss Charlotte's name was mentioned." The judge chuckled again, then drawled on: "That thrilling story you told about her disappearing—the others might've wanted to believe it, but I had my doubts. With all your pharmacological know-how, I had to wonder if you hadn't taken her body home with you, embalmed it, and kept it for your use. I know of stranger doings . . . "

Of course, Placide did, a sickening feeling told me. Beside me, Charlotte remained sitting very still and straight, hands clasped in her lap, but I heard her breath quicken.

"So I sent my girl—" the judge gave a nod towards the darkness at the back door, where I assumed Tansy stood. "One man's servant evasive with another's—I can read that, too. Your Ella was mighty hush-mouthed with my Tansy, giving nothing away, so my girl knew yours had something to hide. And I knew it." The judge's shrewd eyes peered up at Gilbert.

Gilbert glanced away, as did I. Where was Eden in his own house?—a house that had belonged to Judge Placide and where the master had kept a quadroon mistress in the old days. Might that mistress have been Tansy's mother and the once ginger-haired judge her father?

Beyond the screen, I heard only the merest trickle of water in the courtyard fountain. Then a whisper of leaves, a current of air traveled among palm fronds and citrus boughs and the foliage of thorny bougainvillea that climbed the courtyard walls. Nothing more.

The judge droned on: "—little things give us away. Washing day tells a tale. How many dainty garments of one sort and another hang on the line. And I know—" here, he leaned slightly forward and, with thumb and forefinger, took hold of the edge of Charlotte's veil, raised the veil and flicked it over the hat brim. "And I know," he repeated, "just how dainty you are, Miss Charlotte. I watched my girls wash you and dress you and lay you out for dead."

As I heard myself gasp, Charlotte recoiled. And, in a single motion, Gilbert drew her from her chair and away from Placide, wrapping his arms around her shoulders and transporting her to the far side of the loggia. I retreated with them, glancing towards the back door, where Tansy stood, then towards the courtyard, across which lay the front passage to the street door, trying to gauge a way out for us.

"Where's Eden?" Gilbert demanded.

"Well, that makes a change," Placide said. "You want the lady's husband to join you? I tell you for sure, I've been wondering where he is, myself—came to catch up with him tonight, and he's keeping me waiting. Gone to ground somewhere in this convoluted house. Holler for him, Gilbert Crew. Flush him out of the warren for me. I'll just stay put for a bit." The judge put a thick forefinger to his lips—his whereabouts would be our secret.

Gilbert, Charlotte, and I entered the courtyard. Something was wrong in the house, I felt it, and we would be wise to leave it alone, cross the flagstones and get out of there.

"Just to the table, that's far enough," Placide called, as if he saw us through the screen—perhaps he did through a spyhole hidden in the design. "My men are on the street in case Eden comes or goes that-a-way."

Or we try to go out. I heard his warning tone. And I wondered at his bringing men with him to watch the entrance of the house. Had Eden fallen from the judge's favor, and was he now trying to avoid his patron?

"Go on now, holler for him," the judge ordered. "Show him what you brought him."

Gilbert kept hold of Charlotte, she with her head bent down and her cheek pressed against the lapel of his coat, as if she were disappearing into him.

"Mr. Eden," Gilbert called, throwing his voice to the upper galleries. "Mr. Eden!"

A moment passed, and then another, before a door on the second floor gallery opened and Eden stepped out. He looked side to side along the gallery, then came to the railing and peered over, squinting to make us out. "Dr. Crew? What on earth?" Then he noticed me. "Mrs. James?"

"Mr. Eden," I said with a nod.

"To what do I owe . . ." Eden's voice trailed away.

"Sir," Gilbert began, "we must speak—"

Eden cut him off, saying: "This is not a convenient time. It's getting late and—"

Gilbert cut him off right back: "I've brought someone to see you, Mr. Eden."

No easing into the revelation now. Let Eden know that Charlotte was here—have everything out at once with Eden and Placide together. And while they declaimed from gallery and loggia, arguing whatever point had brought the judge there to lurk behind a screen, Gilbert, Charlotte, and I might slip out of the house. Escaping was much on my mind.

Charlotte turned her face upward, and the lamplight caught the angle of her cheek. Eden gripped the balustrade and stared down at her. "Madame?" He cocked his head and leaned further over the railing, the lamplight shining upward illuminating his jaw and deepening the lines across his brow. Eden studied his wife as if she were a puzzle he did not know how to solve. Then he exhaled her name: "Charlotte."

"Sir." This was the first word that Charlotte had spoken since our entering the house. And after saying it, clearly and with some volume, she took a step away from Gilbert, out of his embrace, only keeping one hand on the cuff of his sleeve.

"What trick is this?" Eden's eyes darted towards Gilbert, then back to Charlotte.

"None," she said. "I'm here, Victor."

Eden stood still a full minute before he moved, almost soundlessly, along the gallery towards the spiral front staircase. He disappeared from view at the top of the dark stairwell, then reappeared, coming into view on the lower stairs. First, came his stocking feet, no shoes, then his black trousers with braces over the shoulders of his white shirt, and then his ashen face. As he approached the circle of light, I observed that his trousers were rumpled and the buttoning of his shirt was off a space, the top button lacking for a buttonhole. No starched collar, no tie, no frock coat nor jacket. I had never before seen him disheveled. Had he come home to his empty house after a day's work, loosened his clothing, and fallen asleep in a chair until Gilbert's shout disturbed him? Yet Eden did not seem groggy with recent sleep, but alert with nervous excitation, genuinely astonished at the sight of his lost wife.

"How can this be?" Eden whispered, still staring at Charlotte—stricken. That was my impression. A silent conflict within him played out on his features: eyes widened, then narrowed, brow furrowed, then smoothed, jaw clenched, then slackened, at last, his face resolving itself into an expression of incredulity. He lowered himself onto one of the three remaining chairs, the other three behind the screen. Charlotte, Gilbert, and I remained standing. "Where . . .Where have you been hiding yourself?" Already, Eden had looked in Gilbert's direction, and then he spared a sharp glance at me.

Not a word from the judge on the other side of the screen.

"There was the wreck on the river road, and my coffin broke open," Charlotte said, and Eden flinched. "Dr. Crew discovered I was alive. He believed something was wrong—terribly wrong." A tremor ran through her voice, but she continued: "He took me to Mrs. James and Ella, who nursed me to health."

"You have been hiding my wife from me." Eden shot the words at Gilbert, the transgressor in Eden's eyes.

"Out of concern for Mrs. Eden's safety," Gilbert said.

"Damn your concern. All this time—" he glared at Charlotte—"you left me to mourn for you."

"And did you?" The sharpness of Charlotte's tone surprised and apparently offended her husband, whose posture stiffened. He did not reply, and Charlotte spoke again: "I was afraid to come home, afraid what happened to me was your doing."

"What do you mean—what happened to you?"

"I was with child, Victor, did you know? Sick every morning, when you insisted we go to Testament. Even if you hadn't noticed, your hostess knew, and she disapproved. One more baby, one more distraction for you, might even stir old feelings for me—just when your patrons and your friends had such plans for you." Determination had strengthened her voice, and Charlotte stood separate from Gilbert, no longer touching his arm. "They couldn't have that. If you remembered your better self, you might think of the example you set for your children. You might think twice about your part in Judge Placide's cruel schemes."

Had Charlotte forgotten who listened on the other side of the screen, or knowing the judge heard her, was she daring him to contradict her? But Placide remained silent, hidden. I might have heard his breathing, but Eden did not know to listen for it.

"Someone at Testament poisoned your wife, Mr. Eden," I said, knowing the judge was my audience, too. "You, sir?"

"I miscarried," Charlotte said. "Was that the intent?—or to kill me and the child? Your doing? Or hers or any of them—and you doing nothing to stop them?"

Eden came to his feet. "How dare you say that to me!"

"Then protect me from them!" Charlotte shouted back at him. "Protect your children. You're not the Placides' slave." She caught her breath. "Are you?"

Eden looked away from her then, around the courtyard, towards the stairwell, up at the gallery, anywhere but at his wife.

"Is that your answer?" Charlotte said, dropping her voice.

Eden cut his eyes back to her, wincing as if he had been stung. Like Gilbert, I gazed on Charlotte, and I wondered if I had

414

known her at all, marveled at her fierceness that overcame her trepidation. I had imagined myself speaking for her, playing Paulina to her Hermione, chastening Leontes, or Eden, for his cruelty to her. But Charlotte spoke for herself.

"Does it matter, Victor," she said, "which one mixed the tisane, which one added a drop of this or that to the cup, which one left behind a poison bottle to be found among my things? You were the one who knew how my mother had died. And you, with all of them, were so quick to give me up for dead—even if any one of you knew I wasn't."

Was Judge Placide, voyeur and eavesdropper, enjoying this—little Mrs. Eden dressing down her husband? I glanced towards the screen, then away as, out of the corner of one eye, I caught a shimmer of movement on the second floor gallery: the silvery gray tabby mouser that Gilbert had given Charlotte was padding along behind the railing.

"You are overwrought," Eden said, sounding at pains to prove that he was not.

Charlotte shook her head. "No, Victor. I am clear. I have imposed long enough on the kindness of Dr. Crew and Mrs. James. If you would be your own man, if we could start again elsewhere, for our children, I would try again to be a wife to you."

"Charlotte, you are in no position to bargain with me," Eden said.

I could have slapped him but held back. Gilbert controlled himself, too, clinching his fists at his sides as he spoke: "You endangered your wife, sir. You owe her something."

Eden looked askance at Gilbert. "And what is that? What do I owe a woman who's lived with you—in secret? And before that, all those house calls, all that show of concern for my children. Spare me—I understand too well."

"But you don't, Victor," Charlotte said. "He's not like you."

Eden rounded the table, jostling it as he came towards her.

415

I took her hand, pulling her aside as Gilbert blocked the way, lunging forward and catching the tilting lamp before it overturned. Eden must have mistaken my brother's sudden maneuver for an act of aggression, for he as quickly shifted out of Gilbert's way, putting some distance between them. Gilbert replaced the lamp on the table, while Eden drew himself up to his greater height, and Charlotte and I edged away from her husband, nearer to the fountain by the vine-covered wall. We had all shifted and reshaped ourselves, like the shadows around us as the light had moved.

We stood motionless, but I sensed motion along the gallery, this time not the prowling cat. Tilting my head, I discerned a dark, billowy form, gliding past the rail, disappearing at the top of the enclosed staircase. An invited visitor, or one of Mrs. Placide's revenants, uninvited? Perhaps a former mistress of the house, or a former servant out to haunt old Judge Placide. At any moment, might spirits in white stockings come cantering over the flagstones?

Gilbert had become aware of the movement, too, glancing upward, then back to the scene in the courtyard. Charlotte had not seemed to notice the stirring above nor the impending change in the atmosphere, so intent was she on speaking to Eden, attempting to reason with him, as if something salvageable remained in his character. She asked him for Amy and Wilfred's sake to help her find a way, somehow, towards reconciliation.

A thread of scent of patchouli unwound from the stairwell and traveled the air into the courtyard ahead of the figure that reappeared at the foot of the stairs, shape out of shadow. In the glow of the courtyard lamp, Helene materialized, blowzy in a loose-fitting, bottle-green gown, holding a cut-glass goblet full of red wine in one bejeweled hand.

"Victor!"

We all took notice then. The puffed sleeves of her gown slipped off her shoulders as Helene turned her back to us, revealing that her bodice was unbuttoned. With her free hand, she lifted her unpinned henna-colored curls from her neck, saying to Eden: "Do me up, Victor." Ah. Her presence explained Placide's interest in Eden's whereabouts, I thought. Potiphar's wife had caught her man. And now, unbeknownst to her, she had been caught by Potiphar.

Cocking her head over one shoulder, Helene cut her eyes towards Charlotte and smirked. That was just one of the things the Placides did—show contempt. Spying, snooping, gathering the secrets of the people they exploited were other things. I assumed Helene had been listening from the gallery as her husband listened from his own place of concealment. What had brought her downstairs, not at the moment of Charlotte's appearance in the courtyard, but now? Had Helene perceived Eden weakening towards Charlotte, the possibility he might succumb to her beauty, if not to her moral argument? Helene would put a stop to that. Again, her back to Eden, she wriggled her shoulders. But Eden did not speak nor move nor button Helene's gown.

"What are you waiting for, Victor?" Helene said. "Your wife's permission? As far as the world knows, she's not even here—*she's dead.*"

Gilbert took a step closer to Charlotte and me, and Helene eyed us.

You've been playing parlor games, Dr. Crew, you and that naughty sister of yours. Haven't you? A little conjuring." She smiled crookedly in Charlotte's direction, then said to Gilbert in an exaggerated drawl: "Oh, Dr. Crew, so devoted to a lady in distress. Hid her and had her. You can't tell me you didn't. I sense these things—it's my gift."

Would that the midwife had never lifted the caul from her face.

"Your gift." At last, the judge had spoken.

Chapter Fifty-Four

"Help me up, girl." The judge's voice sounded from behind the floral-painted screen. Labored noises followed that signaled Placide rising—huffing and puffing with low groans and muttered curses. Eventually, the judge lumbered around the screen into the lamplight, one hand gripping Tansy's shoulder and the other an unlit stub of a cigar. I could not make out if Helene were more confounded by the appearance of her husband or of her maidservant. Eden looked as if he might be sick, but neither of the Placides paid him any mind in that moment of their locking eyes on each other.

Then, Judge Placide chortled at his wife's dismay. "The girl works for me," he said. "They *all* work for me." He cast a baleful glance at Eden. "And when they get themselves caught diddling my wife, they work for me *forever.*"

Tansy brought Placide forward to the iron chair that Eden had abandoned. But before Placide would sit, he sent her back behind the screen to fetch the cushion. Meanwhile, he said to Eden: "You've been upstairs a long time with my wife, kept me waiting to surprise you. Then, lo and behold, young Crew and Mrs. James arrived with Miss Charlotte to keep me company."

Tansy returned with the cushion, and the judge settled himself, grating his teeth as he bent his gouty knee, then turning his grimace into a malevolent smile.

"What a tangled web! Why, you've made yourselves a hooraw's nest—every last one of you," said the judge. "Most entertaining! Better than those séances of yours, Helene. But look here, there's six of us, and Tansy to tap and moan—we could hold a séance yet."

Helene's mouth twitched and her eyes shifted, lids blinking rapidly, as if she were calculating, then recalculating what to do to recover herself. She took a sip of her wine—fortification, perhaps—then addressed her husband: "With all your spying around, Royce, you must know what these two have been up to—fooling us all." She wagged a forefinger at Charlotte and Gilbert; Helene would make the judge her ally in condemning them.

But Placide, not so easily distracted, mimicked her gesture, wagging his own forefinger at her. "Mighty droll, Helene. Chastising little missy and the doctor. Isn't she droll, Eden? Slipping out of your bedroom, you sorry son-of-a-bitch."

Eden did not contradict the judge's assessment of him, but Helene drew herself up, ignoring the sleeve dropping from her bare shoulder, acting the queen in disarray, saying: "You disgust me, Royce. Filth and nastiness—that's what you're made of."

"While you are sugar and spice and everything nice." Placide's small eyes became slits, through which he watched her.

"I've always been an ornament for a man—first for Daddy, then for you," Helene said, preening for all the men present. "Your gracious hostess, your finder and keeper of secrets. For years and years, I've put up with your indulgences, Royce—and your *peculiarities*. And then, one day I up and said to myself: *Helene, why shouldn't you have one beautiful man for your own?*" Lifting her glass, sloshing wine over the rim, Helene spun to face Eden. "*Victor.*"

As far away as Eden stood from me, I felt the air move with his shudder.

I imagined all of us were in some degree of shock. No, maybe not Tansy, who had waited in the shadows all her life and seen everything. Maybe not the judge, omnipotent through his minions and with the power to offend and shock as he pleased—but Eden, Charlotte, Gilbert, and me. I heard Charlotte's ragged breathing, stopping in a short gasp before resuming. How would she, my brother, and I escape from these people?

"Victor," Helene repeated, still fixed on him. "Don't worry yourself. Royce will tidy up the mess—he always does. And he and I will make things up between us—we always do—to our mutual advantage." Helene spoke as if it were reasonable for her to betray her husband, insult him, and call on him for his gallant assistance, all in the space of an evening. Despite her dreamy tone, echoing the one she used to carry herself into a trance, Helene spoke as if she were insensible to the cold spot in the courtyard—the iciness with which her husband regarded her.

Eden extended one hand towards the judge in some approximation of a conciliatory gesture, then let the hand fall. "Judge Placide, sir,"—Eden struggled to find his voice. Then, when silence would have served him better, he rushed headlong: "I've done everything you've asked of me, sir—better than you required, you've said so. Plans ahead of schedule, under cost, every detail to your specifications. But this—" his glance sliced towards Helene, then back to the judge. "Mrs. Placide insisted that I . . ." Eden faltered, perhaps on the way to making an unchivalrous excuse for cuckolding the judge.

I suspected that Helene had coerced Eden into bedding her, played on his obligations to Placide as she demanded that Eden serve her as well. Placide could have stopped the pair of them at any time that night, but he had waited until Eden finished his command performance before humiliating the pair of them. A man might not concern himself with a woman's willingness or ardor, but a woman wanted to believe that the man for whom she hankered desired her in return. And a man who allowed himself to be used by a woman, in the judge's eyes, was no man at all.

"Fool." The judge sneered. "I don't rightly recall offering you a piece of my property."

"Sir, I swear to you," Eden said. "I'll do anything you ask to make amends—*anything*."

"Victor?" Charlotte whispered. I heard her fear in his name.

"But you're already making amends," Placide said, "for my pulling you out from under one of your earlier errors in judgment."

"Please, sir." Eden bowed his head, but I suspected his show of contrition was only for his getting caught.

"Does your little wife know you have not always been as clever as you would have us believe?" Placide said and, without waiting for Eden to answer, went on patronizing him: "No economy in design if the building falls down. Annex of an orphanage in Baton Rouge, Miss Charlotte, picture that—plenty of injuries to go 'round. Maybe two or three little orphans buried in the rubble. Nobody counting."

When it had pleased the judge, he had exercised his power to destroy Eden in Charlotte's eyes, if Eden had not already accomplished that. I saw the anguish in her face.

"An accident, Charlotte," Eden said. "The foreman, the laborers all made mistakes. I—it was a terrible accident. Judge, you said so, yourself."

The judge replied with a dismissive snort.

"You said if it were up to you, sir," Eden continued, hardly suppressing his wounded pride, his anger, "you'd have had the bones crushed with oyster shells for tabby concrete—the way you did with slave bones before the war."

Was this Eden's ill-considered attempt to get his own back?

"A turn of phrase," Placide said, brushing his fingers through the air as if dispersing the words. "A figure of speech." An exaggeration, the judge would have us believe. But I recalled boasts he had made to Bartholomew years ago, and I wouldn't put anything past Judge Placide.

Charlotte shut her eyes, and the tears that had welled in them spilled down her cheeks. A silent minute passed, in which Gilbert stepped nearer to her and offered his handkerchief.

With the six of us in the little courtyard and Tansy somewhere in the shadows, I spared a thought for how the scene might be staged for a theatrical production. Hadn't plays of old been performed in courtyards? Here, with a gallery above serving as a balcony and a painted screen serving as an arras, those around me had concealed themselves, then made their entrances. How did one manage a crowded stage—directing the eyes of the audience as well as the movement of the actors? Movement and countermovement, Ambrose had told me, drawing all eyes to an action, all ears to a speech. And now, while the rest of us were still, Helene was on the prowl.

Having woven her way among the potted lemon trees, Helene re-emerged into the lamplight, her eyes grown dark and a queerness of expression flitting across her features. She looked around her as if she had just arrived on the scene and was, for the first time, taking in the stony countenances of her husband and Eden, Gilbert and me, sparing only a glance for Charlotte. Then Helene heaved a sigh and murmured: "Poor Margaret"—as if nothing that had passed between Eden and Placide held any meaning for her. "Margaret could have done it, you know—poisoned Charlotte to get rid of the baby."

Charlotte opened her eyes. Gilbert stepped in front of Charlotte, extending one arm in a protective gesture to keep her behind him, to shield her as he addressed himself to Helene.

"But Margaret didn't do it," Gilbert said. "Margaret believed she was the only one Victor Eden wanted, the only one with whom he—" Gilbert paused, changed direction. "Margaret didn't believe Charlotte was with child. But you, Mrs. Placide, knew that she was and gave her an abortifacient."

"Helene?" Eden said. Had he really no idea?

423

Helene approached him and touched the placket of his shirt, where the buttons were misaligned. "What if I did, Victor?" she said. *For you*—I saw her mouth the words to Eden out of her husband's line of sight, as if she might still deceive anyone.

"If Helene put a drop too much pennyroyal in your wife's teacup," the judge said, "I'm sure she'll tell you, Victor, that Charlotte's supposed death was an *accident*."

"That's right," Helene said. "Her collapse was an accident, sure enough. And Dr. Baldwin, himself, declared her dead before Royce got her out of the house."

"How dare you?" Charlotte said to Helene. "How dare you decide—"

"Now, missy," the judge interposed, "that's enough. My lady-wife depends on me to straighten out the tangles, and I see the way. Think of this—your husband has employment for life, traveling all across the South for me, designing and building prisons. Better than living in one, don't you agree? Why, from now on, Victor won't set foot in New Orleans. And your doctor friend will be traveling right behind him, dosing up convicts. And here you are, Miss Charlotte, with us still. Exhumed—shall we say?—from the alligator's lair." The judge smacked his lips with egregious satisfaction while Gilbert's expression indicated he was prepared to shove Placide into the alligator's lair.

Helene turned to her husband: "I mixed the same recipe for Charlotte that I've mixed time and again for myself, as Tansy's my witness—to get rid of your babies, Royce. And I'm still here." She opened her arms with a flourish, wine swirling in her upraised glass, presenting herself in proof—but of what?

Still here and still loathing her husband for more than twenty years after he took her only child away from her, the one Placide had not sired and would not raise. Had Helene shocked him, angered him? If she had hoped to sting him with the news of her refusal to bear his children, she had wasted her venom. The judge's first wife had already brought him heirs, now grown and carrying on his bloodline; he was satisfied there. Helene had merely brought him more property and, of course, her glamor and her gift. He hardly seemed perturbed now, and his nod to Tansy told the story that whatever the girl witnessed for her mistress she had reported to her master.

"What of the vial of poison?" I said, exchanging the role of audience for actor. I saw Eden flinch, then dart a glance at Placide, whose brow lowered and frown deepened. "If the tisane were not deadly to Charlotte, drops from the vial mixed with the tisane might have been. Isn't that possible?" I surveyed the faces, all turned to me, and glimpsed Gilbert's nod.

"A sedative, that was all," Eden said—at long last, admitting his knowledge of it. "To pacify my wife after her outburst in the afternoon. I couldn't have her insulting Judge Placide."

Charlotte sucked in her breath, and as I turned to look her way, Gilbert had taken hold of her arm and was easing her to sit on the edge of the fountain.

"You rendered Charlotte unconscious to please the judge?" The question escaped me before its implication dawned on me as Placide loosed a low, malignant rumble of amusement. "But then you all thought she was dead by mistake—from your various concoctions, one hand not knowing what the other was doing when—"

I broke off, catching sight of the warning in my brother's eyes, the shake of his head. Say no more his demeanor told me with more subtly—and urgency—than I'd ever before seen him convey. Then, I saw that Charlotte was trembling, and a cold sensation passed over me. What had Placide insinuated on our arrival?—that Gilbert might have preserved Charlotte's body for his use. And Placide, supposing her dead, had watched his servants undress her before they robed her in Helene's castoff dressing gown. I was very nearly sick.

"I wanted her corpse out of my house," Helene muttered through her teeth.

The lamp had burned low, no one turning up the wick. I tried to focus, not to lose track of those around me—how they responded or failed to respond to one another. But Eden by the stairwell and Gilbert and Charlotte by the fountain receded from my sight into the shadows, as I must have receded from theirs. Even Placide at the table, with all his bulk, had lost delineation. Helene, the hazy shape in the center of the courtyard, lifted the goblet she still held to take a sip, a glint of light passing through the dark liquid. Then the judge spoke, his voice rising above any murmuring around him and any humming in my brain.

"Something keeps niggling at me," Placide said. "Tansy, bring that thing to me."

Tansy retreated to the back of the house, and while she was gone, Helene fidgeted with her sleeve, then took another sip of wine and clicked one of her rings against the glass.

Tansy returned with the thing she had been sent to fetch—a poniard, which she presented, hilt first, to the judge. Taking it, he said slowly, as if the idea were just coming to him: "You all were at the inquest. Weren't we given to believe Colonel Duvall was stabbed with his own weapon?" Placide looked around him.

No one answered him, no one moved, but unease traveled the room.

"But how can that be right?" the judge said. "You see, I come to find out that *this* poniard, which I gave as a present to my friend Duvall, was still in his house. The estate agent brought it to me, and here it is." He rotated the poniard by its handle, then set it on the table near the lamp. "And, here's the odd part—*my* poniard, which ought to be in my house in town is missing. You have the answer to that, Helene? Spirits telling you anything?"

Helene nearly tripped on her hem as she approached the judge. "Spirits are telling me that poor Margaret murdered her husband. She knew as well as I do that you had one of those nasty things in your study, too." Helene waved her free hand towards the poniard. "Took it and killed him, didn't she?"

Eden spoke under his breath: "You warned me, Helene, not to walk out with her."

"Well, now. Killings can be arranged," said the judge. "You know that, Helene." We've done it, I imagined him thinking. "And weapons provided."

"Witnesses can be arranged," Gilbert said, more to the judge than to his wife.

"And blame laid on poor Margaret, as you call her," Charlotte said with returning strength, "who is not here to defend herself."

"Who would have died in the colonel's place, if he hadn't protected her," I said.

We had become a chorus addressing Helene, all of us, for I was almost sure that Tansy had muttered something from the darkness.

"Why did you hold the séances?" I asked Helene. "You don't actually believe—"

"To put Charlotte to rest, settle her fate—settle Victor's with me." Helene set her voice afloat on the humid night air. Was she, even now, pretending herself into a trance, as if that would protect her from the consequences of what she had done. Enough light remained for me to see Helene smiling when she added, "And then I wondered if the ghost of Frank Duvall might really come back looking for his flask. He never wanted to be without it."

Gilbert wouldn't let her spirit guide take over. "I understood, Mrs. Placide," he said, "that Mr. Eden intended to marry Margaret Duvall before misfortune intervened."

"Then you misunderstood," Eden broke in. "Margaret *misunderstood*."

427

"Oh, but she was very clear about it to me at the Placides' town home—before the séance," Gilbert said. "And again, when I visited her at the hospital, she spoke with great conviction that you, sir, would be coming to her rescue."

Eden's lips hardly moved, but I heard him: "The woman's out of her mind."

"Sadly so," Gilbert agreed. "But she, like Mrs. Placide, is very attached to you."

"Clearing the field, Helene," the judge said, as if he were gently chiding her. "First, Charlotte, then Margaret—more's the pity that came by way of the colonel—so you could be with your beautiful man. You can't tell me I'm wrong."

Helene stood facing her husband, her back to me, and she seemed to quiver, leaning against the table's edge. "No, Royce," she whispered, "I can't tell you you're wrong."

"And you can't tell me that I'll be next to go," Placide said, "not if you rely on Keogh and his dunderheads to do the job for you. Hmm. . . First, he botches what you paid him to do, then bears witness against your intended victim. Oh, I see it all now."

Helene sighed, lowering the hand that held the goblet, inverting it and spilling the remaining wine over her hem. Then she let the stem of the goblet slide through her fingers before she released the delicate glass to drop and splinter on the flagstones.

Was she faint? Ill? With a physician's reflex, Gilbert started towards her.

"No, Gilbert—stop." Charlotte came to his side, caught at his sleeve.

Helene stood a flagstone away, holding the poniard—taken with one hand while her audience had watched the wine glass drop from the other. The blade was a narrow glint against the dark green drapery of her skirt. The judge, still seated at the table, spread one hand over the place where the weapon had lain, then turned his eyes towards Gilbert. If Helene had taken the poniard to do more harm, or harm herself, Gilbert was the one standing nearest to her, the one to stop her, if he could.

Eden might have noticed Placide's gesture, too, and realized that Helene now held the poniard, or not. Whatever the case, whatever prompted him—even if it were the tabby cat rubbing its body along the back of Eden's trouser legs—Eden moved closer to the edge of the circle of pale light. Helene cast her gaze on him and smiled, welcoming his approach in that instant before she turned away from him, raised the poniard, and threw herself at Charlotte.

In the blink of an eye, Gilbert was between them, shielding Charlotte's body with his own, as Helene ran the poniard into his side, piercing the fabric of his coat. I heard him groan, saw him pull away from the pain Helene must have inflicted, bringing Charlotte with him—or she bringing him, supporting him as he stumbled with her towards the blackness of the stairwell. Gilbert must have caught a breath—I was still holding mine—for he turned back to prevent Helene from lunging again. But Eden, a heartbeat ahead of him, held the wrists of her upraised arms, Helene still gripping the handle of the dagger.

Beyond us, Placide's voice rolled forth, his words indistinguishable to me. But, as the courtyard brightened, I supposed he had commanded Tansy to light another lamp. Helene's face caught the illumination. Then, without parting her lips, as if an unseen hand were clamped over her mouth, she created an eerie squealing deep in her throat. I believe it was the sound of madness trapped inside her body.

Eden, a head taller than Helene, looked over the crown of her tousled hair at Gilbert, then beyond him, his eyes following Charlotte as she took a few steps up the staircase. Still, Helene struggled against his grasp of her wrists held above her shoulders. She pulled and strained forward, away from him, her efforts causing them both to totter, as if they were locked in an awkward dance, endeavoring to keep their footing. For an instant, Eden looked again at my brother, and then Helene's hands slipped from their bonds—or had Eden let her go?—and all the ferocity with which Helene had fought to free herself was released. Her arms descended with that force and her fists shot back—she could not have stopped them—against the man behind her as Helene launched herself forward from Eden towards Gilbert. But as she did so, Eden, not Gilbert, cried out in pain, for in one of Helene's fists had been the poniard, which was now lodged in Eden's ribs.

Helene continued on, tumbling forward, her right hand flailing behind her for the weapon gone from her grasp. Collapsing against Gilbert, knocking him back onto the lower stairs, she must have knocked the wind out of his lungs. I heard him gasping as, in the next instant, Helene was on top of him. I was beside him then, grabbing handfuls of the fabric at the gaping back of her gown, as she clambered over my brother. The volume of her skirts might have cushioned the jabbing of her knees into his groin and abdomen, but her fingers dug into his shoulders and her bosom smothered his face. Helene was pushing herself upward to reach Charlotte, who had not recoiled. Instead, Charlotte, who had dropped to her knees beside Gilbert, pushed against Helene, as he twisted beneath her, and I yanked at her bodice until the three of us forced Helene away—to be caught by Tansy.

That was what happened, wasn't it? What I might tell myself in retrospect, although, from moment to moment, I could not have been sure of anything.

I sank down on the darkened stairs with Gilbert and Charlotte beside me, outside the circle of light in the courtyard. Only then I remembered to breathe, one breath after another—like thoughts that came and fled, like tales told of scattered leaves and violet petals and slivers of glass that broke apart, then reassembled themselves. While I breathed, Charlotte opened Gilbert's coat where it had been pierced, folding back the gray wool from the white cotton shirt beneath, the shirt pierced, too, and marked by a circle of blood. Gilbert put his hand to the spot, and Charlotte laid her hand over his. "It's nothing at all," I might have heard him say as he leaned close to her—before all of us looked again at Helene.

Tansy held her mistress, folding Helene's arms over Helene's body, restraining her, even as she crumpled into Tansy's loveless embrace. Judge Placide did not move from his chair. Eden stood, stunned, a moment longer where he was when he had let go of Helene. Then, he pulled the blade from his side and dropped it and dropped himself to his knees. The blood soaked through the fabric of his white shirt, flowed down his rumpled trousers, and pooled about him on the flagstones.

Gilbert and Charlotte went to him and eased his lying down. She folded her cloak as a pillow for his head while Gilbert tore away the bloodstained shirt to examine the wound. She ran to the back of the house and returned with clean towels, a bowl, and a ewer of water. As Gilbert pressed a towel over the puncture to staunch the bleeding, Eden shut his eyes and hissed his breath through his teeth. Charlotte left again and returned with Gilbert's medical bag. She anticipated his every need, pouring water, handing him another towel as he bathed the wound, cradling Eden's head in her lap, then raising his head and shoulders, allowing Gilbert to apply the bandage and secure it. Eden leaned against Charlotte while Gilbert drew the wide ribbon of gauze over his ribs and abdomen and across his back, winding it around and around him, Charlotte smoothing the gauze as Gilbert worked, her hands brushing past his.

Chapter Fifty-Five

Judge Placidé summoned his men from the street outside the house, and a pair of them carried Eden, weak from loss of blood, to the upstairs bedroom—in which he had earlier obliged the judge's wife. Meanwhile, Helene had fallen ill after her violent outburst in the courtyard, retching over the flagstones while clinging to Tansy, near to fainting against the girl's shoulder. Had Helene imbibed some of Eden's pacifying drops in her wine? Perhaps he had hoped to send her back to her own bed feeling too unwell to make further demands upon him, for women who made demands—amorous or moral—grew tiresome to him. Of course, Eden could not have foreseen Dr. Baldwin's vigorous treatments, reviving Helene with salts of hartshorn and dosing her with castor oil. Then, Dr. Baldwin and another of his colleagues, who had been rushed to the scene by Placidé's coachman, turned their heroic attentions on Eden, himself.

"May they bleed him dry, probe his wound, and starve him on a diet of beef tea," Gilbert muttered for my hearing alone. Eden was not his patient, and Gilbert would stay away.

But Charlotte went to her husband's bedside. Meanwhile, Amy and Wilfred remained in my and Ella's care, and I conveyed messages and carried news back and forth between houses.

On the morning of the second day of his convalescence, Charlotte asked her mother-in-law and Narcisse to join her in nursing Eden. She had explained her reappearance to them, so she confided to me, as a temporary affliction causing her to forget herself. Widow Eden, for her part, was so distraught for her son that she could not help but take comfort in Charlotte's

433

ministrations to him. "Some dreadful misunderstanding occurred between them—I may never know what," Widow Eden told me, and I doubted she would ever want to know. "But Charlotte is here to stay," she added, making me wonder about conversations held out of my hearing. Eden, full of pride, had been brought low and might have begged Charlotte's forgiveness, and she, for reasons of her own, might have granted it in a resolution akin to that of *The Winter's Tale*, when Hermione's grace outshines her husband's penitence.

Despite Gilbert's twinges of pain where the tip of the poniard had pierced him and his bruises from the fall against the stairs—reminders, he called them—he returned to work, willing work to consume him and prevent him speculating on the future.

A clerk from the judge's office delivered documents giving Gilbert notice that he should close his clinic soon, unless he were able to hire someone to replace him. That was hardly likely, considering the meagerness of the new wages offered to him—not the generous terms with which the judge had once teased him. Gilbert was required to begin work for Judge Placide at a private prison northwest of New Orleans—somewhere near the Texas border, was my impression, convenient to lumber camps and plenty of heavy work involving the cutting of railroad ties and the laying of tracks, the building of the New South. Through the judge's patronage, Gilbert would avoid—and protect Charlotte, Ella, and me from—the legal complications, penalties, and punishments that could have resulted from his deception and our participation in it if he dared refuse the judge's terms.

Without an appointment, Gilbert went to Placide's office to challenge the judge's orders, or renegotiate with him if that were possible. My brother waited an hour to receive a five-minute audience with the judge, which Gilbert relayed to me. While Gilbert had stood before Placide, who sat behind his broad mahogany desk, the judge made clear his word was law.

"You made off with a gentleman's wife, Dr. Crew—alienating her affections from her lawful husband. Oh, she sees her duty to him now, sure enough. But supposing your actions become common knowledge? Wouldn't be pretty for her reputation. And how many gentlemen would allow you in their homes to treat their children and thus give you the opportunity to dally with their wives? Your medical practice wouldn't be worth—" Placide finished the sentence with a snap of his fingers. "And you don't make a living on your charity cases, do you?"

"No, sir," Gilbert replied, knowing that, if Placide chose, he could punish Charlotte and ruin Gilbert in New Orleans and beyond, as far as his influence extended.

"I am giving you a chance to redeem yourself, to make amends to those you have wronged with your obfuscation of truth—and what a court would consider nefarious actions," the judge said without a trace of irony. "My old friend Rufus Baldwin signed a death certificate, so for his sake I've decided to allow Miss Charlotte back among the living without unduly embarrassing him or anyone else. Unless someone crosses me." Placide smiled, letting his words register on Gilbert, before continuing: "With you working for me in one state and Eden working for me in another, wife and children in tow, Miss Charlotte need not be branded a trollop in public—and her little children need not be shunned from polite society. You see my point?"

"Yes, sir."

"Very good." Placide's venomous smile widened.

"For how long, sir," Gilbert asked, "am I obligated?"

"Oh, that's a conversation for another day." The judge waved him off as if shooing a fly.

✝ ✝ ✝

I understood what Gilbert had to do and sympathized with how he felt about the re-enslavement of men whose crimes were as likely to be based on desperate circumstances as on villainy. "Keep them alive, Gil, if you can," I said. "But most of all, for me, keep yourself alive."

We agreed that Charlotte and her children could stay on with Ella and me if Charlotte and her husband did not come to an arrangement. But Gilbert and I both thought they would. Eden would recover, and they would reconcile.

On the afternoon of the third day of Charlotte's return to Eden, Narcisse brought a letter to Gilbert from Charlotte, which he read through more than once before sharing it with me. Charlotte had begun with apologies for the trouble and distress knowing her had brought to him and Ella and me. Charlotte had a habit of needless apologizing and effusive thanking for small things. I skimmed the first page of her sorries and gratefuls, written in a careful hand. Then on the second page, I followed the increasing raggedness of her penmanship, reading of Eden and his devil's pact with Judge Placide, which now struck me as eerily similar to Gilbert's own. Charlotte wrote:

Victor admits very little. I wish he had trusted me with his secret, the mistake he made so early in his career. That he did not causes me to wonder if he feels guilty for more than accidental error. How else could Judge Placide have bound him so completely in obligation?

Victor insists he had no part in Colonel Duvall's death, saying only that Helene warned him the colonel was watching him and Margaret, and he shouldn't walk with her. I think you are right that Helene intended Margaret to be alone when she was accosted in the alley. Except that was not the case. And Helene's lie to Victor turned out to be the truth—Colonel Duvall was watching Margaret, and he saved her life.

Victor has told me he was tiring of Margaret and would have broken with her without Helene's interference. Then, when Helene could not control him with threats to expose him to the colonel, she threatened to expose him to the judge—all the while professing her endless love for him, as if her obsession were proof of love—and putting Victor in a terrible position, so he said, between his patron and his patron's wife. But I have my doubts *about his claims of being unaware of Helene's scheming. I believe she had her eye on him even before he married me. And Victor has been aware, all along, of what he does for Judge Placide to advance himself and would not tolerate my questioning him or his master.*

I understand women find Victor handsome, how he stirs their feelings, and how susceptible he is to the admiration of others. But I can accept no excuse from him, if he were to offer one, for his dangerous associations. What would have become of Amy and Wilfred if I had died at Testament? That is my nightmare.

Victor needs me now, and that has made him a little sorry.

Please share this letter as you see fit with Miss Lenore and Ella. I owe you all what explanation I can give, along with my gratitude for sanctuary. I am strengthened by my true friends and by my children, whatever happens in the time to come. I don't know what the future holds for Victor and me. Since my conversation with him this morning, he has become very quiet.

When I think of Helene Placide, I feel some pity for her in her circumstances and more for Margaret Duvall. I do not forget my own frailties. I think of you.

God bless you.

Charlotte

✟ ✟ ✟

The next day, when I called on Charlotte, we did not speak of how she felt about my brother, only of the subject of her duty, Eden. Then, returning home, I brought Gilbert the news that neither he nor I had expected to hear. "Dr. Baldwin says there's an abscess in the pleura and soon the lungs will be overcome with infection," I said. "Victor Eden is delirious with fever."

"Is he?" Gilbert said. "And what of Charlotte?"—for she was his concern.

"She does more than duty requires," I replied.

The following day, what the future held for Eden, which had been a mystery to Charlotte, came clear. Eden passed over

Jordan—if there is any place to go beyond the fog at the riverside.

Narcisse fetched Amy and Wilfred and brought them to the Widows Eden at the elder widow's apartment, where women and children closed themselves in to comfort one another. There, Ella and I joined them, bearing covered dishes, pies, and gingerbread.

At the inquest, Judge Placide set the tone for the coroner's decision: accidental death. Gilbert gave the briefest of testimony, saying only what was required of him—that he had witnessed the accident. Then, Dr. Baldwin presented his expert opinion that Mrs. Placide, while in a trance state, had unwittingly stabbed Mr. Eden, who had died of his wound. Any contribution Baldwin's treatments had made to that outcome went unmentioned, but the old doctor did hint that supernatural forces had been partly responsible. Thus, Helene's gift had saved her, and the judge tidied things up for his wife—although, perhaps, not quite as she would have wished.

The day before Eden's funeral, Helene began her journey to the Magdalene Ladies' Lunatic Asylum, where she would be reunited with her friend, Margaret Duvall.

"Helene will enjoy that," Placide told Gilbert and me over coffee in the study of his cluttered mansion in town. "The ladies can reminisce about their mutual beau." For, even though the judge had come to excuse Margaret of culpability in the colonel's death, he was convinced she had lost her reason and should not return to society.

Placide had commanded Gilbert's presence that day for a discussion of their impending business arrangement. I had come along to be a silent, mitigating presence—since Gilbert had made me swear I would not plead on his behalf to the judge. Instead, controlling my revulsion at Placide, I nodded at him with civility, even as he brazenly surveyed my person—dress, shawl, hat, gloves, and the oval of my face, which was the only part of me I had left uncovered.

While I sipped coffee, Placide gave detailed instructions to Gilbert before wandering to other topics, puffing on his cigar. "My wife recognized something in you, young man," the judge said in his insinuating tone. "Could be, she saw a piece of herself. Obsession—there's the common thread. Helene was bound and determined to clear her way to Victor Eden. And weren't you just as set on clearing a path to Miss Charlotte's door? You can't tell me I'm wrong."

But even if Gilbert had cast Eden as a villain and himself as Charlotte's rescuer, my brother had come to understand the path would never be clear of loss and sorrow. I saw the pain in Gilbert's eyes as Placide opined about young Widow Eden. "You are in no way situated to think about her, young man—you have work to do. And don't delude yourself that she's only a peach of a girl. She's got spite in her, too."

Judge Placide saw in others what he saw in his own looking glass.

"If a man takes a wife, he's got to keep her under his control—and don't I know it," the judge said, winking at me as he held forth to my brother the wisdom of the old days. "We had to guard against bonds of affection then—still do—can't allow blurring of the lines between men and women, rich folks and poor folks, whites and blacks, neither."

But lines blurred, whether or not allowed, perhaps even between the living and the dead.

"Rules used to be clear," the judge said. "And if your wife was soft on the servants, if the children—light and dark—played together too long, too late in childhood, well, Master, beware. Children's games are a prelude, softness is a prelude."

"To what, sir, may I ask?" I heard myself asking Placide.

"Disorder, Mrs. James. Chaos. All hell breaking loose."

Tansy came to take the coffee cups away, while Placide rambled on as if she were not there to hear him. "Hate to do it," he said. "Gal's mighty useful to me. And Helene has given me grief, Lord knows—but she is my wife. And I have decided one of these days, before too long, I'm going to send Tansy to look after her mistress."

I darted a glance at Tansy, who did not bat an eye.

Gilbert waited until Tansy had left the room before he said: "After all her service to you, Judge Placide, you're saying you'd send her away? Your dutiful daughter." The imp of the perverse spoke out of my brother's mouth.

"What?" Placide frowned. "You think Tansy's my offspring?"

"Isn't she, sir?" Gilbert asked.

"You've got that wrong," the judge said. "Tansy was sired by a black buck belonging to my late father-in-law, sure enough. Even if she—like you—ever wondered otherwise. It was Tansy's mother who was white."

Gilbert shot a look towards me. I had once remarked to him that men were not the only ones who ever consorted with servants. And a white woman who did and whose baby differed from her in complexion would be unable to pass off the child as her husband's.

Looking from Gilbert to me and back, the judge slowly smiled. "I'll let you two in on a little secret," he said, "why it's so fitting for me to send the girl to the asylum. You see, Tansy's mother was the young and wayward daughter of Testament Plantation—Miss Helene, herself."

I looked towards the doorway through which Tansy had disappeared, wondering how far out of earshot she was now. "Does Tansy know?" I asked.

The judge shook his head. "I've never told her. No sense in dividing the girl's loyalty. And Helene still thinks I got rid of the child."

"So you never told your wife otherwise," Gilbert said.

440

"What! And insult her powers of perception? No, indeed," Placide said. "And Helene has yet to see what's been right in front of her face all these years."

Withholding the truth might have seemed a trivial meanness in the judge's mind, but what could revealing the truth have been to Tansy, who had been born before the war? A world of difference—for in those days, hadn't a child's condition of bondage or freedom been tied to the mother's condition? Although, one might argue that marriage to Judge Placide was a kind of bondage for Helene. And employment by him was bondage, too.

At the front door, while Tansy handed Gilbert his hat and bag, I studied her face for the cunning eyes of her mother, only finding her expression more inscrutable than ever.

Then Gilbert ventured to draw her out: "Do you think you might prefer caring for Mrs. Placide over staying here with the judge?"

Tansy released a quick snort, expressing her answer even before she gave it: "Judge not locking me up in a madhouse, no, sir. I ain't the one who's crazy."

✛ ✛ ✛

Gilbert and I rode in my carriage to call for Charlotte at her mother-in-law's apartment and escort her to her husband's funeral. On the way, traveling at a sedate pace, we passed Madame Joubert's Hat Shop and, through the shop window, I glimpsed Jeannie showing hats to an elderly lady while keeping up an animated—no doubt, flirtatious—conversation with a young gentleman, possibly the lady's grandson. I wished the girl joy of him. As Gilbert, too, glanced towards the shop, he must have been thinking of Charlotte—imagining if he, not Eden, had been the one to amble into the shop to find her trimming a straw bonnet with a yellow silk butterfly—so wistful were Gilbert's eyes.

The elder Widow Eden was not well enough to attend the funeral, for the loss of her last son had devastated her. "Amy and

Willie are my only comfort," she said, hugging her grandchildren to her, "and their sweet mother." Whom the old lady was, at last, coming to appreciate, I surmised.

The weather that afternoon was crisp and clear, no need for umbrellas in the cemetery. Gilbert stood with young Widow Eden, who was cloaked and veiled, her gloved hand resting on his coat sleeve. After leaving New Orleans, he would recall that sensation of the slight pressure of her fingers on his arm and remember, too, the intimation of her cupid's bow mouth and her dark eyes through the veil. Gilbert would write to me of these and other memories when the whirl of recent days was past and protracted time weighed on his heart and mine.

By the Eden tomb, I stood arm-in-arm with Ambrose Parr, hardly paying attention to the funeral ritual. Instead, I turned over in my mind the jagged fragments of my invented tale as if they were pieces of glass within a kaleidoscope, revolving into a design. Perversity, betrayal, and murder were the shadows—charity, loyalty, and love were the shapes emerging to catch the light. Yes, I was close to completing my stage play, soon to share it with Ambrose.

Judge Placide eyed Gilbert, and I surveyed the judge, who looked bloated and unwell, in my opinion. Dr. Baldwin hovered at his side. Few other mourners were in attendance, and Mr. Keogh was absent, laid up after a nasty fall down his tenement staircase, so I gathered from a conversation near me. I also overheard whispered talk among some of the mourners about Death coming in threes. But in the Placide's circle there had been only two deaths, Duvall's and Eden's. The plaque bearing Charlotte's name had been removed from the outer wall of the Eden tomb, leaving hardly a mark.

When the service ended, I suggested that Gilbert travel with Charlotte to her mother-in-law's apartment in my carriage without me. "Go on ahead of me," I said. "Ambrose and I will catch up to you."

Gilbert pecked my cheek before he joined Charlotte in the carriage, where their goodbyes would not be overheard. The next day, he left New Orleans.

✢ ✢ ✢

I wrote often to Gilbert, three or four letters to every one of his, and only summarize a little of our correspondence here. I informed him that Eden's house on Dauphine, which Charlotte had called a danger, was enmeshed with Judge Placide's holdings, and Charlotte realized nothing from the sale of it. Her mother-in-law was now taking a rest cure, and Ella and I had invited Charlotte, Amy, and Wilfred to stay again with us. The children were thriving, Amy surpassing me at the spinet with her rendition of *Plaisir d' Amour*. Willie was becoming quite the little gardener, spading and weeding under Ella's supervision and saving her back. Charlotte joined me in work at the shelter and taught some of the women what she knew of trimming hats and stitching flowers and butterflies from scraps of velveteen and satin. Gilbert wrote that he appreciated the news, and I had the impression that Charlotte's correspondence with him was less frequent and more reserved than he had hoped. She had suffered, I reminded him, and we must give her time—there was little else Gilbert could offer in his current situation.

Letters from my son were rarer than those from my brother, and I planned to pay Allan an unexpected visit in Virginia after visiting my daughter in North Carolina in the fall. Arabella was now in an interesting condition and had asked me to be with her for her lying in. In months to come, I would be a grandmother, myself, still shy of forty. But would I be a wife for a fourth time, with all the attendant duties and limitations? As much as I enjoyed Ambrose's amorous attentions, I thrilled at our theatrical collaboration. Already, at Ambrose's suggestion, I'd begun revising my play, the better to highlight the talents of certain actors in his company—and the better to mask the identities of individuals on whom certain characters were founded.

Perhaps my foray into playwriting had heightened my sense of finding meaning between the lines, for I knew that Gilbert spared me details of his life and work among the convict labor. As winter deepened, influenza made the rounds of the lumber camp, he wrote, without mentioning he, too, was miserably ill—but I read it in his poor penmanship. With few words for his own condition, Gilbert recorded how, in the course of his duties, he found some peace in knowing the tasks he performed were still in keeping with his profession. And, as he patched up men whom the judge had ensnared, he recognized the bond he shared with them.

"When Charlotte once asked me if I would ever work for Judge Placide, I'd answered that nothing would induce me. But I was wrong," Gilbert wrote to me. "Before going away, I didn't want to speak to Charlotte of my obligation to the judge, knowing how her husband's entanglement with him had diminished Eden in her eyes—and now I, too, am one of the judge's creatures. As I treat the men here for cuts and welts and broken bones, for malnutrition and exhaustion, while a little weary, myself, I often think of Ella's parting comfort to me: *Miss Charlotte would make a pact with the devil for her children's sake. What you doing for her sake—for all of us—that's your pact. Miss Charlotte knows who you are.*"

Gilbert ended the letter with another remembrance: "A few certain words in Charlotte's first letter to me are still my balm and bane: *I do not forget my own frailties. I think of you.*"

✤ ✤ ✤

Maybe death does come in threes, for, by late June, a third death had come. If Judge Placide had not actually believed in his immortality, he may have believed he had bought himself more time with his ever expanding acquisition of property and labor. But he had not. According to Dr. Baldwin, who brought me the news and who had been present on the occasion, Placide had expired at his dinner table in mid-sentence while entertaining guests with a nostalgic anecdote.

"Took a quick breath and choked on his syllabub. Ever hear of such a thing?" Dr. Baldwin said. "Why, Mrs. James, I promise you, his cook makes puddings smooth enough to slide down a baby's throat. I told Tansy—*strike him on the back, girl!* But first she dropped the tray and everybody else's dishes went flying before she got to the judge. Terrible—Judge Placide was purple by the time she reached him and got in a few whacks on his back before he passed."

From Dr. Baldwin, I also learned that Tansy would not be joining Mrs. Placide and Mrs. Duvall at the asylum. "Much as the judge toyed with the notion—just about to send her off. But his heirs are so mightily impressed with Tansy, they've put her in charge of housekeeping and want her to stay at Testament forever."

Then, Dr. Baldwin left me on my front porch with one more piece of news: the judge had failed to will Gilbert's servitude to the next generation of Placides. His passing ended my brother's exile from New Orleans.

I wrote to Gilbert, and he must have written back the day my letter arrived, his response full of vague hopes and concrete plans to reopen his clinic. Then, Charlotte sent him a letter, which she showed to me first. She had enclosed watercolors by the children and a sketch of her own. Amy's picture was of yellow and purple flowers, and Willie's, which required an explanatory note, was of their tabby mouser on patrol in the side yard among the catnip plants. The children had posed for Charlotte's sketch, sister and brother sitting in the front hall on the bottom stair, and Charlotte had drawn Gilbert beside them from memory, at their request. I had left it for Charlotte to give Gilbert an inkling of what to expect on his return to Rampart Street.

My brother's pulse must have raced as he climbed the steps of the front porch, where Ella and I met him at the door. Gilbert dropped his bags, and Ella caught his hat. In the heat of the summer afternoon, his hair was matted on his forehead, and sweat ran down his neck, dampening his collar. My heart lurched when I saw how thin and worn he was, but his face was alight. Ella shooed him ahead of us along the draughty downstairs hall and out the back into the garden, which was in bloom with midsummer flowers.

Amy ran to meet him, slipped her hand into his, and led him towards the shade of the loquat tree. There, on a wicker *chaise longue*, Charlotte reclined in a loose-fitting spring green dress figured with a pattern of leaves that Gilbert might have confused with the dappling of light and shadow in the garden around her—he was that dazzled by the sight of her. Willie smiled up at Gilbert but would not leave his mother's side. His little hand pressed to her swelling abdomen, he was waiting for a tiny, unseen, tangible foot to kick against his dimpled fingers.

"Three healthy children, Gilbert," Charlotte said, smiling up at him. "I was promised." In proof, she held out to him the hand the fortune teller had read long ago, and he kissed her palm.

If Charlotte would have him—and I wagered she would—Gilbert would marry her. I envisioned them living out their days and lingering in this old city, which was well-accustomed to the vagaries of human nature, explicable and inexplicable, through time after irredeemable time. As for myself, I foresaw another journey, another exploration of shadow and light, concealment and revelation, entanglement and liberation, which might well begin tonight in Mr. Parr's box at the theater.

About the Author

Rosemary Poole-Carter explores aspects of an uneasy past in her novels Only Charlotte, Women of Magdalene, What Remains, and Juliette Ascending, all set in the post-Civil War South. Her plays include The Familiar, a ghost story, and The Little Death, a Southern gothic drama. Fascinated by history, mystery, and the performing and visual arts, she is a member of the Historical Novel Society, Mystery Writers of America, and the Dramatists Guild of America. A graduate of the University of Texas at Austin, she was a long-time resident of Houston, where she practiced her devotion to reading and writing with students of the Lone Star College System. She now lives and writes by the Eno River in Durham, North Carolina.